ISABELLA

QUEEN WITHOUT A CONSCIENCE

A HISTORICAL NOVEL

BY

RACHEL BARD

© Copyright 2006 Rachel Bard.
All rights reserved. No part of this publication may be reproduced, stored in a retrieval
system, or transmitted, in any form or by any means, electronic, mechanical, photocopying,
recording, or otherwise, without the written prior permission of the author.

Note for Librarians: A cataloguing record for this book is available from Library and Archives
Canada at www.collectionscanada.ca/amicus/index-e.html
ISBN 1-4120-9212-4

Printed in Victoria, BC, Canada. Printed on paper with minimum 30% recycled fibre.
Trafford's print shop runs on "green energy" from solar, wind and other environmentally-friendly power sources.

TRAFFORD
PUBLISHING™
Offices in Canada, USA, Ireland and UK

Book sales for North America and international:
Trafford Publishing, 6E–2333 Government St.,
Victoria, BC V8T 4P4 CANADA
phone 250 383 6864 (toll-free 1 888 232 4444)
fax 250 383 6804; email to orders@trafford.com
Book sales in Europe:
Trafford Publishing (UK) Limited, 9 Park End Street, 2nd Floor
Oxford, UK OX1 1HH UNITED KINGDOM
phone +44 (0)1865 722 113 (local rate 0845 230 9601)
facsimile +44 (0)1865 722 868; info.uk@trafford.com
Order online at:
trafford.com/06-0966

10 9 8 7 6 5 4 3

Copublisher
Literary Network Press
P.O. Box 13523
Burton, Washington 98013

Library of Congress Control Number 2006904245

Cover Design by Leslie Newman

Seal of Isabelle d'Angoulême courtesy of City of Angoulême

Map by Kajira Wyn Berry

Also by Rachel Bard

Queen Without a Country, a historical novel

Navarra: The Durable Kingdom

Newswriting Guide: A Handbook for Student Reporters

Editing Guide: A Handbook for Writers and Editors

Best Places of the Olympic Peninsula

Country Inns of the Pacific Northwest

Zucchini and All That Squash

Isabella's World and Time

A Historical Prologue

Isabella of Angoulême was born into a "France" that few Frenchmen would recognize today. It had no precise borders, no central government and no common purpose.

King Philip II was undisputed sovereign only of the Ile de France, a small territory centered on Paris. It was surrounded by dozens of semi-independent duchies, counties and vice-counties, many of them much larger than the king's domain.

One of these was the County of Angoulême, the fief of Isabella's father, Count Aymer. Angoulême lay within Aquitaine, the large and prosperous duchy in the southwest of France. Count Aymer was virtually independent. Like his fellow magnates he nominally held his fief as a vassal of his king; but his power over Angoulême was nearly absolute. He and his counterparts could ignore or defy the king if they wished, and they frequently did.

Still, the King of France and most of his vassals usually agreed on one goal: drive out the English!

The quarrel went back to 1066 when Duke William of Normandy invaded and conquered England. As King William I of England, he continued to assert overlordship of his native Normandy—a strategically located duchy in the northwest of present-day France, just a half-day's sail across the Channel from England.

The English added to their possessions in 1154 when William's great-grandson, Henry II, inherited Anjou in central France from his father, Geoffrey Plantagenet, Count of Anjou. (Hence the terms Plantagenet and Angevin to refer to the English dynasty of this period.)

1

Then in 1152 when Henry II married Eleanor of Aquitaine, heiress to the great Duchy of Aquitaine, her vast territory too became part of the English dominions on the Continent.

From these secure toeholds the English continued to claw their way toward the heart of France while the French resisted at every opportunity.

In 1186, the year of Isabella's birth, the English hegemony in France was at its peak: from Normandy in the north to Aquitaine and Gascony in the south, and comprising Brittany, Maine, Anjou, the Touraine and Poitou in between. These English possessions were about a third the size of present-day France.

The adversaries were well matched: Henry II of England, powerful and rapacious, and Philip II of France, astute and a master of intrigue.

During Isabella's lifetime the battles raged, led by these kings and their sons and grandsons. By the year of her death, 1246, England's long Continental decline was well underway and France was close to becoming the strong, cohesive monarchy it would be for centuries to come.

Because of her birthright and her marriages Isabella found herself now on one side, now on the other, in these struggles. Because of her character she sometimes chose to lead her own fight for her own interests, anticipating the Shakespearean "a plague on both your houses." No matter where she stood, she could be adored, admired or decried, but she could not be ignored.

Readers who wish to know more about Isabella's world and time are encouraged to consult the Bibliography on page 355.

France & England in Isabella's Time

Isabella

1243

I know what they're saying about me. They think I'm all wrapped up in prayer and repentance and don't hear or see what's going on around me. But I've heard them—the gossipy nuns whispering to each other in corners.

Just because I don't answer when they talk to me they've decided I'm deaf or nearly so. That suits me very well. The high prioress, Lady Blanche, thinks so too and that suits me even better. I've no desire to endure her chatter and her sanctimonious pity. If I've learned anything since I came here to Fontevraud Abbey it's the wisdom of keeping to myself with my mouth shut and my eyes and ears open.

Only yesterday, when I was sitting in the abbey's common room with my needlework and my psalter, Sir Robert de Beaumont came to call on Lady Blanche. I often take my work to a bench at the far end of the room, where I can look out the low window to the gardens. Sometimes my companion, Louise de Rochemont, comes with me, but this day I was alone.

The other end of the room is much more inviting. There's a big fireplace with comfortable chairs and benches drawn up around it in a half-circle. That's where most people who come in tend to settle, as Sir Robert and the prioress did yesterday.

They're old cronies, I've heard—maybe more. Sir Robert's a tall, loosejointed gentleman and he sat right down like a cricket on a beanstalk, ready for a chat. But it was a while before Lady Blanche felt comfortable. She's a buxom little person and what with her stiff white habit, she had to wriggle about a bit before she came to terms with her chair.

"Now, I've been away up in Normandy for a year and you must tell me all the news," said Sir Robert. "First of all…" he lowered his voice and I knew they were looking at me and he was asking who I was. I kept my eyes on my book and moved my lips as though I were reading the psalms.

"Oh, that's Queen Isabella—you know, the widow of King John of England and wife of Hugh de Lusignan. We're quite set up to have such a royal person here at the abbey! But you needn't whisper. She can hardly hear, and besides she's busy repenting."

"Oho, that one!" said his lordship. "Still remarkably handsome, isn't she? She must be at least fifty."

I was pleased that I was still thought handsome. And even more pleased that he'd guessed I was only fifty. I was fifty-seven.

"But what's she repenting? Surely not her youthful indiscretions, after all this time. Everyone knows she jilted her fiancé here in France when King John came along and she married John instead. But that must be forty years ago and more."

"No, my friend, there's been many another indiscretion in Queen Isabella's life. You must have heard that after John died she ran off to marry the son of her old lover, before John was cold in his grave." She sighed in her distress at human foibles. "Though I've heard she didn't have much reason to mourn John. He was no saint—carrying on with his obliging lady friends."

I couldn't repress a bitter smile at that, but thank goodness they weren't looking at me but at each other, sniggering. Lady friends a-plenty, did my John have, and not all of them what you'd call ladies!

"But why is she here?" asked Sir Robert, hitching his chair closer to his companion. "Tell me all, my dear!" He must have done something rather naughty because I heard the prioress squeak.

"Careful! She may be deaf but she's not blind. Time enough for that later."

That's right, I thought. Don't waste time. I want to hear what she tells you.

"She came nine or ten months ago," said Lady Blanche. "She was disgraced when she and her husband, Hugh de Lusignan, were accused of trying to poison our blessed King Louis. Then she and Hugh had a falling-out, and she had nowhere else to go. Surely you heard about that plot against the king?"

"I heard the rumors, but I had no idea the Lusignans were in on it."

"Well, they were. Some people think she put her husband up to it and some say it was his idea. Thank God they didn't succeed."

So people were calling me an assassin! My lips quivered. To hide my agitation I folded my hands and bowed my head as though I were praying.

The Prioress went on, as pious as the Pope. "I suppose I should say 'poor lady' and I do try to find it in my heart to forgive her for all the evil she's done in her life. We must pray that the Lord God will have mercy on her."

"My dear Blanche, I'd no idea she had led a life you could call evil. I thought she was simply a beautiful, highborn woman who made unfortunate choices. Misguided and impulsive perhaps, but evil…?"

I peeked through my fingers. Sir Robert was leaning toward Lady Blanche, who looked as smug as a puffy-chested pigeon that's just laid an egg.

"Yes, my friend. Greedy and ambitious too, I fear. She wanted to be a queen instead of a mere countess. And then to turn into such a jealous wife, oh dear!"

The prioress was becoming less pious by the moment. I didn't dare look but I could imagine her round little face tensed and prissy, her eyes glittering like a cat's when it's after a mouse.

Just then a lay brother came in to see to the fire and made such a clatter with his tongs on the stones that I couldn't hear what they were saying. When he'd left the gossips were still at it.

"What's more," said the prioress, "they say that she and her old lover Hugh managed their share of sweet trysts, all the time she was married to John."

Sir Robert clapped a hand to his brow.

"Evil, was she? Yes. May she truly repent, with the help of our Blessed Virgin, who pities all sinners." Her voice fell dramatically, like a priest intoning a prayer.

I picked up my needlework and bent over it.

"So here she is, sheltered and safe, in spite of it all?" Sir Robert sniffed.

"Of course. We are bound by our charter to give protection to any who are sick or penitent. She appears to be both."

"Your charity is amazing, my dear Blanche. To take her in, after such a life of adultery, betrayal, deceit and murder. You are a true saint. And will she be here long?"

"For the rest of her life, though she may not know it. We've had instructions from the very highest authorities to keep her here. If she decides she's had enough of the cloistered life, or if that wishy-washy Hugh takes a notion to want her back, we'll have to take appropriate measures."

She shot a look at me, aware that she had been speaking too frankly and perhaps too loudly. Their voices fell to a murmur. I turned my head so they couldn't see my face, flaming with anger.

Silence. I risked a glance. Robert had raised Blanche's hand and was pressing it to his lips.

I got up, gathered my belongings and walked toward the door, doubly outraged. It was dreadful to learn that I was a prisoner, though I had no doubt I could get around that if need be. But even worse was the prioress's sorry story of my life. Because she had it all wrong. It hadn't been like that. It hadn't been like that at all.

Isabella

1200

2

I was nearly fourteen when my parents, the Count and Countess of Angoulême, summoned me one wintry day to give me news that would turn my life upside down.

I'd been in the gardens behind our palace playing hide-and-seek with Adèle. Adèle was the daughter of one of my mother's ladies in waiting, Anne Beaufort. Lady Anne was charged with my care and upbringing. On the whole I liked her. She was kind and indulgent and didn't make too many rules about my life.

I didn't especially like Adèle. She was only ten, but since my parents had provided me with no brothers or sisters, she was the only playmate I had. She had tight-curled brown hair and a pudgy face that puckered when I scolded her. She was like a little puppy who trotted after me, hoping for a kind word.

It was one of those January days when the sun blazes so brightly that you'd think spring was around the corner. But the beech trees that stood against the courtyard walls were bare as skeletons. When our game took us near the henhouse we saw the chickens lined up on their roosts, fluffing up their feathers to keep warm. Off by the far wall two horses were running about in circles. When they whinnied we could see puffs of white breath. A couple of stableboys were making a half-hearted effort to chase them into the barn. Other than that we had the whole silent expanse to ourselves. The invisible city of Angoulême outside the walls was quiet too except for quick footsteps clattering along the cobbled streets. Sensible people would likely either stay inside or hurry home on such a chilly day.

In spite of the cold Adèle and I were chasing about so energetically that we grew quite warm and threw off our cloaks. There was a good deal of shrieking and falling down. I'd just won a game so Adèle had to give me another forfeit. I now owned her two favorite dolls, little stick figures wrapped in bits of cloth and with faces painted on their wooden heads.

"Mademoiselle Isabella," came a high, whining call. The footman Alois was hurrying toward us where we stood almost hidden by the tall gray-green sage plants in the herb bed. He looked annoyed. I suppose he'd been searching all over. When he told me Count Aymer and Countess Alix wanted to see me at once, I was excited. Maybe they were going to tell me I could have the new horse I'd been begging for.

I pulled on my cloak and ran in through the great hall and up the stairs to their tower room. My father was sitting in his big chair before the fire with my mother beside him. The room was so warm that I felt perspiration running down my face. I was acutely aware of my tumbled hair, my torn skirt and my father's disapproving gaze.

He was a large, imposing man who was away a great deal and never had much time for me. As my mother often reminded me, he had to see to the governance of the whole county of Angoulême and all the chancy relations with his neighboring counts and dukes and lords, to say nothing of the King of France.

Today he reminded me of a menacing brown bear. He must have just come from hunting; he was completely enveloped in his long fur cape. His unsmiling, square-jawed face was red from the wind. He was holding out his hands to the warmth of the fire and rubbing them.

With his first words he stunned me.

"Isabella, your mother and I have just agreed that you will be engaged to Hugh le Brun of Lusignan, Count of La Marche. It's a very advantageous marriage. You'll thank us for this some day."

I could only stare at him.

"When Hugh's lands and ours are joined, between us we'll be as powerful as any duke or count in France. We'd be able to withstand King Philip himself. Though I pray we will never have to do battle with our king." His face became even more somber. "So, since God did not grant us a son to carry on the family fortunes, you as our daughter will have the privilege of ensuring the future of our line and adding to our possessions."

I thought for the hundredth time it wasn't fair to blame me for not being a boy.

My mother, my beautiful goldenhaired mother whom I adored, beckoned me to her. She put her arm around me and I relaxed, taking in her scent—today it was lavender. I leaned my head against her silk-clad shoulder. Her voice was like honey.

"We've agreed to this betrothal for your sake, Isabella. We want the best for you. As our only child, of course you'll inherit all of Angoulême. But when Hugh le Brun came to us and asked for your hand in marriage, we saw at once what it would mean for you. Just think, my dear--you'll be one of the wealthiest women in France and a countess twice over. Won't that be lovely?"

"But I don't even know this Hugh whatever! And he doesn't know me."

"He may not know you," said my father, "but he knows very well who you are and what you'll inherit. He's well aware that when we're gone he, as your husband, will become Count of Angoulême. From what we know of him as head of the Lusignan clan, he'll fill that role very well."

"Don't frown, Isabella," said my mother. There was a touch of vinegar in the honey now. "Haven't I told you over and over again that frowning brings wrinkles?" I raised my hand and brushed it across my forehead. I always wanted my mother to approve of me, and besides, I knew she was right. Her own brow was as smooth and white as that of the marble Madonna in the cathedral, though she must have been at least forty.

"Now we must get practical," said my father. "Hugh le Brun has only recently become Count of La Marche. He'll be away from home for some time, visiting his new vassals. But it's none too soon for you to become accustomed to your husband's family and your duties as the future Countess of La Marche. So you'll go to live at your fiancé's castle at Lusignan until you're married. Hugh's brother, Count Ralph of Eu, will serve as your guardian while you are there."

I stiffened in my mother's arms. I'd hardly heard of Lusignan though I believed it was far to the north of our sunny Aquitaine. She gave me a squeeze.

"You won't be alone, Isabella. Lady Anne and Adèle will go with you. You'll like Sir Ralph and his wife. Now why don't you go to your room and ask Anne to help you change into a fresh gown before dinner? You might do something about your hair too."

I walked out. The silly little dolls I'd won from Adèle still dangled from my hand. I trudged up the stone staircase and along the dark corridor to my room. Lady Anne wasn't there and I didn't call her. A servant came in and lit a few candles. I climbed up on my high bed to think. I crossed my legs and sat with my elbows on my knees, my chin in my hands. It seemed an age since I'd been in the garden playing childish games.

After a while I noticed the dolls, sprawled ungracefully on the coverlet. I sat them up facing me.

"You," I said to the girl doll, "are Isabella." To the other I said, "And you are Hugh le Brun." I turned back to Isabella. "And you are going to marry Sir Hugh. What do you think of that?" They stared at me with their dull black eyes and said not a word.

"But Isabella," I scolded the girl doll, " if you're going to be the Countess of La Marche, you must do something about your gown." I jumped down and searched in my chests until I found a lace handkerchief. When I wrapped it around the doll and tied it at the waist with a blue ribbon, she still looked silly.

After a hesitant knock Adèle came in.

"When you didn't come back, I worried. Did they say you could have the horse?"

I'd forgotten about the horse.

She saw the doll in my hand. "Ooh Isabella, how pretty you've made her! Is she an angel?"

"No, she's supposed to be me, when I'm a countess."

"But you won't be a countess until after your mother Countess Alix dies. That's what my mother told me."

So I explained to her about being engaged to Hugh de Lusignan, and having to go to Lusignan, and becoming Countess of La Marche.

Her eyes widened with surprise.

"How exciting! But won't you be lonely, off there without any one you know?"

"Oh, you're coming too, Adèle, and so is your mother."

Her round little face crumpled with worry.

"So it will be just the three of us, and a lot of strangers?"

"I suppose so. But my mother says I'll like it once I get used to it."

We discussed what Lusignan would be like, without much enthusiasm. Neither of us wanted to leave our familiar home. I tried to think of a bright side.

"I do think it will be lovely to be a countess. Maybe you can be my lady in waiting, Adèle."

She giggled, then did her best to come up with another positive aspect.

"And if we're going to make that long, long journey to Lusignan, they'll certainly have to give you your new horse."

Anne Beaufort

1200

3

"I...don't...want...to...go...to...Lu-...si-...gnan!"

With each syllable Isabella stamped her foot and tossed her head. This made it difficult for me to brush her hair.

"Do stand still, my dear. However did you get so many tangles?" Her hair was long and very fine, a beautiful soft gold. One day, I knew, she'd be vain about it. Now it was just a nuisance to her because it had to be brushed so often.

"Of course you don't want to go," I said. We were in my chamber of the palace at Angoulême, just before our departure for Lusignan. Adèle, already wrapped in her cloak so she looked like a woolly little cocoon, watched with solemn sympathy.

"I don't want to go either. But we'll just have to make the best of it. Your father and mother and Sir Hugh have decided we must go. There's nothing we can do about it."

I'd been in Countess Alix's service for ten years, ever since my daughter was born and my husband died, all in the same month. The countess preferred sitting at her husband's side in the council chamber or accompanying him on his tours of the county to playing the role of mother. She'd gladly entrusted little Isabella to me when she saw that I didn't mind supervising the nursery or exercising some discipline. As for me, with one child already, it wasn't much trouble to take on another.

I'd grown fond of my high-spirited charge. When I felt I was making headway in reining in her impetuosity and hot temper I was gratified. When I didn't I told myself I was learning the virtues of patience and persistence.

Standing there, warm and dry in my familiar chamber, dreading the cold January journey awaiting me, I looked around. Mentally I said goodbye to the deep blue carpet; the blue-and-rose wall hangings—I'd embroidered them myself; the graceful folds of the fine wool drapery around my big bed and Adèle's little one; the rosy glow of the fire still burning merrily on the hearth. I wouldn't be there to watch as it died. I gave Isabella's head one last smoothing with the brush.

"Yes, we must make the best of it. And who knows, Isabella, we may find that Sir Hugh's castle is quite pleasant."

She looked at me suspiciously. She knew perfectly well I didn't think so at all.

It took us six grueling days to get to Lusignan. We were a party of a dozen: the countess and myself and our daughters, another of her ladies in waiting, four men-at-arms and three muleteers. Each night we'd stop with some vassal of Count Aymer. The countess was always greeted with respect and pleasure and seemed happy to linger in the dining hall, chatting with her hosts. She was used to the rigors of long hours on horseback. Isabella and Adèle and I weren't. All we wanted was to sup and go to bed.

Isabella was sore and cross every night after a day of struggling with her horse. She'd been given the new one she'd longed for, a pretty little chestnut-brown mare with a black mane. Isabella called her Jolie. She seemed docile enough at the start, but soon decided she'd show who was in charge. She had an ungainly gait when she trotted, so the unhappy rider bounced up and down like a cork on a table. When she walked she'd stop to munch on whatever wisp of roadside greenery caught her eye. Sometimes she just stopped for no reason, and wouldn't budge until the countess sent one of the men to put some sense into her. By the end of the journey it looked as though Isabella was beginning to get the upper hand, but her temper and her backside were suffering.

We arrived at Lusignan on a dark, damp day. I thought wistfully of Aquitaine, far off to the south, where the sun was undoubtedly shining. When we looked up to the castle, perched on a high bluff above the River Vonne, we saw a lifeless pile of gray stone. Even the town that hugged the road up from the river seemed devoid of life except for a few men bent under heavy loads of hay or firewood on their backs. Trudging wearily uphill past close-packed humble wooden houses, they paid us no attention except to move to the side as we approached. Once three ragged children emerged from a narrow dark side alley to stare openmouthed at this unaccustomed procession, rattling and jangling its way up to the castle. As we passed the stone church, by far the most

14

imposing building in the town, a black-cassocked priest came through the tall arched portal and watched. He nodded gravely when I smiled at him.

When we reached the castle on its promontory and drew closer through the clammy mist, the huge wooden gate was securely closed. No one was there to greet us. It was midafternoon but already the sky was darkening.

"Go knock on the postern gate," said the countess to one of the men. The rest of us waited with dull resignation in the thickening mist. The only sound was the animals snorting and pawing the ground. The men were restive too, hoping the business here wouldn't take long so they could get down to the village inn to dry out. They were as eager for their ale as the horses were for their oats.

Finally the gate opened. There stood Ralph de Lusignan, Count of Eu.

"Remember to call him Uncle," Countess Alix whispered to Isabella.

He didn't strike me as an uncle I'd have chosen. He was short, wiry and bushy-headed, nervous and jerky in his movements. His lips were pursed together tightly and seemed frozen in an expression of disapproval. Or perhaps he had a chronic stomachache.

He let us into the bailey, the great walled enclosure that contained the castle and its various outbuildings. When I dismounted my legs were stiff and my feet numb. Isabella was sagging with tiredness and discouragement. The castle didn't live up to our hopes. It consisted of a row of one- and two-story stone buildings that jutted out from the west wall. At either end of the row rose a menacing tall tower. A few wooden structures dotted the grounds, stables and piggeries and storehouses and such. I smelled something horrid. I saw next to me a damp, rotting stack of hay where two optimistic goats were nosing about looking for something to eat. Everything was cheerless and untidy, nothing like the courtyard at Angoulême where the count insisted on neatness and efficiency and the countess took pride in the gardens. Adèle, standing groggily beside me, reached to take Isabella's hand. Normally, I fear, Isabella would have snatched her hand away. Now she was too disconsolate.

The countess had been conferring with Ralph. She beckoned to us to join them. I was proud of Isabella when she smiled at him politely and said, "I am pleased to meet you, Uncle Ralph." He looked down at her, gave a sort of grunt, then gestured toward one of the castle buildings.

"She'll be lodged in there," he growled. "We've cleared out three good rooms, plenty of space for her and her ladies. My wife Alice will help them get settled." He patted Isabella's head and she looked up at him in surprise. Then he walked back to where he'd come from, his heavy-booted feet striking the flagstones like hammer blows.

Lady Alice emerged from the larger tower and walked to greet us, her smile broadening as she came. I felt my spirits lift in spite of myself. She was rosy-cheeked, double-chinned and brisk. Her voluminous dark-blue cloak couldn't conceal the fact that she was considerably rounder than her husband. What hair could be seen was gray and curly. Most of it was tucked up under a smart blue silk cap.

"Welcome, welcome to you all," she said cheerily. "Not too nice a day to be out on the roads, but now you're here we'll soon have you inside and dry." She took charge at once. In short order our belongings were brought in and stowed away.

I looked around my new home. I saw two beds, a table, a chair, a pair of chests and a scattering of rushes on the floor. Nothing to soften the somber stone walls. A grimy candelabrum held one lone stub of a candle, unlit. The fireplace was bare. A little fading daylight came through the two narrow windows. It was even colder than outside. My depression came back.

I walked into Isabella's chamber, next to mine and just as dreary. Countess Alix was supervising the putting away of her daughter's possessions while Isabella looked on glumly. Lady Alice smiled at me.

"I've just been telling Isabella to cheer up. Your lodgings may not look like much yet, but we'll soon bring in some comforts to make things cozy for you. We didn't have much notice, I'm afraid. And once you have nice fires on the grate you'll feel better. I'll send a lad in to lay them now." She bustled out.

Out in the courtyard again, saying goodbye, Isabella lost what composure she had. She clutched at her mother's cloak and buried her face in its folds, sobbing. "Please, please take me back with you," she begged. "I hate it here, I don't want to stay here."

The countess sighed.

"Now Isabella, be reasonable. We've been over this time after time. You must realize you're not a little girl any more. You must start thinking of yourself as a future countess. Before long you'll meet Sir Hugh, and when you're married he'll take you traveling about with him. You'll stay in castles far finer than this with plenty of lords and ladies at your beck and call." I could almost see the visions of lording it over lesser folk dancing through Isabella's imagination. The countess knew her daughter better than I thought. The sobs subsided.

"Meantime, you'll have Lady Anne and Adèle for company and Uncle Ralph and Aunt Alice will take good care of you."

She kissed her daughter, then signaled to a groom that she was ready to mount. He cupped his hands for her foot and she sprang gracefully up onto her saddle. Looking down, she said, "And of course we'll come to see you. Didn't we promise you that? Now dry your eyes, Isabella. It's nearly sundown and we must be on our way." And away the whole party went, to the jangling of harness, thudding of hooves and riders' urgings of their steeds. The silence that fell as the last horse disappeared through the gate was almost palpable.

Isabella, watching dolefully, sniffled and wiped her eyes. I put my arms around her and led her inside.

The next morning we breakfasted with Lady Alice in the dining hall. I took heart when I felt the warmth of the fire on the hearth and saw the chunks of fresh-baked bread with big bowls of warm goat's milk on the table. When we'd finished, I got up to take the girls back to our rooms. Alice reached up to take my hand.

"Don't go yet. Let's get acquainted."

We sat down again.

"I'm so glad you've come." She beamed at us, and I believe she really was glad. "It gets pretty lonely here, with just Ralph and me and our retainers, rattling around in this old castle. I expect you're finding it very different from Angoulême. I visited your mother there once, Isabella, so I know what you're used to. And to tell the truth, since we don't spend a great deal of time here, we haven't done much to brighten things up. Our castle up in Normandy is much nicer. Maybe we'll all go there for a visit, later this spring." As she chattered on, I found it soothing. Adèle looked at her trustingly. But Isabella sat sullenly, her lower lip pushed out, refusing to be cheered up.

"Meantime, we'll do whatever we can. Let's get started. What would make you feel more at home, Lady Anne?"

"I'd like to send for some of the furnishings of our chambers at Angoulême, since it seems we'll be here for some time."

"I'm sure Ralph can manage that. How about you, little one?" She turned to Adèle.

"I'd like some honey to put in my warm milk. We always had honey at home."

Alice patted her on the shoulder. "So you shall have honey here. Isabella?"

"I'd like to go home." Isabella stared obstinately at her hands folded in her lap.

Alice's voice grew gentler. "I know this is quite hard for you, getting uprooted, leaving your parents and being set down in some stranger's home. You may not believe it, but I know some of what you're feeling, my dear." She had a faraway look in her pale blue eyes. She sighed, then smiled.

"Yes, once I too was very young. When my parents sent me off to live with a strange family I was only ten, much younger than you. I remember I cried myself to sleep every night. I've never forgotten that terrible time."

Her eyes came back to Isabella's sulky face. "Now don't give me that look, as though you think I'm inventing this to make you feel better."

"Were you supposed to marry someone you'd never seen, like me?" The girl sounded half skeptical, half curious.

"No, I knew him. But I didn't like him at all. He was a little bully, and he used to trip me up and laugh when I fell down. Then he'd pull my hair to make me get up."

I must have looked shocked. She said quickly, "Oh no, that wasn't Ralph. As it turned out, the marriage never happened, though I never knew why. Years later my parents arranged the betrothal with Ralph, and he never, ever pulled my hair!" She chuckled and gave Isabella a little hug, trying to coax a smile out of her.

She didn't quite succeed, but the girl let herself be hugged.

The weeks crept on. We adjusted as best we could. I discovered that beneath Ralph's crustiness a soft heart lurked. He made dolls for Adèle. He helped Isabella with Jolie. Before long the beast became obedient as a trained monkey on a string.

Occasionally some of Ralph's Lusignan connections came for a visit, usually of several days' duration. This involved a great deal of loud talk and parties of hunters going out with falcons on their wrists, coming back with rabbits and small birds in their gamebags. After such an expedition, I looked forward to dinner. Normally the food we were served tended to be dreary—pasty gray stews of indeterminate meats, instead of the well-spiced roast pork and plump, steaming game pies we'd enjoyed at Angoulême.

Alice and Ralph had never had children, so this adjustment was perhaps as hard for them as it was for us. They certainly did their best. Alice arranged for the village priest to came once a week to school the girls in Latin. She and I taught them needlework. Isabella was too impatient to stay quietly sewing for very long, but she did learn to hem a wimple passably well.

Meantime we all wondered when we would see Hugh le Brun, the reason for our presence at Lusignan. When we heard he was on his way and might arrive before Shrove Tuesday, Isabella suddenly became full of curiosity. She asked me over and over, "What do you suppose Hugh will be like, Lady Anne?" I tired of saying, "How can I possibly guess?" and told her I expected he was short, skinny and bald with a harelip, but a kind heart. After that she let me alone and badgered Ralph and Alice to tell her about him.

They weren't much more help. She did manage to extract a few facts. He was about thirty-five. He had fought bravely in the Holy Land against the infidels. He was called Hugh le Brun –Hugh the Brown--because of his dark complexion and brown hair. The Lusignans had so many Hughs in the family that they had to find nicknames to tell them apart. They didn't consider Hugh le Brun particularly handsome, though some might say different. And they themselves hadn't seen him for five years. It was very little to go on.

"You'll have to wait and see for yourself," they said.

Hugh le Brun

1200

Early in 1200 I found myself at Nôtre-Dame Cathedral in Rouen to meet King John of England for the first time.

My liege lord, Richard the Lionheart, had died the year before. Now his younger brother was on the throne and had summoned me to renew my oath of fealty to England's kings.

Like all those who'd fought at Richard's side I mourned his passing. He'd been a leader any knight would be proud to follow: tall, handsome, openhearted and brave. I hoped that John would prove to be the same.

He received me in a splendid hall in the cathedral's Tour St. Romaine. Morning light poured through soaring arched windows that pierced the thick walls. The room was so spacious, and the vaulted ceiling rose to such dizzying heights, that the group of men standing by a window toward the other end seemed dwarfed. One wore a crown. He was rather short and stocky, and bedecked with so many gold chains and jeweled rings that I'd have thought they'd make him stoop under the weight. As I drew closer I saw that he was dark-complexioned, with black hair and a neat little pointed black beard. So this was King John.

He walked to a gilded throne in the center of the room and seated himself. His courtiers and I followed and stood before him. There were no other chairs. One of his men whispered in his ear.

"Sir Hugh de Lusignan," he muttered. It was less a greeting than a reminder to himself of who I was. Perhaps he'd been receiving so many vassals that he had trouble keeping them straight.

"My liege," I replied.

"Sir Hugh, we welcome you to Rouen. Normandy is the original homeland of the English kings and has been favored by them ever since my noble ancestor William of Normandy conquered England, a hundred and thirty years ago. Since Rouen is and has always been the capital city of the Duchy of Normandy, it is appropriate that we receive our French vassals here." He was giving me a history lesson I didn't need. I decided John was not at ease making conversation and made speeches instead. I was sure he'd made this one many times before.

"It is indeed appropriate, my liege. I know that your brother Richard cared deeply about Rouen and directed that his heart be buried in this very cathedral. It is a tribute to his memory that as his successor you have chosen to receive your vassals here."

He reddened, half rose and raised a fist. I thought he was going to strike me. Two of his courtiers stepped forward, whether to join in the attack or to restrain him I don't know.

John sank back on his velvet cushions and glowered at me. "What I do here today has nothing to do with my brother Richard, his heart or any tribute to his memory. I am my own man. Remember that. Now shall we get back to the reason you have come? Are you prepared to swear allegiance to your overlord, King John of England?" His face was still mottled and I could hear his quick breathing as he tried to regain control of himself.

"I am, my liege."

"Then kneel."

I knelt. John held out his hands and I placed mine between them. His hands were warm and trembled slightly. His burst of temper must have pervaded his whole body. I looked up into his black, unreadable eyes.

"I, Hugh de Lusignan, swear to serve you, John of England, as my lawful king and to forswear allegiance to any other lord or king, from this day forward. I swear to do homage to you for the lands I hold under your suzerainty and to defend them against your enemies."

"I accept your oath, Sir Hugh." He released my hands and gestured that I should stand. "Sir William, our steward, will acquaint you with our further wishes." Without another look he rose, turned his back and left. His short fur cape swung behind him like an angry tiger's tail.

Sir William, a straight-standing soldierly man, told me that John wished to grant me the overlordship to the county of La Marche, to the east of our Lusignan lands.

"The King is aware that as leader of the clan of Lusignans you command a considerable body of his subjects. He is confident that you and your allies will do all in your power to maintain the peace and insure the loyalty of his vassals in La Marche."

I was at first astonished, then gratified, then amused.

"So I am now Count Hugh of La Marche. Well, King John clearly grasps the means of making sure his vassals will remain loyal to him. But I can accept a bribe as happily as the next man. Thank you, Sir William, and please convey my thanks to the King."

We went straight to the conditions of my countship. Sir William wasted no words, and our business was concluded with dispatch.

Still trying to take in what had happened so swiftly, I walked out from the austere quiet of the cathedral into the teeming, noisy streets of Rouen. It was midmorning and cold and damp. Rain or worse would come soon. I pulled my cloak closer about me and my hat down over my ears. When I entered the cathedral square I realized it was market day. The place was crowded with stalls and tables laden with all kinds of wares from woolen hose to earthen pots to wheaten loaves. Citizens were pouring in from every side, in a hurry to buy and sell before the low-lying clouds let down their freezing deluge. I forced my way through the crowds, ignoring pleas to buy a fine fresh fish, a wedge of goat cheese, a leather jerkin, a basket of wrinkled little apples. I was briefly tempted by a huge pot of steaming soup, sending out rich aromas of onions and herbs, but I was more interested in starting homeward.

Pushing on, I smiled when I saw one enterprising fellow who'd led his brindled cow with her bulging udder into the center of the throngs. "Here's milk for all, buy it now, couldn't be fresher, straight from the cow," he bellowed. My smile changed to a curse when I stepped into a puddle of foul-smelling dung the beast had just deposited on the cobbles. I lunged to avoid a man who was flourishing a squawking chicken that he held by the feet, then banged my shin on a cart of enormous yellow rutabagas.

I escaped as fast as I could, found my squire and our horses and set out southward. I'd had enough of cities, kings and turnips. All I wanted was to be out of Normandy and back in my familiar Poitou. I knew my brother Ralph was expecting me at our family castle at Lusignan.

But I couldn't go directly. Thanks to King John's largesse I had to make a quick detour through La Marche to establish myself with some of my new vassals. I sent a message to Ralph about the reasons for this change in plans. In a way I was glad of the delay. I knew that at Lusignan I'd meet for the first time my fiancée, Isabella of Angoulême. I viewed the prospect of marriage without much enthusiasm.

My betrothal to Isabella had taken place the year before. It was a business matter, no more. When Count Aymer and I came to an agreement he didn't volunteer much information about his daughter, beyond the fact that she was only thirteen. Betrothal could take place at once, but the marriage should wait a while.

"She's been well brought up," he said, "and she's generally respectful to her elders." (Among whom he may have included me, for I was thirty-five.) I inferred from his reticence that she was probably no beauty, perhaps even ill-looking. That didn't disturb me. I wasn't looking for a love match. All I hoped for was an amenable wife who could produce enough sons and daughters to insure the succession to our joint lands of Angoulême, Lusignan and now La Marche.

By early March I was home. When I walked into Lusignan Castle's great hall, windblown, damp and weary, Ralph seemed glad to see me, though with Ralph you couldn't always tell. His habitual expression was one of melancholy disillusionment. Still, he squeezed out a thin-lipped smile and clapped me on the shoulder.

"Come into the dining hall when you've put yourself to rights, Hugh. I'll have them stir up the fire and warm us some wine. And shall I send down to ask Father Etienne to join us? He's been pestering me to tell him when you arrived."

"By all means." Father Etienne, the village priest, had taught me my Latin and heard my childish confessions. Over the years I'd come to respect his judgment as much as I valued his friendship.

He arrived just as I'd settled before the fire in dry hose and tunic and Ralph had sent for the wine and bowls of figs and nuts. The priest folded his long frame into a comfortable arrangement with his legs stretched out toward the flames and sighed with content. In my home he could cease playing the part of shepherd of souls and be as worldly as he pleased. Etienne's interests stretched far beyond the little town of Lusignan.

He raised his pewter mug in salute and asked, "So, Sir Count, must we bow down before you, now that you're master of everything from the River Vienne to the River Cher? And to the south all the way to Aquitaine's borders, if I'm not mistaken? Did you find your new vassals suitably respectful?"

"Not so much respectful as indifferent. None of them seemed inclined to pick a fight with me or anyone else. They don't much care who claims their fealty, as long as they're left alone. But I've been away five years. Tell me what's new hereabouts."

Etienne pursed his lips and scratched his tonsured head. "Well, three aged parishioners were seriously dampened last week when the rain poured right through the church ceiling. They've taken to their beds with ague, fever and outrage. I called on them and told them I was sure a generous benefactor would soon be here and then we could manage a new roof. Is that the kind of news you had in mind?"

"No," I grinned, "but I'm sure the benefactor will be happy to oblige. Ralph, surely you can think of something a bit more momentous."

"I can," said Ralph. "At least it's been momentous for Alice and me to have a young person and her ladies staying with us these past two months, turning up you never know where all over the castle and grounds. As you know, your intended, young Isabella of Angoulême, is living here. I expect Alice will bring her in presently."

"Yes, I suppose it's time we got acquainted."

My expectations being so modest, I was wonderstruck when my sister-in-law brought Isabella into the room. I had just raised a flagon of wine to fill my goblet, and I almost spilled it.

"Here is our ward, Isabella of Angoulême," said Alice matter-of-factly. "Isabella, this is Sir Hugh, come to see us at last."

This was not the shy plain child I'd expected. Tall for her age, slim, she was more like a budding young woman than an awkward little girl. Her fair hair, with glints of gold, fell in soft ringlets to frame a perfectly oval face. There was the merest hint of curiosity in the slightly parted lips and the intent gaze from her eyes, blue as cornflowers. For half a dozen heartbeats we took stock of each other.

"I've been looking forward to meeting you," she said. She held out her hand. I rose to take it and quickly dropped it, I felt so awkward and confused.

For the first time in my life I was smitten by female beauty. Since my brief early marriage and my young wife's death, I'd known many women, as any soldier does, but none I wanted to know better after one or two encounters. In an instant all that had changed.

During the next few weeks Ralph and I surveyed the walls and fortifications, discussed repairs and improvements and conferred with stonemasons and carpenters. As the days passed, though, I found myself wanting to spend more time with Isabella. Oddly enough, we became comfortable with each other almost at once, in spite of the difference in our ages. Maybe we both found something that had been missing in our lives. I'd had no younger brothers and no sisters at all. Isabella was an only child. She'd had to learn to depend on her own resources, and had acquired more maturity than you'd expect in a fourteen-year-old. Yet I soon found her moods could change as quickly and unexpectedly as a butterfly flits from flower to flower.

After I'd been there about a week, on a rare day of brilliant sunshine, we went riding. The sky had never been so blue and anything seemed possible. We walked our horses down the winding road through the town. When we passed the old church, I stopped and told Isabella, "That's where I was christened."

She surveyed it and announced, "Well, *I* was christened in the Cathedral of Saint-Pierre at Angoulême, and so was my father before me. It's ever so much bigger and handsomer!"

When we reached the Vonne, Isabella, who had been riding sidesaddle as a lady should, swung her leg over the saddle in order to ride astride. She looked at me as though expecting a protest. By now I knew better. She would do what she would do. And thus, more evenly matched, we had a good run on the road that ran beside the narrow, swift-flowing stream. We were both full of high spirits and shouted at each other as we raced. I won by only half a length.

Isabella was an excellent horsewoman, I was glad to see. She had a sure hand with the reins, and was absolutely fearless. However, she clearly didn't like coming in second.

As we slowed our horses to a walk, she was scowling.

"I would have won if you hadn't swerved in front of me back at the last turn. I couldn't make this stubborn horse go fast enough to head you off."

"Never mind, Isabella. Ralph told me he'd helped you train the horse to mind you better. Maybe now she's ready to be given her head more. Next time she finds herself in a race we'll see what we can do to liven her up."

We rode back along the lane that led up the side hill to the castle gates. It was just wide enough so we could ride side by side.

"Well, it was a good gallop, anyway, Hugh. I do love to ride! But I hardly ever had anyone to ride with at home except one of the grooms."

"You haven't told me much about your life at Angoulême."

"Well, mostly, I was lonely. I didn't see much of my parents. They were too busy, or off somewhere. I didn't have anyone to play with except Adèle, Lady Anne's daughter."

"Maybe I can be your playmate," I ventured. She looked at me quickly to see if I was joking. We were still feeling each other out, like a pair of dancers trying to establish a common rhythm. "I mean it. It's a while before we'll be married, but in the meantime I think we can be good friends."

She bent her head and her long hair hid her face. I wondered if I'd alarmed her by speaking of marriage. We hadn't mentioned it yet. Then she looked up, brushing her hair aside, and her face was transformed, joyful. Her words poured out like water released from a dam.

"I've never really had a friend. I was so worried about whether I'd like you. Nobody would tell me anything about what you were really like, not Uncle Ralph or Aunt Alice or my father. I supposed they all knew things about you they didn't think I should know. So I had all these ideas about a big old ogre and you're not like that at all. I'm so glad!"

"I didn't know what you'd be like either. I knew I'd have to get along with you, no matter what. But I never dreamed you'd be so...so...pretty. And so nice!" My words seemed meager, compared with what I was feeling. I reached out to take her hand and we rode along a few minutes quietly.

I don't know what her thoughts were, but mine were not the lustful ones you might expect. I wasn't fantasizing about the time when she'd be old enough for me to bed her. No, I was wondering at my good luck in being the guardian of this exquisite being who had fallen into my hands like an exotic, fragile little bird. All I wanted was to protect her and make her happy.

From then on we never lacked for things to talk about. For one thing, she was curious about my soldiering. On a wet day when we couldn't go out riding, we sat at the table after breakfast for an hour or so while she asked question after question. She wanted to know where and when I'd gone into battle and whether I liked it.

"Not especially. It's just something one must do. Though when I was with Richard in the Holy Land..."

"King Richard of England? I knew you'd been to Palestine, but I didn't know you'd been on King Richard's Crusade. How heroic!"

I'd never felt much like a hero, but seeing her wide-eyed admiration, I warmed to the role.

"Yes, I was in his army and a finer leader I never hope to have. He knew how to fight, and he kept all his men as determined as he was to drive the wicked unbelievers out from the holy places."

"And did you really drive them out?"

I had to remind myself that when all this happened, Isabella would have been only five. Though tales of the Third Crusade had spread all over Europe at the time, it was a whole new story to her.

"Not completely, more's the pity. We couldn't take Jerusalem. Richard was brave but he wasn't foolish. Old Saladin was a fiendishly clever enemy. He'd poisoned the wells for miles around, and he'd burnt the farms and orchards. So our army would have perished of hunger and thirst before ever reaching the city."

"So you all just gave up?"

"Yes, but it wasn't as disgraceful as it sounds. Richard and Saladin signed a truce. It was really quite fair. We Christians could keep control of the cities we'd taken, and pilgrims would be free to go worship in Jerusalem."

"Then what happened?"

I took a handful of raisins from the bowl before us and chewed, remembering the flurry of packing up, the mixed feelings of relief and disappointment that the Crusade was over.

"We all came home. Richard promised us that we'd go back, but last year he died."

"Yes, I know. And John is now King of England."

"He is, and my liege lord. We'll see what kind of warrior he'll be. I doubt if he'll lead any crusades."

"Why not? Isn't he brave enough?"

"I don't know, but in any case he's too busy right here. He and King Philip are fighting about the English lands in France."

"Yes, my parents have told me about that. They said even our Angoulême might be fought over. So what will happen, Hugh? Will John win, or Philip?"

She was supporting her chin with her clasped hands, watching me intently, as though I knew the answers to all the world's questions. I'll confess, I enjoyed being the schoolmaster. Nobody had ever hung on my words as she did, and I loved looking at her, alert, taking it all in, her eyes fixed on mine.

"We'll see. There's a truce right now, but it's not likely to last long. Neither Philip nor John trusts the other farther than you can blow a feather. Sooner or later, one of them will start the whole thing over again. But there's this to fall back on: when you and I are married, we'll have a domain bigger than King Philip's little patch of France, and we won't have to be afraid of anyone who challenges us, English or French."

She sat thinking this over. Then in one of her sudden shifts she pounced on a new subject.

"When we are married, Hugh, where will we live? Here, at this castle?"

"Sometimes. But it needs a lot of work to make it suitable for the Count of La Marche and the Countess of Angoulême. All these improvements Ralph and I have been talking about will take some years. No, I expect at least at first we'll spend most of our time at Angoulême. Your father told me we'd always be welcome at his palace there."

"Well, it's more suitable than Lusignan but it's not very grand, in fact it's quite small. I think it needs a new tower, Hugh. I want to be the grandest countess in France, and live in the grandest castle!" She jumped up and paraded around the room, chin high, eyes half-closed, hands held stiffly at her sides, looking as haughty as she could.

I laughed. Apparently my little bride-to-be had high ambitions.

Soon after that I had to leave. If war should break out again, I needed to make sure all my new lords in La Marche would support me.

The day I left was one of those sunbright days when the deep heart of France basks in the soft warmth of early summer. Isabella came out to the courtyard to say goodbye. Ralph and Alice had tactfully left us alone. She stood looking at me while tears streamed down her cheeks. I was amazed to feel the sting of tears in my own eyes. I put my arms around her—she came just to my shoulder—and held her close, then turned brusquely to mount my horse, not trusting myself to speak.

I knew then she'd begun to truly care for me. As for me, leaving her was one of the hardest things I'd done in my life. I rode down the hill and onto the plain. The wheatfields were green and shimmering in the sun. Bur for me it might as well have been gray, icy winter.

John

1200

5

In early July of 1200 I had alarming news: Hugh le Brun and Count Aymer of Angoulême had agreed to some sort of alliance. Though Hugh had recently pledged me his fealty I wasn't sure of him. If he was in league with Count Aymer anything could happen. That slippery count could switch masters as easily as a weathervane swings with the wind. There was nothing for it: I'd have to interrupt my tour of Aquitaine, call on Hugh and remind him who his king was.

On a fine midsummer day I set out with my entourage from Poitiers to Lusignan. In spite of the heat I wore a long velvet cape, black as is my custom, that fell over my horse's flanks almost to the ground. I wore my crown. I wore a gold chain with a ruby pendant about my neck. My horse was as well dressed as his master, with a scarlet rump-robe embroidered with the three gold lions of the Plantagenet coat of arms. The gilded bells on his bridle made a pleasant tinkling sound. My herald rode ahead of the procession, ready to sound his horn to warn off any heedless herdsman who might bar the royal passage with a flock of bleating, unruly sheep. Behind me twenty knights rode two abreast. The hoofbeats of their horses on the hard-packed roadway were like the rat-a-tat of tabors accompanying the jingle and clank of armor and harness. Small wonder that when we met other riders they'd draw deferentially aside and bow. Sometimes if they appeared highborn I'd nod graciously and raise my hand in acknowledgment. The moment I'd passed they'd begin whispering excitedly while my knights and I swept along.

In just one year as King of England I'd learned what was important: dress in your finest, let the people see you, keep moving about your realm.

As we neared Lusignan our road followed the banks of the Vonne. I watched the river's lazy flow and brooded about the Portuguese princess I might have to marry. What if she proved as dull a creature as the woman I'd just divorced? What a dough-faced, silent, barren stick Isabel of Gloucester had been! I was well out of that marriage. I wasn't eager to embark on another. There wasn't much I could do about it, though. My mother had seen to that. And when Eleanor of Aquitaine made up her mind it took a brave man to argue with her.

"John," she'd said when I called on her in Poitiers, "you've wasted ten years without producing any heirs. Now that you're king and rid of that worthless wife, you must remarry. I've sent envoys to Lisbon—an alliance with Portugal would be extremely desirable."

She's right, of course, I thought gloomily. It's a king's duty to procreate. But I'm just not quite ready to tie myself down again. I'd have liked to be footloose a little longer, free to chase any skirt that took my fancy.

I brightened when we came to an inn between the road and the river. I suddenly felt a powerful thirst.

"Sir Robert, we'll stop here. We've earned a rest and a drop to drink," I called to the leader of the knights. While we were dismounting another party arrived. The small courtyard was soon a confusion of dismounting riders, hostlers leading off the horses, the innkeeper bowing and scraping and asking us in, and servants standing about gawking at these lordly guests stopping at their humble inn.

Amid the bustle I saw a pretty girl still on her horse, looking around and taking it all in. She saw me staring at her and smiled.

"What a luscious little morsel," I thought. I longed to get my hands on her, though she looked as though she'd barely reached puberty. Those days I was powerfully attracted to pretty young things, the younger the better.

"Sir Robert, who is that lass?"

"I'll find out, sire." He went to speak to the man who was helping the girl dismount. The three of them made their way through the crowd to me.

"This is Ralph de Lusignan, Count of Eu, and his ward Isabella. She is the daughter of the Count of Angoulême."

She'd let down her hood and I saw the cloud of ash-blond hair that fell to her shoulders. I couldn't take my eyes off the lovely face, all youth and innocence.

Sir Robert went on, "And this, Sir Ralph and Lady Isabella, is King John of England." For just a flash her eyes met mine. I thought I saw a sauciness that hinted at an eagerness to grow up.

"Well, shall we go in and refresh ourselves? I would be pleased if you and the Lady Isabella would join us, Sir Ralph."

I was glad of this chance encounter. The Count of Eu was influential in Normandy, where most of my strength on the Continent was concentrated. Even more important, he was brother to Hugh le Brun. I hoped I could get Ralph to give me some inkling of Hugh's intentions.

When we were settled in the big, dark public room of the inn, which smelled not unpleasantly of spilled ale and roasting fowl, the innkeeper brought refreshments from his cellar. The cider was so cold it misted the pewter flagon. I drank gratefully.

I began questioning Ralph. Yet at the back of my mind, like the vision of the last ripe plum on the tree that you put off the pleasure of plucking, was the consciousness that Isabella was sitting across from me. Soon I could talk to her and look my fill.

It wasn't easy to pry information out of Ralph.

"I'm on my way to Lusignan. Is that your destination as well, Sir Ralph?"

"It is."

"And have you been traveling long?"

"We've been two weeks on the road, all the way from my castle in Normandy."

I couldn't imagine why these two were traveling together. Ralph's thin, beak-nosed face disappeared briefly as he raised his mug and took a long draught.

"And the Lady Isabella, do her parents have lands in Normandy too?"

"Not that I know of."

Isabella broke in. "No, I begged Uncle Ralph to take me with him because I'd never been to Normandy."

More mystification. Why "Uncle" Ralph?

"And Sir Ralph, you think Sir Hugh will be at Lusignan when you arrive?"

"I'm sure he will."

Isabella spoke up. "We know he'll be there because he sent word that he'd expect us on this day or the next. He promised he'd be there to meet us. He's my fiancé, you know."

I put my goblet down with a thud. I couldn't hide my surprise. I had no idea the alliance between the two houses had gone this far. The girl looked sideways at me with an impish little grin. Part of me wanted to slap her, part wanted to press my lips against that adorable mouth.

"So you're to be the Countess of La Marche? When will the happy event take place?"

"That's yet to be decided," Ralph interceded gruffly.

Isabella told me, "When we get there and my father comes we'll set the date for the wedding. My mother told me I'd be a countess twice over—of Angoulême and La Marche." When she was excited she was a little girl; her voice rose and her words tumbled out.

Then her smile faded. She turned to Ralph. "Oh, how I hope my mother will come too! Do you think she will, Uncle Ralph?"

"You've asked me that a dozen times, and I still have no idea. We'll have to wait and see."

He banged down his mug and rose.

"Now we must be on our way, Isabella. We wouldn't want Hugh to get there and wonder where we were."

I rose too, hoping to delay them. Before I could say a word he flung some coins on the table, whisked her out the door and shouted to their attendants. The door banged behind them.

I finished my cider, considered briefly and told Sir Robert, "We'll spend the night here at Le Breuil, instead of pressing on to Lusignan. I believe it would be better to arrive in the morning instead of late at night."

At first Robert looked alarmed. Where would he find lodging for twenty knights in this mean little village? But he rallied.

"Very wise, my liege. That gives them all night, after Sir Ralph arrives, to prepare a proper welcome for you." Good lieutenant that he was, he went off to make arrangements.

That night I sat up late in my room with a jug of wine and my thoughts.

I was pleased that I'd have a chance to see Aymer as well as Hugh. But I was worried about this new coming together of the Lusignans and the Taillefers, Count Aymer's clan. I told myself I'd have to break it up somehow.

By the time I finished the wine my mind was made up.

"Never mind what my mother thinks I should do," I said to the empty jug. "This time I'm going to be my own man. To the devil with the Portuguese princess. I'll marry the sweet little Isabella instead."

John

1200

"It's not much of a castle," I said to Robert de Thorneham when we rode into the bailey at Lusignan the next day.

He surveyed the scraggly gardens, the gaps in the stone walls, the stables and hencoops looking as though a strong breeze would flatten them into so much firewood.

"Right you are, my liege," he boomed. His deep bass voice made even his most trivial remarks sound important. "Can't compare with ours in England. I'd say what they need here is a good steward." Sir Robert, as my chief steward, knew whereof he spoke.

The servingman who had been lolling against the weathered door of the main tower came to attention as we approached and leaped to seize the brass handle—in need of polishing, I noted. He ushered us into the great hall. As he was taking my cloak and hat Ralph de Lusignan came to meet me. I asked him if Hugh le Brun had arrived.

"No. He sent word he'd be here before sunset. But Count Aymer and Countess Alix are expecting you," he said, grumpy as ever. "The count is waiting in the tower room."

So Count Aymer was here! Good. I'd have time to talk to him and assess his commitment to his new alliance with the Lusignans before broaching my plan to marry his daughter. Once that was settled I could deal with Hugh. Everything was falling into place.

Before Ralph led me up the stairs I cast a look around the dim hall, hoping to glimpse Isabella. But in vain. I supposed she was with her mother, whom she'd so longed to see.

I found the count settled in Hugh's private chamber. It was pleasantly cool after the heat I'd been riding through, but that was about all that could be said for it. Furnishings were sparse and utilitarian: a narrow bed with dull gray curtains, a chest, a table, a few chairs. No rugs or tapestries, no stools for weary feet, no woman's touch.

Aymer invited me to sit in a tall armchair beside the table. He was a big man, thickset but muscular, elegantly groomed, self-confident. He stood until I motioned to him to sit down. I felt more at ease when we were eye to eye.

"Sir Aymer," I said, "I'm very glad to find you here. I would have called on you later in Angoulême, but this is much more convenient. You'll understand that in my first year as King of England and ruler of the lands I inherited from my late brother, King Richard, I am anxious to meet my vassals in France and assure myself of their loyalty."

I'd been making the same speech all over Aquitaine. Usually it was just a formality, but not this time. "I'll be frank with you. I know that some time ago you swore allegiance to King Philip. Fortunately Philip and I are at peace, since our truce last May. However, hostilities may well resume when the truce period expires. If that should happen I would not like to think of you in the ranks of my enemies."

He looked mildly questioning, waiting to see where this was leading. I remembered what my mother had once said: "In negotiation, John, when you ask for something you must be prepared to offer something in return, but not right away; lead up to it."

I went on. "First, let me ask you: Is it true you've forged an alliance with Hugh le Brun of Lusignan? And you're planning to marry your daughter, your only child, to Hugh?"

"That is true."

"I've recently granted to Hugh the lands of La Marche, to add to his already considerable possessions. I expected that would insure his continued loyalty to England. But when you two are allied by this marriage, and between you control such a large and rich territory, you'll surely do fealty to the same lord. Will it be Philip, or John?"

Before replying he poured each of us a small goblet of a pale, sweet wine from a pitcher on the table. He took a sip. "You are right. Hugh and I will control a very large area. Our joint domains will in fact be larger than the Ile de France where Philip reigns. We've discussed the matter of fealty. I think Hugh would agree with me when I say that we wish to make no commitments until the need arises. Why seize the oars when the seas are calm?"

There was more arrogance in this than I cared for. And just as I'd guessed, he would need a good reason to declare himself in my camp. He looked down and fidgeted with the hem of his tunic, as though bored and waiting for the interview to be over.

"I may be able to offer you an inducement to ally yourself with the King of England, who is also Duke of Aquitaine, Duke of Normandy, and Count of Poitou, and whose possessions surround yours on three sides."

He inclined his head to indicate he had heard me and was waiting for more.

"Consider this. Isabella marries me instead of Hugh. An alliance with England is certainly preferable to one with a mere Lusignan, don't you agree?"

It took only a moment for him to grasp the situation. His eyes met mine and for the first time he smiled, with what I took to be admiration for my clever scheme.

"Indeed, my liege, how could I refuse such a generous offer?"

The detached adversary became the enthusiastic collaborator. Within half an hour we had settled on a course of action.

After Hugh arrived, I would meet with him and ask him to reaffirm his loyalty. Then, as though to test it, I would send him off to take messages to some of my most distant vassals. That would keep him out of my way while we proceeded with the rest of our plan.

I would go on with my royal progress through Aquitaine. Aymer and his countess would tell Isabella that her wedding to Hugh was to take place in August. They'd take her back with them to Angoulême to prepare for it. They'd send out invitations to their noble friends and vassals. Everything would ostensibly be in preparation for the wedding of Isabella and Hugh. I would appear at the end of August, and the ceremony would be held in due course-- but with a different bridegroom.

There was, of course, one glaring hole in this fabric of intrigue: the bride's consent.

"Now as to your daughter Isabella. I had the pleasure of meeting her yesterday. I could see, even on such brief acquaintance, that she is a girl of some spirit." He sent me a knowing glance. I surmised he guessed she had captivated me.

"She appeared to be looking forward eagerly to seeing her fiancé and preparing for the wedding. It may not be easy to persuade her of the wisdom of the change in plans."

He placed the fingertips of his hands together and studied them pensively, as though considering whether to wear the blue doublet or the brown. He looked up with a faint smile.

"Not at first, perhaps. It may take some dissembling. But I think I can find a way to bring her around."

"I hope you can dissemble credibly, my friend?" I asked him. By now, after our plotting and a few more glasses of wine, I felt that we were, if not exactly friends, at least men who understood each other perfectly.

"I am a past master at dissemblance."

I raised my glass to him. I liked this man's smooth craftiness.

"Just one thing, my liege, before we quit the subject. Isabella's mother and I had made it a condition of Hugh's marriage agreement that he was not to take Isabella to his bed until she is sixteen. We would expect you to hold to the same condition."

Before I could reply—I would have to agree, of course, dismaying as this was—the door opened. At the threshold stood Countess Alix, bringing a burst of color into the drab room. She was all in scarlet, even to the lacy scarf over her golden hair. I'd thought my mother the champion of dressing for the occasion, but here was someone who could rival even Queen Eleanor. She was perfectly poised and strikingly beautiful for a woman who must be in her forties. I thought I could see how Isabella might look in twenty years or so.

Then my heart gave a lurch as Isabella followed her mother into the room. In a blue gown that matched her eyes and a sash of the same gold as the ringlets that framed her face, she looked like a fledgling angel.

Aymer rose and presented his wife to me. He turned to his daughter. "I think you met King John yesterday, Isabella. Now he is our guest, and you may greet him again."

I went to meet her, holding out my hand. She took it, bent her head briefly, and looked at me with all the audacity she had shown at the inn when prattling about Hugh and her forthcoming wedding. But her voice and words were respectful.

"I am pleased to see you again. I hope you are well."

I managed to blurt out a reply, then with relief heard Aymer speak to his wife.

"King John will be with us until Hugh arrives, then he will go on to Limoges."

The countess smiled at me as though I'd done her an immense favor.

"We're honored to have you as a guest, even though we're only surrogate hosts for Hugh. Perhaps some day soon we may entertain you at our own castle at Angoulême."

"Yes, that may be, I hope so, it well may be." I hardly knew what I was saying. My eyes were fastened again on Isabella. She, however, had forgotten me.

"Will Hugh come soon, Father? He promised he'd be here to meet us yesterday but he wasn't. And Uncle Ralph and I hurried so to come on time."

"Don't whine, Isabella. We've just had a messenger from him. He hopes to get here before evening."

Lady Alix said, "Now, my lord King, would you like to rest for a time? We've tried to make a chamber comfortable for you, but you must ask for anything you find lacking."

I was conducted up another dark, dank flight of winding stairs to a room considerably more agreeable than the one I'd just left. A small but cheery fire had been lit on the hearth, to dispel any chill that might come with sunset. A large bed was curtained in rich red hangings. A cushioned chair was drawn up to a table where, in a pool of light from a tall fat candle in a silver candlestick, I saw a flagon of wine and a bowl of nuts and fruits.

The countess had urged me to ask for anything that was lacking. Alas, I couldn't ask for what I wanted most: Isabella. It was agony to know that she was so near, yet so inaccessible. I walked to the window, where I had a full view of the bailey.

I heard hoofbeats approaching. It was Hugh and his party of two knights and their grooms. As they rode through the gate the high walls threw back the sounds of stamping hooves, clanking armor, the whinnying of horses glad to be home. I saw and heard the bustle of dismounting, tossing of cloaks and swords to servants, shouts of instruction.

Hugh was soberly dressed in some nondescript brown garments with no plume in his hat or tassels on his hose, as he'd worn when I saw him in Rouen. When he took off his hat his russet hair was disheveled and as bushy as a fox's tail. He looked tired.

Ralph came out to meet him. Before the brothers had exchanged a dozen words, Isabella shot out of the castle door like a hound after a hare. She ran headlong toward Hugh, then caught herself and stood stockstill before him. They took each other's hands and she looked up at him with pure, undisguised affection.

There were no embraces, no touching except the clasped hands, but their faces shone with such joy that I had to turn my eyes away. When I looked back, they were sitting on a bench, talking. I couldn't hear a word but their happiness at this reunion was so evident that even Ralph smiled almost benevolently at them. After he left they stayed another ten minutes. Isabella must have said something that surprised Hugh because he rose and looked around. They walked inside, still holding hands, Isabella skipping to keep up with Hugh's long strides.

I was hot with jealousy, then cold with fury. I knew that Isabella would be mine eventually. But would she ever look at me as she looked at Hugh?

I hated him with all my being.

Hugh le Brun

1200

7

Just past Midsummer Day I was at last on my way back to Lusignan. Following the winding course of the Vonne, my two men and I rode through fields of ripening barley, not quite ready for the scythe, still green-gold. When a breath of wind arose, it moved over the grain and sent waves marching across the fields, as measured and inexorable as the billows of the sea. Here and there a patch of blue signaled a field of flax. In the meadows the cattle looked up gravely as we clop-clopped by, then went back to the serious business of grazing.

Sometimes we passed country folk on the road: a woman on a donkey leading another donkey on a rope, an oxcart so loaded with hay that the driver was almost invisible. A very small boy was herding two large balky black-and-white goats. When he saw me looking at him he flicked his little willow-whip at them and urged them on—"Hup there, hup there, be alive!" They increased their pace very slightly. I smiled at him and saluted him with my own whip.

This was my country, this Poitou, where I'd been born and raised. I loved it. I was content. More than content: I thought myself the happiest man alive.

For one thing, the visits to my new vassals in La Marche had gone well. They were agreeably surprised to find me so accommodating, after their years of trying to get along with their former suzerain, Eleanor of Aquitaine.

"A most demanding mistress, Queen Eleanor was," said Hubert of Belloc, lord of a prosperous domain near La Trémouille. "Always sending her men around to poke into our affairs and make sure we weren't holding out any revenue due to her."

"If you promise to be honest with me," I assured him, "I'll leave you to manage your demesne as you think best." I'd found it usually worked best to begin on a footing of trust rather than suspicion. Time enough to play the heavy-handed seigneur later, if need be.

Hubert pledged on his honor to serve me loyally, as did the others. With my mind easy on that score, I could give myself up to the anticipation of seeing my Isabella again. I could hardly believe that only three months before I'd thought of my betrothal with indifference. Now, God willing, Isabella's parents and I would set the date for our wedding.

I spurred my horse to a gallop as the track up through the town of Lusignan leveled off at the castle entrance. When my men and I rode into the bailey, I'd hardly dismounted when out Isabella flew like a little whirlwind to greet me. We walked across the parched dusty grass to a stone bench against the farther wall, under a huge sycamore. Sitting in its deep cool shade, sheltered from the heat and brightness, we paid no attention to the men shouting, armor clanking, and horses stamping their hooves, not twenty feet away.

Isabella was a surprise. She'd grown, not in stature but in maturity. Her hair was not hanging free, but was pulled back and coiled in a knot on the nape of her neck. Her dress, a filmy pale-gray gown, caught at the waist with a band of green linen, was more womanly. This was not the heedless girl who used to throw on any old garment to go galloping through the countryside with me, riding astride like a boy.

She giggled. "Why are you staring at me, Hugh? Because I'm not the simple little girl you once knew?"

"No, you aren't. But I like the new Isabella very much." I pressed her hand gently, realizing I'd been holding it ever since we sat down. She returned the pressure and we sat quietly, getting used to being together again.

"Well, if I look different it's because of my mother. She and my father arrived yesterday, My mother told me it was time I dressed like a lady. She said it was disgraceful that Aunt Alice let me go around like a raggle-taggle gypsy. She's already made me change my clothes twice today."

"So I expect I must compliment your mother, though I was perfectly happy with the other Isabella."

Then she was all curiosity about where I'd been and whom I'd seen. I told her about visiting a half-dozen of my new vassals.

"Did you tell them you were going to marry the daughter of the Count of Angoulême?"

"I did indeed, and they were suitably impressed, to a man. I'd like to think it was because the fame of your beauty had spread, but more likely it was a decent respect for a prudent political alliance."

40

More questions: Which of my vassals had the largest estates? Would they be invited to our wedding? And—"Will you be making a progress like this around La Marche and Lusignan when we are married? Will I go with you?"

"I will indeed from time to time. And of course the count will want his countess at his side when he calls on his vassals. She'll dazzle them with her beauty so they won't notice when he raises their rents. Now, enough of questions—or do you have any more?"

"Yes." She was suddenly very serious. "Hugh, why didn't you ever tell me you'd been married and you had a son?"

I was so dumbfounded I stammered.

"It just wasn't—I never thought—Oh Isabella, I'm sorry! I wasn't trying to keep anything from you. But it never seemed that important and it had nothing to do with you and me."

She said nothing, still staring me accusingly.

"But how did you know?"

"A tall young man came to see Uncle Ralph last week and stayed about an hour. I didn't meet him but I saw them talking in the courtyard, so I asked Aunt Alice who that was. She told me it was your son Hugh and that his mother was dead, but that was all she'd tell me. She said I should ask you if I had any more questions."

It was my turn to be silent. I'd meant to tell her some day, of course. But it was true, I'd never thought it had much to do with our relationship. Some things, I was learning, mattered much more to women than to men. I took her hand again but she withdrew it.

"All right, Isabella, maybe I should have told you this sooner. It was so long ago. I was only seventeen. My uncle Geoffrey, who was head of the Lusignan family, arranged it. He was a good friend of his cousin, the Count of Lezay, and the two of them decided the count's daughter Agatha and I would make a good match, good for the family. She was just my age. We took to each other—at seventeen, it's not hard to imagine one's in love!" I stopped, trying to remember how it had been.

"Was she pretty?" Her voice had a hardness I hadn't heard before.

"I thought so at the time, but do you know, now I can hardly remember what she looked like. Anyway, we were married and in about a year our son Hugh was born. But it was a hard birth and poor Agatha died when the child was only three days old."

"And then what? Who took care of that little baby? Surely not you, Hugh."

"No, I knew little enough about being a husband, much less a father.

Everybody agreed it would be best for my son to be raised by his grandparents down there at Lezay. So he was, and I was glad enough not to be in charge. I wasn't around much when he was young. I was off on the Crusade, and then serving King Richard here in France. But I've been trying to pay more attention lately because he'll be Count of La Marche some day. He needs to learn responsibility."

She was very quiet, not looking at me but out from our haven of shady coolness toward the expanse of hot dry grass between us and the castle. I put my arm around her shoulder. She held herself stiffly, then relaxed. I tried not to let my arm weigh too heavily.

"So will you forgive me for seeming to keep secrets? I didn't mean to. I would have told you all this sometime. Don't you see that young Hugh makes no difference to you and me?"

Silence.

"Yes, I guess so." Then, more animatedly, "But Hugh, you must let me meet him soon. Just think, I'll be his stepmother! I'll have to make sure he behaves!"

We both laughed at the thought of a slight fourteen-year-old taking on the upbringing of a hulking seventeen-year-old boy.

"Good, I'll try to arrange it. And he'll certainly be at our wedding. But now we must find out when that will be. Let's go in. I must pay my respects to your parents, and talk about setting the date."

"Before we do, you'll never guess who's just arrived."

"Who? Some bear-baiter, a troubadour ready to sing for us, a band of pilgrims on their way to Rome, some mighty bishop?"

"Much more mighty. It's King John of England."

I'd not expected to come on John so soon, after our brief and not very pleasant encounter in Rouen. I had an unaccountable sense that something was not quite right.

"Why has he come to Lusignan, do you think?"

"My father says he's calling on his new vassals—just as you've been doing, Hugh. He must have heard that my parents were to be here, and he came to make sure they would stay loyal to the Angevin side. There's going to be a dinner in his honor tonight."

"In that case, I'd better make myself presentable as soon as possible."

We started toward the castle. Glancing up I thought I saw a head quickly disappear from an upper window of the tower. Again, that faint foreboding. But I forgot it when Isabella said "Hugh, I'm so glad you're back!" We walked inside, swinging our clasped hands.

I still felt myself the happiest man alive.

Isabella

1200

Hugh and I stepped out of brightness and sunshine into the chill gloom of the castle entry hall. Chill and gloom, but not silence. We could hear shouting, pounding and banging from the kitchen, where everyone was frantically getting ready for the evening feast. Hugh peered through the arched doorway and reported, "Looks like roast goose for us tonight. I see two noble big birds being plucked this very moment."

Aunt Alice, looking flustered and with her cap askew, appeared from somewhere. "Oh, Isabella, your parents want to see you at once in the great hall. And Sir Hugh, King John has sent word that as soon as you arrived, you were to go up to his room in the Melisande Tower." She went off to the kitchen and I heard something about "A flagon of the best Bordeaux for the King, and quickly."

In the great hall servants were making a great racket as they set up long tables. Boys were bringing in logs to stack by the hearths. Two men were gathering up the old rushes and sweeping the floor, followed closely by another who strewed fresh ones. In a pocket of calm at the far end of the room my mother and father sat at the head table, waiting for me. They were talking in low voices. When they saw me they broke off. Something about this encounter reminded me of the day when they'd called me in to tell me I was to marry Hugh. Had that been only six months ago?

"Good, there you are, Isabella," said my father. "Come sit down and pay attention. As you know, we've come to Lusignan to talk about your wedding. Now that we've discussed it with King John, we've decided it should be at the end of August."

I'm afraid my voice rose as it does when I get upset. Lady Anne had often told me to watch myself.

"You mean *this* August? I thought it wasn't to be for at least a year. So did Hugh. And why isn't he here, doesn't he have something to say? It's his wedding too, you know. And what does King John have to do with it?"

My father frowned.

"Don't be shrill, daughter. As for Hugh, he'll join us when he can. King John had some urgent business with him."

He looked at my mother. She gave the tiniest of nods. He continued.

"It's true, we'd thought the wedding wouldn't be so soon. But things have changed. King John has just told us that he expects to engage King Philip in battle again before the end of the year. He needs to be sure we'll support him. In his view, the sooner you and Hugh are married the more secure the alliance will be of two of his most loyal and powerful vassals. So he's asked us to hold the ceremony before the end of the summer."

That made sense. But so far I'd thought of Hugh as a friend, the friend I'd never had. We'd talked about marriage, but as something far in the future. Was I ready?

"Besides," said my mother, "you and Hugh seem to be compatible. In fact, Ralph tells us you've grown fond of each other. We thought this would please you."

My father resumed.

"Since John must leave tomorrow for southern Aquitaine he wants to be assured that the marriage will take place soon. We thought that was a reasonable request."

My mother put on her most persuasive smile. "Remember, you'll soon be a countess with many responsibilities. Sometimes we have to put aside our personal feelings and do what's best for the family and the county. Surely you can understand that."

I tried to think like a countess-to-be.

"Yes, I guess so. Hugh's already told me that he's King John's man. He said the Lusignans have been subjects of the Angevin kings for a long time, and he sees no reason to change. But I thought you were pledged to King Philip. Won't he be cross if you go over to John?"

"He may well be," my mother said. "We'll just have to cross that bridge when we come to it."

"If we change from Philip to John, shouldn't he give us something in return?"

"He should indeed," said my father. "Congratulations, Isabella. You're thinking like a countess already. You may be sure I'll not let John forget that he owes us a very large favor."

We heard a creak as the massive door opened. Hugh was standing there, looking dazed. My father beckoned to him to join us. The scraping and sweeping had subsided and the hall was now quiet. Hugh sat beside me. We exchanged a quick look. His lips were pressed tightly together, and his face was flushed and darker than usual. If King John had given him the same news I'd just had he should have looked happier.

My father was speaking. "Well, Hugh, has King John given you the word—that he wishes your wedding to Isabella to take place by the end of August?"

"He has. And I think I can appreciate his reasons." His face was losing its dark flush. He turned to me. "It's sooner than we thought, Isabella. Are you ready to become the Countess of La Marche?"

I looked at his honest face, the steady brown eyes, the openness and kindness. I felt calmer. It was as though a windstorm had suddenly subsided to a gentle breeze. I put my hand in his.

"I'm glad if you are." We smiled at each other, for the moment forgetting we weren't alone.

Then, though, Hugh's anger came back. He told us the rest of his interview. John had ordered him to take a message to one of his Welsh vassals.

"He says the information is too important to trust to an ordinary messenger. But it will take weeks for me to get there and back."

He looked at my father.

"I must say, Sir Aymer, it seems strange, his sending me off like this when the time is so short to the wedding he's so anxious for. But I can't refuse him." He ran his fingers through his hair so it stood up all over his head like a bushy cap. It made him look like a little boy come in from play. A very worried little boy.

"He must have his reasons. How soon must you go?"

"In two days' time. But first, tonight in fact, I must go to Lezay and Fontenay to recruit some of my Lusignan relatives to accompany us. He's already told Ralph that he must go too. King John expressly required that we take a large enough body to represent him properly."

My parents were taking this remarkably calmly.

"Well, the sooner you leave the sooner we'll see you at Angoulême," said my mother cheerfully.

Hugh walked slowly to the door. I had to say something. I tried to keep it light.

"I'll be there waiting for you, Hugh. And don't worry. No matter how long you're gone, we can't hold the wedding without you."

He couldn't manage a word or a smile. He sent me an anguished look and left. The door gave an ominous thud behind him.

I was so cross at King John for sending Hugh off the very day he'd come home that I thought I'd refuse to come to the banquet in his honor and said so. But my mother told me I must absolutely be there.

"You absence would be unforgivably rude. The King particularly asked if you would be present. It's in our interest to please him and entertain him suitably. As long as he holds your father in his favor we could see a great rise in our fortunes. Now go up and change. You must wear something suitable for a state dinner. I think the green brocade."

I hated the green brocade, so stiff and heavy, like a suit of armor.

"Ah, here is Anne. She will help you. Now I must see how the cooks are doing." She swept out of the room and on to the next task.

An hour later I was at the foot of the winding tower stairs where I paused to tie the sash I'd taken without Anne's notice. I was wearing a soft, supple gown, a rose-tinged gold. It had taken only a few pouts to persuade Anne that it was more suitable than the green brocade.

"I'll be much more comfortable, because it's so loose," I said.

"Well, perhaps. But it does seem a little snug on top."

Anne still thought of me as a child and dressed me accordingly. I, on the other hand, had discovered that I was becoming quite shapely. At last, after what seemed like years of waiting, my body was changing in the most wondrous way. I was enchanted with it. Standing there in the shadows, I tied the sash snugly. Then I placed my hands at my waist and swept them up to brush them across my breasts. Through two layers of silk I could feel my nipples rising. I felt a delicious little shudder and smiled though I hardly knew why.

I heard a rustle and glimpsed a dim figure emerging from the dark alcove under the stairs. It was King John. He must have been watching me. He moved swiftly and silently to stand behind me, then put his arms around me. For a moment I felt his hands on my breasts. Then he released me. I heard a long sigh.

I was surprised, speechless, trembling.

"I'm sorry if I startled you. I've been waiting until you came down so I could escort you to the banquet hall."

His tone was polite and proper and told me nothing, but when his eyes met mine I felt drawn into their black depths. I remembered how intently he'd stared at me in the tavern. A new sensation—giddiness, confusion—overcame

47

me. I looked away, and John gently took my arm.

As we walked along the short corridor that led to the great hall he spoke calmly as though nothing had just occurred.

"I wanted to have a moment to tell you I am sorry to have sent your fiancé off so suddenly. I know it must be distressing to you. But I assure you that it was necessary. I had to have a messenger I could trust absolutely. And Sir Hugh will return well before your wedding date. So, Lady Isabella, no hard feelings?"

Before I could think of an answer there was a flourish of trumpets from the herald who'd been waiting to announce the King's arrival. The double doors to the great hall stood wide open, with a page in the King's scarlet-and-gold livery standing at either side.

All the other guests were assembled, and all eyes were on us as we walked in. I tried to look as though it were an everyday occurrence for me to enter a grand banquet hall on the arm of the King of England. For a moment I felt almost like a queen.

Anne Beaufort
July 1200

hen I saw who escorted Isabella into the great hall I caught my breath in surprise: the King of England, no less! She was blushing just a little and no wonder. It was the first time in her life she'd received so much attention from such a great person. I was glad to see that she kept her poise. I glanced at her parents. They looked surprised too, but not displeased.

The crowd in the hall remained standing and watched attentively while John led Isabella to the head table where the Count and Countess of Angoulême, the Countess of Eu, two of John's stewards, and the Bishop of Poitiers stood waiting. He seated her at her mother's right, then took his place between her parents. At that signal the rest of us to took our seats and neighbors murmured to each other about the lovely young girl who was being so favored by the King.

I hadn't seen such an impressive gathering since we'd come to Lusignan. Sir Ralph and Lady Alice didn't entertain much. We usually took our meals in the small dining hall near the kitchen. Isabella's mother and father must have plunged into action the minute they'd heard the King was to pay us a visit. Besides their own lords and ladies who'd come with them from Angoulême they'd somehow managed to assemble a dozen or so Lusignan vassals from the area. Their crowning achievement was the presence of the Bishop of Poitiers. There was, in addition, a large contingent of John's knights. We must have been at least two score in all, and everybody decked out in such finery that the dingy old hall took on a most festive look.

As we settled ourselves, all eyes were on our royal guest. King John was a study in dark elegance. He wore a black cape embroidered in gold over his black velvet tunic. A massive gold chain with a ruby-studded cross hung about his neck. The jewels in his crown glinted and sparkled, reflecting the light from the tall candelabra that were lined up around the room. His hair was short and dark. His pointed little black beard gave his face a triangular look. He reminded me of an alert mouse as his eyes darted about surveying the room.

His companions at the table had dressed in such a variety of brilliant colors that the King's somber splendor stood out even more. Lady Alice in her scarlet gown was, fortunately, several places removed from the bishop in his ruby-red cope or their combination might have blinded the beholder. Sir Aymer was all in mulberry. Even the Countess of Eu had been transformed from our familiar Aunt Alice into a well-rounded vision in sapphire-blue with rows and rows of pearls at neck and hem. She wore a countess's tiara perched on her gray curls. Her round face beamed with goodwill. Amid all this ostentation Isabella, my unaccountably sweet and demure Isabella, in her pale gold-rose gown, shone like a rare pearl among gaudy gems.

I found myself surrounded by strangers except for Lady Angeline Clafond, who was on my right. She was an old friend from my days in the countess's service.

"What an excellent view we have from here," she said. We were just a few seats down one of the two long tables that had been set up at right angles to the head table. "And how your Isabella has changed! I'd hardly have known her. She's quite the young woman, and so beautifully dressed. My compliments, Anne. You've done wonders with our awkward duckling."

"I can't take all the credit. Lady Isabella is developing a definite fashion sense on her own." I'd noticed the sash at once.

It became difficult to converse then because servingmen were tramping in bearing heavy platters and bowls and thumping them down on the tables. First came great tureens of steaming lentil soup, which they ladled into the silver bowls at our places. I'd hardly managed half my bowl when I had to push it aside because mountains of food were being heaped on my plate: roast venison; a fish pudding swimming in a sauce of wine, ginger and mustard; and a slab of simmered beef. Not to mention an onion pie, thick slices of fresh-baked bread and wine goblets kept filled by assiduous stewards.

It was a relief when entertainers appeared and one could pause to draw breath. A trio of musicians—vielle, tabor and flute—in patchwork red and yellow danced merrily into the hall and set themselves up in the space between the two long tables. They made up in volume what they lacked in musical ability. After ten minutes of hearing a flutist shrilling and a drummer pounding away not an arm's length from my ear, I was glad when they strolled on around the hall.

Devoting myself to my plate again, I did my best with the venison and the fish pudding but couldn't face the beef. It was in a sauce with a good deal more garlic than I care for. I noted that Lady Angeline's appetite, too, had flagged. We looked at each other ruefully. The knight across from us, who'd cleaned his own plate in short order and mopped up every drop of gravy with chunks of bread, eyed our leftovers hungrily. I gestured to him to help himself. "Better me than the hounds in the corner!" he cried and happily complied. Perhaps King John kept his men on short rations when they were on the march.

I looked up at the head table from time to time, and saw that though Countess Alix tried to make conversation with the King, she couldn't get much response and gave up. He was more interested in attacking his venison and keeping the page at his shoulder busy replenishing his goblet. Sometimes he spoke a few words to the count on his right. Once I saw him lean forward to look past Lady Alix to where Isabella sat. I thought I saw him catch her eye, but I couldn't be sure.

Finally the clatter of knives on trenchers and silver platters died down. When most of the guests were nibbling on tarts and sweetmeats, King John signaled to the trumpeter who'd been standing at the door. He advanced into the room and blew a blast that immediately silenced the chatter. John rose. Even with his crown he looked short. His eyes were fixed on a spot on the far wall somewhat above the head of the last knight at the foot of the table. His voice was rather high and didn't carry well. However, his words were as regal as one could wish.

"Good people of Lusignan and Angoulême, we are honored that you have come here to do honor to us. We value your allegiance to the crown of England. We will not forget you when we have successfully established our claims to the lands in France that King Philip withholds from us."

He looked at Sir Aymer and Lady Alix beside him, and down the table to Lady Alice, nodding at each. "We are grateful to the Count and Countess of Angoulême and the Countess of Eu for their hospitality. We are only sorry that two of our vassals who should be here and receive our gratitude as well are absent: Hugh de Lusignan, Count of La Marche, and his brother Ralph, Count of Eu. It was necessary to dispatch them on urgent royal business. However, we fully expect them to return in a few weeks' time. Then on August 26 the wedding of Sir Hugh and Lady Isabella will take place at Angoulême. This is a union that we welcome, uniting as it does the houses of two of our most distinguished vassals.

"Perhaps we will see many of you there, because we plan to attend the wedding after finishing our tour of Aquitaine."

And that was that. Preceded by his herald and his pages, he strode out of the hall, which began to buzz with conjecture and discussion.

"What business could have been so important that Sir Hugh couldn't stay to be congratulated on his upcoming wedding?" Lady Angeline wondered.

"I have no idea. I only learned of it two hours ago. Poor Isabella was very upset. But she seems to have gotten over it."

"Well, no matter what they say, I thought King John looked and acted like a strutting little fop. I saw his brother King Richard once and this one can't compare."

The gathering was getting rowdy. The Englishmen were shouting at each other. Pewter goblets crashed to the floor and pools of wine spread among the rushes. Sir Aymer looked pained, perhaps as much at what this was costing him as at the unseemly din. Lady Alix and Aunt Alice rose, gathered up Isabella, and left. It was time for me to go too. I said goodbye to Lady Angeline and found Adèle with the children near the foot of the table. We made our way through servants bringing more wine, a pair of knights threatening each other with dire fates—"Just draw your sword and say that!"—and a small pack of dogs snarling over bones that had been tossed in their midst. My head ached from having taken more wine and food than I liked and from a vague uneasiness about what King John might be up to.

Once we were back in Angoulême everybody became caught up in the preparations for the wedding. Isabella was overjoyed to be home again. She reveled in her new status: bride-to-be of the noble Hugh de Lusignan. Soon her room and mine were overflowing with gowns in every state of preparation, lace petticoats, silk capes, furlined cloaks. Seamstresses came daily to stitch and gossip and order the girl to stand still while she tried on their creations.

As the weeks passed Isabella became more anxious about Hugh. She'd ask me or anyone else who would listen when we thought he'd come home. Nobody, of course, had a clue.

"At least he could send us a message," she'd complain.

Sometimes she'd run out to the city gates, five minutes from the castle door, and stay for an hour looking down the long road that climbed up from the river. Then she'd come back dejected. "The only messengers I saw were my father's men, going out with his invitations to the festivities." Then she'd brighten.

"Well, if he doesn't get here in time, we'll just have to put off the ceremony."

One afternoon, I remember it was August 16, just ten days before the wedding, I was called to the count's chamber. He and the countess were looking very worried.

"Lady Anne, thank you for coming. We've had some very bad news and we want you to be with us when we tell Isabella. She'll be here shortly."

Before he could say more, in she ran. I could tell from her face that she was hoping they were going to tell her Hugh was on the way. The count took both her hands, then put his arms around her. This was most untypical of his usual role as the stern parent. I think Isabella could tell something was dreadfully wrong. She moved out of his embrace and looked with apprehension at him and her mother.

"What is it, father? Why have you called me?"

"My daughter, you must be brave. We've just had tragic news. I won't mince words. Your fiancé, Hugh, was attacked by a band of brigands in Normandy. He fought bravely but he fell. He is dead."

She stared at him in disbelief, then clasped her head in her hands and fell in a heap on the floor. Her mother and I both ran to help her up. Lady Alix led her to a chair and knelt beside her, smoothing her hair, murmuring to her. But the girl was sobbing now, hardly able to take in what her mother was saying.

"My poor little daughter. This is a shock to all of us but so much worse for you. We are so sorry, so terribly sorry. There, there, Isabella, let me dry your tears. My dear, I know that now you may think you'll never get over it, but believe me, you will in time."

Isabella shook her head violently back and forth. She was gasping, speechless, staring at her mother.

"Now let Lady Anne take you to your room. She'll sit with you until you sleep." I helped Isabella to her feet. She always wanted to do what her mother wished, and let me lead her away.

"I'll have them bring up a bowl of warm milk and honey," said the countess.

I said, "Yes, that might be a good idea. And also would you ask cook to make up a draught of motherwort?" I remembered how I used to give a younger Isabella motherwort tea when she had a temper tantrum and needed calming. It might help her sleep.

This was no tantrum, though. This was a wound to the heart.

John

1200

When I arrived in Bordeaux toward the middle of August I was pleased with myself. My progression around Aquitaine had been productive. I believed I'd done well in persuading the nobility to be well disposed to their new king and to stand ready to support England if war should break out. I'd done just what my mother had told me I must do.

When I'd seen her in Poitiers the month before, she'd impressed on me how important it was to woo these independent, opinionated local lords. She sat on her throne in the great audience chamber in the Poitiers palace, her chin in the air and her fierce blue eyes fixed on me: Queen Eleanor at her most didactic. I stood before her, trying to erase the memory of all the times I'd been called before her as a naughty little boy and lectured on the duties of a prince of the blood.

"John, you must never let your attention stray from your vassals in Aquitaine. They might go off in any direction unless we keep reminding them of their allegiance to the Angevin kings."

She'd never had much faith in my potential as a strong ruler in the pattern of her husband and my older brothers. But now I was the only son left and she was determined to make me measure up. I, for my part, was just as determined to show her how masterful I could be. Between us, perhaps we would make something of me.

I was glad to visit Bordeaux. It was a city where one could feel at home, what with the stout English ships in the harbor and English merchants walking the streets talking about the wines they were loading onto the ships. My main purpose here was to call on Archbishop Hélie, a delicate mission. I wasn't sure how he'd receive me. I needed the sanction of the church for my wedding to Isabella. I hoped this powerful churchman would stand by me.

"We're always glad when we're favored by a visit from any of your family," he said when we met. We were in his palace across from the Cathedral of St. André. His tall arched window looked out on the huge pile of stone, so decked out in carved angels, cherubim and seraphim, devils and sinners that it looked like some mad priest's fancy. But I was more interested in archbishops than architecture. I looked at my companion, a pudgy soft man who had surrounded himself with comforts: ample chairs softly cushioned in purple velvet, thick Turkish carpets, priceless tapestries and silver bowls of sugared fruits. The scent of some heady incense came from a brazier in a corner, more powerful than I cared for.

"I wish we could come more often," I said. "Queen Eleanor told me that Bordeaux is a city she holds dear. She asked me to tell you she regrets not visiting you for some years."

"I thank you," he said. He sounded like a plum pudding talking. "Your mother has always been a good friend to Aquitaine. We thought when she conferred the dukedom on her son Richard that he'd be equally attentive. But it seemed Richard came to these parts only to do battle, or when he had some grudge to settle with one of his vassals."

His plump lips turned down at the corners as though he'd tasted something bad. He must have guessed that I bore no good will to my departed brother or he wouldn't have spoken so plainly.

Then I invited him to come to Angoulême to officiate at my marriage to Isabella.

"She is the daughter of Count Aymer and Countess Alix of Angoulême. The marriage will forge an alliance between them and England. It will mean much greater security for Aquitaine. You would do us a great honor by lending us your presence."

I waited nervously for his reaction. I said nothing about Isabella's engagement to Hugh le Brun. If the archbishop was unaware of it I saw no reason to be the one to tell him. I was more concerned about his objection on the basis of my separation from Isabel of Gloucester. But he surely knew that the Pope had given his official approval to the dissolution of that marriage. When it is sufficiently pushed the church can find justification for divorce. In this case it was consanguinity, though the subject was conveniently forgotten during our twelve-year marriage and wasn't raised until it became plain Isabel would bear me no children.

Archbishop Hélie beamed at me like a child who has just been given a sweetmeat.

"Your Highness, any prelate would give his mitre to marry the King of England to such an illustrious heiress."

So off we set the very next day. Besides my fifty knights our party included five churchmen who would assist the archbishop in the ceremony. We rode hard to reach Angoulême by August 26, the date set for the wedding. I was nervous. I wasn't afraid the count had changed his mind. But I wondered how—or if—he'd persuaded his headstrong daughter to give up Hugh and marry me.

I had another worry. What if, in spite of the many tasks I'd charged him with, Hugh sped so fast to Wales and back that he'd return to Angoulême before the wedding? I'd counted on his arriving after the fact. Could I possibly forestall him? If so, how?

I turned in my saddle and beckoned to Jacques Motan, a clever, crafty knight who'd often undertaken delicate missions for me before. He wasn't at all surprised when he heard what I wanted.

"But no murders or maiming, Sir Jacques. And don't tell me anything about your plans. All I'm interested in is the result. Of course there'll be a generous gift if you succeed."

"Leave it to me, my liege."

There. I'd done what I could. Now I could give myself up to anticipation of my wedding. Over and over my mind's eye took me back to the vision of Isabella as I'd seen her at Lusignan, my last night there. I'd gone to wait at the foot of the tower stair for her to appear so I could escort her to the dining hall. I was standing in the shadows under the stair when she came down. Unaware of my presence, she stopped to arrange her clothing. Her dress was a lovely color, like ripe peaches, but hung on her like a loose bag. She was carrying a long golden sash. When she tied it around her slender waist, accentuating her swelling breasts, she was suddenly no longer a child but a bewitching, nubile young woman. I watched in silent, hungry fascination. She looked down at herself with approval, then drew her hands slowly up from her waist to linger on her breasts, then move up to her throat. I stepped quietly from my concealment to stand behind her and put my arms around her. She turned her head to look up at me like a startled bird. But she didn't cry out or move away. We stood there a moment, perfectly still, alone in the gathering dusk.

I released her, took her arm and asked, "Shall we proceed to the hall?" We weren't seated next to each other and had no conversation during the long dinner and the entertainment. Sometimes, though, our eyes would meet. I could tell she was seeing me in a new light.

Since then I'd often relived the moment at the foot of the stairs. I hoped that she did too.

Finally on the afternoon of August 25 Angoulême on its high rocky plateau came in sight. The sky was lowering. Lightning flashed on the horizon as my men and I pounded up the flinty road to the town. The massive city walls that loomed above us were already splashed with raindrops, dulled from their rosy sunlit glow to a damp gray.

"Only a summer storm," I told myself. "Hardly an ill omen for my wedding day."

I urged my horse on, tired as it was from a long day's riding, and galloped through the city gate. We were drenched, but briefly. As we entered the town the sun broke through and clouds of steam rose from stone walls, cobbled streets and my horse's flanks. Townsfolk came out from shops and shelters, resuming their business of buying and selling, gossiping and hurrying on their little errands. Some, recognizing me, cried, "Vive le roi Jean!" My mood changed in an instant. I sprang from the saddle in front of the count's palace. Even the indignant complaints of the Bordeaux churchmen as they shook out their sodden finery couldn't dispel my good cheer.

Count Aymer and Countess Alix greeted me and assured me that Hugh hadn't returned. After I'd changed my dripping clothes for a warm woolen robe and dry hose we conferred in the count's chamber.

Aymer told me of his ruse to get Isabella's consent to our marriage.

"She was inconsolable at first, or course, when we told her Hugh had been killed in an ambush by robbers during his return journey. She went to her room and cried and wouldn't see anyone except her lady in waiting for three days. We gave her some time, then my wife got us over the next hurdle."

The countess took up the story. "Yes, and it wasn't as hard as I'd feared. I comforted her and told her we all felt her sorrow. But I told her life must go on. When I suggested she might marry you she didn't fly into a rage at such an idea, as I'd been sure she would. She just looked at me, not saying yes and not saying no. I told her you'd already asked if you might have her hand and that you were disappointed to learn she was promised to Hugh. So we waited a few more days while she thought that over."

"I have a notion," said the count, looking at me shrewdly, "that she had an idea you might have taken a fancy to her."

"Also," said the countess, "she'd been looking forward to the grand wedding. 'What a pity it would be to stow those gowns and jewels away,' I told her.

'And think of the dozens of noble guests we've invited. They're all prepared to admire you and wish you well. Think how much more impressed they'll be to see you marrying a king instead of a count.' I'm afraid she is rather vain."

"So what with one thing and another she finally came around, just like that." The count slapped his knee and looked at me for approbation.

I thought there was more to her being so agreeable than vanity or even the titillation of marrying a man whose passion she'd aroused. Isabella was an ambitious little maid. Small wonder, considering how power-hungry her parents were.

"Well done, my friends," I said. "I'll confess I was worried. Not only about your daughter, but also about the possibility of Hugh arriving before the ceremony. But I believe you and I have taken all necessary measures. You've managed extremely well. I won't forget it."

Isabella

1200

11

It was August 26, my wedding day.

Brides are supposed to be happy and full of hope on their wedding days. Walking down the aisle of the Cathedral of Saint-Pierre, my hand on my father's arm, I was too worried to be completely happy. What would it be like to live with a man I hardly knew? John seemed to be attracted to me, though he certainly hadn't said so. But what did he really think of me, did he truly want to marry *me*, or was it only for the political reasons my father had explained? And would I be able to live up to what he'd expect of me? I was even fretting about whether I was suitably gowned. Was my lovely blue dress, with all the pearls, elegant enough?

All these questions whirled in my head while I walked sedately toward the altar. The familiar cathedral, where I'd gone to mass so many times, seemed strange—bigger, brighter, with hundreds of candles lighting up the nave that was usually so dim and shadowy. I was intensely aware that a crowd of nobles from all over Poitou were watching my every step. I heard murmurs. I wanted to look but knew I shouldn't. I could imagine what they were whispering about. Until this very moment they'd had no idea I was marrying the King of England instead of Hugh le Brun. No wonder they were confused. I was too.

Everything had happened so fast! After that terrible day when I'd been told of Hugh's death, matters had been taken out of my hands. My parents had been so persuasive, urging me to see the wisdom of marrying John. I'd agreed. I was still numb, hardly able to realize what had happened. It was easy to be dazzled by the thought of being a queen. At once we plunged into another flurry of wardrobe planning. It was decided I must have a new wedding gown, suitable for a queen rather than a mere countess. It was sky-blue, embroidered all over with silver and bordered by bands of tiny pearls. I adored it.

Then only yesterday John had arrived. I hadn't seen him since he'd been at Lusignan, a month ago. But I'd had no more than a glimpse of him last night, when he came into the castle and went straight to confer with my father. My mother said it wasn't proper for me to see my bridegroom the night before the wedding.

And now—now I'd almost reached the altar and there he was. He stood very straight with his back to me, facing the archbishop. He was all in elegant black velvet and wearing his crown. He could have been a stranger. I managed the two steps up without tripping over the hem of my gown. It was very full-skirted and I hadn't had time to practice walking gracefully.

I let go of my father's arm and stood beside John. He gave me a quick survey from top to toe.

"You look absolutely beautiful," he whispered. "The gown suits you perfectly."

That was reassuring. Perhaps I would get through this ceremony without any undignified lapses. Then I looked at the archbishop and I was unnerved all over again. I'd thought our bishop of Poitiers impressive. This ecclesiastic from Bordeaux far outshone him. He wasn't very tall, but with the lofty two-peaked mitre on his head he looked like some holy giant. Under his long embroidered cloak I glimpsed the rich purple of his cassock and the jeweled cross at his neck. When he gestured to us to kneel my eyes fastened on his ring. I'd never seen such an enormous ruby.

I had plenty of time to regain my composure. While we knelt before him Archbishop Hélie spoke at considerable length. I supposed it was the church's special wedding ritual for royalty, but I hardly understood two words of the jumble of Latin. Then he faced the altar and mumbled on for a time, with his hands clasped and his head bowed. His assistants, red-robed churchmen but not nearly as magnificent as the archbishop, waved their censers. I came very near to sneezing at the incense but managed to suppress it. The archbishop turned and delivered a long homily to John and me, about ruling wisely, trusting in God to help us, and maintaining heaven's holy harmony in our married life. We promised to do so. Then came more rapid Latin, which I took to be his pronouncement that we were now man and wife.

A bishop removed John's crown and held it on a cushion while the archbishop sprinkled a few drops of holy oil on our heads. John's crown was replaced. I'd assumed somebody would put a crown on my head too—wasn't I now King John's queen? But the archbishop told us to rise, then made the sign of the cross in the air. He led the way down the aisle with his bishops and the chanting choir behind him.

Leaving the cathedral on John's arm, I could look around freely at the crowd. I could even smile. Like flowers following the sun, all heads turned as we paced down the aisle. The ladies nodded and smiled. The lords doffed their plumed hats in salute. I felt more self-confident with every step. I stole a glance at John. He was very solemn. I decided that was how a king looked when receiving the respectful attention of his subjects. I stopped smiling and looking about, and did my best to assume a queenly expression.

All of us—bride, groom, archbishop, bishops, parents and noble guests—then walked the short distance from the cathedral to the Taillefer palace. My father's great hall was cool and made even more welcoming by boughs of greenery that had been hung about the walls, with posies poked into their branches. The room quickly became crowded with church dignitaries, lords and their ladies, knights and their pages. I stood beside John and my parents, still dazed, still trying to realize what was happening to me. Servants were already coming in bearing platters of meat, pitchers of wine, bowls of fruit, all the bounty for the banquet to come. It was noisy, but it was a joyful kind of noise. Children were romping and rolling on the floor like carefree puppies. A burst of chords erupted from the musicians tuning up in a corner. When they were satisfied, they began a fast-paced dance tune, with the tabor beating out the rhythm for the lute and the vielle. I looked hopefully at John.

"Isabella, I have an idea you're fond of dancing," he said.

"I am! Aren't you?"

"Not particularly. But perhaps dancing with you would change my mind."

My mother intervened. "Please forgive us, my liege, if we take your bride away for a short time. Her wedding gown would prove a little cumbersome for ease in dancing."

In my chamber, I changed to the same peach-gold gown that I'd worn that night in Lusignan, when John had come upon me so suddenly at the foot of the stairs. I wondered if he'd notice. While Lady Anne brushed my hair back and arranged it in a ladylike chignon I relaxed at last.

"How did I look, Anne? Could you tell how nervous I was?"

"My dear, you looked as calm and lovely as a swan swimming in a pond. I was proud of you."

When I returned to the hall John came to me at once. His eyes flickered and I knew he'd noticed what I was wearing.

The musicians had subsided into a more decorous air since nobody was dancing. Perhaps the guests had hesitated to begin before the King did.

He took my hand and led me a little apart from the crowd. Everyone was discreetly leaving us alone, but they were watching and whispering. John put his hands on my waist and turned me about so he could survey me from all sides.

"My dear Isabella, you've transformed yourself!"

"What do you mean? How transformed?"

"Why, you've grown up at least by two years since we were in the cathedral. Lovely as you were, you were like a pretty doll or a child playing at dressing up. Now you look more sixteen than fourteen." He drew me to him and tilted my head so he could look directly into my eyes. "You are enchanting," he murmured.

I felt the velvety softness of his tunic against my bare arms.

Nobody had ever wooed me like this.

"Are you glad, Isabella?" he asked softly. "I know this hasn't been an easy time for you. But are you happy it's turned out as it has, that we're now man and wife?"

"Oh, I am! Of course before Hugh died I was looking forward to being the Countess of Lusignan. But since that couldn't happen, I'm glad to the Queen of England instead."

He laughed. It was the first time I'd seen John laugh, though it was not much more than a few barks.

"But you're not yet the Queen of England, my love. Of course, for me and all my French subjects you are. But you won't truly be recognized as England's queen until we can go to England and arrange the coronation."

"And when will that be?" It dismayed me to realize how little I knew about my future, how little anyone had told me.

"Not for some months. I'm afraid I still have a great deal to do here in France first."

I drew away and looked up at him, startled and disappointed.

"You mean you're going to go off again? And I suppose I'll have to stay here at home with my parents while you're gone? If that's the case, why did we have to get married in such a hurry?"

"Now don't pout, my love." He took my hands and looked into my face, all seriousness. "You'll be with me wherever I go, I promise. Don't you realize that John loves Isabella, and wants her by his side always?"

"You've never told me so, you know."

He leaned toward me. "Now I'll tell you so." His lips on mine were cool and soft. He didn't prolong the kiss—just enough for me to begin to wish it would go on and on. I felt a little giddy. My first kiss. Hugh had never kissed me.

Suddenly I felt guilty. Had I betrayed Hugh's memory? Then I imagined him saying in his kind, sensible way, "You mustn't grieve for me forever, Isabella. You have all your life ahead of you. Whatever fortune offers you, accept it and be happy!"

I decided that I would always do whatever I could to be happy. I had no doubt now that as John's queen, I was well on the way to a blissful future.

And long after the end of that eventful day I could still feel John's lips on mine.

Hugh le Brun

1200

12

"**W**hat a wild and horrid country that Wales is!" Ralph said.

We were heading toward Angoulême from Boulogne where we'd met after our separate missions for John. We were bringing each other up to date as we rode along.

It was a fine summer day, half an hour after sunrise. Before long, the August heat would beat down on us, but so far we felt invigorated by the cool freshness. Dew still spangled the grass along the road. Our horses stepped along smartly.

I had calculated that we had plenty of time to get to Angoulême. We'd arrive well before my wedding day. I was as full of joy and anticipation as any country swain about to wed his milkmaid. I could hardly wait to see Isabella again.

We could hear our two squires chattering behind us. They were lads of our Lusignan clan, both called Robert. They were already looking forward to dinner.

"We'll have proper French wine with our meat today," said Cousin Robert.

"Nothing like that piss-and-vinegar they call wine in England," said Nephew Robert.

I grinned.

Ralph, though, was not so light-hearted. His narrow face, never particularly cheery, was furrowed with misery and his whole body sagged. He went on with his tale.

"When I finally found Sir William, he was snuggled down in his barony at Radnor. I gave him John's message about meeting in Winchester in September, and he glared at me as though I were a stupid potboy. He roared like a wounded boar, something about, 'By God's teeth, why does that foolish king waste my time by telling me what I already know? John sent exactly the same message a month since. You can tell your little king that I'll come if I feel like it.' And he practically pushed me out the door."

I hadn't liked Wales any better than he had. I'd found it a land of trackless wilderness, steep mountains and rude castles where the chieftains perched, eyeing each other suspiciously, ready to gather their men at any imagined threat and go out to stick swords into each other.

"My story isn't much different, brother. When I finally found Lord Llewellyn's castle, up in the north, he wasn't there. I was supposed to tell him to chase after a neighboring lord who's done John some sort of injury, and teach him a lesson. His steward told me Llewellyn had left a week before to launch a surprise attack on Ranulf, the enemy in question. He'd done just what John wanted, and my whole trip was useless."

"I wonder what tale Geoffrey will have to tell, " said Ralph. John had sent our uncle to Normandy. "He must be home by now."

All at once it came to me how similar our experiences were. This was more than coincidence. Had John deliberately sent all three of us off on wild goose chases? Why? My head almost ached as I tried to sort it all out. I felt we must get home as soon as possible.

I told the others we'd have to step up the pace, and so we did, as much as the roads would allow. They were quite dreadful for a while, with deep furrows of hardened mud and washed-out stretches where we had to descend steep rocky slopes, then scramble up the other side. But presently we found ourselves traveling a smooth, dry track beside the Charente River. Now we could urge our horses to gallop, without fear of breaking their legs in potholes. Some kind landowner, years before, had planted poplars along the road. In the shade of the tall close-set trees we found a welcome respite from the sun that was hot enough to broil our brains.

Ralph, my elder by some fifteen years, was plainly weary. Yet he knew how important speed was to me and didn't complain. I kept hearing Isabella's words—"Don't worry, Hugh. We can't hold the wedding without you," but I still felt panicky.

On August 24 we were close enough that I felt we could stop and rest. The river flowed quietly along, tempting to thirsty horses and dusty riders alike. A meadow sloped gently down to the river's edge. We dismounted, led the horses to the shore and let them drink their fill.

"My feet feel like fried sausages trying to burst out of their skins," said cousin Robert.

I took off my boots. So did Ralph, and we sat on a low bank, dangling our feet in the cool stream. The two lads threw off their tunics and hose and jumped into the river to splash about like a pair of otters.

What fools we were! While we sat there a gang of rough fellows rushed down to our riverbank. Ralph and I sprang to our feet, but too late. Before we could get to our swords and daggers that we'd flung down with our clothes, the ruffians were upon us, grabbing our weapons, brandishing them and jeering.

I say we were fools because we should have been more cautious. We knew these were dangerous times for travelers. When there's no war going on, foot soldiers with nothing much to occupy them go on a rampage, robbing and assaulting anyone they come across. Ever since the end of the Third Crusade, a few years before, they'd multiplied like beetles in a dunghill. Some were unemployed mercenaries and some were luckless fellows who'd lost their lands to the enemy. None had any regard for the law.

But I soon found out that these were no common mercenaries.

While we were fighting them with our fists—all we had—the thieves jumped on our horses and rode off. One of them turned in the saddle and shouted with a wicked grin, "I almost forgot. King John asked us to wish you a very pleasant journey."

The words hit me like a blow to my midriff. This confirmed my worst suspicions. John had planned this fiendish scheme to delay my return to Angoulême.

There we were, bereft of horses and weapons and supplies, for we hadn't even taken the saddlebags off the horses. At least we had kept our money pouches on our persons.

"And the dastards didn't take our boots," said Nephew Robert, trying to find a silver lining.

There was nothing for it but to trudge along the road until we came to an inn. It was well after dark when we found one. By morning the innkeeper had procured horses for us. It took us another full day and a half to cover the remaining distance. I was frantic with anxiety. At last, late on the morning of August 28 we rode into the bailey of the Taillefer castle at Angoulême. It was very quiet. Nobody was about except some grooms who were saddling a pair of horses. I dismounted and went inside, to find Count Aymer and Countess Alix dressed as though for a journey.

We stared at each other. Count Aymer had always been very good at concealing emotion. But he was not so successful in trying to display it. I believe he was hoping to express shock and surprise, but it looked more as though he had an acute stomachache. Countess Alix, on the other hand, after only a moment's hesitation smiled her lovely smile and exclaimed, "Hugh! We heard you were dead, that you'd been killed on the way home. Yet here you are!"

"Where is Isabella?" I shouted.

She placed a hand on my arm. "Hugh, Hugh," she said, " calm yourself and listen."

In short order they told their story.

King John had asked Count Aymer for Isabella's hand two months ago, said the count, but withdrew when he learned that she was betrothed to me. All was ready for the wedding when word came that I had been killed in an ambush.

"Isabella was very distressed to hear it," said the countess.

Then John, who was among those invited to the wedding, renewed his suit.

"When we told her about it, she thought only a little while, and agreed," said the count. After a pause, "We were surprised."

"We had expected her to mourn you longer," said the countess, with a pretty mixture of sorrow and wonder.

The wedding had taken place on the date scheduled, just two days ago, and the couple had left yesterday for Chinon.

"And we are about to join them there," said Count Aymer.

My face burned red with anger. I was clenching and unclenching my fists, hardly able to avoid striking him.

"But you're welcome to stay and recover from your journey," said the countess, still pretending that this was a civil conversation. "Our people will provide anything you need."

They were edging toward the door. I flung past them, ran to my horse and signaled Ralph to follow me. He and the two Roberts stared open-mouthed, then scrambled to get into their saddles and join the flight.

As we galloped on, I told Ralph what had happened. I was almost incoherent in my fury. Loyal brother that he was, he agreed that revenge was imperative.

"We'll make for Lusignan first," I said. "I pray Geoffrey is there. Then we'll ride out through La Marche and rally our vassals. By God, we'll make John suffer for this!"

Isabella
August-September 1200

13

The morning after the wedding and the feast I woke suddenly from a vivid dream.

I'd been standing with John in the great hall. "He's really quite good-looking," I thought. "I like his eyes, so smoky-black. And his black hair, with just a little curl. I wonder if his beard is as soft as it looks. I wonder what it would be like if he kissed me."

Then he did. I was wishing he'd never let me go. But a tall, sour-faced man I didn't know came and pulled me away. "Careful, Isabella!" he said. "Don't be too happy too soon. How well do you know this man?"

That's when I woke and sat up, frightened. I wondered what it meant, if anything. But gradually the memory of John telling me he loved me took over and I forgot the dream. I lay down, stretched luxuriously and pulled the coverlet up to my chin. The curtains of my high bed were tightly drawn and I was snug and warm. I closed my eyes and gave myself up to reliving the whole exciting day, the day when I married the King of England.

I was drifting off to sleep again when Anne Beaufort came in, pulled open the bed curtains and told me she had a message from King John.

"He says to tell you he's sorry, but he's just learned we must leave for Chinon this morning," she said. "He said to let you sleep as long as possible, but now we must get ready for the journey. I've already packed your chest and your bags."

I was still tired from all the ceremony and festivities. I would have liked nothing better than to spend the day lying about and being waited on. I considered whining and arguing until I got my way, as I would have done when younger But now my husband the King requested my company. Hadn't he told me "John wants Isabella with him always"? I jumped down from the bed and docilely allowed myself to be dressed. Ann had brought a bowl of milk and a rusk, which would have to do for my breakfast.

When I came down to the hall I saw John, already in his traveling cloak and pacing nervously about. My parents were there too, also impatient. My mother was tapping her foot. Nobody had noticed me yet.

"I'll go see to the horses," said my father. "The sooner you're well out of town, the less chance of an untimely encounter."

I wondered what that meant, but I was still too drowsy to try to figure it out.

"Good, there you are, Isabella," said John. "Now we can leave."

I rubbed my eyes and yawned.

"Why are we going to Chinon in such a hurry?"

"I've just learned that important visitors I'd arranged to meet there are on their way. We must be at Chinon Castle to greet them." He'd hardly glanced at me. Where was the tenderness of last evening?

"I'll explain once we're on our way."

My father hurried in.

"The horses are saddled and ready, " he said. "And your troops have already left."

My mother kissed me. "Travel in safety. We'll follow you within a few days."

We all mounted quickly—John and I, Lady Anne and Adèle, our maids, John's stewards and four of his knights. We hurried through the town as though in flight. But when we were riding along the river road on the plain and had caught up with the rest of the troops, John signaled to the leading knight that we could all slow our pace. At last he gave his attention to me and gestured that I should ride close by his side. I still felt curious about the hasty departure.

"I'm sorry, Isabella. There was a rumor that a band of brigands was waylaying travelers around Angoulême. I think we're well away from them now. Are you all right? Did you sleep well, my love? You're looking particularly beautiful this morning. A good gallop must agree with you." He took my hand and raised it to his lips. "Will you forgive your husband, whose only care is for your safety?"

This was the John of the night before.

"Ah, you smile at me. So I am forgiven?"

"Yes, of course. But John, can you tell me now who these people are that we must go to Chinon to meet?"

"They're Queen Berengaria and her party. She's the widow of my brother Richard. You may not have heard of her."

"Of course I have. She was once the Queen of England. But why is she coming to see you?"

"She has some foolish notion that England owes her a huge sum of money as her inheritance. She pretends that she's in dire need. But I must put her off somehow."

I thought a minute. "Of course you must. My father's often told me that we mustn't agree to the requests of everyone who asks."

"And your father, I believe, has amassed quite a fortune out of being so thrifty."

The closer we got to Chinon the more convinced I was that I wouldn't like it. From the plain I looked up to see a long chalk-white rampart crowning the cliff that overhung the river. The walls bristled with towers and buttresses. Far below an untidy earth-colored town huddled between river and cliff.

Our party straggled through the town and up the twisting narrow road to be faced with a high, forbidding stone wall, unbroken except by a small arched opening with an iron gate. A soldier unlocked the gate and a pair of armed horsemen cantered out. On their crimson shields the three golden Plantagenet lions cavorted. The men greeted John respectfully, eyed me with curiosity and led us through the gate.

The news of John's sudden marriage must have barely reached Chinon. Of course they wondered about me. I sat up in the saddle, held my head high and took a firmer grip on the reins.

As we came into the vast, hot, dusty bailey, completely surrounded by stone walls, I looked around in dismay. This was like no castle I'd ever seen. It was enormous and desolate. I could make out unkempt garden plots, huts and stables. Far down at the end stood a squat structure that might be a chapel. But where did people live? Half a dozen towers were fitted into the walls. Their small square doorways led, I supposed, to dark interior chambers as unwelcoming as what I saw now. I shivered in spite of the heat. Angoulême and Lusignan seemed cozy in comparison. Clearly this monstrosity had been built to repulse enemies, not for courtly gracious living.

John, however, seemed enamored of the dismal fortress.

"By my faith, this is the way to build a castle! I haven't been here since long before Richard died. I see he added two towers. Look, Isabella, how well the defenses are placed. Four towers along that south wall, and another down at the end. There's no way an enemy could get close without being seen."

I'd already dismounted with the help of one of the knights. I felt as droopy as the scrawny, discouraged bushes that lined the walkway to the nearest tower. All I wanted was to get out of the sun and lie down. Three days of jolting travel in the heat of August had nearly exhausted me. I staggered, then righted myself. John leaped down from his saddle and ran to me. I leaned against him gratefully.

"Isabella my love, forgive me. How could I run on so? Of course you're tired. We'll go in at once and see if they've done what they should to make things comfortable for us."

They had indeed. I was agreeably surprised when John led me through one of those forbidding doors into a well-furnished chamber, nothing like what I'd feared. My eyes flew to a high bed with a dark red canopy, a beautiful carved chest festooned with golden wreaths that shone in the dim room, and a throne-like chair all red and gold. Wherever I looked I saw richness and elegance. Tall gold candlesticks stood in each corner, the candles not yet lit but ready to chase the shadows when night fell. Instead of the grimy rushes I'd feared, a soft rose-colored carpet covered most of the stone floor. A fireplace was laid neatly with logs. Sprays of lavender sprang from a silver vase on a table.

"John, how beautiful! Is the rest of the castle like this?"

"I'm afraid not. This is my mother's room. She must always have things just so, wherever she goes."

So this was Queen Eleanor's room. I knew nothing of my mother-in-law beyond what all Europe knew. She was a high-spirited beautiful woman who had brought the Duchy of Aquitaine with her when she married Henry II of England; a woman who was often at odds with her husband and who didn't hesitate to persuade their sons to go into battle against him; and, they said, a woman with a softer side, who invited knights and damsels and troubadours to gather around her when she held her Courts of Love.

"Then I'm grateful to her. And to you too, for having a mother with such elegant tastes. When will I meet her, John? Is she glad you've married me?"

"She is, to her credit. I stopped to tell her of our plans the last time I went through Poitiers. She agreed this was a much better match for England than the Portuguese princess she'd been trying to push at me. And the one thing my mother cares about most is what's good for England."

"This is the first I've heard of any Portuguese princess! Was she beautiful?"

"I have no idea, but I doubt it. I never saw her and I never wanted to marry her." He smiled and kissed me on the cheek "But from the moment I saw my beautiful Isabella, I knew I wanted to marry her."

He gently smoothed my hair and I nestled in his arms. With my cheek against his tunic I inhaled the scent of leather and wool, a whiff of lavender—familiar smells yet now linked to John and to this moment. He pressed me closer and looked down at my face. I didn't understand what was happening to me. I'd never felt this pull toward another being, this urge to prolong the closeness, to feel his strong arms about me. Was this what they called love?

"I must leave you now, sweetheart. I'll send the women in with your things. Get a little rest because I fear our guests will be here soon. But we'll soon be rid of that bothersome old onetime queen. And then, my sweeting, we'll be all alone here, just the two of us."

When John left I poured myself a cup of cool water from the silver ewer on Queen Eleanor's marble-topped table. Then I climbed onto Queen Eleanor's bed. Rest had never been so welcome. I watched drowsily as two servants brought in my traveling chest and Anne told them where to put it. The last thought that came to me was the memory of the disturbing dream. But how silly. There was nothing wrong with being happy. And I was married to a king, to John, who really did love me, and whom I was getting to know better every day. How could I not be happy?

Isabella
September 1200

When John escorted me to the dining hall later that afternoon, I felt like skipping.

"Just think, John, this will be my first official appearance as your queen!"

He didn't answer but tightened his clasp of my hand and half-smiled. John didn't smile very often or very broadly and hardly ever in company. But I was coming to recognize the look on his face when it was just the two of us and he looked at me as though we inhabited our own little world where nobody else could intrude.

In spite of what John had said I'd been hoping the rest of the castle would display at least some of the elegance of Queen Eleanor's boudoir. But the dining hall was cramped, with a huge wooden table occupying most of the space. A tarnished silver candelabrum lacking a few candles hung over it, giving off a dim light. From the cold hearth came the smell of stale ashes. Some effort had been made to spruce things up: a white linen cloth on the table and a silver goblet at each place. The floor appeared to have been recently swept.

John barked an order to a servant to bring more candles and to light a fire.

Two women and a man were standing near the window. A sunbeam wandered in and illuminated the face of the younger woman. This must be Queen Berengaria. Her face was pearl-smooth and unlined. Even from across the room I caught the serenity of her expression and the steady gaze of gray-green eyes. She was dressed all in white—widow's garb, I knew. A wimple concealed most of her hair but on her forehead two curves of dusky brown showed, like the wings of a wood thrush. A delicate jeweled tiara rested on the snowy wimple. She was certainly not the grasping crone I'd been expecting.

"Will I ever look so queenly?" I asked myself, brushing back an unruly lock. I was jealous, but at the same time I wanted to know this woman better.

John was greeting her. I heard her introduce her companions, Sir Hugh de Vendeuvre and his wife Charlotte, who had come with her from Troyes. They turned to me and Berengaria quickly stepped forward and took my hand.

"And you are Queen Isabella. They've been saying that John had found the prettiest girl in France for his bride. I see he did indeed!"

"Thank you, you are very kind," I murmured.

Berengaria turned to John. "I congratulate you, brother."

His eyes had darted between us during this brief exchange. He grunted what might have been a thank-you, then said, "Well, shall we seat ourselves?"

Anne Beaufort, two of John's knights and a churchman had joined us. Berengaria was on John's left and I was on his right. In spite of the candles and the fire, it was hardly a festive scene. Servants brought platters of roast pork and fowl, bowls of stewed turnips and cabbage, apple tarts and heavy puddings, more fitting for December than August. The guests spoke in subdued tones if they spoke at all. John did nothing to encourage an easier ambience. I was too shy to initiate any conversation.

I was glad when my neighbor, Charlotte de Vendeuvre, addressed me. She complimented me on my gown and my complexion. She asked how I managed to look so fresh in spite of the heat, but didn't wait for an answer. She even found favorable things to say about the castle: "So solid! Such high walls! One feels quite safe here."

I nodded. "Yes, it's far better fortified than any castle I've seen."

"I was so privileged that Queen Berengaria asked me to come with her! We're here to talk about her inheritance, you know."

"I know, the King told me. That was why we hurried here from Angoulême."

"Yes, well, my husband has been helping the Queen compose her claim, and King John has sent word that he'd settle it all if we'd come. So we came."

She paused to chew daintily on a pigeon leg, dropped the tiny bones on her plate and picked up another.

I was curious about this worldly woman. "Do you travel much? Have you been to Paris?"

"No, and I long to go. King Philip came to see us in Troyes once, though. But he left after only a half-goblet of wine and a bit of fish. A rather meager man, King Philip. Ought to eat more. Now your husband, I see, has a proper respect for his dinner."

I turned to see John eating stolidly, as though it were his duty to dispose of all that was put before him. I'd already learned he wasn't one for table talk. He didn't stint himself on wine, but it seemed to make him morose rather than merry.

Hugh de Vendeuvre, on his wife's other side, had gotten her attention so I could relax and look around the table. Berengaria was deep in conversation with the bishop. The two knights were eating and drinking as though it were their last meal and exchanging what must have been lewd stories, judging from their muffled snickers.

I looked at John and saw him staring at me. He leaned to kiss me on the cheek. I rather liked that. Let the world see that the King of England has married for love.

He plucked a plump grape from a silver bowl and asked, "Have you tried these, my little one? They are delicious." He put the grape in my mouth and let his fingers slide gently over my tongue, then withdrew them and sealed my lips with a kiss. I felt again that strange tremor of excitement and unease. He drew back and watched me as I swallowed the grape. I glanced around, but the others looked unconcerned if they'd noticed at all. I drew a deep breath. John went back to mopping the gravy on his plate with a chunk of bread. When it was polished clean he stood up and raised his goblet, bowing slightly to Berengaria.

"To your health, sister. You and your friends are welcome at Chinon. Tomorrow we will meet with Bishop John and my chancellor to go over the settlement I am prepared to make. Until then, let my people know if you desire anything, and sleep well." He strode from the room. I thought I heard sighs of relief from some in the company.

I rose and walked around the table to Berengaria.

"It's still early. Will you come visit me in my chamber? Then you'll see that not all the castle is as dreary as where we are now. Or perhaps your lodgings are pleasing?"

"Well, pleasing may not be quite the word. They're adequate, shall we say." She sounded amused but tolerant. We walked out to the barren courtyard, still baking though the sun had sunk an hour ago below the battlements on the west. As we walked along I explained I was staying in Queen Eleanor's chamber.

"Then I can believe you when you say it's not like the rest of the castle. From what I know of her she loves her comfort."

"Do you know her well? I've never met her, though I hope I will soon now that I'm her daughter-in-law."

"I feel I know her well, though I seldom see her now. But she arranged my marriage and we traveled together to Sicily so I could go with Richard on the Crusade."

We entered my cool, dim room. Someone had lit the tall candles, and the gold wreaths on Eleanor's chest reflected the mellow glow. Berengaria looked around in admiration and stood by a window to make the most of a faint breeze.

"John said his mother had demanded the walls be broken through so she could have these windows." Berengaria smiled but didn't comment. I urged her to sit in the thronelike chair. I poured each of us a cup of water, then perched on the bed.

"So you had an arranged marriage? I did too, though Queen Eleanor didn't have anything to do with it. It was just between my parents and John."

"I've heard it was rather sudden."

"Yes, it was. I was supposed to marry Hugh le Brun of Lusignan, you know. But after he was killed, and after I got over feeling so dreadfully upset about it, my parents told me John had asked for my hand. I was sort of in a daze and I thought, why not? Since I can't have Hugh I might as well be a queen. And do you know, now I'm beginning to enjoy myself?" I smiled at her, feeling shy at having spoken so freely.

She looked at me in bewilderment.

"But Isabella…" She stopped, and there was such shock on her face that I couldn't imagine what was the matter. She was silent, trying to gather her thoughts.

"Isabella, I'm so sorry to be the one to tell you this. But you'll find out sooner or later. There's been a grievous misunderstanding. Hugh de Lusignan is not dead. We saw him with his brother at Tours on our way here. He was very much alive three days ago."

I stared at her in incomprehension. Then I shrieked, "They lied to me, they lied! All of them lied!" and I fell back on the bed, wailing. I saw Berengaria standing over me, wringing her hands and wondering what to do.

Anne, who must have heard me cry out, ran in. Through my sobs, as though from far away in a dream, I heard Berengaria tell her what had happened.

"I'm so dreadfully sorry I told her. What was I been thinking of? What can I do?"

"No, no, I'm glad you did. I've wanted to but I didn't dare." Anne put her arms around me and murmured, "There, there, my pet."

"I'll go then. It's best for her to be with you, not a stranger."

"Yes, I've seen her through many a stormy time. But she didn't deserve this. Of course she takes it hard." She smoothed my hair. I could imagine it was my mother's cool, soft hands comforting me. Then I remembered how my mother had deceived me.

I heard, clearly, Anne's words as Berengaria left.

"Don't feel it's your fault. It's John who will have to answer for this."

John
September 1200 15

The morning after the dinner with Berengaria and her party I carefully considered what to wear. I settled on one of my favorite tunics, a finespun blue wool, then threw a cloak of blue silk about my shoulders. I held up the small polished-bronze mirror I always carry with me and admired the way the gold cross around my neck gleamed against the deep blue.

"An excellent choice, my liege," said my man Albert while he adjusted the drape of the cloak. "You look very royal but not ostentatious."

I looked at him suspiciously. Was this his veiled implication that he thought I usually wore too many jewels? Never mind. I accepted the compliment. In my nervous apprehension I needed all the reassurance I could get. And it wasn't because of my bothersome sister-in-law and her infernal demands for her inheritance. No, it was Isabella I dreaded meeting.

The previous evening while I was planning how to put Berengaria off, Lady Anne had knocked on my door. She told me bluntly about Isabella's discovery that Hugh was still alive.

"She must have an explanation. She is suffering grievously."

I could almost feel the heat of her barely controlled anger. She went on.

"I've known of this subterfuge ever since Countess Alix told me, so I could keep Isabella from learning the truth accidentally. Now it's up to you, my lord, to mend the situation. If you can."

This was insolence. I half rose, ready to threaten her with some punishment and order her from the room. But she wasn't subject to me. She left, and I sat glowering.

Though I'd known Isabella was bound to find out some day, I'd hoped it would be much later and I could tell her myself. I wasn't prepared. What would I say? At least I had all night to think about it. By morning I had my story well in hand. In the dining hall I found Isabella at the table, between Lady Anne and Adèle. Lady Anne was urging Isabella to eat. When I entered, she rose, took Adèle's hand, and left without a word or look in my direction.

My bride's eyes were red and puffy and her face looked drawn, as though she had not slept. I sat down beside her and took her hand, but she angrily took it back.

"Isabella, I've just heard the news. I see that you've heard too. I couldn't be more surprised." Her face was a blank. Her blue eyes were wide and unblinking. Her lips trembled.

"The man who brought me the story of Hugh's ambush and death was one of my most trusted informants. I had no reason to disbelieve him. He must have been bribed by some enemy for who knows what reason. You may be sure I'll track him down and get to the bottom of this. It was a monstrous and cruel deception."

She looked down and began toying with the bowl of oat porridge before her, lifting spoonfuls up and letting them drop back into the bowl. I was desperate to have her believe me.

"I'd never have suggested our marriage if I'd thought Hugh was alive. But I had every reason to think he'd been killed. We all did. So when I asked your parents for your hand, it was in good faith. When you finally consented to be mine, I could hardly believe my good fortune." That part at least was true. She pushed the bowl aside and narrowed her eyes to scrutinize my face as one would a page of writing, trying to read some meaning in it. I took heart.

"Tragic as this news is, we're man and wife now. You are my queen and I love you dearly. Nothing can change that. I think you've come to care for me too, at least a little. Am I right?"

I ventured to take her hand again, and this time she let me hold it.

"We mustn't look back, my love. Soon, just as I promised you, we'll go to England and you will be crowned my queen at Westminster."

Her face was less closed. She didn't smile, but she was listening. I sensed I was winning.

"Remember, Isabella, when you told me on our wedding day that you were glad to be Queen of England instead of Countess of La Marche?"

At last she spoke, angrily. "Of course I remember! But that was when I thought Hugh was dead. Now things are different." Suddenly she was a lost child. "Couldn't we go home to Angoulême before we leave for England? I want to see my mother."

I wanted to comfort her, to let her know I loved her and would take care of her. I wanted her to forget Hugh had ever existed. I had to keep talking.

"You'll see your mother, my love, very soon. She and Count Aymer promised me when we left that they would come here as soon as they could. They should arrive tomorrow or the next day. They'll stay until we leave. That will cheer you up."

I was still holding her hand. I rose, drawing her to her feet.

"Let's walk out for a bit for some light and air, before I have to see Queen Berengaria."

She obediently accompanied me to the bailey, where the sun was just coming over the walls and where the early-morning coolness made walking still tolerable. It had rained in the night, and patches of green grass showed here and there. Yesterday they'd been smothered in dry dust. Even the scraggly daisies and calendulas along the walk had taken heart, with their petals polished and their stems upstanding.

I rattled on, hoping to turn her thoughts in a new direction.

"So, Isabella, you'll have company while I go to Paris. I must see King Philip. He's asking for 30,000 marks. Everybody demanding money! I'll put Berengaria off again with no trouble; all I have to do is promise to send her settlement, then forget about it. But King Philip is another matter."

She stopped suddenly. I'd caught her attention.

"Why must you see King Philip? You told me you and he had settled everything, when you signed the truce in May."

I was surprised when she showed an interest in governance. Except for my mother I'd known no woman who understood the possibilities of royal power. I imagined a day when Isabella and I were tied by the bonds of physical union as well as our ambitions. That time hadn't come. Soon (but not yet, John, not yet! I had to keep telling myself), she would respond to my ardor with the passion that was so far unawakened. Then, who could stop us? My mind had raced from King Philip to the marriage bed, where I would have liked to linger. Isabella tugged at my arm.

"Is Philip threatening to break the truce? I thought it was to last for a year."

"No, my clever little queen, he is not. But I did promise to pay him 30,000 marks before I leave for England. In return he promised not to invade my lands while I'm gone. It's a bribe. A shameless bribe. But I had no choice."

The words hung in the air and neither of us said anything for a minute. We seemed to be back on a friendly footing. I thought it was safe to return to our earlier conversation. I wanted to be sure of her trust in me.

"Never mind all that now. I beg you to put my mind at rest. Can you tell me you believe me when I say I had no idea Hugh still lived, when I made you my wife?"

She looked at me gravely. "I must believe you, John. After all, I have no choice either, have I?"

Hugh le Brun
September 1200

16

Since I was a boy they've called me Hugh le Brun—Hugh the Brown—because of my dark hair and swarthy complexion. It was so I wouldn't be confused with another Hugh in the Lusignan clan, who was yellow-haired and fair.

In September of 1200, though, they could have called me Hugh le Noir. Black was my mood, and my hopes had sunk into a mire of dark despair. Isabella was lost to me.

"It wasn't her fault though," I said to Ralph. "She wouldn't have thrown me over and married John unless he'd convinced her of my death. He managed that very cleverly, just as he arranged that attack on us so we wouldn't arrive before the wedding day."

Like so many of our conversations, this one was punctuated by pounding hoofbeats. Our words were jolted out of us as we kept our horses at a trot. We were on our way to Lusignan from Angoulême where I'd learned of Isabella's wedding to John. The heat had abated somewhat, and I thought I detected a tang of autumn in the air. The fields along our way were a sea of ripening grain where a few farmers were already out swinging their scythes. I felt envious of men who had no more worries than getting in the harvest before the rains came.

I glanced at Ralph. His face was scrunched in a perplexed grimace.

"I don't know about that, Hugh. She's a lass with her eye on the main chance. And she'd have had plenty of encouragement from her parents to aim for a queen's gold crown rather than a countess's silver circlet."

I didn't pay much attention. Ralph always took the dark view. I knew as well as I knew my name that Isabella had really cared for me and looked forward to our marriage.

Be that as it may, my immediate task was to make John suffer. My oath of allegiance to him was meaningless now. Once we'd found our Uncle Geoffrey we'd all make for Paris and ask King Philip's support in our war with John.

Geoffrey had always been as close to me as Ralph, and I thought of him as a brother. He and I had fought side by side in King Richard's army during the Crusade. Geoffrey was the firebrand of the family. He was always for attack, no matter the odds. Where Ralph stewed and I smoldered, Geoffrey boiled.

He was waiting for us at Lusignan.

"It's monstrous!" he rasped, when I'd told him the tale of John's perfidy. He ran his fingers through his long, graying hair. His black eyes, flecked with gold, glowed like molten coals with his outrage. "King Philip must know of this. It's an insult to our whole family. Are we off to Paris, then?"

"We are," I said, "but first we'd be glad of a slice or so of bread and a bowl of soup or whatever's on the fire. Then as soon as we can find fresh horses and assemble a few retainers, we'll be on our way."

Though he'd had no warning (we had no time to send a messenger) King Philip received us within half an hour of our arrival at his palace on the Ile de la Cité in the heart of Paris. He was seated in the grandest audience chamber I'd ever seen. It was twice as long as our great hall at Lusignan. The sunlight that streamed in through the tall windows bounced off polished wood paneling. Tapestries on every wall glowed as though illuminated from within. There hardly seemed need for more light, yet dozens of candles in the massive chandelier were blazing away even at midday. Philip sat on a throne at the far end, with two of his courtiers nearby. He beckoned to us to approach.

I'd been curious to see if he'd changed since I'd last seen him. That had been two years ago when he so abruptly left the Crusade. He'd been co-leader with King Richard, but Richard outshone him and Philip resented it. Richard was a tall golden-haired warrior, commanding and vigorous. Philip was slight with a short beard and dull brown hair that fell untidily to his shoulders. His dark, thin face had a perpetual look of annoyance. After a few months he'd gone home, pleading acute dysentery. We Crusaders jeered. If that were an excuse to desert, most of us could have followed him. Everybody knew it was a case of acute jealousy.

The Philip I saw now could have been a different man. He sat with the light from a window behind him so his face was somewhat in the shadow. Even so, I could see that he'd become a self-assured monarch, wearing his crown proudly and holding his head high. His hair was smooth and cut short, like a close-fitting brown cap. He'd shaved his beard.

He invited us to sit in the chairs facing his throne.

"Greetings, and welcome to our city and our palace. Now tell me what portentous matters bring three noble Lusignans to Paris?"

"My lord King, we have come to make a complaint against King John of England, and to plead for your support in our battle for retribution."

Philip looked alert. I was sure he had a good idea of the nature of my complaint.

"Continue," he said.

I told, as briefly as I could, the story of how John had deceived Isabella and stolen her away from me. I tried to keep my emotion in check, but I think Philip could see that this was more than a case of pique. A man's heart had been wounded and his honor besmirched.

Geoffrey added a point I'd forgotten.

"My lord King, my nephew would want to make it clear that our whole clan feels this affront. It has wiped out any loyalty we had to King John. We will be honored if you will accept our fealty to you as our rightful sovereign, from this day forward."

Whereupon he knelt on one knee. Ralph and I followed suit.

Philip stood up at once. "Rise, rise, no need to prostrate yourselves before me. I welcome you as vassals of the French crown. In return for your pledge of loyalty to me, I will defend you against any unlawful attacks."

We all sat down again. I felt that now we were getting somewhere. What could be more unlawful than John's atrocious behavior?

"Then will you join us in seeking retribution from John?" I asked.

Philip looked at me for a half a minute before he answered. His hand strayed toward his chin, as though seeking a beard to stroke. When he spoke, at first I thought he was trying to soothe me, because his voice was as suave and mannered as that of a priest offering absolution.

"After what you tell me, I can understand your frustration, Sir Hugh. I was aware that John had married Isabella. I knew that her parents had agreed to the match. They led me to believe that you had agreed too, though I could not imagine why you would yield so easily. I know you Lusignans, and your hot heads."

Geoffrey broke in. "Forgive me, my liege, but we must act quickly. John may escape before we can catch him. Will you help us?"

"No."

The word snapped out like the crack of a whip. His eyes were as piercing as steel-pointed arrows, letting us know that he'd been conciliatory long enough. Now he was the imperious ruler, laying down the law to his subjects. "I can't go to war with John now. The truce we signed last January still holds. As part of our agreement then, he is to pay me 30,000 marks before he returns to England. I would have to forfeit that payment, as well as go back on my word, if I broke the truce and attacked him. There is, you know, honor between kings."

Geoffrey was getting so red in the face that I knew I'd have to speak up and forestall any words he'd regret later.

"Of course we can understand that. But without your help, we can do nothing. We have only half a hundred knights we can count on. John has his whole army. If you agree that he has acted unlawfully, and if we are your loyal vassals, aren't you obligated to help us defend ourselves against our enemy? Especially since he's your enemy too?"

Philip rose, looked out the window as though considering my question, and looked back at us. His thin-lipped smile acknowledged the sense of my argument, but there was no mirth in the smile. "Strictly speaking, Sir Hugh, you are right. And when the time comes, I'll make John accountable for his insult to you. You may be sure of that. Now, however, I can do nothing."

Geoffrey couldn't contain himself. He roared, "Then just what do you advise us to do? By our Lord, the King of England is a thief and a liar! He must be made to suffer!" Philip looked at Geoffrey quizzically. "Indeed, he should suffer. Perhaps Sir Hugh could challenge him to a duel? I believe your nephew would prove the stronger."

Was he joking? We couldn't tell. He turned his back decisively and walked to the window. I looked where he was looking, toward the huge half-built stone towers of Notre-Dame Cathedral, at the other end of the island. Maybe Philip could take comfort from this impressive evidence of his generosity and piety, but I could not.

The interview was over. We would have to pursue John on our own.

Isabella

September 1200

17

oward the end of September the charms of Chinon, not much to begin with, began to pall on me.

My parents had come and gone. While they were still there John made his trip to Paris to see King Philip. I was glad to have their company during that week. We didn't talk about anything very important—my wardrobe, gossip about events back in Angoulême, ways we would improve Chinon Castle if it were up to us. The subject of my sudden marriage to John never came up, nor did I want it to. I was fairly sure my parents had connived with John to deceive me about Hugh's death. But most of the time I succeeded in burying the thought. I didn't want to believe they or he could do anything so wicked. It was easier to pretend everything had been as they'd said.

Sometimes I'd see my mother looking at me strangely, as though wondering what had happened to the child who used to hang on her every word and try desperately to win her approval. I'd want to cry out to her, "Yes, I am different, Mother. I've learned disillusionment and I'm learning how to be self-sufficient. And it's your doing." But we didn't talk about that either.

Then my father had word that he must return to Angoulême. The morning they left was one of those days when summer seems finally to be loosening its grip. Standing in the dusty bailey while the horses were being saddled, I looked up to see the sun shining as glaringly as it had for months but without quite so much deadening heat. There was even a cool breeze. To the west a few tattered gray clouds scurried across the sky. Dry, rust-brown leaves blew about in little whirlwinds and rattled across the paving stones.

The walls around me were as impassive and prison-like as ever. Yet I felt none of the desolation of other partings from my mother. This time I hugged to myself the knowledge that soon I too would be leaving Chinon. I was going to England. I was to be crowned a queen.

A squire helped my mother to mount her horse. I was used to hoisting myself onto a steed without assistance. Now for the first time I noticed the grace and dignity of my mother's ascent, the way she settled effortlessly into her saddle and allowed Lady Anne to arrange her flowing skirt in becoming folds to conceal her legs. I thought I might change my ways.

She leaned down and took my hand. I looked up into her face and saw anxiety. She was probably expecting an outburst of tears.

"I hope you'll have time to come see us at Angoulême before you go to England," she said.

"I hope so too. But I don't know what John's plans are. We'll have to wait and see." We didn't seem to have much more to say to each other.

My father was anxious to leave. With a final pressure from my mother's hand and a wave from my father, they rode off toward the gate.

And there I was with no company except John, Lady Anne and Adèle. Chinon, being a fortress rather than a royal palace, was seldom visited by the Plantagenets, so there wasn't a complement of resident lords and ladies. Adèle had made friends with the cook's ten-year-old son but I wasn't eager to seek companionship among the household help. Though ten or so of John's knights were lodged in various towers we saw little of them. They were a rough sort and were usually either hunting or, at John's behest, riding out in search of spies and enemies.

John spent a good deal of time in the small audience room next to his bedchamber. His rooms weren't nearly as opulent as mine, but he did have a small Persian carpet before the fireplace. Servants kept the fire ablaze with man-sized chestnut logs of an evening.

When going over his accounts with his steward or dictating messages to his secretary, John would seat me next to him. From time to time he'd absently take my hand, smooth my hair or squeeze my shoulder. I was used to this by now, but I began to feel like a pet dog with no purpose except to look pretty and amuse my master. I didn't like being so passive. I was bored.

I liked it better when someone came from England. I wanted so much to learn about my future realm. I'd listen carefully, storing away such nuggets of information as which Welsh lords were making trouble or what the King of Scotland was up to. Then there were the restive English barons. A great deal of John's attention went to keeping them pacified.

Often he and his visitors conversed in English. Then I was lost. It sounded like the jabbering of monkeys compared with the graceful French I was used to. Yet I knew I should learn it. Finally it occurred to me to ask John to teach me.

"When we're in England I suppose I'll pick up the way of talk in time. But couldn't you help me get started? I'd think our subjects would be pleased to hear me address them in their own tongue."

He looked surprised. He wasn't prepared when I showed signs of taking my future royal duties seriously. Then he gave his little bark of a laugh.

"Not a bad idea, not bad at all. Yes, it would be well for you to learn what you can. But I wouldn't make a very good teacher, my dear. As it happens, my old friend Hugh, the Bishop of Lincoln, will arrive tomorrow. He's a learned man. I'll ask him to give you some instruction."

The good bishop, a very kind, very old man, was able to spare me two hours. My education began. After that whenever a visitor fluent in both languages came to Chinon I learned a little more. I'd practice with Lady Anne, who'd picked up some English from a brother-in-law who'd lived in London.

On the whole, though, life in Chinon was dreary. John and I were getting used to each other, but so far we didn't have much common ground. I was learning that he could be moody and silent for hours or days. At meals we were seldom alone. Lady Anne, Adèle, a few of his knights, and perhaps visiting churchmen or lords from the surrounding towns would join us. John left it to others to make a show of sociability. Even when he and I were alone together he'd seldom start a conversation. Sometimes I found myself remembering how Hugh and I used to talk for hours.

Often, in company or not, I'd catch John looking at me intently as a hawk with its eye on a rabbit. It was almost frightening. It reminded me of the way he'd stared at me the first time I met him in the tavern by the river.

One day when we were alone in his audience chamber I caught his eye, his hungry eye. On an impulse I jumped from my chair and flung myself down in his lap. I threw my arms around his neck and kissed him lightly on the mouth. Instantly he clutched me and began kissing my forehead, my eyes, my throat. Then he sought my mouth and held me so close that I was almost breathless. While our lips were joined I was intensely aware of how soft his beard was and how I was pressed against his chest, with only a thin layer of silk between my flesh and the rough wool of his tunic. I was a little afraid and I pulled away.

He rose so quickly that I had to catch hold of the table to keep from falling. He strode to the door, but paused when I addressed his back.

"If that's what you've been wanting, John, why didn't you say so? After all, I'm your wife."

He whirled around. His face was suffused with a dull red. He spoke in a voice I'd never heard before, rasping, harsh, as though choking down anger.

"You know nothing about being a wife, Isabella. And the time hasn't come for me to teach you. For the present, you'll do me the favor of not setting yourself up as a brazen little temptress." He was gone.

I was abashed and resentful, like a child admonished unfairly by a severe parent. What had I done wrong? It was only a prank. Yet under my ill humor I was gloating. I sensed I'd learned how to move him. It was a lesson I wouldn't forget.

I didn't see him again for two days. This wasn't the first time he'd gone off for half a day or overnight with no explanation so I didn't think much about it. And in truth I was glad. Now was my chance to escape from the deadly confines of the castle. I'd wanted to go riding out in the fields and along the river. But when I'd asked John he was adamant.

"Not unless I go with you. You'd have to go down through the town and across the river to find good riding trails. There are too many ruffians on the roads and lurking in alleyways."

Now he wasn't here to deny me. I ordered a young groom to saddle my mare, Jolie, who had by now become obedient but hadn't lost her spirit. The boy stammered, "But my lady, the King said…"

"I know what the King said. He said I wasn't to go riding alone. Very well, you'll accompany me."

The poor lad, somewhat slow-witted, had nothing to say to that. Off we went through the main gate. At a cautious walk we made our way down the steep cobbled streets of the town and across the bridge. At first the groom hung back in a deferential position, but when we came to a fine level straight trail through the fields I beckoned him to join me in a race. I gave Jolie her head and we had a glorious gallop, laughing and urging our horses on. My hair flew in the wind, and I felt as though the horse and I were one swift, smoothly moving body. The race ended in a tie, though I suspected the groom held back on purpose. I hadn't felt such joy and freedom since I'd gone riding with Hugh.

When we arrived back in the castle courtyard, the groom again in the rear, I was shocked to see John waiting. He was furious. He seized the groom's arm and shook him.

"You stupid, disobedient lout, how dare you go against my orders?"

I was afraid he was going to strike the boy. "That's not fair, John. He was obeying my orders. Don't punish him. Please, let him go."

With a glare John released the poor youngster, who led the horses off to the stables, trying to look as though he weren't there. I spoke in a rush before John could start on me.

"I know you told me I couldn't ride without you. But either you aren't here or you're too busy. For weeks I've been cooped up like a prisoner. I've seen nothing of the countryside and I've seen enough of this castle to last me the rest of my life!"

I glared at him as he'd glared at the groom. He calmed down. He actually smiled.

"What a little spitfire it is! I'm sorry. Of course it hasn't been easy for you. I've been thoughtless, but I'm not an ogre. We'll go riding together soon, maybe tomorrow."

It wasn't tomorrow, it was in three days. And it wasn't the gallop by the river and through the forest that I'd longed for. It was a sedate ride of about half an hour to visit one of John's vassals who lived just beyond the River Vienne.

I knew John was proud of me and wanted to show me off. I knew it was my duty to help him to maintain the fragile ties that bound his vassals to him. But I thought they and their frumpy ladies were a sorry lot. When we entered the hall a half-dozen men stood around the huge fireplace, laughing, talking loudly and calling to the cupbearers to keep their mugs full. A fine cheerful fire blazed on the hearth, but puffs of smoke escaped into the room. At least the chimneys at Chinon drew properly. Then I got a whiff of the sour smell from the trampled, musty rushes on the stone floor. They must not have been changed for weeks. Even the acrid smoke was preferable. I looked at Lady Anne and she too was wrinkling her nose in disgust. I was glad when John led me across the room to where the lady of the castle, Blanche, was sitting with her companions. A little fire of rosemary and thyme stalks burned nearby in a brazier, dispelling the stench from the old rushes.

The ladies hardly knew how to take me. They couldn't very well include me in their gossip about their children, their troubles with their household servants or their husbands' bad habits. So they pretty much left me alone. The men's talk was getting louder. I overheard their gory tales of hunting exploits and boastful accounts of their bravery as Crusaders.

After a short time Lady Blanche remembered her manners and invited Lady Anne and me to come with her to her chamber to wash off the grime of the journey and arrange our clothing before the meal. The two others started back to the great hall ahead of me. Alone, feeling my way along the dark passageway, I was about to round a corner when I heard my name. I stopped. Two men who must have just left the latrine were talking.

"So at last we get to see Isabella, the King's poppet. A toothsome little sweetmeat, isn't she? No wonder he keeps her all to himself up there in his stronghold."

"Ah, but the tale is, he hasn't bedded her yet. Her parents forbade it until she's sixteen. If I were in his place I'd ignore that and have her between the covers in two minutes. What sport we'd have! She's ripe for the plucking, anyone can see that."

"What I hear is, the only way he can stick to his promise is to pay a private visit every so often to Madame Albertine on the Rue Charles. You know the one I mean?"

"Ay, and a handsome lass she is. But only kings can afford the likes of her."

"Well, this king has always managed to find willing bedmates, for free or for a price. What I'd dearly love to see is how long it takes when he's back in England and settled in with his Isabella for him to seek out another Albertine."

They moved on down the corridor. I waited a few minutes, wishing desperately I hadn't heard them. I stood there in the gloom, fighting back angry tears and trying to come to terms with this shattering glimpse of how the world saw the man I'd married. I had no doubt of the accuracy of the picture. It explained a great deal.

After a time I felt calm enough to rejoin the company. For the rest of the day and during the ride back I mulled over what I'd learned. I said hardly a word to John. I doubt if he noticed, being in one of his withdrawn black moods. I didn't confide in Lady Anne. This was my affair, no one else's. It was up to me to try to comprehend John so I'd be prepared for whatever life brought when we were truly King and Queen, man and wife. Married life might not prove as idyllic as I'd dreamed.

The very next morning John announced that we were to prepare for the long-anticipated journey to England. The news lightened my spirits marvelously.

"How soon do we go, John? Shall I tell the ladies to start packing?"

"Yes, the sooner the better. I hope we can leave day after tomorrow. On the way we'll stop to see my mother at Fontevraud Abbey."

That pushed everything else out of my mind. At last I was to meet the legendary Queen Eleanor.

Isabella

September 1200

18

When we rode down a lane and into the great courtyard of Fontevraud Abbey I drew my breath in sharply, pulled my horse to a halt and stared. It was like a city. From the enormous church with its spiky towers a network of streets and paths radiated, leading to substantial buildings and, in the distance, fields of grain. Flower gardens, vegetable patches and beds of herbs filled the spaces between the buildings. Black-robed nuns and a few monks walked purposefully and quietly along the paths.

A white-robed figure materialized beside us and announced that she was Abbess Marie, sent by Queen Eleanor to greet us. She was as generously proportioned for an abbess as the church was for a church.

"Queen Eleanor wishes to see King John first, then Queen Isabella. You know the way, I believe, my king. Meantime, if you wish, Queen Isabella, I will be pleased to show you around our abbey." Tired from riding and full of curiosity, I dismounted gladly while John went off to see what his mother would demand of him. His expression was ludicrous—half defiant, half fearful, like a small boy being summoned for punishment.

In an hour, though, I didn't see the half of it, because my plump guide had to stop and catch her breath every ten steps or so. Moving or standing still, she was as loquacious as a magpie. At first I couldn't take her seriously. She looked like a large white egg waddling along the stone-flagged walks. Only her towering, stiff-starched headdress gave her the dignity of her office.

"As you see, we're quite self-sufficient here. The abbey church, of course, is the center of it all."

"Yes, I can believe that." By sheer size, with its sprawling annexes and lofty towers, it announced its supremacy over the whole complex. Its tawny golden stone seemed to glow with sunlit warmth even on this cloudy day.

"Over there to the west you see our dormitories. Most of them house the sisters of the order and the noble widows who have come here to retire from the world. Queen Eleanor lodges in the house with two turrets, halfway down the lane. She says she hopes to end her days here. Poor lady, that could be soon. May she find peace and repose as her end approaches." She crossed herself and cast a stern glance at me to see if I would do the same. I complied.

I knew the Queen was old but somehow I'd never thought of her as old enough to die. While I tried to look suitably solemn the abbess took my arm and moved briskly for five paces. Stopping with a wheeze, she pointed. "That farthest dormitory at the end is the refuge for fallen women who have repented. Queen Eleanor, bless her, cares for the unfortunate as well as those who are well off."

"How long has Queen Eleanor had this abbey?"

She let out a cackling laugh that led to a fit of coughing. "It isn't hers, my child. It belongs to the Order and has done for a hundred years. But the Queen and all her family have been wonderfully good to us. It's become a tradition for the Angevin monarchs to donate generously to the maintenance and enrichment of the abbey. We never forget them in our prayers."

She peered at me from her little button eyes.

"And may you and your good husband King John remember that in years to come."

It hadn't occurred to me to think of myself as a benefactor of worthy causes. How wonderful it would be if John and I could make some munificent gift to Fontevraud Abbey and thereby earn the gratitude and devotion of its nuns. Not to mention, when the time came, their prayers for our eternal souls.

"I'm sure we'll remember," I smiled at the abbess. She gave a little nod.

A veiled sister, one of the nuns who were sworn to silence, approached. By her gestures she indicated it was time for the abbess to take me to the Queen.

The Eleanor I saw when the abbess delivered me to her chamber was far from what I'd expected. I knew the reputation of Eleanor of Aquitaine: Wife of two kings, mother of ten children—two of them kings, two of them queens. An indomitable woman, renowned for her ability to take charge of any situation.

I'd envisioned a tall, regally clad woman, an erect and redoubtable presence. The room would be brightly lit to show off its royal occupant amid her rich furnishings.

But when the door closed behind me I could hardly see her. The gloom was relieved only by one candelabrum in a corner and the flickering light of a fire. Draperies covered the windows. The room was airless and hot. When my eyes became accustomed to the dimness I made out a chair by the fire in which the Queen seemed to be dozing. Her head was bent. Her hands were folded in her lap.

I stood mute, wondering what to do or say. She looked up.

"So there you are, Isabella. Bring the candle here and put it on the table so I can get a look at you."

She straightened her back and sat erect. Her voice was as strong and commanding as her words. What had appeared to be a limp insensible old woman was now every inch a queen. When I set down the candle I could see she wore an ermine cape around her shoulders over a gown of deep blue wool. Her hair was covered by a white wimple, held in place by a delicate gold circlet. Her pale austere face showed lines of aging, but this was clearly a woman who had been very beautiful and knew it. She did not smile.

Standing before her I felt diminished. She was totally unlike the only other queen I'd met, Richard's widow Berengaria. During our brief acquaintance my awe at Berengaria's dignity and beauty had given way to liking. I'd come to see that she had human qualities, that she might even become a friend. Not so with Eleanor. I was transfixed by the steady gaze of those cold blue eyes, the silent assessment. Despite the heat of the room I felt chilled.

"John chose well."

I managed a half-smile. I felt like an ungainly duck in the presence of a swan.

"John tells me that although you've been married two months you haven't lain together. Apparently your parents made it a condition of the marriage that it should not be consummated until you are sixteen. Is that your understanding?"

"Yes. My mother told me so. She said that John had agreed."

"John will agree to anything to get what he wants." Her lips curled scornfully. "Your parents were overly cautious. As far as I'm concerned, only one thing determines when a bride is ready to become a wife. Have your monthly flows begun?"

"Yes. Last spring."

"Very well. I told John and now I tell you: it is your duty to procreate and the sooner you start the better. The English throne requires an heir. John seems eager enough to take steps to become a father. I hope that you are just as determined to mother a son and that your enthusiasm will match his."

After one long look to make sure I'd fully understood, she turned her head and closed her eyes.

I walked slowly toward the door while her words sank in. I'd given no thought to becoming a mother. I'd dreamed of lying with John and of the pleasures of the bedchamber. But motherhood had been far from my mind. Eleanor's words were a shocking reminder that there might be much more to being a queen than crowns and gowns and an attentive king.

When I came out into the hall John was waiting. He was indeed attentive. He seized my arm and his black eyes searched my face. He looked as agitated as a kettle on the boil. First his lips trembled and he seemed about to smile, then he became as solemn as a bishop. His very beard seemed to quiver.

"Our time has come at last, Isabella. Are you glad?"

"Yes," I whispered. But in truth I was apprehensive as I was glad. John led me down the hall to his chamber—now ours.

John
September 1200

I woke to see her beside me, sleeping soundly. She was curled up in a ball as though hugging herself. Her face was childlike and innocent, but her lips were curved in a little smile: the smile of a woman who has learned something children don't know. I could hardly believe that only yesterday we were more like polite acquaintances than friends or lovers.

How sweet she'd been, my darling Isabella. I'd never known love like this. Of all the women and girls I'd taken to bed, none had made me feel so protective, so eager to please them as much as they pleased me. How different from my first night with my first wife, an unfeeling lump of a woman then and colder and stiffer with every year of our marriage.

Isabella had been warmer and more eager to partner me in our lovemaking than I'd dared to hope. We'd fall together almost in a frenzy, then when our appetites were appeased we'd draw apart, murmuring and caressing each other, then doze until one of us woke. Then we'd talk. For the first time we talked with ease, without constraint.

"You've never been to Normandy, my love, have you?" I remember saying drowsily while we lay holding each other close.

"Never," she said and tickled my ear. "Why?"

"It's been practically a part of England ever since my great-great-grandfather came from there to take the crown as the first Norman king of England. It's a friendly land. They like me there. They'll like me even more when I show them their beautiful new queen. We'll go right through Normandy on our way to Cherbourg. It will be our honeymoon and we can take all the time we like."

She raised herself on an elbow.

"Not all the time, John. Didn't you say you'd arranged for the coronation to be in October? I wouldn't want to miss my own coronation!"

"And so you won't, my sweet. But if we dally along the way, what harm? We can always put the ceremony off a few days."

"So we can. After all, we're the King and Queen! We can do what we like."

I laughed and pulled her down.

"And can you guess what the King would like now?"

Now a few hours later, as dawn crept through the windows and I watched her, I gloated over my good fortune in capturing this bewitching creature, so young and unspoiled, for my own. She opened her eyes.

"Good morning, John." Her voice was a whisper but her smile was a radiance. "Now we are truly man and wife, aren't we?" She raised her arms above her head and stretched with the luxuriant languor of a cat before the fire. She kissed her fingers, then placed them on my lips.

"I think now I will tell you I love you."

She gave my beard a little tug. Suddenly she sat up, pulled the curtains aside and jumped down from the high bed to the floor. She was as light and quick as a kitten. She ran to the window.

"Oh John, what a lovely day! It would be heavenly to go out riding. They must have horses here—they have everything else."

Shafts of golden morning light streamed through the window. I could see every curve of her slender young body in its diaphanous white shift.

I wasn't quite ready to go riding.

"Of course, my love. We'll go find some horses if that's what will please you most. But it's early yet. Let's lie a little longer and stay warm under the covers."

I held out my arms. After a moment she scampered over and climbed back into bed. I pulled the coverlet up over our heads.

I heard a tap at the door. I could hardly believe anyone would interrupt the King in his nuptial bed. It must have been my imagination. The tapping became an insistent pounding. I heard a familiar voice, the deep bass of my chief steward, Robert de Thorneham.

"My King, I beg you to forgive me. But we have urgent news. May I enter?"

Hoping to put him off, I growled, "What can be so urgent that it can't wait a few hours?"

"It has to do with the Lusignans, my lord."

I felt Isabella tense in my arms.

"Come in, Robert."

I opened the bed curtains and put out my head. The heavy oak door creaked open, and he strode in. He was perspiring as though after a run. Probably he had indeed run all the way from the household knights' quarters. He was a large, heavy man. It took him a moment to catch his breath.

"Hand me that cloak on the chair, please, Sir Robert. Wait for me in the anteroom. Then I'll hear what you have to say."

I leaned down and whispered to Isabella, "Never mind, it's probably nothing. I'll join you in a few minutes. Close your eyes. Rest."

She looked at me wide-eyed, almost in terror. We'd never talked about it, but she knew as well as I did that the Lusignans would never forgive me for snatching Hugh's bride from him. I wondered fleetingly if her concern were for me or for Hugh. No time to think of that now. I kissed her, got out of bed and pulled the curtains closed.

Robert stood in the anteroom waiting for me, nervous and fingering the ruby clasp of his cloak. It was a jewel I'd given him. Robert shared my appreciation of precious gems. I was glad to bestow them on him if it kept him loyal and trustworthy.

His broad forehead was creased with worry.

"One of our messengers has arrived with word that Hugh le Brun and his brother and uncle and two-score or so of their knights are riding toward Le Mans. Our informant overheard enough to believe they intend to ambush you as you ride north toward the Channel."

I was speechless with shock and anger.

"We must assume they know you've sent the army on ahead and that we have only a handful of knights."

I'd felt safe from Philip, in view of our recent agreement. It hadn't occurred to me that other enemies might be lurking. I'd been thinking only of riding with Isabella and a small party, carefree and unencumbered by a large army. Now what should have been my honeymoon was more likely to be an ignominious flight.

"Where were they when your spy saw them?"

"Within a day's ride of Orléans. But they must be well beyond it by now."

I was too full of resentment to think clearly. Why should this happen when all I wanted was to go back to bed with Isabella?

Robert was looking more anxious by the moment.

"Do you think we can catch up with our army before the Lusignans intercept us?"

"I do, my lord, if we leave today—by noon, I'd hope."

"Do what needs to be done, Robert. And thank you." As he was leaving I thought of one more thing. "And Robert, please find someone to send the

Queen's women to her."

Back in our chamber while I was getting dressed I told Isabella what was happening and that we'd have to leave quickly. The alarm had left her face. She seemed calm. I couldn't tell what she was thinking. She obediently got out of bed and looked around for her clothes. Just then Anne knocked and came in. I left them and went to report events to my mother. She would probably scold me for not keeping the army with me.

"But," I would tell her, "Isabella and I have made a promising start at producing an heir, just as you wished." That would please her.

Hugh le Brun
September 1200

20

After King Philip dismissed us so summarily we walked silently down his grand staircase and into the glare and bustle of the city. The three of us stood there a minute, unnoticed by the Parisians going about their late-afternoon business. They didn't look too different from the citizens of Poitiers or Angoulême or any other city I'd ever been in, though there were a lot more of them. Some were neat and prim, some rough and ill-dressed, some hurrying as though late for an appointment, some dawdling as though looking for an unwary citizen whose purse might be snatched. We saw pretty women, tottering crones and boisterous drinkers making their way between taverns. None gave us a glance.

In a way, I was glad to be invisible. Geoffrey was still fuming and glowering, ready to strike the first person who dared to look at him. Ralph was hunched over, sighing like a lost soul, holding a hand to his stomach as though in pain. Ralph's digestion always suffered when he was upset. I was betwixt the two, but more angry than discouraged. I threw an arm around Ralph's shoulder.

"Let's walk down to the river and look for a wineshop," I said. "We need to decide what to do next."

"Right," said Geoffrey. "That's what you need, Ralph. A dose of good red wine always helps a pain in the gut."

We made for a narrow, crowded, dark street and headed for the glint of bright water ahead. Geoffrey led, shouldering his way through the jostling, chattering, shouting throng. Ralph and I followed close in his wake, Ralph holding his nose. These folk weren't all well washed. The trough down the middle of the road, meant to carry garbage to the river, was clogged with foul-smelling waste, hardly disturbed by a mean trickle of water. When we emerged on the bank of the sun-dappled Seine

00

we stopped to drink in the fresh air and look around. We marveled at the dozens of big and little boats ferrying people and goods back and forth across the river. A breeze made the water choppy, and the smaller boats bobbed about like corks.

"Makes me seasick just to look at them," Ralph moaned.

We turned and surveyed the huddle of mean buildings that lined the narrow road above the river. Most were ramshackle, with weatherbeaten wood walls all aslant and slates missing from the roof. But here and there was a straight upstanding shop with a small, neatly swept yard. One of the nearest seemed semi-respectable and displayed a huge wine barrel by its open door.

"Come on," Geoffrey growled. "Here's a likely spot. Let's go in."

It was small, crowded and noisy. The ten or so tables were all occupied, but we finally found three seats at the end of a table in the corner. As soon as the pitcher was slammed down Geoffrey poured himself a mug and drank half of it in a gulp. Ralph took a few sips and waited anxiously for results.

I filled my mug, then asked, "How many men can we find to go with us after John?"

For a half-hour we counted and recounted the supporters we could depend on, tried to guess John's whereabouts and likely movements, and made plans to intercept him. But at last we had to admit we needed better information. John was a wily enemy and might go off in any direction. Rather than guess where we might find him, one of us would have to go at once to Chinon, where he'd been last reported, and trace his movements from there.

I volunteered. I had to keep moving. If I sat still I'd brood over my wrongs to the point of despondency. I'd find myself remembering Isabella's bright, laughing face, wishing I'd ever worked up the courage to kiss her, wishing I could recover the happiness of only a few months ago. But I couldn't live in the past. I needed action, any kind of action, to fuel my anger and resolve.

While I went to Chinon, Geoffrey and Ralph would rally as large a force as they could. We agreed we'd meet in a week at Tours.

That decided, we raised our mugs in a toast to comradeship and brotherhood (by now we were a little tipsy) and Geoffrey went further.

"Death to King John!" he roared.

A few drinkers who heard this cheered. So did a strapping bargeman who had just come in.

"Let me get a cup in my hand and I'll drink to that!" he called to Geoffrey. He began edging his way through the crowded room toward our corner.

"And down with King Philip!" Geoffrey shouted, encouraged by his audience's enthusiasm. "A man who doesn't keep faith with his vassals doesn't deserve to be king!"

Ralph, emboldened by a quiescent stomach, added his two sous' worth. "And while we're at it, down with this filthy, stinking city of Paris! I'll be heartily glad to shake the dust of your town off my feet!"

I heard a muttering from the men at the next table, then the whole room erupted in angry cries and raised fists. The bargeman was no longer eager to drink with us and joined the chorus. "Who do you think you are, outlanders, to come here and insult our king and our city?" He was almost upon us.

Geoffrey would have gladly taken him on and the whole crowd too, but Ralph and I saw the wisdom of escape. I'd noticed a small door behind our bench. I pressed it. It opened. "Save your blows for your real enemies!" I said to Geoffrey. Ralph and I pushed him through the door, then tumbled after him onto the muddy path above the sullen river, now reflecting a gray sky. Nobody followed us. It began to rain. We sloshed on until we found the stable where we'd left our horses and grooms, and were off.

So as it turned out we shook not the dust, but the mud of Paris off our feet. And glad we were to be out of the city and heading for our familiar countryside. We rode hard and fast, stopping only for a few hours of sleep. Toward dusk on the second day we saw the massive tower of Chartres Cathedral rising from the plain, a huge dark presence silhouetted against the overcast western sky—funereal black on leaden gray. I shivered, fearing it was an omen of bad luck to come. The immense shape grew more awesome the closer we came. Speechless with wonder, we rode slowly through the humble town until we reached the small square in front of the cathedral. We reined in our horses and bent our necks back to look up at the soaring spire. None of us had been to Chartres but we knew its fame. We'd heard, too of the great fire that had destroyed much of the still uncompleted structure a few years ago.

"I'd have thought there'd be only a pile of rubble," said Ralph. "But that one great tower still stands, and they've made a good start on rebuilding the other." Just then the sun, nearly set, emerged from the clouds and sent beams of light to flood the cathedral façade. The stained glass windows gleamed like amethysts and rubies. I took heart. Perhaps God was on our side after all.

At Chartres we separated. Ralph would go north to his castle in Normandy, where he'd try to rally his vassals. Geoffrey would head for Poitiers and Lusignan, where most of our clan lived. And I'd go to Chinon and pick up the trail of my quarry.

Anne Beaufort
September 1200

urry, hurry, hurry.

The enemy could be anywhere. Look around you. Above all, hurry! Catch up with our army. Maybe they're around that next bend.

The need for haste was on everybody's mind while we rode toward Cherbourg, that September of 1200. John was as jumpy as a bear at a baiting. Isabella was cross at having to leave the comfort and warmth of Fontevraud Abbey so precipitately. I was almost as cross, and fully as nervous as John.

The first day or so weren't so frantic. We rode along the Vienne, past patchy little farms and through villages that huddled close to the river. In such open country an ambush would have been unlikely. Our pace was fast but controlled. In the forefront rode John's heralds and six of the dozen knights who guarded us. Then came John with Isabella on his left. Isabella's maid Hortense and I were close behind them. Behind us were John's personal servants and the beasts that bore the baggage. Then, in an orderly column in the rear, rode the rest of the knights, all armorclad in mail hauberks and with their squires at their sides.

It was strange to see signs of ordinary life going on while we were under such pressure. We passed a huddle of huts along the road, not even a village, where an old woman was calmly and deliberately spreading grapes and plums on a cloth to dry in the sun. I almost envied her. What would it be like, I wondered, to live so oblivious of the deadly games of kings?

On the third morning we left the open meadows. Lead-gray clouds hung low over the land and even the horses seemed depressed, trotting stolidly along with heads lowered. We rode through a forest of ancient oaks whose branches met and entwined over our heads. What daylight there was barely filtered through. The road was still damp from recent rain. There was no sound except the soft plop, plop of the horses' hooves and the muleteers' cries, urging their animals on.

Riding just behind John and Isabella, I saw how he'd turn in his saddle to make sure all was well behind him. Then he'd peer into the forest as though expecting a shower of arrows to fly out. He clutched his cloak about him. He sank his chin into his high fur collar and pulled his wide-brimmed hat down over his forehead. His eyes darted from side to side like those of a cornered ferret.

When Isabella glanced at him in concern he didn't meet her eyes. His fearfulness was catching. Before long I too felt uneasy in this gloomy tunnel. We were rushing along like rabbits pursued by the hounds, with no idea where the hounds were. Then it began to rain in earnest. John became even more fidgety. Isabella put her hand on his arm. I couldn't hear what she said, but I clearly heard his snappish reply.

"Afraid? What am I afraid of? I'm not afraid, I'm cautious. If we aren't watchful we could be attacked at any moment."

He barked at the knight riding ahead of him, "Go fetch Sir William." I supposed this was William de Cantilupe, an old Crusader and one of John's stewards. I'd never met him but I'd heard of his reputation as a brave warrior and a shrewd leader.

Sir William, who'd been riding in the vanguard, appeared almost at once. He looked considerably more composed than his master. He'd hardly arrived when John accosted him.

"Do you have any news, Sir William? Have you sent spies ahead to La Lude and Le Mans? Could the Lusignans reach Le Mans before we do? Do you think they'll wait to attack us there?" His voice rose in pitch with each question. "Or maybe they're behind us! Do you think they're hiding in the forest? They're just the types to jump out on us when we least suspect it." By now he was almost whining, like a child who feels the world is treating him unfairly.

Sir William waited impassively for John to finish.

"If there had been anything new to report, my liege, I would have told you at once. We've sent men to scout ahead, of course. But I doubt very much if the Lusignans are in Le Mans. That's your city and has been since last year. Nobody would let your enemies in the gates. I believe they must be still behind us. We have loyal men posted along the way who are keeping a good lookout. They'll send word quickly if they see any sign that we're being pursued. Also, as you doubtless remember, we've sent men out to spread false tales of what route we're taking. Now I must get back to my post."

John pulled his collar even higher over his face and sat hunched in his saddle, watching as Sir William rode back toward the head of the column.

Isabella brightened.

"Well, Sir William says we're in no immediate danger. That's good news, isn't it, John?"

He looked at her as though she'd awakened him from a dream, and raised his hand in signal to resume the march.

But before we'd gone a dozen yards we heard the thud of rapid hoofbeats. I was convinced a party of horsemen was about to overtake us. Sir William wheeled and rode to the rear, calling to the knights to follow him. They drew their swords even as they spurred their horses. After a moment's hesitation John rode after them.

Isabella and I waited, pressing closely together. I could see how tensely she gripped her reins with one hand, the wooden pommel of her saddle with the other. I peered toward the rear, but I could see nothing except a distant crowd of milling knights, servants, pack horses and grooms. Rain continued to fall relentlessly.

"Anne, it must be Hugh. Do you think I should ride back and beg him to let us go on?"

"No, I don't. Let's just wait and see. Your husband's knights are likely to be a match for whoever it is." I hoped I sounded calmer than I felt.

After what seemed ages but must have been only a few minutes, John came riding back, followed by a half-dozen knights. He was holding his head high. His hand rested on the gilded scabbard of his sword. Timidity had been replaced by cocky self-confidence. What a strange man, I thought.

He smiled broadly at Isabella.

"Why so pale, my love? There's nothing to fear. These stout men are routiers my mother sent to help guard us."

I knew what routiers were: mercenaries, soldiers for hire. Count Aymer had sometimes employed them when he couldn't round up enough of his own vassals to go on some foray. They were swarming all over Europe these days looking for employment, what with no big wars to keep them occupied. The new arrivals looked uncouth but brawny. If Eleanor had engaged them she'd probably paid them well, after making sure they were trustworthy.

"They do look stout, John. I'm greatly relieved to see them. But can only six men, no matter how strong, really help if we're ambushed?"

"Nonsense, Isabella. Those pitiful Lusignans probably have no more than a dozen of their henchmen in their party. We're more than a match for them now."

He called William de Cantilupe and his other steward, Robert de Thorneham, and told them we'd halt at Château-la-Vallière, just ahead, though it was not yet noon.

"My vassal, the Duke of Vaujours, will be glad to give us food and shelter."

"I don't think that's wise, my liege," said Sir William. "We're still some days away from Le Mans. It would be folly to delay now. We won't be safe until we're within the walls." He looked as stern as the priest who'd taught me Latin and who scolded me when I made a mistake.

"True, a stay at Château-la-Vallière would be well deserved," said Robert de Thorneham. I sensed he knew his master would rather be mollified than preached at. "We've been going at such a pace, we're all near exhaustion. But think how relieved we'll be when we reach Le Mans, where we're very likely to find your army waiting for us. As you know, my lord King, once we're reunited with them we can proceed at a more leisurely pace and stop when you wish."

John nodded and muttered a grumpy "Very well." We all took our places and the whole procession set off once more. At least the rain had stopped.

The journey seemed endless. We rode through beech forests showing such brilliant gold that they seemed burnished with sunlight though the sky was still a lowering gray. We rode past silent lakes bordered by green-black pines. When I drank in their pungent, bracing aroma I sat a little straighter in my saddle. Sometimes we rode for hours without seeing anyone, then came out to fields tawny with ripening grain. We'd see men with worn, brown faces who rested on their scythes to watch us. We rode through little villages that at first looked uninhabited. Grimy women with thin children trailing them came out of their hovels to watch. I wondered if they had any idea who we were. They gazed at us expressionless, without so much as a bobbing head or a shout of recognition that this was the party of their liege and his queen.

For three more days we pressed on. We stopped every night with some vassal who had to scramble to feed and lodge this large party that descended on him. Exhausted after a hard day's ride, we'd sit down for supper, glad to be dry and out of the saddle. John and Isabella always left the gathering early, holding hands, with eyes only for each other. At first I offered to help Isabella prepare for bed, but she told me she wouldn't need me, that she could manage with her maid. It wasn't hard to guess, from the way she looked at John and the way they sought each other's company, that married life was agreeing with her. I was happy for her and tried to forget my misgivings about John's character.

At last the square bulk of the Cathedral of Saint-Julien came into view, looming above the high walls of Le Mans. We crossed the River Sarthe by a graceful arched bridge and began the ascent to the city. At the top John stopped, looked around and became more loquacious than he'd been for days.

"See those walls, Isabella? The Romans built them. That's how old Le Mans is. They knew what they were doing, those Romans, placing so many lookout towers around the city. It would have been hard for an enemy to get near it. Still is. My grandfather Geoffrey was Count of Maine. He lived here and my father was born here. He loved this city, so do I. We'll stop at the palace of the counts of Maine."

"I hope it's not like Chinon," said Isabella. I'd been hoping the same thing, remembering how grim that other castle of John's family had been.

"Like Chinon? Of course not. No, this is a palace right on the town square, not a fortified castle. It's true there was an old castle, and a fine sturdy one it was too. But I had to knock it down last year when it looked like King Philip was going to take the city."

Was this the same John who'd been beside himself with fear just a few days ago? If he could go about tearing down castles maybe he wasn't the lily-livered coward I'd thought. Or was this merely blustery John, bragging about something that might or might not be true?

We rode through the narrow gate and into a pleasant tree-bordered square. Isabella and I looked at a row of imposing tall houses, trying to guess which one was the palace of the counts of Maine, while John went to confer with his guard.

Shortly we heard a mighty three-note blast from the herald's horn: ta-DA-da. Knights poured into the square from surrounding streets until our small party was the center of scores of cheering men. John pulled off his hat and waved it in the air, shouting greetings in return, reaching down to clasp his lieutenants' hands.

We were safe at last.

After a few days in the palace of the Counts of Maine life seemed more bearable. Since it was always kept ready for a visit by the English monarch and was staffed by a complement of attentive and able servants, we could quickly settle in, dry out and recover our equanimity.

Isabella and John were in the royal apartments on the second floor. I was on the third floor in a big room with a fine view. Below the old Roman walls John was so proud of stretched the fertile plains of the Sarthe where fields of grain were punctuated here and there by woodlands and villages.

One of the things I liked about this palace was the broad marble staircase instead of the dark winding tower stairs of Chinon. Another was dressing every day in a fresh dry gown. During our wet ride from Fontevraud Isabella and I were dismayed to see how bedraggled and mud-spattered our garments were getting. We decided to wear the same clothes day after day, saving the rest for better times. Now better times had come.

One afternoon we went into the great hall and spread on a table all the exquisite gowns and mantles she'd assembled for her wedding journey—the journey that had turned into a mad flight. The palace staff included dressmakers, so we were assessing what needed to be done. It was the first time we'd really been able to talk. She spent most of her time with John. But he'd gone hunting today.

She held up the blue and silver gown she'd worn for her wedding.

"I thought this would do for my coronation gown, but I wonder now. It was a little tight before and I felt awkward in it. What do you think, Anne?"

"Well…I suppose we could let out the side seams. Let me take a look."

There was a knock on the door. At Isabella's "Come in," William de Cantilupe entered.

"I beg your pardon for disturbing you, my lady, but a messenger has come from Angoulême with an inquiry from your parents as to your welfare and your whereabouts. They are very concerned, and have sent messengers to Fontevraud also. Perhaps you would like the man to return with a reply." As usual, he spoke with formality but complete self-assurance. I was used to seeing him in his bulky armor. I was struck by his tall lean figure as he stood there like a soldier at attention.

"Oh yes! Of course they're worried. Please have him take them my respects, and tell them that we finally arrived here in safety, and John and I are well. And tell them I will send another message before we leave for England. And thank you, Sir William." When she smiled at him I thought some of his reserve melted a bit. He bowed his head slightly, nodded to me, and after a "Thank you, my lady," he was gone.

Isabella was quiet a moment, looking at the door he'd closed after himself.

"I think that's a man my husband is fortunate to have as an adviser," she said. "Remember how sensible he was when we thought we'd be ambushed in the forest?"

"Yes, but I also remember how sharply he spoke. Perhaps the King is used to his ways."

"Oh no, he isn't. In fact last evening he was complaining to me about Sir William's manner. 'I may have to give him a reprimand,' he said, 'and remind him of his duty to show me more respect.'"

"And what did you say?"

"I didn't say anything. John was in rather a temper. But I think I'll speak to Sir William. A word from me might have more effect on him than a scolding from John."

I laughed and gave her a hug. "Isabella my pet, you are becoming quite the cunning queen!"

We were still standing by the table where the blue gown was spread out. I picked it up.

"And speaking of queens, we must decide what to do about this or you may find yourself walking into Westminster Abbey in your shift."

Hugh le Brun
September 1200

22

For hours I'd been lying awake on my rock-hard narrow cot in the silent dormitory of the Vendôme Abbey. I knew my uncle Geoffrey and my brother Ralph were awake too. I'd heard their sighs and restless turnings. When the abbey bell tolled midnight the slow, heavy clangs were like the final knell for my hopes. I raised myself on an elbow to whisper through the blackness.

"Geoffrey? Ralph? Since you're awake too I think we'd best have a talk. Let's go outside."

We carefully made our way along the rows of our sleeping companions and crept down a long passage, guided by a glimmer of light that grew brighter and brighter. We came out to the cloister garden, where the full moon cast its flood of cold light. One could almost count every blade of grass if one had nothing better to do.

I sank down heavily on a stone bench in the gallery. The others joined me. Ralph's yawn ended in a long descending groan. Geoffrey held his head in his hands.

"We might as well admit it," I said. "We're never going to catch them. And even if we did, what could we do with only twenty men?"

"If that no-good son of yours had turned up with the ones he'd been sent for, we wouldn't be in this barrel of sour pickles," growled Geoffrey.

I held my tongue.

We'd met at Tours as planned ten days ago. Since then everything had gone wrong. First, I couldn't get anyone at Fontevraud to tell me or even guess when John had left and by what road. Doubtless those who knew had been bribed to keep mum. Second, and worse, Ralph and Geoffrey had had little luck in gathering men. Our vassals were sympathetic but they politely pointed out that we hadn't been attacked.

"As your vassals we're required to go to your aid if you've been assaulted by our enemies," they said. "But you haven't. King John did you a monstrous injustice, but he didn't seize any territory. We'd serve you loyally if he had, but not for this."

The fact that it was the busy harvest season may have had a lot to do with their reluctance. At any rate, twenty men was the sum of our force. Nothing had been heard from Young Hugh, who was supposed to be rallying troops from Lusignan. We waited two more days hoping he'd arrive. Then we heard rumors that John was traveling toward Nantes, taking the western route to the Channel. So off we chased, only to learn our information was false. Back to Tours, still no contingent from Lusignan. A new rumor, also false: John had been seen in Vendôme, far to the east. Another two days wasted. Now here we were, glad to have the hospitality of the brothers at the abbey but utterly discouraged.

I was pretty sure I spoke for all of us.

"No matter why we're in this pickle barrel, the fact is we've wasted three weeks and we're no closer to our quarry than when we started. Should we go on?"

"That wicked John," said Ralph. "He's such a sly one, he must have been sending out men to spread all those lies about where he is and where he's going." He yawned again. "I've had enough. It's time to call it quits."

He began to rise but Geoffrey grabbed his arm and yanked him down onto the bench.

"Quits? *You're* ready to call it quits? What if I'm not? What if Hugh's not? Don't be in such a rush to get back to bed." But he couldn't seem to work up his customary roar.

I'd never felt so weary in body and soul. Ralph was right.

"I've had enough too. No point in quarreling about it. We've failed for now. That doesn't mean we can't try again. John's sure to come back from England in a few months. He has to if he's going to hold his French inheritance. And when he does, by God, I'll get my revenge."

"Next year, then. Next year we'll be ready for him." Geoffrey rose, sounding tired yet relieved. Ralph was already disappearing into the passage. For some time I stayed alone in the cloister watching the almost imperceptible descent of the moon. When it sank behind a row of cypresses and I could no longer make out the outline of shrubs and columned arcades I too turned back toward what was left of my night's rest.

The words repeated themselves in my brain: "Next year I'll be ready."

On the way back to Lusignan I had plenty of time to think. I was in no particular hurry and let my horse clop along at his own pace. My squire and the five other men with me were glad enough to slow down. We'd all been rushing so aimlessly over the countryside that it was a relief to know we were going home, not to some problematical encounter with a slippery enemy.

We crossed the Loire near Tours. It had been a warm autumn day in the Touraine. The river was lower than I'd ever seen it so we could ford it with no need of a bridge. I looked at the wide expanses of dried mud and sand and the sluggish stream that flowed along the narrow channel. "That's you, Hugh," I said to myself. "Feeble and defeated, with desolation on every side." Then I laughed at how I was wallowing in self-pity. The Loire would become a broad blue river again, and surely I'd get my life back on course too. The prospect of avenging myself against John gave me a purpose.

I'd accepted the fact that Isabella was lost to me, though I'd always cherish the memory of her gaiety and fresh young beauty and how close we'd become. Lost too was the dream of how we'd have a son, two sons, daughters, and insure the future of united Angoulême and La Marche.

That was past, gone. My mind was now consumed with two things: vengeance, and concerns about my son. Why had he failed to do as he'd been told? Why hadn't he brought his recruits to Tours? By the time I rode into the castle bailey at Lusignan and dismounted I was half furious at him, half worried that he'd had some accident.

"Send my son to me," I shouted to the guard at the gate even before my feet touched the ground.

"Sir Hugh, he is not here."

Stable lads scurried to take my horse's reins and lead him away. Jonas, my manservant, came to help me out of my heavy leather coat and leggings.

I snapped at the guard, "Not here? Well, where is he then?"

Jonas spoke before the discomfited guard could answer.

"Sir, I believe he is hunting."

"*Hunting*? When he should be doing his father's bidding?" I caught myself. These men had nothing to do with the matter. I tried to control my temper.

In the hall I sent for old Pierre Chastillon, my house steward. He'd served our family as long as I could remember and knew more about what went on among the many Lusignan connections than anyone else. He shuffled in, talking from the moment he entered.

"So you've come home at last! Welcome, my lord. Have they brought you some wine, and water to bathe your face? Fie, what are they thinking! Oh good, here they come at last."

Somewhat shrunken and not very steady on his legs in his later years, he was as bright-eyed and eager to help as ever.

"Never mind all that, Pierre. What do you know about Young Hugh?"

His face, wrinkled as a prune, lost its good humor.

"Ah yes. Young Hugh. A bad business." He stopped to cough and to gather his thoughts. I'll say this for Pierre, when he had something to report he started at the beginning and went straight to the end with no detours.

"He got your message, my lord, when you asked him to assemble men to help in your pursuit of King John. He made a good start, went over to Couhé and Saint-Heray, and persuaded them to volunteer a half-dozen men. He brought them back here, then went off again. At Lezay, though, his cousin Simon took a hand. You know how Hugh's always looked up to Simon, almost like a big brother he's been. From what I heard, Simon was all excited about a stag that had been sighted in their forest, a giant creature with broader antlers than anybody'd ever seen. He told Hugh they absolutely had to bring it down. I understand Simon promised Hugh to help him round up all the men he needed as soon as they got the stag. Well, they went out day after day and the clever beast would just show himself, then go bouncing off. Playing with them, he was. I kept sending men down to remind Hugh what he was supposed to be doing, and he'd just send word back that it would be only one more day and they were sure to get their quarry."

He paused to cough again. I poured him more wine.

"Should have gone myself. And I would have, if I could get myself on a horse these days."

"No, no, Pierre, you did what you could. So Hugh and Simon are still blundering about in the woods and the six men he did find are hanging around waiting for orders?"

"Oh no, they gave up after a week. Said they were tired of wasting all this time and had work to do at home. Can't blame them."

"And Hugh? When did you hear from him?"

"Yesterday he sent word that if they didn't get the stag he'd come back."

"You'd better send a man at once to tell him his father demands his presence." I glowered into my goblet. Then I got up and put my arm around Pierre's thin shoulders. "Thanks, my friend. You couldn't have done more."

A grin broke across his seamed face.

"Glad you're back, my lord. It's high time."

I sat on, finishing my wine. I'd always felt my son was easily led astray by his own enthusiasms and those of others. But I'd hoped he'd grow out of it. Now this, the worst example yet. At eighteen he was still unable to set a straight course and stick to it. Where was his sense of duty to the family? How could he let himself be carried away by Simon's frivolous urgings? It didn't bode well for the time when he'd take over as the leader of the Lusignans. As my only heir, he should be showing more responsibility. My irritation was flaming into anger. If he'd walked in then I don't know if I could have kept from striking him.

Fortunately for him I wasn't there when he finally appeared the next day. Early in the morning a messenger came from Angoulême, respectfully begging me to come for a meeting with Count Aymer on a matter of great importance.

At first I laughed. It was preposterous that Count Aymer, who'd done me such grievous harm, should be so blithely resuming our relationship as though nothing had happened. Then I became curious. I decided to go, and at once. I badly needed some distraction from my woes. Pierre could deal with Young Hugh.

"It was good of you to come," said my host, suave and finely dressed as ever.

"And on such short notice!" said Countess Alix, all in violet and with every golden hair in place.

If they hadn't changed, their great hall had. It was hard to believe it was only four months since I'd been in this very room. That was the last time I'd seen Isabella, when John sent me off to Wales. Then it was bare and cold, like my state of mind. Now there was a blazing fire on the hearth. Attentive young men kept it well fed. An expensive colorful tapestry showing a hunting scene hung on one wall. The decanters on the table were silver instead of pewter. I smiled, realizing the explanation: John's generosity was evident, his gratitude for certain assistance in arranging his marriage.

The count, seeing me smile, tried to reciprocate but smiling never came easily for Count Aymer.

"Shall we sit down?" He took his place at the head of the table and gestured to me to seat myself at his left. The countess was on his right. A servant filled our goblets with cool, foaming ale. The countess offered me honeyed walnuts from a crystal bowl.

What next, I wondered. I waited.

"Yes, Sir Hugh, we're glad you came. Now to our business: you remember that less than a year ago when we met in Rouen we discussed the desirability of uniting our lands of Angoulême with yours of La Marche through a marriage."

Seeing my face darken, the countess broke in quickly. "And nobody is more sorry than we are that what we planned did not take place."

The count hurried on.

"The reasons for such a union are strong as ever. So we would like to put it to you again." He looked at me, the picture of honesty and rectitude. "You may be aware that my niece, Mathilde, is still unmarried. She is the daughter of my older brother Wulgrin, who died ten years ago. Though she has never pressed them, her claims to Angoulême are probably as strong as Isabella's. She has been frail for some time, but seems to be recovering. I am her guardian. I think I could convince her that it would be desirable to marry you."

The countess gave me her sweetest smile, as though discussing the outlook for fair weather. "She has been considered quite pretty. She's still young, only thirty-five I believe. She should be able to bear several children. So you will have other heirs if anything should happen, God forbid, to your son Hugh."

"What do you think? Would you like time to think it over?" The count watched me with cocked head, like a robin listening for a worm.

I sat back, considering this strange proposal. My first thought was to wonder what King John would make of an alliance arranged without his knowledge. But that was the count's affair, not mine. My second was a pang of guilt that I could even think of marrying someone else, having been so attached to Isabella. My third was that the idea made a great deal of sense, in view of my worry about what a weak reed Young Hugh might prove as the lord of Lusignan. Fathering another son or so would be a reassurance. The sooner I set about it the better. In only a minute, I had made up my mind.

"I see the wisdom of your suggestion. Please, on my behalf, ask the Lady Mathilde for her hand. And let me know when we may hold the ceremony."

So it was that I married Mathilde d'Angoulême on November 5, 1200, just having passed my thirty-sixth birthday. My bride was neither pretty nor young, being quite plain and I suspected somewhat older than thirty-five. But she was brave and sweet-natured in spite of her fragile health. She proved a good companion. During all the years of our marriage she never gave me the slightest cause for complaint. Nor did she give me any children.

John
September 1200

After arriving safely in Le Mans I could finally relax. I was ready to settle in and enjoy a week of domestic dalliance with my bride before we journeyed to England. In two days my complacency was shattered.

I was in the audience chamber of the counts of Maine, where I'd been talking to the bishop about the city's revenues. As the current count I was entitled to half the taxes, but the bishop had the task of collecting and disbursing them. I had an idea he'd been holding something back from my share. He was an angular man with thin straight lips and deepset yellowish eyes below pale eyebrows He had a nose as sharp as a falcon's beak. His bargaining was sharp, too. We'd just come to an understanding when Robert de Thorneham rushed in.

"I beg your pardon, my lord bishop, but we have important news for the King," he wheezed. As usual, my steward was in such a hurry that his substantial body was hard pressed to keep up with his sense of urgency.

The bishop rose, folded his wide-sleeved black robe about his spare figure and glided out. Secular squabbles weren't his concern.

Robert wiped a beefy hand across his forehead and puffed a few more puffs.

"We've been talking to some travelers who've recently been in England. They say that King William is getting testy up there in Scotland. He's saying publicly now that you promised him those border counties and since you haven't kept your promise he'll take them by force."

"What! He's claiming Northumberland and Cumberland? What an underhanded ingrate that William is. I merely told him last year that I'd take his request under consideration."

116

I fumed. Just when my problems seemed solved here came this annoyance.

"Can we believe these travelers, Robert? Maybe it's a false rumor."

"I doubt it." Robert sank with a thud into the chair the bishop had just vacated. "They've just come from York, and they seem reliable. It's unlikely that King William will do anything rash before your return to England, though. He's not a total fool. Still, you'll want to keep one jump ahead of him. It might be well to depart soon. Better safe than sorry, eh my liege?" Robert was given to producing timeworn aphorisms as proudly as though he'd just made them up.

He was right, of course. I valued Robert's counsel. It generally coincided with what I was about to decide myself. In that it was unlike what I often heard from William de Cantilupe, who'd preach at me and urge some course of action that involved unpleasantness and disruptions.

On my way to tell Isabella we'd have to leave the snug haven of the counts' palace I ran into Sir William.

"Ah my liege, there you are. I have important news. It seems the King of Scotland…"

"I know, I know, Sir William. We've already had that news." William was half a head taller than I was and I hated having to look up at him.

Undeterred, he went on. "I believe that you should prepare to leave immediately for England."

"Of course we should. I've already given orders to Sir Robert to that effect. I suggest that next time you think twice before coming to me with stale news and unnecessary advice."

I pushed past him without waiting to see his reaction.

I found Isabella in the great hall, a spacious chamber with high arched windows looking out over the city walls to the meadows and forests below. Isabella was seated at the far end of the room near the fireplace, her back to me. At a nearby table Lady Anne was busy with thread and needle and a jumble of garments. She barely glanced at me when I came in. She and I hadn't been on good terms ever since she'd berated me for deceiving Isabella about Hugh's death.

Isabella hadn't seen me. She held her hands out toward the flames, then clasped them and breathed deeply. She stood, raising her arms high over her head and stretched, luxuriating in the warmth. I loved watching her when she didn't know I was there. She had such an unselfconscious grace. I stood at the door a moment, gloating over my good fortune. This enchanting being was mine, all mine.

She was wearing a full-skirted, tight-waisted green gown. Her flax-gold hair fell softly to her shoulders.

"You look like a spring daffodil greeting the sun," I said as I crossed the room.

"What a pretty speech!" She smiled and put her arm around my waist. That lightest of pressures excited me. It took only the merest touch from Isabella, just a brush of her hand against mine, for me to want more of her, all of her.

"I may look like a flower in the field, but I feel like a near-drowned rat that's come in out of the rain. This is the first time I've been truly dry in a week. It's heavenly here! My compliments to the thoughtful counts of Maine for putting so many fireplaces in their palace."

"On their behalf I accept your thanks. It's indeed comfortable here. Now you see why I feel so at ease in Le Mans. I'm glad you do too, and how I wish we could stay! But my love, we must be off again. I've had word that King William is making trouble in Scotland, and who knows what else might be brewing. I've been gone six months. It's high time for me to see to my English affairs."

The brightness left her face. Isabella, I was learning, loved her comforts. Even with her rosy little mouth in a pout, though, she was adorable.

"Just when Anne and I have almost brought order to my wardrobe we must pack everything again and take to the road? Will we have to rush the way we did to get here? What about that leisurely honeymoon you promised me?"

"It's beginning now. We'll leave tomorrow but this will be no flight from pursuers. We'll make our way to Cherbourg as slowly as a pair of tortoises."

She giggled and I smiled too, at the thought of two lumbering creatures plodding across the fields and orchards of Normandy.

"Tortoises in the daytime, but at night we'll be turtledoves. Just so we reach London in good time for your crowning as Queen of England."

At mention of her coronation she jumped up and clapped her hands.

"That reminds me, John. We've been trying to decide what I should wear for the ceremony. I really must have a new gown. I thought I could wear the blue one I wore at our wedding but it's far too tight now. Anne says we could let it out and add some gussets, but it would look very strange. Isn't that right, Anne?"

Anne looked up and smiled but said nothing.

"Please, John! I've been seeing myself in violet satin with a white mantle. If you wear your elegant black, just think how grand we'll look together!"

This was a serious matter. I sat down.

"I'm afraid we can't afford any new gowns, my love. I've spent far more than I should have, what with all the extra men and horses and mules we had to hire these past weeks."

The pout again. I hated to see her unhappy.

"But perhaps we can manage a new silk cloak to go over your wedding dress and hide the repairs. If it's violet it would set off your blue prettily. Yes, that's the thing! I'll wear a purple cloak over my black tunic. Your blue and violet would go very well with my black and purple."

She looked doubtful. I took her face between my hands and kissed her. Wrapped up in each other, we hardly noticed when Anne gathered up her work and left.

"Don't be disappointed about your gown, my pet," I murmured into her ear. "Don't you know that Isabella is the most enchanting creature on earth, no matter what she wears?"

She smiled, and her light kiss on my lips told me I'd won her over.

"And between us we'll present a splendid spectacle to the guests in Westminster Abbey. When they see such a beautiful queen by my side they'll be positively dazzled. I know the English well enough to be sure that a little dazzlement never hurts. It leads to a proper awe for the monarchy."

"It sounds like a game! First we dazzle them, then fill them with awe. What comes next?"

"Why, when they're awed enough and it comes time to tax, the money flows in all the more freely."

The journey across Normandy passed without incident, except for the daily miracle of how our passion kept growing. By the time we reached Cherbourg we still hadn't had our fill of each other. The Channel crossing put a temporary stop to all that, though.

Poor Isabella was miserably sick our whole time at sea. The galleon was crowded and smelly. The weather had turned stormy so we bounced about on the waves with sickening swoops. I'd made this voyage dozens of times, but even I felt queasy.

The seas at last subsided toward sunset and I saw her come cautiously on deck. She was pale. Her shoulders drooped. I took her arm and led her forward.

"Is the worst over, John? I know I look like a guttersnipe. I couldn't find the energy to wash or change my gown. My maid was in no condition to help me. Neither was Anne. But oh, how I've been longing for fresh air! Are we almost there?"

I pointed toward a wall of chalk-white cliffs directly ahead of us. They were tinged with rose in the setting sun's rays. Above them rolling green fields receded into the distance like billows of the ocean surging toward an unseen shore.

"The Isle of Wight," I said. "The beginning of England. In two hours I'll be back in my kingdom."

Isabella stood straighter and stared fixedly at the approaching land.

"Our kingdom," she said.

Isabella

October 8, 2000

King John, with all his enemies pacified and subdued, returned to England at the time of the feast of St. Michael. He came with his wife Isabella, daughter of the count of Angoulême, whom he had married overseas with the consent of King Philip. He had put aside his first wife in the previous year on the basis of their consanguinity. The next day, John wore the crown at Westminster, and his wife was crowned queen.

Ralph, Abbot of Coggleshell, chronicler of the life of King John

First the sudden blare of the trumpets, piercing the quiet as John and I stepped into Westminster Abbey. Then the long slow walk down the nave of the vast church while the organ played a solemn hymn. John marched ahead of me, preceded by his chancellor, his treasurer and three earls bearing the swords of state. I was accompanied by a bishop on either side. I heard the choir somewhere behind me singing an anthem but I couldn't make out the Latin—something about "Let mercy and truth go before thy face." Tall candles in sconces fixed to the lofty pillars along the nave lit their immediate surroundings brilliantly, and I could see faces turned toward me, the gleam of scarlet cloaks and jeweled headgear. Beyond there were shadowy areas where I sensed rather than saw that the immense abbey was crammed with nobles, merchants and churchmen. All were standing and craning their necks, come to see what kind of queen their king had chosen. To see me! I glanced up once but the ceiling was quite invisible, it was so high and dark. I felt I might sink under the weight of my ermine-trimmed ceremonial robe, and I gripped the arm of one of the bishops. I wanted so desperately to appear grown-up and composed that I clenched my teeth to keep my chin from trembling.

When I reached the transept I ascended a few steps to the high altar where

John was standing before the archbishop. This, John had told me, would be Hubert Walter, Archbishop of Canterbury, primate of all England. I knelt before him; I was too petrified to look up and kept my eyes fixed on his red vestment only a few inches from my nose. It smelled musty like a garment recently unpacked from a chest.

The archbishop spoke at some length but I hardly heard, I was so nearly dizzy with excitement. Then he told me to rise, removed the gold circlet from my head, dipped his hand in a silver bowl held by an acolyte and anointed my head with the holy oil. A bishop held out a cushion and the archbishop took from it a ring and put it on my finger.

"Let this ring, worn by Matilda, the wife of your royal husband's illustrious great-great-grandfather, King William the First, be always a reminder to you of your duties to your king and your people."

I looked in awe at the gold circlet with its huge ruby that seemed to glow with an inner fire. What a fat finger Matilda must have had! The ring hung loosely but I held my hand carefully so it wouldn't slip off.

I liked the anthem that came next. The choir exhorted the English people to "rejoice in their Queen's virtuous prudence." As the strong voices, all in unison, delivered this message to the assembled cream of the English people, I composed my face in what I hoped was an expression of virtue and prudence. It was too bad I had my back to my audience.

Now the archbishop had been handed my crown and I saw it for the first time. It was of gleaming gold, its wide solid band topped by two fleurs-de-lis made of pearls embedded in delicate gold petals. It looked heavy. The archbishop held it high for the spectators to see, then placed it gently on my head. I was so transfixed that I hardly felt the weight. It was no more burden than one of my lace caps.

I looked up at John, standing beside me, but he was staring straight ahead. Then the archbishop's stern baritone doled out more momentous words:

"Now Isabella of Angoulême, we proclaim you, by the grace of God, henceforth to be Queen of England, Queen of Ireland, Duchess of Normandy, Countess of Maine, Countess of Anjou, Countess of Touraine, Countess of Poitou, Countess of Aquitaine and Countess of Gascogne."

So many titles! Was I really ready to be a queen, a duchess, a countess? The anxiety came back. My robe was too big, my ring was too big, and I was reminded of how Adèle and I used to borrow our mothers' gowns and play at being grown-up.

I came to myself to realize the archbishop had stopped speaking. The last words of his benediction hung in the silence.

"Now may our Lord bless His handmaid the Queen, who by His will is the partner of her royal husband. Rise, Queen Isabella."

John took my arm and helped me to my feet. We turned to face the lords and ladies who had come to pay us honor. I heard a murmur that I hoped was approval. Here at the high altar we were bathed in light from three tall gilded candelabra. All eyes were on me. I should acknowledge this attention, but how? These were not people I knew. What did they expect from me?

Hesitantly, I raised my right hand and smiled. I heard a shout from the rear, "God save our King and God save our new Queen!" John put his arm around me and squeezed me to him, a familiar gesture. Then he turned my face up to his and kissed me. This must have been what the crowd was waiting for, and a cheer rose that filled the great church with glad sound. When quiet returned, John spoke. His voice was no match for that of the archbishop, but where his words did not reach his gestures made his meaning plain.

"We thank you, loyal Englishmen. We rejoice with you in this welcome to our Queen. Now let us all celebrate together in Westminster Palace where the coronation banquet awaits."

So often a long-anticipated event isn't the turning point one had expected, but when I left Westminster Abbey with the crown of a queen of England on my head I became a different person, just as I had known I would. With every step, as John and I led the procession down the nave, I felt taller, older, more self-confident, more queenly. I could relax and bathe in the admiration. I could cast more than a fleeting glance at John and we could exchange a few words.

"You've enchanted them, Queen Isabella."

"And I've never seen you look more regal and resplendent, my lord King."

It was true. He'd flung his purple cloak back over his shoulders and now I could get a good look at his rich attire. He paced along like a walking black velvet jewel case, with sapphires, rubies and emeralds at wrist and belt, on his fingers and set into the heavy gold chain around his neck. For the first time I saw him wearing the crown of state, which he didn't take on his Continental travels but kept safely locked in the royal treasury in London. It was like mine but more massive and had three fleurs-de-lis where mine had two.

We marched out from the dim church into the blinding sunlight of the courtyard, followed by the archbishop, his bishops, the other church dignitaries, John's noble companions and the still-singing choir. The organist was playing now with noisy abandon. The triumphant chords poured out from the church, almost drowning the babble of the crowds who hadn't been invited in. Cheering and throwing caps in the air, they were massed before us where we stood on the church steps. It was a warm, crisp London afternoon. The River Thames below the palace caught the rays of the sun and its waters were transformed into a sheet of rippled gold.

While John and I stood there above it all, a magnificently clad footman came and removed our cloaks. My hand rested lightly on John's arm, not for support now, but to show that we were partners, as the archbishop had said. I looked up at him and we smiled at each other. I believed we envisioned the scene the same way:

Behold, Londoners, your King and Queen. Are they not a splendid sight? Admire the dark elegance of the King so richly jeweled and the delicate beauty of his golden-haired Queen. How fortunate you are in your monarchs!

John and I led the procession along a red-carpeted path to Westminster Palace. The crowds pressed close, tossing flowers and calling out with huzzahs and cries of "Long live the King and Queen." I basked in the sun and the adulation.

"Now, my little bride, do you still think it's better to be the Queen of England than the Countess of La Marche?"

I knew what he was really asking: Had I forsaken all thoughts and regrets about Hugh? To be sure, I'd not thought about Hugh for weeks, not since we'd outrun the Lusignans and come to safety at Le Mans. But would I ever completely forget him? That chapter in my life was over, but one can't erase memories.

I knew what John wanted to hear. My answer came from my heart.

"I do, John. You are my husband and I love you and I love being the Queen. I can't imagine any other life."

He stopped and took me in his arms. I turned up my face. We kissed.

The crowd cheered.

Isabella

1200-1201

25

"After six months here, I'm afraid I find the English rather stodgy and unrefined. What do you think, Anne?"

"I agree, my lady. They certainly don't have the wit and fine manners of our French nobility. And they do seem to drink a great deal at dinner. It makes them even ruder."

It was the evening of Easter Sunday. We were lodged in the suite reserved for royal guests of the archbishop's palace at Canterbury. John and I had just been recrowned in Canterbury Cathedral. John lost no opportunity to wear the trappings of royalty before his people. This was his third crowning.

I'd soon tired of the din and confusion of the banquet that followed the ceremony and had left John to his roistering knights. I was exhausted after so much traveling over half of England. John had felt it necessary to meet face-to-face with as many of his vassals as he could. Since our coronation at Westminster we'd been to Guildford, Marlborough, Malmesbury, Gloucester, all over the Welsh March, to Lincoln and even to Newcastle and the old Roman Wall. There in the north our long, cumbersome procession with its barons, knights, outriders and creaking wagons paused so John could treat with King William of Scotland, whose demands had brought us so hastily back from France.

Now, thankfully, I could settle for a while and rest.

Of course I'd enjoyed all the chances to stand by John's side as his queen, but I was not quite as tireless a traveler as he. It was heavenly to be here alone with my old friend while she bathed my face and brushed the tangles out of my hair. Though I'd acquired three or four other ladies-in-waiting, all chosen by John from the wives of his English barons, I couldn't feel completely at ease with them. Anne was my only confidante, my only tie to the past.

I smiled at her remark about the uncouth manners and fondness for wine of our hosts.

"I hope you didn't suffer any rude advances this evening?"

She looked at me a moment as though wondering what to answer, then her infectious laugh erupted. She put down the brush and drew up a chair near mine. In company Anne usually managed to look the soul of circumspection, a proper middle-aged lady whom nothing could ruffle. But when we were alone together she could relax. She was bursting to tell her story.

"I did receive unwanted attentions. But you'll never guess from whom, and who my savior was. You couldn't see from the head table, but I was seated between Robert de Thorneham and some Saxon noble. Horace was all I caught of his name. I knew Sir Robert was a famous trencherman, but I must say Horace gave him a good run. I never saw so much roast beef and stuffed capon go down two gullets so fast. Of course it helped to wash it down with plenty of wine. We had very little conversation, they were so devoted to their meal. Finally, when the puddings and sweetmeats had been served and the page had refilled their goblets for the sixth time I suppose, Horace hiccuped and turned to me. Maybe he was remembering his duties as citizen of the host country to make his foreign guest feel at home."

"What did he look like, this Horace the Saxon?"

"He was not exactly prepossessing. Tallish, thinnish, baldish, with a wispy blond beard and a beaked nose like a parrot's. Not to mention smelling like an old wine vat. But I tried to look polite." She straightened her face and assumed her dignified public expression.

I was laughing now too, picturing the scene. Anne went on, mimicking the Saxon's slurred, rumbling speech.

"'Quite the mousy little creature, aren't you?' said he. 'I thought all you French ladies could talk a man's head off.'

"'For all you know,' I said, 'I could have been chattering like a magpie but you were making so much hubbub with your tankard and your knife and your platter and your roaring for wine that you wouldn't have heard a syllable.'

"'Ho, so that's how it is! Well, lucky for you, my lady, I like a woman with spirit.' And he put his arm around me and tried to get me into his lap."

"Oh my dear, how awful! What on earth did you do?"

"There wasn't much I *could* do. He was very strong, and he had me in such a grip that it hurt. But my savior turned out to be Sir Robert, bless him. All the drink hadn't totally dulled his good sense. It took him a while to hoist himself up out of his chair, he's such a great heap of a man. But he managed, and he yanked Horace by the collar and jerked him to his feet. He growled at him like a mad lion. 'You'd best mend your manners, my friend. Don't you know this is lady-in-waiting to the Queen of England?'

"So I escaped. The last I saw of them, Horace was trying to fight Sir Robert, but Sir Robert just picked him up and sat him down in his chair. For all I know, they went at the wine again and ended the evening the best of friends."

"Poor Anne! But good Sir Robert. I'm so glad he was there to rescue you."

"As it turned out, I had still another champion. When I reached the door on my way out, there was William de Cantilupe. He must have been watching all the time, ready to intervene if need be. I must say he was kind and courteous, not so withdrawn as he usually appears. He said the incident was most unfortunate, and asked if I'd been injured in any way.

" 'I shall certainly report this to King John,'" he said, 'and I shall advise him to remove Horace Wyndham from his body of household knights. Meantime, my lady, let me accompany you to your lodgings, to make sure you are perfectly safe.' Which he did, and here I am, perfectly safe."

She sighed and I took her hand. Though she made it seem like a joke, she'd been distressed by the assault, harmless as it turned out to be.

"We can't have this kind of thing, Anne. Remember that time in Lincoln, when John was closeted with King William and we went walking in the town with my other ladies? And we got separated in the crowd and some local oaf saw you alone and tried to get familiar with you? You look altogether too pretty and nice for your own good sometimes!"

"Well, I can't help being what I am. I try to think the best of everybody, I'm sure. What can I do about it?"

"I've been thinking about this, Anne. I believe we should send for Adèle to come to England. If you're seen as a respectable widow with a twelve-year-old daughter, you'll get fewer unwanted attentions." Anne had decided to leave Adèle in Angoulême with her grandmother while we were in England. I hadn't realized until I saw her radiant face how much she missed her daughter.

"Oh my lady, I would be so very pleased, if you are sure she'll be welcome. I know she's not at all happy staying with my mother. The child has seen nothing of the world, nothing at all, and it worries me that she's growing up such a little provincial."

"Then it's settled. I'll talk to John about it and I'm sure I can get him to agree."

An hour later when John appeared he wasn't as morose as he sometimes became after an evening of carousing. He did, however, seem extraordinarily tired. Maybe this pace we were keeping up was beginning to tell on him, too. All he wanted to do was to take off his leggings and belt and tunic and prop his feet up on a stool before the fire. I sat by him and smoothed out the furrows in his forehead and massaged the back of his neck.

"Ah, sweetheart, that feels good," he sighed. "What a wearisome evening it's been. I know I have to put on a show of being the great all-powerful monarch, but sometimes I feel nothing's accomplished. Tonight the best thing that happened was that Hubert Walter didn't tell me again that I was neglecting my Christian duties." Hubert, the Archbishop of Canterbury, had chastised John more than once, and the memories rankled.

"Do you sometimes wish you could just eliminate him, as your father was said to do with *his* troublesome archbishop?"

One of the first tales I'd heard on arriving in England was of how King Henry was so angry at Thomas à Becket that he ordered his men to murder the defenseless archbishop in Canterbury Cathedral.

John turned on me in a cold fury. I shrank, almost afraid he was going to strike me.

"Don't ever joke about that, Isabella! My father never gave that order, he never wanted Becket killed, and he did penance for his unwitting part in the deed. Haven't you heard how he wore sackcloth on a pilgrimage to Canterbury, and bared his back and ordered the monks to lash him with hundreds of strokes? Our whole family was in disgrace for years. You'd do well not to be such a gullible little sponge, believing every wild tale you hear."

"I'm sorry, John. I hadn't heard that part of the story. Of course, I don't believe your father would have ordered the murder, any more than I can imagine you doing such a horrid deed."

He was still glaring at me like a maddened bull. Then he sank back in his chair and sat brooding for a few minutes. I tried to think of a change of subject. It was John who broke the silence, but not with an apology for his outburst.

"Come to think of it, there was one other good thing tonight. William de Cantilupe seems to be learning how to conduct himself. I had to reprimand him a while ago and he's learned his lesson. Tonight he asked very civilly for a word with me and gave me a useful bit of information. He said one of my knights, Horace Wyndham, had been abusive and almost injurious to one of your ladies. He himself witnessed the incident. We can't have that kind of behavior. I told him we would have to send the fellow from court, and he agreed."

"I'm glad to hear that. The lady in question was Anne, and she told me the whole story. She said Sir Robert was a powerful champion, and Sir William was helpful and sympathetic."

Though Anne's name had been mentioned, I felt this wasn't the time to bring up the subject of having Adèle join her. John was still too touchy, and I knew he wasn't well disposed toward Anne. I'd never known why. Then it came to me: Why did I need to ask his permission?

You are the Queen of England, Isabella. You are the King's partner, not his subject. If you wish the daughter of your lady-in-waiting to join your court, that's your affair. Besides, Count Aymer and Countess Alix are Anne's employers, not John. They send a regular stipend for her expenses, and will certainly add something for Adèle.

I sat there staring at John while I absorbed this new reality: I no longer had to assume my elders were in charge of my life. Not even when this particular elder was my husband.

"Why do you look at me so intently, my sweeting? Have I bit of pudding in my beard? No need to hesitate, just tell me so." He'd regained his good humor.

"No, I was just thinking how interesting it was about Sir William. You must have handled him extremely cleverly, to make him change his ways like that."

I did indeed find the steward's softened manners interesting. It looked as though he'd begun to see the value of suggestion over highhandedness. Perhaps it was time for Sir William and me to get to know each other better.

John
1201

26

Our grand tour of the kingdom had been strenuous but worth the time and effort. Many of the barons hadn't been called on by an English king for decades, and they'd gotten altogether too high and mighty. I did my best to show them a monarch they'd do well to respect and obey. I'd even put a burr under the saddle of that troublesome old Scot, King William the Lion, what with my ostentatious tour all along his southern border. It shortly appeared that the lion's growl was worse than his bite.

Now, after the coronation and Easter festivities at Canterbury, which were hardly restful, we'd come with our court to Winchester to take our ease for a time.

I was looking forward to showing Winchester Palace to Isabella. When I led her into the great hall, she stopped short in amazement.

"This is beautiful, John! It's so big! I was expecting just another cold old barn of a place like so many of the castles we've been staying in."

"King William built it," I told her. "When he conquered England, he needed a castle strong enough to keep his enemies at bay, and an audience chamber that would impress his subjects. But by my father's time, what kings needed was a royal residence, not a stone-cold fortress. So he added onto this hall, and did a lot to make the living quarters more pleasant."

"Was it your father who put those lovely big tapestries on the walls? From what you've told me, King Henry didn't have time or taste for pretty things to look at."

She ran to look at a tapestry and called out, "Oh John, how beautifully it's worked! It's a hunting scene, and here's the deer flying away and the huntsman blowing his horn! You can almost hear it!" She cupped her hands to her mouth and produced a creditable blare.

I covered my ears with my hands. "Careful! You'll frighten the deer right out of the picture!" She giggled, and I walked over to examine it. "That was one of my mother's additions, I think. But you're right about Henry's tastes. He wanted plenty of room, but he didn't care if there were rushes on the floor or carpets. To please my mother, though, he went well beyond bare necessities. After all, he imprisoned her for fifteen years, a lot of that time right here. The least he could do was make it agreeable for her."

"There's so much I still don't know about your family. Now you must tell me why on earth the King of England put his Queen in prison, even if it was in a pleasant palace."

We'd continued our stroll around the room and up onto the red-carpeted dais. The well-polished table of state stretched across its whole width, almost from wall to wall. We sat at its center as though presiding over a banquet, though the hall was empty and our words echoed from the stone walls.

"It's a long story."

"Of course it is. So do begin."

As we'd grown used to each other, she'd often asked me to tell her more about my childhood and young manhood. When I did, it was usually a lazy recalling of this or that while we were in bed. Somehow we'd never gotten around to my mother's long imprisonment, which had begun long before Isabella was born.

"I'm sure you know that my mother and father were at each other's throats a lot of the time, far more often than when they managed to be civil to each other."

"I have indeed heard that. And I hope devoutly that such behavior doesn't run in the family."

"Well, you may also have heard that my older brothers plotted to rise up against our father. They went so far as to ask the King of France to help them. The long and short of it is that the King accused the Queen of encouraging them. In fact, he suspected she was conniving with King Louis. Louis was her former husband, and she'd lived with him long enough to produce two daughters before they divorced. I expect my father was always a little jealous."

"And had she been conniving?"

"Who knows? I wouldn't put it past her. She was spending most of her time in Aquitaine. It would have been easy to keep in touch with Paris. But I doubt it. I think that even after their differences she still bore Henry some love, certainly some loyalty, as the father of her children. Anyway, he decided he had to keep her from making more trouble, so he snatched her away from Poitiers and shut her up in Salisbury, then here at Winchester. I will say, though, that he built her a chapel and a fine suite of chambers, just for her and her ladies. You'll see them."

"Fifteen years! That does seem hard on poor Queen Eleanor. Promise me John, that you'll never, never imprison me!"

"I do so promise, unless you give me sons who turn against their father." I sealed the promise with a kiss.

Both of us, I think, were half joking, half serious.

I sat there, remembering living in this castle as a very young boy. Those had been the happiest years of my life. I was only six when Queen Eleanor was brought here. None of my brothers were around to claim her attention. I had her all to myself. By the time I was about eleven, though, I was more often with my father. By the time I was fifteen, when my mother was given her freedom, I was already involved in our family squabbles and making life difficult for my father. How long ago it seemed. Now I was learning for myself how hard it is to be a king.

Isabella rose and pulled me to my feet.

"No moping, my lord. Let's go on with our exploration. I can't wait to see the queen's house. Is your mother likely to come again, to claim it as hers?"

"No. I think she's perfectly happy to stay in France for the rest of her days."

"Then it's all mine! I think I will require you to make an appointment whenever you wish to come see me."

"In that case, I request a private audience immediately."

Arm in arm, we left the great hall, walked out into the spring sunshine and passed the herb garden. Several of Isabella's ladies were seated on benches nearby with their embroidery. I glanced at them, then asked Isabella, "Who is that slim, dark-haired girl standing by Lady Anne? She's a pretty little thing."

She turned toward where I was looking. "Oh, that's my old playmate Adèle. She's Anne's daughter. She came over to join her mother a few weeks ago, because Anne was missing her so much. I told Anne it was all right—I hope you don't mind?" She waved at the girl, who smiled shyly and waved back.

"Well, it's one more mouth to feed, when our court expenses are already far too high."

"Oh, you needn't worry about that. My parents are already sending an allowance for Anne, remember? They'll just add something on for Adèle."

"All right then. She doesn't look as though she'd eat much, anyway."

We went on to the little stone house on the other side of the garden. We passed through the anteroom, off which the rooms for the ladies-in-waiting gave, and on into the Queen's chamber. Isabella stood at the door and gasped with delight.

"It's absolutely elegant, John! I can tell at once that Queen Eleanor has lived here."

She danced about like a butterfly flitting from flower to flower, peering into corners, opening chests and cabinets, examining a silver ewer and looking at herself in a mirror with a jeweled frame. Then she jumped up on the high gold-canopied bed and leaned back against the soft silken pillows. She sighed languorously, beckoned me and announced, "The Queen will now receive the King."

My private audience lasted well into the dinner hour.

A week later a messenger came from France with an alarming letter from my mother.

"My very dear son," she began, as well she might. I was the only son she had left, and her only hope for ensuring the succession to the throne.

She begged me to come to France to see to my affairs. She reminded me that my nephew Arthur was a growing threat and was being encouraged by King Philip to challenge me for the crown of England. As if this weren't enough bad news, she said the Lusignans were rising. They'd be able to gather a far greater force than the year before when they chased me across Maine.

"You must raise an English army and come as soon as possible," she concluded.

I read the letter again, feeling resentful. Did she realize how shaky my support still was in England, no matter how hard I'd been working these past few months? I'd heard complaints, punished evildoers, put King William of Scotland off, collected taxes, and replenished the treasury. I'd dealt temporarily with the barons' insolent demands. Did she think I could just drop everything and leave?

Obviously she did. I had to admit she was right. It would be foolhardy to delay. We must hold the Angevin territories in France at all costs.

I looked up at the travel-weary messenger, waiting patiently—or perhaps not—for his dismissal and his dinner.

"Did the Queen ask you to give me any further message?"

"Only that she wishes you to send word by me as to when you will embark."

"Very well. After I've met my council, I'll give you that word."

I sent for my justiciar, Geoffrey Fitz-Peter. He had served as second-in-command to my brother and my father and ruled for them when they were out of the kingdom. He was not only trustworthy, but also wise in the ways of what a king could or could not do. Calm in crisis, he had a long, deeply furrowed face that reminded me of a benevolent horse. Behind that disarming exterior, though, was the brain of a keen, ruthless strategist.

I also summoned my two stewards and Godfrey de Lucy, the bishop of Winchester. It would take all of us to come up with a way to persuade my fractious barons to lend me their support and their troops.

First, though, I knew I must do something at once to deter the Lusignans.

"We can't let Hugh and his henchmen think they're free to do as they like," I said, when we were all assembled in my chambers. "But how can we do any damage to them, when they command so much of La Marche and Angoulême, and we have no force there to attack them?"

"Perhaps we could deal them a blow outside their homeland," said William de Cantilupe. "Haven't I heard that Ralph de Lusignan has some holdings in other parts?"

Then I remembered something Isabella had told me. Her "Uncle" Ralph, as Count of Eu, had a castle at Driencourt, at the northern reaches of Normandy. For a time she'd feared she'd be sent to that faraway place while waiting for her marriage to Hugh.

"Of course!" I said. "That's the answer. We'll take Driencourt. They'll never expect that. It's probably defended very lightly. My seneschal in Normandy can round up some men and take it before the garrison knows what's happening."

"A clever move," said Robert de Thorneham. "That will put the fear of King John into the Lusignans' foolhardy hearts."

I sent for a messenger at once, to take the orders to the Normandy seneschal.

Now, what to do about raising an army?

The bishop, himself one of the most powerful men in the kingdom, knew his fellow barons.

"They won't be easy to persuade. They keep looking back to the good old days, when they were like little kings in their baronies. They hated it when your father cut their privileges. Now they're taking it out on you."

"I know all that, Sir Godfrey. There's no need to dwell on the same old obstacles. We must come up with a practical plan."

He pressed his lips together as though holding in a reply. Then his face became bland. He remained silent while the others all began talking at once. The justiciar, Geoffrey, prevailed.

"Perhaps the first step is to send out your orders to your vassals to prepare to join you for the expedition. All those who owe you military service will either agree to meet you at Portsmouth, or they'll refuse. Thus you'll know who is with you and who is against you—and you can take steps against the latter."

Everybody looked relieved and welcomed this suggestion. Though it wasn't a final solution it was immediate action.

"Excellent, Sir Geoffrey. I'll have my clerk send out the writs tomorrow."

After that, we discussed how quickly we could embark from Portsmouth for France. We agreed on May thirteenth. I sent this word to my mother's messenger.

As the courtiers were leaving, Geoffrey Fitz-Peter held back and asked me for a private word.

"If I may, let me suggest a way to make sure of sufficient support from your barons." I agreed to listen. Within two minutes he outlined his plan. Within another two minutes I saw how devilishly clever it was.

I clapped him on the shoulder.

"Brilliant! It should work—it *will* work. But let's keep it to ourselves. Not a word of this must leak out. When the time comes, I won't forget you." We smiled at each other in complete agreement.

The smell of fowl roasting on the spit drifted up from the kitchens below.

"We'd best go down to dinner. But first, will you drink a glass of wine with me?"

I raised my glass. "To success!" I said.

"Let the barons beware," said Sir Geoffrey.

Isabella

1201

The chamber at Portchester Castle where John and I were lodged was noisy, which didn't do much to improve my temper. I looked down from the window that overlooked Portsmouth Harbor. It was growing dark but I could see a dozen ships at anchor. Small boats were ferrying goods out to them, then rushing back to get a new load. They looked like so many waterbugs with flying oars for arms. On the quayside men ran about like ants, each intent on his own task. Carts rumbled over the cobblestones. Horses neighed. Men shouted. My head was beginning to ache.

"How can we possibly be ready to sail tomorrow?" I asked John.

He answered absently. He was busy getting dressed to go down to the hall to meet his barons.

"They'll manage, even if they have to work all night. We sail at first tide, ready or not. No Peter, not those boots. What are you thinking of?"

"John, please, please, can't I go to this meeting with you?" I'd asked him before and he'd said no. He said no again.

"It's not women's business, Isabella." He was still preoccupied with donning his royal garb: black leggings, soft leather boots polished to a fare-thee-well, gold-embroidered tunic, jewels, gold chains, everything he needed to make him look and feel like a king at this crucial parley.

I knew it was crucial. It was the last chance to take stock of men and money and to make sure all was as ready as could be for resumption of the battle with King Philip for our lands in France.

"That will do, Peter," John said when his valet had placed the gold crown on his head and he was satisfied with his appearance.

As soon as the man was out the door, I resumed my arguments.

136

"Why may I not be present? When I was crowned Archbishop Hubert called me your partner. Shouldn't your partner be by your side when it's such an important meeting?"

To tell the truth I was impelled as much by inquisitiveness as by the need to assert my status. I wanted to be in at the end of this exciting story.

John had told me part of it: how he'd ordered the barons who owed him military service to meet him at Portsmouth. They were to bring their knights and sufficient money to pay their expenses during the campaign. Many of them demurred, though. They refused to come unless he guaranteed their traditional privileges. They wanted to return to the days when they ruled like kings in their own domains, free to dispense justice and levy tributes, unbeholden to any king. John had been furious at this show of independence. When he'd threatened to seize their castles, they were alarmed and backed down. John had told me all this with glee, proud of how he'd shown who was in charge. He was sure he'd prevail.

The rest I'd heard from William de Cantilupe. I'd met him by chance one day just before we left Winchester while I was on my way to hear mass. Several of my ladies were walking along the brick walk through the gardens that led to the chapel. As I drew near I heard them talking and laughing. I was surprised to see Sir William part of this merry group. Perhaps he's not always the hardworking, unsmiling functionary, I thought.

Though it was May, the breeze was fresh and cool. I asked one of the ladies to go back and fetch me a shawl. Sir William fell in by my side as I walked on toward the chapel.

I asked him what the news was of the barons' revolt.

"John tells me he's got the upper hand," I said. "I could hardly believe that those ferocious subjects of his would cave in so easily. How did he manage it? What have you heard, Sir William? Have the wolves become lambs?"

He was more than forthcoming. He told me that to carry through on his threat, John had been preparing to attack and burn down the castle of one of his staunchest English lords, William of Albini. At the last minute the hapless lord offered his son as hostage if John would desist. John did desist—but held the lad prisoner and threatened to kill him if there were any more insurrections.

"They've been quiet since then. But I'd be surprised if they'd turned into lambs. There's still a lot of fierce resentment at being called to cross the Channel and fight in France."

That was a week ago. The confrontation would come to a head tonight. From what Sir William had said, there was a real chance that the barons could gain the upper hand. I had no wish for this, God knows, but I very much wanted to be there, to see these fearsome barons in a body and to see how John handled them.

But John had said no.

After he left, I waited impatiently for hours. Lady Anne and Adèle were with me for a while. At first I was glad of their company. My former playmate and I were settling into a new relationship. At twelve, she'd grown taller and had become quite pretty, with her long dark ringlets and hazelnut-brown eyes. When we were younger, she'd deferred to me because I was older and bigger and she was somewhat afraid of me. Now she treated me with respect because I was the Queen, but she'd also gained a certain dignity and self-confidence. She wasn't simply somebody I could push around, but more of a little sister, who might become a friend. I liked her.

This evening, though, I didn't like anyone, I was still so annoyed with John. At last I told Anne and Adèle that they might as well leave. I would wait alone. And wait I did, pacing back and forth between my chair by the fire and the window. There'd been no letup in the frenzied activity. Now, under torchlight, it looked like a scene from purgatory. Finally I called my maid and changed into my nightdress (a silky rose confection, one of John's favorites) and lay down on the bed. I was just dozing off when the door opened and in he came. I was determined to have the first word.

"So. What mighty deeds have you and your men accomplished?"

My sarcasm was lost on him. He walked in like a conquering hero, swept me off the bed and into his arms and gave me a resounding kiss.

"Now they know who their King is and why they should obey him! My sweeting, you would have been proud of me. What a pity you weren't there."

I repressed my angry retort because by now curiosity was stronger than resentment. However, I intended to be as cool with him as I could. I slipped out of his embrace and sat down.

"Since I wasn't there, you must tell me all about it."

He did, still so full of the story that he couldn't settle anywhere and paced about the room.

"Well, they came here as ordered, two dozen of the mightiest lords of the kingdom, with their money and hundreds of their men. But I knew they'd been complaining to anyone who would listen about having to leave their homes and go abroad for a foreign war. Once we got to France, I doubted if they'd serve me with the dedication I needed. So what do you suppose I did?"

"I have no idea."

"First I had my treasurer collect all the coin and gold they'd brought. And a goodly pile it was, my sweetheart! You would have been amazed! We had to send for two more chests. Once that was secure and locked up, they stood before me, sullen as beaten hounds, waiting for instructions for departure tomorrow." He stopped, looked around, and asked peevishly, "Why is there no wine here?"

"Because, my lord, I ordered none to be brought. I had no idea when or whether you would return. However, we can certainly send for refreshments now."

He stamped to the door, hallooed and gave instructions to the page who came running.

He went on with his tale. His black eyes were flashing, and his beard quivered as it did when he was excited.

"I thanked them for their 'loyal support.' I was really ridiculing them, and it wasn't lost on them! Then I asked my justiciar Geoffrey Fitz-Peter, who was beside me on the dais, to stand up.

" 'Sir Geoffrey,' I told them, 'will be my deputy here in England while I'm in France. If you have any complaints while I'm gone you may present them to Sir Geoffrey.' You should have seen their faces then! Mouths hanging open, wondering what I was up to. I soon set them straight. 'Because, my lords, in view of your reluctance to fight for England, you may all go home, and take your knights with you.'"

A servant came in with wine and a bowl of nuts and figs. John poured himself a goblet and sank into a chair.

"Then I thanked them for the tithes they'd brought and I pointed to the chests. I told them that without their generosity, I wouldn't have had the wherewithal to hire soldiers in France. That was about it. They were so thunderstruck, they just stared at me trying to take it in. Some of them began to grumble, but what could they do? Nothing. So they left."

He took a handful of nuts and chewed, watching me, waiting for my praise.

I was a little thunderstruck myself. So this was what a king could do. It smacked of deceit, but on the other hand, what a monstrous joke he'd played on those horrid barons!

"King John, I congratulate you. What a clever scheme! Tell me though, did you have it in mind even when you sent out the orders to the barons from Winchester?" I knew he could act decisively but it was often on impulse and rashly, with dire results. This would have taken a great deal of planning.

"I did. I put it to Sir Geoffrey, no one else, and he saw at once how well it could work. 'Brilliant,' I believe he said. So now, since my chicken-hearted barons won't be going to France, I don't need to be afraid of desertions or treachery. And when we get across the Channel, I'll see how things stand with Philip. If I decide it's time to hire mercenaries I'll have all the money I need."

"Well done! Shall we celebrate your victory? Shall I send for more wine?" I'd forgotten how cross I'd been, how I'd determined to be cool and withdrawn. I felt only astonished admiration.

"No, I think I'm ready to celebrate in a more intimate fashion."

He stood, lifted me onto the bed and bent over me. He ran his hands gently over my cheeks and traced the outline of my lips with his finger. Very slowly, he inclined his head and brushed his lips against mine.

There was a knock and Peter poked his head in the door. Perhaps he wanted to atone for his selection of the wrong boots.

"Do you wish more wine, my liege? And do you wish me to assist you now with your preparation for bed?"

"No thank you, Peter. I believe the Queen and I will manage on our own tonight."

Hugh le Brun

1201

"God saw that none were rendering him glory and he was displeased. He turned aside and his anger consumed him so greatly that instead of the peace we had enjoyed, troubles broke out, especially in Poitou."
Chronicle of the Abbey of la Couronne, Angoulême, 1201

In the spring of 1201 God seemed to go to great lengths to punish us in Poitou.

From Poitiers all the way to the Atlantic, fields that should have been green with young wheat were soggy and barren. A severe freeze and ice storm the year before had killed trees and vines. Then torrential fall rains made harvesting and threshing impossible, much less replanting. People who had been able to eke out a living on their plots, albeit a poor and chancy one, now suffered from near-famine. Whole families, poor and hungry, wandered about the countryside, hopeless and ready to steal or kill to keep body and soul together. The church viewed it as divine vengeance.

It had been a dreadful spring for me too, with one piece of bad news after another for our Lusignan clan.

First we heard that John's forces in Normandy had taken Ralph's castle at Driencourt, near Eu. Then we learned that even before the loss of Driencourt, John had seized Ralph's holdings in England. Most serious of all, an army of two hundred warriors under the famous and feared English knight, William Marshal, was poised to make a sweep of Normandy and Poitou. John had instructed them to seize the castles and lands of those lords who refused to submit. Geoffrey's castle at Moncontour was sure to be on their list.

Finally I heard that John himself had landed at Cherbourg in early June.

The vow I'd made the year before when he escaped to England burned in my brain: "Next time, I'll be ready."

It was time to keep my vow. I sent swift messengers to my half-brother Hugues de Surgères and to our kinsmen at Lezay, Angles and elsewhere, as well as to a dozen other Poitevin families who were not close kin, but longtime allies.

I asked for their pledges of support. As soon as I received them I planned to go to Paris. Surely now King Philip would come to our aid. I waited impatiently in Lusignan, almost alone. Neither Ralph nor Geoffrey was there. The former had gone to Normandy to see for himself what condition his castle was in and how great a force was holding it. Geoffrey was at Moncontour, strengthening its defenses. My son Hugh wasn't at home, just when I needed him to act his age and accept his responsibilities as a member of the Lusignan clan. He'd gone off to Paris to hear a rabble-rousing priest who was urging a new Crusade. Still, I couldn't blame him too much. At his age I too had been caught up in the Crusading fever.

While I waited, my wife Mathilde was almost the only company I had. As she'd become increasingly unwell, she spent most of her time in her tower chamber. I'd made it as pleasant as I could for her, carving out a larger window so she could look out from her bed at the green valley of the Vonne below the castle.

On this warm, windless day I'd spent the morning with my overseer, checking on the supports of the north wall. There'd been a Lusignan castle on this high ground for three hundred years. I suppose every lord of Lusignan in all that time had worried about the north wall, which topped a very steep slope that fell to the river. With every severe rainstorm some of the soil slid downhill. Repairs were made: we piled sod around the base of the wall and its towers. We set huge rocks in place to hold the structure together. We planted trees on the slope. So far we'd managed to stand steadfast on our promontory. I meant to see that we stayed that way. When I'd made a thorough inspection and felt reassured, I went in from the heat of the day to the cool of the empty, echoing great hall. It was time to spend an hour with Mathilde. I walked briskly up the winding staircase. Though I was thirty-six, I could still climb those steps as nimbly as when I was a boy.

Ordinarily Mathilde and I sat in companionable silence. It was painful for her to use her voice, and I was glad of the peace and light in her chamber, where I could sit quietly and almost forget my troubles. Today she must have been feeling stronger. She was propped up against her pillows and seemed to want to talk. She was a good woman, and I know it grieved her that she hadn't been able to be a real wife to me.

I watched in concern as she forced out the words. Her lips were as pale as her colorless face. She strained with the effort not to cough. Her voice gathered strength as she spoke.

"Have you heard anything from Young Hugh?" she asked. She hardly knew my son but she was aware of how much I worried about him.

"Not since he arrived in Paris. I can hardly believe that hothead priest Fulk de Neuilly can be serious about preaching for a Crusade. But Hugh isn't the only one who's been taken in. His cousin Simon de Lezay has gone to Paris too, and dozens more lads from our Poitou, they say. Mathilde, do you remember the last Crusade?"

"Of course I do, it was only ten years ago. I know what you're thinking. That time, there were three great kings to lead the Crusaders, and today there are none. We need another like your King Richard."

"God rest his soul."

We were both silent for a moment.

"But who is there to step up and take the lead?" I said. "Not King Philip—he's already done it once. Not King John—too busy squabbling with his barons at home and King Philip in France."

"And maybe too wrapped up in his little..." She stopped. Mathilde had always been careful to avoid talking about the girl who'd jilted me. I respected her for that.

"That's all right, Mathilde. You may mention Isabella. It seems a long time ago when we were engaged. I hardly think about her nowadays. I spend more time thinking about John."

"Too much, maybe." Sometimes when Mathilde spoke as gently as she did now what she said was worth hearing. She sat up straighter and leaned toward me. Her thin face was full of pity. "Hugh, you mustn't let this hatred tear you apart. It's all very well to seek your revenge, but don't let it sour you. You're too good a man for that."

I looked at her in surprise. Was I getting sour? Maybe I was.

There was a knock at the door. Pierre Chastillon, my steward, came in.

"Yes Pierre, what is it?"

"Sir Hugh, Father Etienne is here. He has some news you should hear. He's waiting in the hall."

I turned to Mathilde. "I'll come up before nightfall and tell you what I've heard. Now rest."

She smiled and waved me out of the room.

Father Etienne was far more than a priest to me; he was my friend. Ordinarily his lean, intelligent face was merry and our conversations were far-ranging, not always of church matters or the welfare of my soul. He was as interested in the foibles and conduct of the great and mighty as he was zealous about guiding the worthy folk in our village toward salvation.

Today he was more serious than usual. He ran a hand through his thinning gray hair and folded his lanky frame into a chair. I told Pierre to stay.

Etienne said that a friar from Paris had passed through Lusignan the day before and had taken his supper at the church refectory. He proved quite a chatterbox and seemed to have acquaintances in high places who knew all the gossip. Etienne and his clerical brethren, always eager for news, had picked up a good deal.

"He told us what he'd learned of King John's whereabouts. It seems he went first to Andelys."

"To Andelys, on the Seine? That's where King Richard built his fortress, Château Gaillard. I've always wanted to see it. But why should John go there? Unless to make sure it could be defended against Philip if war breaks out again."

"That may be. Friar Junot didn't know. But he told us something even stranger. John and his Queen went on to Paris. They're lodged in King Philip's palace. He's entertaining them with lavish feasts and spectacles. Friar Junot says that Paris hasn't seen anything like it since Queen Eleanor reigned as the wife of Louis. He himself witnessed an evening party when twenty boats ferried the guests from the royal palace on the Ile de la Cité across the river to Philip's new fortress, the Louvre, and back again. He said there were so many torches lighting the way that it was like daylight. And so many musicians were twanging and tootling and warbling on both banks, it sounded like a barnyard when the fox gets in."

Pierre sniffed and growled, "Fine way to waste money, when the peasants out here are starving."

"True enough," I said, "but what I want to know is why Philip and John are so friendly all of a sudden. Have you any idea, Etienne?"

He rose and stretched, then sat down. It was hard for Etienne, with all his energy, to sit still very long.

"I do have a theory. I talked to the friar for another hour, trying to find out what he'd heard about Philip's affairs. We all know that Pope Innocent imposed an interdict on France because Philip repudiated his wife and married

Agnès of Méran."

"And some of us, myself included," said Pierre, " think it's shameful that a king's subjects should be punished for his misdeeds."

"Yes, well, there it is," Etienne went on. "And of course Philip is suffering too. It can't be pleasant to know all your fellow monarchs are laughing behind their hands at how you've brought the wrath of the church down on your whole kingdom." He grinned. "Oh who would be a king! Anyway, what Philip cares about most is peace with the Holy See. He's obsessed with getting the interdict lifted. If he were to dishonorably break the truce with John, the Pope would regard it as another sin. Philip can't afford that."

"So he's just biding his time?" I asked.

"I think so. Friar Junot thinks so. He's playing the generous host just to lull John into careless complacency. It's part of his game. Then you'll see, he'll go after him when he's on better terms with the Papacy."

I sat digesting this. It made sense.

"In that case, there's no point in going to him now to ask his help against John. We'd get the same answer we did last time: 'Not yet.'"

Then I remembered some idle words Philip had spoken when he dismissed us last year. At least I'd supposed they were idle. I'd hardly paid attention.

"Perhaps Sir Hugh could challenge John to a duel," he'd said.

Perhaps I could! Why not? What a glorious vindication it would be. To settle my grievances for once and all, in hand-to-hand combat with the villain who had wronged me. I'd no doubt I was a better swordsman than John.

"Your face betrays you, Hugh," said Etienne. "What brave notion makes you look so foolishly happy?"

I told them what I proposed to do.

Etienne, as a good churchman, couldn't condone dueling.

"You can't go challenging a king to a duel just because you don't like him."

"But it's not simply that I don't like him. My suzerain did an injustice to me, his vassal. Remember, I was his loyal man at the time. If he refuses to even admit he was wrong, I have every right to challenge him."

Etienne wasn't sure. He stroked his chin and pursed his mouth. "Maybe. I believe I've heard of such cases. They call them judicial duels—to decide a matter of law. Though I've never heard of a challenge to a king."

"Well, a king can't pretend to be above the law. I'm going to go ahead with this, Etienne."

Pierre had been listening to us impatiently. At my last words he set off as fast as his old legs would carry him to look for our swiftest, most trusted messenger to take my challenge to John as soon as I'd composed it.

So much for vindication. Five days later (days when I paced my lonely halls and could hardly sleep, I was so eager to face my enemy), a messenger came from John.

He delivered his memorized words in a toneless voice, looking not at my face but at his own dusty boots.

"King John accepts your challenge to a judicial duel. However, it would besmirch his honor as King of England if he engaged in combat with any of his enemies, the lowly, perfidious Lusignans. Therefore he presents you with a counter-challenge. He has appointed Quentin Proudfoot to meet you in his stead. You may choose the time and place and send your reply by the King's messenger."

The man looked up and asked with more insolence than courtesy, "What reply shall I take?"

I was nearly speechless with anger but I managed to growl, "No reply," turned my back and stamped out of the room.

I'd heard of Quentin Proudfoot. He was nothing but a hired assassin, often engaged as a duelist by men too cowardly to fight their own fights. His record of victories was impressive and so was his reputation for spectacular violence, from slicing off an arm to decapitation.

It wasn't fear of this lethal champion that made me scorn John's challenge, though. I felt contempt for a king so pusillanimous that he had to hide behind his "honor" rather than risk his neck.

Quentin Proudfoot wasn't my enemy. John was. So my fury and resentment continued to smolder, like a banked-down fire ready to burst into flame at a breath.

Queen Eleanor

1202

"Your beauty only grows with the passing years," said Sir William Marshal, after bending to kiss my hand.

"Nonsense, William. We both know that's not true. And I'm long past the time when flattery meant anything to me."

He wasn't abashed. William Marshal was seldom abashed. He smiled as cheerfully as though I'd accepted the compliment. He sat down beside me.

We were on the dais of the great hall of my palace in Poitiers. I sat on my gold-inlaid throne. William's chair was almost as regal. Below us were courtiers, rich merchants, lords and their ladies strolling about. Some, no doubt, looked for a chance to make some request of me. But most had come to see and be seen in the Queen's presence. One such, probably, was the young man in blue velvet who perched on a tall stool far down at the end of the hall. I could see the bow moving across the strings of his vielle. I could see his mouth move so I supposed he was singing, but the chatter was so loud I couldn't make out tune or words.

It was a familiar scene. How many times had I sat just here, presiding over a convocation of bishops and lords of the church; or a gathering of the nobility of Aquitaine, come to repledge their fealty to me; or a gay and festive Court of Love, when troubadours sang and maidens blushed and the garlands on the walls filled the air with the fragrance of lavender and roses.

Abruptly I pulled myself back to the present. This was not the time to reminisce about gallants and garlands. We had urgent matters to talk about.

"I'm sure you know why I sent for you, William. You must tell me what you know of these reports that King Philip is raising an army on the borders of Normandy. Doesn't his truce with John still hold?"

He sighed and turned his earnest, troubled face to me. I could almost see the words arranging themselves in his head. Still handsome at sixty, William had never been a deep thinker or a brilliant strategist. But he could be counted on to accomplish whatever task was given him, on the battlefield or at the courts of kings. He'd served our family for as long as I could remember. He was the bravest, most loyal and trustworthy man I'd ever known.

"Apparently Philip feels he can now break the truce. He'd been keeping John off his guard, professing friendship and peaceable intentions. He even invited him to Paris."

"Yes, I heard of that. What could John have been thinking of? I suppose he felt flattered to be entertained so royally by a fellow monarch."

"That may be. At any rate, after Philip's wife Agnès died last fall he wasn't living in sin anymore. The Pope had no more reason to chastise him so he's lifted the interdict. I fear we can expect to see Philip begin to attack very soon. The Lusignans have persuaded him that John must be forced to make reparations for the injuries he's done them."

I groaned. "Those troublemakers! I sometimes wish John had never married that girl."

"But just as serious, Philip has brought your grandson Arthur into the picture."

"Oh, Arthur! William, what are we going to do about Arthur?"

My feelings toward Arthur were far from grandmotherly, though he was the son of my son Geoffrey. After Geoffrey's death his widow, Constance of Brittany, had encouraged the boy to think of himself as heir to the English throne. "The hope of Brittany," the Bretons called him. My husband Henry and I, however, had always held that our sons came first in the succession. If we should ever run out of sons (God forbid!) it would be time to consider grandsons.

William bent his head with its smooth cap of silver-gray hair, studied his clasped hands and looked up. "The same question has been much in my mind. He's become even more troublesome now that he's fifteen and his mother has finally died."

I shook my head in impatience at the annoyance Arthur was proving. And another annoyance: we *were* almost running out of sons to inherit the crown.

"What if John were to die childless?" I said. "Then we'd have to accept Arthur, and what a mess he'd make of things. That wretched mother of his would keep on running his life from beyond the grave." Constance's pushy aggressive nature had always reminded me of a vixen holed up in her den, defending her cub. "When I heard she'd died it was the first good news I'd had in months."

William looked a little shocked.

I reached over and patted his hand where it rested on the arm of his chair.

"Am I unchristian to rejoice in her death? Well, so be it. You know me well enough not to be surprised at my honesty, old friend."

He looked down at my thin white fingers resting on his brown, weather-beaten hand.

"Like a lily that's fallen on the mud," he said.

For William, gallantry was as automatic as breathing.

"Getting back to Arthur," he resumed, "I'm afraid he's become more of a threat than an annoyance. We've just learned that Philip has knighted him and received his homage for Poitou, Maine, Anjou and Touraine."

"That is monstrous! What right does Philip have to give all our Angevin lands in France to Arthur? I'm surprised he hasn't tried to snatch away my Aquitaine too. William, I think you must go see John at once and impress on him that he must take action. Any day now Philip could start attacking us. John must tear himself away from his little poppet and get his armies ready for the field."

He nodded. "I agree. I'll start tomorrow morning. At the same time, perhaps you should go to Fontevraud Abbey and keep out of harm's way. Surely Philip wouldn't make trouble for you in such a peaceable, holy place. You could send for Arthur to come visit you. Maybe it isn't too late to remind him that you are still head of the family, and to appeal to his better nature."

"Ha! If he has any left. But yes, that might at least buy us some time."

I rose and took his arm as we walked down to mingle with the crowd. We moved slowly through the room, accepting a greeting here, a bow there, until we reached the corner where the young musician had been playing. He was still sitting on his stool. When he saw me he brightened, tucked the vielle under his chin and played a soft introductory chord. His voice was a pleasing tenor. The tune was lovely, in a minor key, almost mournful. I stood and listened, still leaning on William's arm.

> Lady, I am yours and shall be
> Vowed to your service constantly.
> This is the oath of fealty
> I pledged to you this long time past.
> As my first joy was all in you,
> So shall my last be found there too,
> So long as in me life shall last.

I was transfixed. I knew that tune, those words, but from where?

"How do you come to know this song, young man?"

"My lady, I learned it from the first teacher I ever had, Bernard de Ventadour. He told me he'd written it in your honor. I thought I too would play it now in your honor—I hope I've not offended you?" He was so fearful that his voice quavered.

I stood there remembering. Yes, Bernard, the famed troubadour, had played that song for me here at Poitiers, thirty years ago at one of my Courts of Love. Now Bernard was gone, there were no more Courts of Love, and I was old.

Again, I had to wrench myself away from nostalgia.

"No, you have not offended me. You play and sing beautifully. Thank you."

William and I walked on and he saw me to my chamber in the tower. As we said goodbye we agreed that Gerard Delorme, one of my most trusted messengers, would go with him the next day, in order to bring word back to me at once of what developed. Then I thought of one more request.

"When you see John and Isabella, be sure to find out if she's pregnant yet. After all, they've had nearly two years to produce an heir."

I was very tired, but I made myself stay up long enough to summon my majordomo and instruct him to send a message to Arthur the next morning.

My dear grandson:

I was grieved to hear of the loss of your mother. You must be grieving also, for I know she was dear to you. We must trust in the wisdom of our good Lord when our loved ones are taken from us. Will you not come to see me at Fontevraud Abbey, where I plan to spend the summer? Then I may extend my love and sympathy in person. I would come to you, but I am too old for much travel these days. It would do my heart good to see you again after all these years. As one grows older one feels more drawn by family ties. Please send word that you will come. Your loving grandmother, Eleanor.

It was hypocritical, but it was necessary.

Shortly, though, the good Lord took matters into his own hands. Or perhaps it was Philip Augustus.

I'd been back in Fontevraud only a week, still hoping for Arthur's reply, when Gerard Delorme arrived with word from William Marshal. He came at once to my chamber, his blue and white livery splattered with mud, his face red and perspiring from his haste.

His news was dreadful. Arthur, newly empowered and encouraged by Philip, was on his way to Tours to join forces with the Lusignans. As soon as reinforcements came from Brittany, they would attack. They'd learned I was at

Fontevraud so that would be their first target.

"The Queen must leave Fontevraud at once," William had instructed Gerard. "Arthur has vowed to find her wherever she is and take her hostage. She'll be safer at Poitiers, where the city is well fortified and her people are loyal."

William himself was on his way to Le Mans, where John had gone to muster his forces.

For once, I didn't feel in charge of my own destiny. I was like a ball being bounced back and forth by careless players. I knew William was right. I got ready to set out again. Never in my life, even when it was a matter of leading troops into battle, had I pled the excuse of weakness or womanhood when action was called for. Nor would I now, at eighty.

Isabella

1202

ohn and I were finishing a late breakfast at Chinon, where we'd come after being so lavishly entertained by King Philip in Paris. We hadn't dressed for the day yet. Even so I thought we looked quite elegant. John's morning robe was black wool embroidered with silver braid; mine a lace-trimmed blue silk.

Nibbling on a raisin cake, I felt languorous and content. I looked around the room with pleasure. At my urging John had ordered improvements not only here, but in much of the rest of the sprawling old fortress. A new oak table, smaller than the monstrosity that had formerly crowded the room, was covered in white linen and the silver tableware shone. A long pennant with the three golden Plantagenet lions on a field of red hung on one wall. On another was a blue banner with the gold crown and fleur-de-lis of Angoulême. A cheerful fire crackled on the hearth. The stone floor was scrubbed and clean. I drew a basket toward me and drank in the fragrance of pale-pink dried rose petals.

"If Queen Berengaria ever came back, she would find us much more stylish than when she visited two years ago," I said to John. "Remember how gloomy and dingy this room was then?"

He looked at me suspiciously. I realized I'd spoken without thinking about that terrible night when I learned from Berengaria that Hugh still lived, and that I'd been tricked into marrying John. Neither of us had ever referred to it since. I believe we both knew that there were some subjects better left undiscussed. I hurried on--I wasn't trying to rake up old grievances now.

"And now, I love coming to Chinon. You've made it almost as pleasant and comfortable as Angoulême." That was the highest compliment I could think of. I blew him a kiss. He was appeased.

Our domestic bliss these lazy days was hardly disturbed by the occasional word that came of movements by the Lusignans or of King Philip's affairs. "You deal with it, Sir William," John would say to William de Cantilupe, and go back to his wine, his hunting or our bed.

This morning, though, William came into the dining hall in rather more of a hurry than usual. A messenger in the black-and-gold livery of the King of France was close on his heels. William spoke quickly to forestall an angry outburst from John. John hated being interrupted at our leisurely breakfasts.

"My liege, this man insists he must see you at once with an urgent message from King Philip."

John looked ready to throw them both out. But the King of France was the King of France.

He barked at the messenger. "Very well, give us your message. But be quick about it."

The man doffed his plumed hat. He placed one black-shod foot, toe smartly pointed, in front of the other and recited.

"His majesty King Philip Augustus greets his vassal John and summons him to come to Paris to do homage as Duke of Normandy, and to answer certain charges made against him by Hugh de Lusignan, Geoffrey de Lusignan and Raoul de Lusignan." He stopped and waited for John's response.

John sputtered a bit, then exploded.

"Nonsense! Philip and I parted the best of friends in Paris three months ago. He didn't say anything then about this. You must have misunderstood him."

The fellow's face showed no expression. He was only the messenger.

William bent and whispered in John's ear. John nodded impatiently and brushed him aside, but I believe he acted on William's advice.

Fixing the messenger with a contemptuous gaze, he replied, "You may tell your king that it's true I am his vassal as Duke of Normandy. But according to the law, the Duke of Normandy may not be required to meet his sovereign anywhere except in that duchy. Therefore, if King Philip would like to meet me on the Normandy border instead of Paris, I'll be happy to oblige."

I wasn't happy to hear this. I'd found Normandy a rather dull place, not nearly as inviting as Paris. I'd been much admired and sought after at King Philip's court. My taste of Parisian high life had left me eager for more

The messenger continued. He'd been instructed well.

"If you object on these grounds, I am authorized to tell you that King Philip addresses this summons not only to the Duke of Normandy but also to the Count of Anjou and Maine. In that capacity you are required to come to

Paris to do homage, which is long overdue, and should have been rendered immediately on your accession to the throne." The wording was insolent; the tone, carefully noncommittal.

John was more sure of himself now. "As King of England, I may not be so summarily ordered to the court of one of my peers. Tell King Philip that. And again, tell him I will be glad to meet him in Normandy, at the place and time he suggests." He made a dismissive gesture and returned to his breakfast.

The messenger bowed, put on his hat and left. William and John exchanged wry smiles. Then both grew very grave.

"So. King Philip has decided to break the truce," said William. "This message wasn't even serious. He knew you wouldn't agree to his demands."

"Right," said John. "I have no intention of meeting him on the borders of Normandy or anywhere else, unless I have an army at my back."

So much for my dreams of Paris.

During the next few weeks I saw John transformed from an indolent lie-abed whom I had all to myself to a bundle of nerves with a hundred things on his mind. For days I hardly saw him, he was so busy conferring, sending out messengers, enlisting informers and preparing for resumed hostilities. Most important, he had to hire paid soldiers, using the chests of money his barons had so unwillingly given him. There were plenty of available recruits. After every Crusade, men willing to fight for a fee roamed over Europe looking for work.

We were preparing for war. We hoped we had time.

"And now, our Lord God of Hosts, may You bring victory to Your servant John as he goes into righteous battle against his foes." The Bishop of Le Mans pronounced his last words in a dramatic descent down the scale, from a sonorous tenor to a portentous bass.

To John, who had been fidgeting or dozing beside me for twenty minutes, it must have seemed the climactic end of the interminable prayer. He sat up straight. He seized his moment.

"So be it, amen," he called out, and rose. The Bishop's hawklike face turned to him. He glared with his yellow eyes. He doubtless had several more things to say to the Lord God. However, he recovered himself and signaled to the choir and acolytes to begin the march out of the cathedral. We followed, bathed in a swirl of incense and a chorus of Te Deums. Along with the usual crowd of knights and attendants, we walked down the cobbled street to the palace of the Counts of Maine where we'd come from Chinon and lodged for the past few weeks.

It seemed ages since I'd first come to Le Mans, when we sought refuge within its walls from the Lusignans. How frightened I'd been, and John even more so! Now everything was different. This time we were on the offensive, against Philip and his allies. Our information was that the Lusignans had raised a considerable force, and would very likely join Philip on his assault on the Angevin lands in France which Philip now had decided to repossess.

I say "our" information because at last John had agreed that I could be present during his councils. I'd hated being excluded as though I were a turnip-headed ninny. I was able to get him to change his mind because I'd learned the arts of persuasion in bed. Before love, John would agree to anything. After, he was so proud of his prowess that he'd agree to whatever was left on my list.

So on this sweet June afternoon when hawthorn trees showed tender pink blossoms and the sun shone benignly on the daisy-dotted grass in the palace courtyard, we went inside to talk of mortal warfare. William de Cantilupe had just received two messengers with urgent news from the informants who served as John's eyes and ears throughout his continental lands. In the small audience chamber, John sat at the head of the table, I on his left, William on his right. Robert de Thorneham, whom John had just named his seneschal for Poitou, was present, as were Henry Seuvallis, captain of the horse troops and foot soldiers, and the chief of the household knights.

The first messenger gave his report briskly and concisely.

"Your seneschal in Rouen, Guarine de Clapion, requests that you send as many men as you can. Philip has already taken Aumale and is besieging Arques. If he takes it, Rouen will be next."

This was shocking. All were temporarily struck dumb. How had Philip slashed so deeply into Normandy, all the way across the duchy to two of the Angevins' major strongholds on the Atlantic? If he took Arques, he'd have only a two-day march south to reach Rouen.

John's face flushed dark.

"We mustn't lose Rouen. It's always been the key to all of Normandy. We always keep a force in the city to defend it. How many men are there now?"

Nobody knew. The messenger thought perhaps twenty-five at most. Everybody began talking at once, then fell silent when Sir William's voice prevailed.

"I suggest we send a small contingent of our mercenary troops to Rouen at once to survey the situation. We can follow with more troops if the danger seems imminent."

"Good," said John. "How many can we spare?" he asked the captain of the mounted troops. More discussion and argument. The only thing everybody agreed on was that even with the hired mercenaries, John's continental forces were woefully inadequate for an all-out battle with Philip. He'd sent for reinforcements from the English barons who were still loyal to him, but they hadn't arrived.

At a pause, I broke in.

"Maybe we should hear what the other messenger has to say. It might be better news."

It wasn't.

"My liege, I come from Tours. I am to tell you that King Philip has knighted your nephew Arthur. Philip has granted him Maine, Anjou and Touraine. He has also provided him with an army of two hundred knights. Arthur is now in Tours, preparing to lead his army into your ancestral lands, to claim them for his own."

John turned so redfaced I feared he might burst. "By God's teeth! That treacherous boy! How can I be rid of him?" he began in a roar and ended in the whiny falsetto his voice rose to when he was under great stress. He banged his fist on the table so hard that goblets and tankards jumped. So did the messenger.

He finished his report quickly so he could escape before John's anger was directed to him.

"Finally, your spies have learned that Arthur has been joined by Hugh de Lusignan, Geoffrey de Lusignan and others of that clan. Our best estimate is that the combined force Arthur is leading comes to between two hundred fifty and three hundred men, and that his first objective is Poitiers. Your mother, Queen Eleanor, is now on her way to Poitiers from Fontevraud."

Before the babble could begin again, the man bowed and slipped out the door.

My first thought was shock that none of this had been foreseen. What were all those spies up to, if not warning John of impending disasters? Or could it be that warnings had come, and he had refused to take them seriously? Well, he was certainly taking them seriously now.

He stood. I could almost imagine he'd grown taller. Faces were tense as his counselors waited for his words.

"My mother's safety comes first," he said. "That, and stopping Arthur. We'll send a force of twenty-five to go north and join the Rouen garrison. Henry Seuvallis, you will accompany that contingent and keep us informed. I shall leave at once with the rest of our army to head off Arthur from Poitiers."

The word of his mother's danger had transformed him from a worried fumbler trying to go all directions at once into a firm, single-minded leader.

I had only a few minutes alone with John before he was off. While his servants helped him into his leather leggings and his mail coat I stood watching, filled with a growing anguish. We hadn't been separated since our marriage. I hadn't realized how much I depended on his presence and our love.

When he was properly clad, except for his helmet, he held out his arms to me. It was a strange embrace, clasped by steel-clad arms against a chest encased in cold steel. But his cheek against mine was warm.

"What will I do without you?" I asked, blinking back tears. "Will you be careful? When will you come back?" Foolish questions.

"My love, I want you to leave at once for Chinon. Robert de Thorneham will take you. You'll be safer there. I'll send word as soon as I can from wherever I am. You will help me by receiving any messengers who come from the north. Send their reports on to me. Pray for our success. As soon as it's safe, we'll be together again."

I clung to him, then drew back to look into his face. Somehow I managed to smile and wish him Godspeed.

Eleanor

1202

31

Our hasty flight from Fontevraud brought us, toward evening of the first day, to the castle of Mirebeau. In my younger days I'd have ridden on through the night to Poitiers. But I was worn out from the daylong, headlong ride over rough roads. I decided we'd halt here.

I remembered the castle from my travels with Henry during the early days of our marriage.

"It goes all the way back to my great-grandfather, or was he a great-great grandfather?" Henry had said. "No matter. Old Count Fulk of Anjou knew how to build a fine little castle. He planned that tower, the keep, to stand off besiegers. Just shoot arrows at them as they try to come up the stairs, till they're all taken care of."

Revisiting it now, so many years later, I recalled that the castle hadn't offered much in the way of gracious accommodations. I'd probably find even less now. But I was glad to see the tower was still standing, tall and sturdy. This night, safety meant more to me than silken canopies and silver platters.

"Very well, my Queen," said Jean de Brouillet when I told him my wishes. He'd served us since he was squire to my son Richard. He'd risen steadily through the years to become the captain of my personal guard. Except for William Marshal, there was no one I trusted more. He led our small party, which included two of my ladies and six of my knights, through the gate that led to the bailey. This courtyard was, I was glad to see, still well protected by its high walls. But I'd been shocked to find the portcullis down and no guard on duty.

Jean pounded on the door of the keep. Presently the elderly castellan emerged, tousle-haired and scowling at being rudely wakened. But when he saw who his visitors were, he found a smile, introduced himself as Albert Portot, and made us welcome. Unused to visits from his Aquitaine sovereign, he and his small staff had to scramble to provide us with a meal of rabbit stew and chunks of yesterday's bread. Meanwhile his wife, a short dumpy woman who was flustered but full of goodwill, did what she could to make a few of the tower rooms habitable. My ladies and I were climbing the steep, tightly spiraled staircase when there was a fearful noise from the bailey.

I made for the nearest window, a mere slit. I could see dozens of steel-helmeted horsemen in battle armor wheeling their steeds about, brandishing their lances and shouting, apparently waiting for some guidance as to what to do next. It was dusk. Individuals were hard to make out. Then I saw, riding through the gate, a youth in chain mail but no helmet. His long brown hair fell to his shoulders. He was sitting as tall as he could in the saddle. Behind him a squire bore a pennant with a lion, a unicorn and a griffin. It was the insignia of Arthur, who called himself Duke of Brittany. My grandson Arthur. He hadn't come to accept my invitation to pay a visit to his loving grandmother, I was sure of that. He had come to take his grandmother hostage. He looked left and right, up and down. For a moment I thought our eyes met, but it couldn't be.

Jean de Brouillet, peering through an arrow-slit a few steps below me, assessed the situation at once.

"If they attack, we'll have our bowmen posted here in the tower to prevent Arthur's men from getting close to the entrance to the keep. That's a stout oak door, but it could be broken down by a few determined fellows with battleaxes."

There was no thought of retiring to bed now. I went with Jean while he positioned our six soldiers at loopholes from which they could aim their crossbows at the attackers. I asked the castellan to assemble his staff. The dozen men and women included the cook and baker and their assistants, three scullions, a stableboy, a dairymaid, and three men-at-arms. Jean posted the latter near the door, ready to fall on any who broke in. He instructed the others to arm themselves with whatever they could find: cleavers, hammers, brooms, shovels.

Now there was nothing to do but wait.

I'd been in mortal peril many times before. More than once when I accompanied my first husband, King Louis, on his crusade we'd been threatened by attacking Turks and I'd feared for my life. And more than once, in later years, I'd gone into battle to subdue recalcitrant vassals in Aquitaine.

But never had I felt more helpless than this July night in 1202.

We watched, waiting fearfully for the first assault, until it was too dark to make out any details. One by one, fires began to blaze here and there in the bailey, fueled by logs pilfered from the castle's woodshed. Now we could see men swarming around the fires. Did they mean to burn the castle? Then a half-dozen soldiers came through the gate bearing slaughtered lambs and chickens, which they spitted and placed over the fires to roast. Near the gate a tent had been set up and in the firelight I could see Arthur seated on a makeshift bench, watching the preparation of his dinner. He looked lonely and less substantial than he'd seemed on horseback: a vulnerable boy who found himself in a grown-up situation he wasn't ready for. I felt no pity. He'd brought this on himself.

Two men in armor, one tall and one very tall, approached him and sat down on the bench. They conversed earnestly, gesturing toward our tower, looking around, arguing perhaps. The taller man walked over to the castle door and gave it a thump with his mailed fist as though testing its strength. He shouted something to the to the others. I couldn't make out the words but the tone was one of utter contempt.

These, I deduced, must be the dreaded Lusignans. William Marshal had told me they'd joined forces with Arthur. I asked Jean if he thought so too.

"I do. I've seen them at tournaments, though that was some years ago. I'm sure that big fellow who pounded on the door must be Geoffrey and the other's his nephew, Hugh. I wonder how many troops they've brought."

I couldn't see his face, but I could tell from his strained voice that he was apprehensive. We continued our vigil. It was an eerie scene, where dim figures moved about in the dark, lit by the flickering cooking fires. The soldiers had taken off their armor and clustered around the fires, ready to snatch a half chicken or a lamb leg, the minute the cooks began to carve. Swirling blue smoke and the smell of roast meat rose to our windows.

"Surely they won't attack now, if they're getting ready to eat?" I called down to Jean.

"We must still be watchful. It could be a trick, to lull us into feeling safe."

Suddenly I felt my knees buckle and I sank down on the step. In the excitement I hadn't noticed how near collapse I was, but now I felt ready to give up and let events take their course. My two ladies had already fled to their rooms. I hardly blamed them. I longed to unpin my wimple and let my hair hang free. I longed for a basin of water and a cloth so I could bathe my face.

The soldier posted above me noticed my weariness and stepped down to offer to help, but I waved him away. All I needed was a short rest. After ten minutes,

I forced myself to stand up and peer again through my peephole. The bailey had become strangely silent. There was a small group around Arthur's tent, but the fires were dying down. Most of the soldiers had disappeared.

Gradually a new kind of noise broke the quiet. From beyond the castle walls, from the twisting streets of the little town we had ridden through only a few hours before, came a growing din of whoops and shouts, raucous singing, and thumping of running feet. Tense as a stretched wire, I watched the gate, waiting for the first wave of invaders.

None came. For the next half-hour, though the hubbub continued, no one passed in or out of the gate.

The castellan's wife, surprisingly agile for her girth, came up the stairs at a trot.

"Albert told me to tell you not to worry!" she said, her words coming in squeaks interrupted by puffs. "That horrid uproar doesn't mean they're getting ready to attack. The stable boy managed to slip through the gate and back again. He says it's just that the soldiers have been in the taverns and wineshops so now they're all tipsy and happy. Some of them are looking for women, and some have already found a place to stretch out and sleep it off."

Jean and I looked at each other, both thinking the same thing.

"What kind of a leader is Arthur, to permit such a lack of discipline in his army?" I'd thought Arthur ungrateful and untrustworthy. To those sins I could now add incompetence.

"At any rate," said Jean, "there'll be no attack tonight. Do go to your rest now, my lady. I'll have the archers take turns standing guard, and we'll all be the better for a few hours of sleep if there's to be trouble tomorrow."

Immensely grateful for the respite, I climbed to my chamber and roused my ladies to help me prepare for bed. I fell asleep almost immediately.

The next thing I knew it was morning. I woke with a start. I sensed that someone was there in the shadowy room, looking at me. A man. A man in armor. I sat up, about to cry for help, when he spoke.

"Don't be afraid, Mother. It's your son John, come to rescue you from Arthur and the Lusignans. We've won the day."

John, whom I'd always thought the weakest and least of my brood, had done this heroic deed. How? I looked up at him, still taking in his news. I thought I saw strength and assurance in his face that hadn't been there before. The last time I'd seen him, his beard had been a foppish little pointed appendage, barely covering his rather weak chin. Now he'd let it grow. He looked more manly, more like his late brother Richard, though Richard was much taller and his beard had been red-gold whereas John's was black. Could it be that John would turn out to be a bold Plantagenet after all, like his father and brothers?

With tears pricking my eyes, I held out my arms, and he sat on the edge of my bed. We embraced like mother and son for the first time since he was a child.

John
1202

32

Lifting the siege at Mirebeau—if you could call it a siege—wasn't nearly as hard as getting there had been.

Within only twenty-four hours of leaving Le Mans we'd arrived, having ridden all day and all night, wearing out I don't know how many horses. Along the way welcome reinforcements joined us: William de Braose, one of my staunchest supporters, and William des Roches, my seneschal at Chinon Castle, perhaps not quite so staunch. The latter had previously served Arthur in Brittany. When I accepted his fealty, he made it a condition that he'd have charge of Arthur if we captured him. "After all, I know his ways. I'd know best how to keep him from plotting to escape," he'd said. It was easy enough to give him that promise.

Just as dawn was breaking I led the troops into the little town of Mirebeau, my sword drawn, expecting a battle. But we were met only by disheveled, bleary-eyed soldiers staggering about looking for breakfast. A few were armed and made a stab at halting us, but we simply rode over them. At the castle the portcullis was down and there was one dozing man on guard. We made short work of him and rode into the bailey. There at last was my quarry. Arthur and a group of unarmed men were sitting in front of a tent, eating pigeon pie.

"Seize them!" I cried. Within minutes we'd captured one would-be king, a clutch of Lusignans, six seigneurs of Poitou and five of Anjou. I ordered that all, including Arthur, be put in chains. I commissioned William de Cantilupe to go with a dozen men back into the town to round up Arthur's laughable excuse for an army.

Before the prisoners were led off I surveyed them with satisfaction. So many of my enemies, taken in one net! Arthur was the prize. He wouldn't meet my eyes but stood sullenly, staring at the ground. He was like a lad who's been caught out in some mischief and hopes he won't be punished. I'd have to take pains to see that he could never make trouble for me again.

Hugh de Lusignan was another matter. My old enemy--the man whom Isabella had loved before I knew her, the man who still aroused my jealousy, my onetime vassal who'd gone over to the King of France--stood straight despite the chains around wrists and ankles. He met my eyes with no hint of fear or submission. It was as though I were the transgressor, not he. I trembled with rage at his effrontery. It was all I could do to refrain from striking him on the face. Instead, I spat into the dust at his feet.

Then I went into the castle to find my mother. Thank God, she was unharmed, but more unnerved than I'd ever seen her. I'd been preparing myself for some such greeting as, "So there you are. Where have you been all this time?" On the contrary, for once in her life she showed me real affection and gratitude. I believe she'd truly feared for her life, and welcomed the brave son who'd saved her.

It was the first time she'd told me that anything I'd done had met with her approval. I savored it.

"You'll want to go back to Fontevraud now, won't you?" I asked, after we'd exchanged accounts of our adventures. "I'll see that you have a strong guard, whenever you and your people are ready."

She rose, threw on a robe and looked around the bare, cold, charmless tower room as though realizing for the first time how distasteful she found it.

"I know this was the safest place they could lodge me, but I'm glad it was only for one night. Yes, I must get back to Fontevraud, and the sooner the better. But first, John, what do you plan to do with Arthur? And the Lusignans, and the others?"

"I don't know. We'll hold a council this afternoon and discuss all the prisoners. But I can tell you I'd find it hard to forgive Arthur. After casting his lot with King Philip he deserves the worst punishment we can mete out."

"That's true, he's been rash and wicked. But you'd do well to consider carefully before you settle Arthur's fate. Think of what people will say about you if you're cruel and ruthless to your own nephew. Think how much better to win him over and give him recognition and make him an ally. Our support has shrunk, John. You may need all the allies you can gather. And it will be doubly hard to attract them if you mistreat a member of your family."

Her eyes were fixed on mine as though daring me to ignore what she said. This was again Eleanor the imperious, who always knew better than I what should be done.

"I'll remember what you say, Mother." I kissed her and we parted.

"To remember is not necessarily to obey," I said to myself as I left the tower.

The upshot of the council was that, first, our most noble prisoners should be placed, still in chains, in oxcarts with faces to the rear like farm animals being taken to market. Then they would be sent on a slow progress through their own lands, publicly disgraced. That was William de Braose's idea. I thought it a nice touch. After that we'd disperse them to various fortresses in Normandy and England.

As for those in whom I took a particular interest-- Arthur, Hugh de Lusignan and his uncle Geoffrey--something special must be devised.

For the time being, I ordered that Arthur and Geoffrey de Lusignan be imprisoned at Falaise, the stronghold in Normandy where my ancestor, William the Conqueror, had been born. Hugh would be sent to nearby Caen and lodged in the castle William had built there.

I grinned at my companions. "It will do them good to be shut up in those Plantagenet fortresses. They'll have plenty of time to reflect on how puny their strength is compared to ours."

"A wise disposition of your prisoners, my liege," said William des Roches. "Now, there's no reason to delay, I suppose. With your leave I'll set out tomorrow morning with Arthur and Geoffrey for Falaise. With a strong guard, of course."

I'd been expecting that. I still didn't altogether trust William des Roches's loyalty. I suspected he might switch sides again and contrive to get Arthur freed.

I looked at him, pretending to consider, then said, "No, Sir William. I'd prefer that you accompany Hugh to Caen. We will send William de Braose to Falaise."

He looked at me first with disbelief, then with barely suppressed rage. "But my liege, you promised me I'd have custody of Arthur."

"Never mind what I said a year ago. The situation is not what it was." I rose, and the council was over.

I was very weary. But there was one more thing I had to do before I could rest. I sent a messenger to Chinon to tell Isabella of our victory, and to say I'd rejoin her as soon as I could.

Albert, the castellan, had prepared a chamber for me off the entry hall. I found considerably more comforts than I'd expected after seeing my mother's room at the top of the tower. She'd had only a narrow bed and a table. My bed was canopied, if somewhat rickety and with mothholes in the woolen drapes. A chair was drawn up by the fire on the hearth. Albert's wife conducted me, clucking like a mother hen that she hoped I'd find everything in order. She promised she'd send in some wine and a roast capon and whatever else I wished.

It was just getting dark when I finished my lonely meal. I sat on, going over the events of the last three days.

First, the dismaying news of my mother's danger. There'd been no question in my mind that it was up to me to go to her rescue. Who else was there? It was more than a son's duty to his mother. If Eleanor of Aquitaine fell captive to the French, the Angevin cause on the continent would be terribly compromised.

That decision taken, there was the hard ride from Le Mans to Mirebeau. With every hoofbeat I'd felt more excitement, mixed with apprehension, at the thought of the bloody battle to come. The victory without any battle at all was almost a letdown.

That was followed in short order by the exhilaration of taking so many of my bitterest enemies without shedding a drop of blood. So many rich prizes! They'd command handsome ransoms, which would certainly be welcome. The money I'd tricked the barons into contributing was almost gone.

All in all it had been a highly satisfactory undertaking. Yet I still felt restless and keyed-up.

I knew what was missing. If Isabella were with me, I could tell her about my exploits. She'd praise me and kiss me and take my hand and lead me to bed. I dreaded the thought of retiring without her just when I needed the release from tension that a night in her arms always provided. I sat there staring into the fire, longing for her.

At last I went to the door and woke up the page who was sleeping on a pallet just outside. I told him to call for Albert. When the man came, I asked him to find me some willing lass, either in the castle or the town, who could come at once to keep the King of England company for a few hours.

Hugh le Brun

1202

33

I arrived at Mirebeau in high hopes of capturing Queen Eleanor in retribution for the insults I'd suffered from her son John.

I left Mirebeau in an oxcart.

After John's swift victory, he immediately dispatched his most valuable prisoners in this degrading manner. Geoffrey and I had no time even to say goodbye; he was off in one direction and I in another.

I was chained to the sides of the cart, facing to the rear so spectators could get a good look. It was a dreary, shameful journey. Though I knew the end was imprisonment, I was almost glad when, at dusk on the third day, the city walls of Caen and the hulking gray castle behind them came in sight. At least now I wouldn't be exposed to stares and jeers from curious, ignorant country folk who had no idea who I was. I was so dirty and unkempt that even those who knew me couldn't recognize me. I took a bitter satisfaction in the failure of John's plan to hold me up to ridicule from my own people.

At Caen, two soldiers unfettered me, took me firmly by the arms and led me quickly through the great hall and to the main tower at the rear. One of them hurried me down a twisting stairway, past wine cellars and grain storerooms, to a dark windowless chamber carved out of the rock. The floor was hard-packed dirt. By the light of my escort's lamp, I saw a straw mattress and a grimy wool blanket on the floor. A bucket of water and a few candles were on a low wood table.

The soldier lit a candle, fixed it to the table with a drop of melted wax, and left. The iron-barred door clanged behind him. I heard the key turn in the lock. Before I'd had time to feel properly sorry for myself the door opened again and in burst a short, squat man with wild red hair and bushy red eyebrows overhanging his little black eyes. He looked very cross.

"So they've brought me a prisoner, as though I didn't have enough to do already." His low growly voice reminded me of my hound when she thought another dog was encroaching on her territory. He banged a bowl down on the table and looked me up and down. I knew I was a sorry sight: bits of straw clinging to me here and there, rumpled dirty tunic, no hat, torn hose.

"You're Hugh le Brun, Lord of Lusignan, eh? Well, lordship won't do you much good here. I'm warden of this castle, and my name's Gautier. We've had many a prisoner in this dungeon, though few as highborn as you. But I see no reason to treat you any different from the rest. You'll get porridge in the morning and stew at night. That's your dinner in the bowl. Water's in that bucket. That hole in the corner's where you can relieve yourself. We bring you a shovel so you can fill it in and dig a new one every week or so. Any questions?"

"Yes. May I send a message to my wife?"

"King John's orders are, no messages in or out. And if you're wondering how long you'll be here, I have no idea. That's up to the King."

He glowered at me, daring me to ask for something else. I was silent, and he left as abruptly as he'd come.

I'd never felt so hopeless. I'd been in bad situations before. Sometimes when I was fighting the infidels with King Richard in the Holy Land I knew that death could come with the next thrust of a lance. But at least there I was master of my actions. Here I had no alternative but to submit to this ignominy. There was no way out. And to think that it was John, my most despised enemy, who had put me here, was enough to make me mad with fury.

I was angry but I was also ready to drop from weariness after three days of jolting over Normandy. I ate a few spoonfuls of the revolting stew, then lay down on the straw pallet and pulled the blanket over me. It wasn't enough to keep out the damp chill, but I was so tired that, blessedly, I fell asleep almost at once.

The next thing I knew, the grinding sound of a key turning in the lock awakened me. A man came in, put a bowl on the table and left. So it must be morning. I must have slept for twelve hours.

Spooning up the lukewarm porridge by dim candlelight, I brooded on my prospects. Could I possibly bribe Gautier to let me get a message out? With what? I had no coins, no gold, no jewels. Could I convince him that if he'd let me send word to Mathilde of my situation, she would reward him? And even if that succeeded, what could she do next? Ill as she was, she couldn't take on the task of raising a ransom. If my feckless son were around, he might be able to do it. But he was still off on his Crusade, maybe on his way to Constantinople by now.

But wait. What about my brother Ralph? He hadn't been with us at Mirebeau, but up north with King Philip besieging Les Arques. But how to get word to him? Another dead end.

My gloomy thoughts were interrupted when, again, my prison door swung open. In walked a tall man in a fur-trimmed hat and a long black cloak with fur at neck and hem. Some people, I thought bitterly, can dress for this bone-chilling cold. A servant followed him, placed a lamp on the table, and left.

My visitor had a lined, severe face, with a square jaw and a thin-lipped mouth that looked as though it seldom smiled. We stood there assessing each other. I was still not very presentable, though I'd managed to wipe away some of the grime and had brushed the dust and straw off my clothes. I waited for him to speak.

"Sir Hugh, I am William des Roches, your guardian during your imprisonment."

"Yes. Now that I see you I believe you were one of the first of King John's men to break through the bailey gate at Mirebeau where we were sheltering with Arthur."

"I was. And you probably also know I led the contingent that brought you here to Caen."

"So I heard. Welcome to my sumptuous quarters. I am sorry they forgot to provide me with chairs for my guests or wine to offer them."

I saw no reason to be pleasant to King John's man.

"Never mind that. I've given orders that you are to be moved to a more comfortable room. You'll have a chair and if you behave yourself, perhaps even some wine." To my surprise he smiled, but in the dimness I couldn't tell if it was the smile of a gloating victor or of somebody who wished me well.

"Until later, Sir Hugh," and he was gone.

In short order I found myself settled in a room off the great hall. It was small and without a fireplace, but there were a charcoal brazier, a real bed, chairs and a narrow barred window. My door was still kept locked. The meals they brought me were somewhat more appetizing than my fare in the dungeon. My dinners were, indeed, accompanied by a goblet of wine. I was even provided with clean hose and tunic. Gautier brought them, though with ill grace.

"Sir William said to see that you're decently clad and we're to give you washing water too. In all my days as warden here, I've never seen a prisoner pampered like this. What are things coming to if a guilty man can't be properly punished?"

I couldn't imagine.

After a week of boredom, during which I occupied myself by wondering what was behind this consideration from William des Roches, he visited me again. This time he was more loquacious.

"Greetings, Sir Hugh. Are they treating you well?" He sat in one of my two chairs and gestured to me to sit in the other.

"They are, and I'm glad to see you again, so I can thank you for my greatly improved lodging. Surely this isn't at the orders of King John?"

Again the rare smile. This time I saw it as a smile of genuine goodwill.

"No indeed. If he knew, he'd have both our heads. Of course you're curious. So I'll tell you why I've moved you and what I've learned, these past few days, of events since you were captured." He crossed his long legs, folded his arms and fixed me with his steady gaze.

"First, a little history. You may not know that I served Arthur for five years, when he was just beginning to show promise as a leader worthy of his Angevin heritage. I thought he should have been declared King after Richard's death. When John was chosen instead, I believed it was my duty to give John my allegiance. But when I did so, I made it a condition that if John ever went to war against Arthur and captured him, I would be in charge of the boy."

He brushed his hand across his brow as though wiping away unwanted memories. I was watching and listening intently.

"I've now learned that after Mirebeau fell, John sent Prince Arthur to Falaise Castle where he was placed in irons with no way to communicate with the outside world. Your uncle Geoffrey is at Falaise too, probably suffering the same conditions. They are both in the care—if you can call it care—of William de Braose, who isn't known for indulging in pity or mercy."

His face flushed with sudden anger. He pounded his knee.

"*I* should have been sent there. *I* should be the one charged with keeping Arthur secure. It's true he rebelled against his uncle and deserves punishment. But the fact remains that he's next in line for the English throne. He should be treated accordingly."

"So you feel that because King John has not kept his promise to you, you needn't keep your pledge of loyalty to him?"

"Exactly. And I propose to act as quickly as I can to try to free Arthur and enlist support to attack John. I'd expect the Lusignans to join me."

At first I thought he was joking. How could we support him if we were all in prison?

"And that means we must free you and Geoffrey and your friends as soon as possible. But I can't just open the gates and let you go. John doesn't trust anyone, and his men are posted all around the castle, in case of an attempted escape. Falaise is even more strongly guarded. No, you must raise a ransom. John needs money badly. I'm told that he's counting on his more well-to-do prisoners to buy their freedom."

With this encouraging prospect, I took heart. I wished I could do something at once. I rose and paced about the room, then stood before him.

"Then, Sir William, I must get in touch with my brother Ralph. He's the only Lusignan not behind bars. He can begin raising the money. The last I heard he was with King Philip in the north, but that was some weeks ago."

"My information is that Philip left Les Arques when he heard of John's victory at Mirebeau, and headed for Tours. He's said to be planning an offensive against John."

"Ralph will still be with him, I'm sure. Can you send him a message?"

"I can and I will." I liked this man. He wasted no words or motions. He went to the door and called Gautier. When the surly fellow appeared, William instructed him to find his squire and have him come immediately.

"And one more thing. Please have some wine brought to us." Gautier's eyebrows waggled up and down, signaling his deep disapproval. He ran his fingers through his unruly hair, making it stand up like a flaming topknot. But he obeyed.

When the wine came, William filled our glasses and proposed a toast. "To the downfall of King John and the rise of the Lusignans."

I drank willingly, then proposed my own:

"And to the success and well-being of William des Roches, whom I'm proud to call my friend." He smiled. I wondered that I'd thought him stern and unfeeling.

So the plan was set in motion. Ralph, good faithful Ralph, somehow raised the ransoms for Geoffrey and me. Within a month, I walked out of Caen Castle a free man.

Isabella

1202

After John left Le Mans to rescue his mother I felt shaky and insecure. Our palace had no defenses. The sturdy old city walls that John was so fond of were pierced by eleven gates, not all in good repair or well manned.

So I willingly let Robert de Thorneham hurry me off on the three-day journey to Chinon. Once within its stout walls, I could relax. There was, in fact, little to do except relax. Sir Robert wouldn't let me leave the castle confines, so there was no riding by the river or visiting the town. Thank goodness, Lady Anne and Adèle were there too.

The three of us passed many an afternoon sitting at our embroidery, listening to a minstrel, or walking in the garden. Sometimes we all practiced our Latin.

"Adèle needs to work on it and if you'll forgive me, my lady, you could benefit from a little refreshment too." Anne had had a good education, thanks to a father who had for a time studied for the priesthood. She found a few dusty, crumbling manuscripts somewhere in the castle, perhaps left over from King Henry's day. One we particularly liked was a treatise on cookery for a monastery. When we sat at dinner, we'd amuse ourselves (and mystify Sir Robert) by introducing terms from our limited vocabulary into our conversation.

"I wonder," I said, "if there'll be *crustum cum malos* for the sweet?"

"I think so," said Adèle. "When I went by the *culina* the *coquus* was peeling some *malos.*"

Sir Robert appealed to Anne. "Now what are they jabbering about, my lady?"

Anne laughed. "Just about the apple pie they hope we'll have. But Adèle, wasn't it Cook Marie you saw peeling apples? So you should have said *coqua* for

172

a lady cook, not *coquus*."

The fine fat apple pie was borne in at that moment. We all gave it our attention instead of our Latin declensions, to the relief of Sir Robert.

While I was at Chinon the news reached me that my father had died. I tried to feel sorry but I couldn't. For one thing, I'd never forgiven him for the way he deceived me about Hugh's death. And he'd never been a loving father. He was far too wrapped up in building up his power and adding to his lands. He was devoted to my mother, but that was the extent of his family feeling. I was devoted to her too, but even as a child I knew that her affections and attentions were focused on her husband, not on me. I sent her a consoling message.

Finally we received word from John. We were all gathered in the dining hall for the midday meal when the messenger was admitted. He handed me the parchment. He told me that after I'd read it, he was to deliver the message to John's vassals in Poitou and Anjou.

I read it to the others:

"Know that, by the grace of God, we are safe and well, and God's mercy has worked wonderfully with us for on Tuesday, the feast of St. Peter ad Vincula, we heard that the Lady our mother was closely besieged at Mirebeau, and we hurried there as fast as we could. And there, after a hard-fought battle, we captured our nephew Arthur and all our other Poitevin enemies, and not one escaped. Therefore God be praised for our happy success."

The messenger then told me he had been particularly instructed to tell me John was leaving for a short time in Normandy but he'd send for me as soon as possible.

"This is joyful news!" I said to Sir Robert.

"It is indeed. He doesn't give any details, but it must have been a fierce fight. I only wish I could have been there to stand by the King's side in battle."

"Never mind, you've done your part by taking such good care of your charges here at Chinon," said Anne. "With brave Sir Robert to guard us, we've felt perfectly secure."

I went to bed that night filled with pride at John's victory and wishing I were with him.

It didn't occur to me then to wonder who the enemies were that he he'd taken captive, besides Arthur.

The very next day, as Anne and I were getting out chests and garments, hoping for an early departure, we heard a tremendous uproar that seemed to come from just outside the castle walls: shouting, hoofbeats, then what sounded like pounding on the door of the portcullis gate. Sir Robert burst into my chamber, red-faced and breathing hard as he did when he had to move his bulky body quickly.

"My lady, the lookouts on the walls say it's a force of two dozen or so horsemen, looking like they're about to make an assault. I'm going now to the gate to see what it's all about."

Anne and Adèle and I looked at each other in confusion, wondering what we could do. Perhaps barricade ourselves in one of the towers? But before we'd made a move, Sir Robert came back and reported that he'd talked to the leader of the force, William des Roches. I recognized the name. John had spoken of him as one of his powerful Angevin vassals. So what was he doing, attacking his King's castle?

"He says he's no longer the King's man. He's going to keep us all shut up here until John releases Arthur. He's sent word to him that he won't see his Queen again until Arthur is in William's hands. Then they'll lift the siege."

We were shocked, fearful, angry—and helpless. Confined within the walls of Chinon, we had nothing to do but wait and worry. Every morning I woke to the hope that today John, the conquering hero, would arrive and put down the rebels, just as he'd done at Mirebeau. Surely if he could bring off such a daring rescue of his mother, he could do no less for his wife.

We were set free at last but not by John. After ten days Peter de Préaux, one of John's mercenaries, arrived with a large pack of his fearless, merciless fighters. They soon sent our besiegers flying. Peter announced that he'd been instructed to escort us back to Le Mans.

All the way I fretted at the slowness of our progress. I had no eyes for the pleasant autumnal countryside, the smoothly flowing Loire and its broad valley where tight little villages sprouted amid the fields and vineyards. All I wanted was to be safely back in Le Mans, where I'd find John.

Our pace was governed by that of the soldiers, who were in no hurry. They'd had a nearly bloodless victory, they were feeling smug and carefree until the next battle, and they'd been well paid by Robert de Thorneham with more to come when we reached Le Mans. Peter de Préaux indulged them when they wanted to stop and spend some of their new riches in the taverns along the way. There was nothing I could do about it.

When we paused for a meal at an inn in Angers, I said I wasn't hungry and asked the innkeeper if I could rest somewhere while the others ate. He showed me to a small room next to the dining hall. It held a plain uncurtained bed and not much else. I suspected it might be for the convenience of lusty travelers who'd take a lass there for an hour or so. But it was clean and neat, and I lay down gratefully. Anne stayed with me. I knew at once I wouldn't get much rest because we could hear all the conversation through the thin wall.

Robert de Thorneham must have asked Peter de Préaux why he'd come instead of John. Peter had a loud, carrying voice. I had no trouble hearing him over the clatter of jugs and tankards and tableware.

"Oho, that's easy. He was going to come all right. We were up in Normandy when we got the word that the Queen was being besieged. He was all for leaving at once. But we hadn't gone two leagues before a man came from Alençon to tell us that we'd best avoid the town because its lord had just gone over to King Philip after years of loyalty to John."

I couldn't make out Robert's reply but Peter's braying voice came clearly.

"No, it's not so shocking. Lords all over Normandy are going over to Philip. John is losing his support though he won't admit it. Anyway, when we got that news, you should have seen the change in your King. All at once he says, 'We could be surrounded by enemies and not even know it. You go on to Chinon, Peter, and I'll go to Le Mans and wait for the Queen there.' Or words to that effect. So here we all are, safe and sound, and no thanks to John Softsword. That's what they call him now, you know."

This time I heard Robert's reply. By now they'd both probably had so much wine they didn't care who heard them.

"Even after his victory at Mirebeau? I heard he took the castle from a force three times his own, and captured every one of them."

"Ha. So you were taken in too. That's the story he's been telling. You should have been there, my friend. Arthur's army, if you can call it that, was either asleep or drunk when we rode into the town. All John had to do was ride hard to reach the castle, find Arthur and the Lusignans in the bailey without any guards on duty, and put them all in irons. It didn't take bravery, just good horsemanship."

"You're being most disrespectful to your monarch, Peter. Are you planning to desert him too?"

"No danger of that. He pays me too well. As long as he has the gold, I have the loyalty."

His guffaw put an end to the conversation, or what I could hear of it. I sat on the edge of the bed with my face in my hands. Anne sat beside me and put her arm around my shoulders. Neither of us said a word.

Bewildered, I joined the others. We remounted our horses and set off again. All the rest of the way I tried to come to terms with what I'd heard. Every time I thought I had John's character figured out, he proved me wrong. I'd been so proud to hear of his courage and leadership at Mirebeau. Yet apparently the tale he'd spread wasn't what had really happened. Now at the very next challenge, he'd crept like a coward to Le Mans and sent Peter to save us. It reminded me of his fit of nerves when he feared the Lusignans would ambush us during our first journey to Le Mans. Would I ever, ever understand him? I wanted so much to believe in the man I loved.

Just as the hilltop cathedral of St. Julien came in sight, I tired of my brooding. John was unpredictable, and that was that. I took a bit of comfort from the thought that he'd certainly set off as boldly as a bulldog to Mirebeau, even if he'd had an easy time of it when he got there. So what if he'd bragged about a battle that never happened? It wasn't his fault that the enemy was lax and in no condition to fight. And what was most important, he'd succeeded brilliantly in his objective of rescuing Queen Eleanor.

Deep down, though, a nagging annoyance lurked. John had been ready to risk all to rescue his mother. To save me, he'd sent others. I sighed. When I saw him again, maybe none of this would matter. I gave my horse a little kick to encourage it to trot up the hill to the city.

John must have heard us coming. He was waiting at the palace door when we rode into the courtyard. He hurried out, his face alight with relief and eagerness. He helped me out of the saddle and held me close. We kissed.

"Thank God you're safe," he whispered. When I felt his strong arms about me, I forgot my doubts. All that mattered was that we were together again.

Isabella

1202-1203

35

When we were reunited in Le Mans in the fall of 1203, John and I were both so relieved to be safe again, to be together again, that we paid no attention to the world beyond our little court. We were as blissfully happy as ever. Whether he was a brave leader or a coward didn't seem to matter.

One morning when he'd gone to meet with the bishop about something or other, I was standing by the window of our rooms on the second floor of the palace. I was trying to decide between two pieces of silk to cover some worn chair cushions. John and I had our favorite chairs, capacious, with high carved backs and almost like thrones. They were usually drawn up in front of the hearth. On fine afternoons we'd have them placed near the west windows so we could watch the sun setting behind the city walls. The day before, a merchant had come to show me the wares he'd just received from Venice. He was to come back this afternoon to hear my decision. I was holding up the lengths of silk, one over each arm, to catch the morning light when Anne came in.

"Shall I choose the leaf-green with threads of gold, or this brilliant ruby-red?" I asked. "I think perhaps the green. So few of my gowns would look well with that red, such a strong color."

She studied them. "I agree, my lady. But why not have both, one for each chair? King John so often wears black. Just think how well the red would set that off."

"What a wise decision! Thank you, Anne. Now tell me, what are all the ladies gossiping about today?"

"No gossip, or none I've heard. But I've learned something troubling. William de Cantilupe told me how King John disposed of the prisoners he took at Mirebeau."

I wondered fleetingly why William was confiding in Anne. But my curiosity was aroused. I knew by then that Hugh had been one of John's prisoners, but I'd hoped and believed that he'd be treated like the nobleman he was. I'd expected he'd be speedily released, maybe for a ransom, maybe in exchange for a prisoner on the other side. That was how it usually worked in wars.

"And what does Sir William say?"

"He says that Prince Arthur is in Falaise Castle. Nobody has seen or heard of him since he was sent there. And Sir Hugh was sent in chains to the castle at Caen. John ordered that he was to be locked in the dungeon, forbidden to send or receive messages."

I stared at her in shock.

"Forgive me for daring to tell you this, my lady. But I truly thought you should know, in view of the regard you once held for Sir Hugh."

"Of course you were right to tell me. This is dreadful. I'm sure there's some mistake. I'll ask John about it."

"I think you should. Maybe some underling has taken it on himself to shut Sir Hugh up like that. But please, if you can, don't tell the King how you learned of it."

"Of course not, Anne." I knew there was no love lost between my husband and my friend. I had no intention of stirring up trouble.

I was resolved to be the soul of tact. That evening we were sitting in the dining hall after dinner, watching a juggler toss balls in the air. Often he failed to catch them and they thudded to the floor. John had dined well and drunk just enough to make him relaxed and content. He was laughing at the man's ineptitude.

"One more missed ball, and it's off to the jailhouse for you." He shook his fist at the juggler in mock threat.

"Oh no, John, he's only a lad, still learning. Be merciful." I kissed him lightly. "Just as I'm sure you were merciful with all those men you took prisoner at Mirebeau." As soon as I spoke I realized I'd changed the subject too abruptly. John was sure to be suspicious. But he didn't seem to notice.

"Oh, I was merciful all right. Didn't behead a one of them. They're all safe in their skins, hidden away where nobody can get at them and chained down so they can't get at anybody. That goes for Arthur and those rascally Lusignans too, in case you're wondering. Including your old friend Hugh le Brun." He was lounging in his chair but alert now. His searching black eyes were watching me carefully to see my reaction.

"In chains, John? Your own nephew? And noblemen who once were your vassals, and might be again if you show them clemency?"

He sat up straight and banged his fist on the table.

"Why this sudden concern for a foolish lad you don't even know, and for those renegade Lusignans? Maybe you still care for Hugh? Maybe you wish you'd married him after all?" His face was contorted with rage, like a snarling bear that turns on its baiters. I was frightened. I'd seen him direct his terrible anger at others, but seldom at myself and never like this. I'd gone too far. I had to think fast.

"It isn't just Hugh, it's all of them. It's beneath your dignity to lock them up and treat them like beasts in cages. People will think you're afraid of them. John, you're the King. You can do anything you want. You can be vindictive, or you can be just and lenient. Don't you want your subjects to look up to you as a wise, merciful ruler?"

I laid my hand gently on his arm. He shook it off. His face was still fiery.

"Now you sound just like my mother. By God's feet, I'm tired of other people telling me what to do! You're right, Isabella. I'm the King, and I can do what I want. If I want I can demand such a high ransom from your old lover that he'll never be able to raise it. Let him stay locked up until he starves."

There was no point in continuing. I rose, looked at him as calmly as I could, and said, "Well, perhaps you're right. But I'm ready to retire. Please come soon." I leaned down to kiss him, but he turned his head quickly and shouted for more wine.

At the door I turned. John's back was to me. William de Cantilupe had looked up and seen me. I had a sudden impulse. I nodded and pointed to the door. Five minutes later he was admitted to my chamber.

"I feel I can trust you, Sir William. Will you do me a great favor?"

He bowed slightly and looked at me, waiting to know more.

"Can you help me send a message to Hugh de Lusignan? Anne told me he's in prison at Caen."

Over the two years I'd known Sir William I'd come to like and respect him. On the few occasions when I'd asked him for information, he'd always been frank with me. He looked at me, considering my request. I found myself thinking that he was really quite a handsome man, though old enough to be my father. His brown hair was lightly streaked with gray. His face was unlined except for a few fine wrinkles around his steely blue eyes. In his burgundy cloak over sober black tunic and leggings, he stood tall and erect, like the soldier he'd been.

"Will this favor in any way be to the detriment of my liege lord, King John?"

"That's a fair question, Sir William, since as everybody knows I was once affianced to Hugh. No, this is no plot to do harm to my husband. I simply want to tell Hugh that I'm sorry at his misfortune because I still consider myself his friend. After I write my message you may read it if you wish. But I wouldn't want my husband to know of it, so perhaps I'm asking you to do something you consider going behind his back."

"I can understand your reluctance to have the King know. Your request seems reasonable. I'll help you if I can. Let me think." He paced across the room and back.

"Some of the King's counselors are hoping to persuade him to offer ransom terms to his more prominent prisoners. He badly needs the money. If he can be convinced he's not losing face by offering terms we may get him to agree. If so, I can include your message in the one we send to Sir Hugh. But we'll have to give the messenger some reward, since he'd be taking a chance of discovery and punishment."

"Thank you, thank you! As for a reward for the messenger, I still have jewels that were mine before I married John. I can give him some of them, if you think that would be acceptable."

"I'm sure it would. Perhaps you could write your message now. I'll take it away and hold it safe until the messenger goes, which may be within a few days."

I knew why he suggested that. It would be most unfortunate if John came across a letter from me to Hugh. I ran to my writing desk, found a scrap of parchment and scratched out a short letter.

My dear Hugh: We bribed the messenger to include this with the parchment William de Cantilupe will send. I have only a few minutes to write. When I heard of your capture and imprisonment, I was greatly distressed. John told me he'd had you shut up in a dungeon. He said he didn't know when he'd let you out if ever. I told him you were a nobleman and deserved to be treated as such. Then he got very cross and accused me of wishing I'd married you instead of him. That is not true of course, though I have never had a chance to tell you how sorry I was about the way he and my parents deceived you. I'd hoped I could persuade him to let you go but I couldn't. If I could help you I would. Please think of me as your friend. Isabella.

I blotted it, rolled it up and gave it to Sir William. "There, that will have to do. I'll have a pouch of jewels for the messenger delivered to you tomorrow. Thank you, Sir William! You are a true friend."

"You needn't thank me, my lady. I'm happy to have this opportunity to be of service to you."

After he left I sat down to gather my thoughts. Everything had happened so fast. I wondered if I'd been unwise. No; I couldn't bear the thought of Hugh shut up in his prison, blaming me as much as John for his misery.

But I couldn't sit wool-gathering. I had to be ready for John. Would he still be in a temper when he came? Well, I'd been able to wheedle him out of black moods before.

I jumped up and called my lady of the bedchamber, Hortense.

When John came through the door a half-hour later, I was reclining against the bedpillows, my hair freshly brushed and wearing my most seductive nightdress, of satiny rose-petal silk with wisps of lace around the top of the bodice. At first he looked at me sourly, as though determined to keep his displeasure with me alive. Then he walked toward the bed, discarding garments as he came. Within minutes we were in each other's arms. As he kissed my ears, my cheeks and then sought my mouth, I knew his fury had yielded to another passion. I held his face between my hands and looked into his black eyes. Our lips were almost touching.

"John, I'm sorry if I angered you at table tonight. You know that I'm totally yours and I've never loved any one as I love you." I meant every word.

"I know, my love, I know," he murmured, and kissed me. "I shouldn't have doubted you."

After that Hugh's name never came up between us. All was as it had been. My message was sent, thanks to Sir William. I'd done what I could to keep Hugh from thinking ill of me. My conscience was eased.

We resumed our life of pleasure. Every day we rose late, breakfasted late, dawdled through the afternoon, dined in company or not and retired early. Sometimes we had minstrels and players to amuse us at dinner; sometimes there was dancing. John gave me a ruby on a gold chain and an ermine-trimmed red satin robe.

He seemed to have forgotten that he was at war with the King of France. When counselors came to bring some urgent matter to his attention he brushed them aside and said he'd think about it later.

I was present one day when William Marshal, the counselor whom he trusted above all others, told him bluntly, "My lord King, if you do not act soon to check King Philip, you will find he has taken all your lands and England will no longer rule in France."

"Never mind," said John. "When I'm ready I'll take back everything I've lost. Come, good Sir William. Join us in a glass of this excellent Bordeaux wine."

Finally, though, he couldn't ignore the fact that Philip was seriously on the warpath in Normandy. He left for Rouen to drum up support for a counter-offensive. I heard scanty reports and would have known even less if William de Cantilupe hadn't kept me informed.

The news went from bad to worse. John's English-born vassals were abandoning their Normandy holdings and going back to their English estates. A rumor was spreading through Brittany that John had murdered Arthur. Breton barons were defecting, enraged at this violence done to their duke. Philip was now reaping the rewards of John's inertia the past few months and taking castles all over Maine and Anjou.

When Château Gaillard, the mighty fortress on the Seine built by Richard the Lionheart, was besieged and seemed about to fall, I think it broke John's spirit.

In December of 1203 he sent word from Rouen to ask me to meet him at Barfleur, the ancient Angevin port on the Channel. From there we sailed across a choppy, stormridden sea to Southampton. In little more than a year, the English had lost more than half their French lands.

Eleanor

1203-1204

After the excitement of the siege and rescue at Mirebeau, I had to admit I needed to rest. Poitiers was closer than Fontevraud so I decided to go there. As I grew older I found I was more and more drawn to people and places I had known in my youth. There were few of the former left, but Poitiers had been a beloved home ever since my childhood. Here in the palace of the counts during my carefree girlhood I'd been the toast of Aquitaine. After I married Henry, I often came to Poitiers for refuge from the cold, unwelcoming English and their fogbound isle.

I settled gratefully into my customary chamber in the tower with its familiar furnishings. I'd sit in my favorite chair, glad of the soft cushioning for my tired old bones. I'd look out at the two shapely poplars in the garden, bright green columns against a cloudless blue sky. I'd seen them grow from saplings to their now imposing height, almost as tall as my tower.

Resting soon became tedious. My ladies-in-waiting weren't stimulating company—I'd chosen them for pretty faces, noble birth and tractable natures, not conversational brilliance. Besides being bored, I was worried. There'd been no news from John for months. Nor had there been news of Arthur. The last I'd had was of his imprisonment at Falaise. I had no love for my turncoat grandson. I was glad he'd been taken. But I didn't want violence done to him. Knowing my son and his fits of ungovernable temper and his tendency to hold a grudge, I was deeply uneasy.

I sent messages to John but got no reply or a meaningless assurance that all was well and I was not to concern myself.

"I hope to heaven he hasn't resumed his do-nothing life with that child bride of his. Maybe the silly tales the people tell are true after all. Maybe she's seduced him by witchcraft to keep him captive to her charms." I snorted, then realized I'd been thinking aloud. Lady Maurienne deTournon, my companion for the day, smiled and went on with her embroidery.

Shortly after Easter of 2003 I finally received some news. John of Valernt, a Benedictine friar who'd served my son as trusted messenger on other occasions, brought it. I received him at once in my chamber.

Brother John bowed to me and pushed back the cowl of his black mantle to reveal his smooth, earnest face and even smoother pate, ornamented by a barely visible fringe of gray hair.

"My Lord King has instructed me to bring first to you, then to his vassals in Normandy and Bordeaux, this communication. It is in two parts. The first is written. The second I am to deliver orally. Here is the parchment where you may read the first part."

I read it quickly. It had little of news. After greeting the Lady Queen his mother and the other dignitaries, he asked us to listen to Brother John, "who has seen what is going forward with us, and who will be able to apprise you of our situation. Put faith in him respecting those things whereof he can inform you. Nevertheless, the grace of God is with us …"

The document was witnessed by William de Braose. I knew him to be the man who had been in charge of Arthur at Falaise.

I returned to that word "nevertheless" and stared at it. Apparently what Brother John would tell me was so horrendous that one might expect God to take His grace away from the King? But God, it seemed, had not done so.

I looked up at the friar. He now gave me the oral message. He'd memorized his words well. He released them without emphasis, like drops of water dripping from a rainspout.

"These are King John's words: 'To our sorrow, our nephew Arthur left this world on Thursday of Holy Week past. We mourn for him and pray for his soul. We ask you to do the same. Yet in all misfortunes God shows His mercy to His people. With Arthur's death, the warring between him and his King, which has taken so many lives, will now be ended.'"

I thanked Brother John. After I wished him a safe journey on the rest of his mission I gave in to growing shock and disbelief.

What was unsaid was as terrible as the words I'd heard. If Arthur had died a natural death, John would have said so. If one of John's lieutenants or servants had killed him, John would have said so, denied any responsibility and fixed the blame. I could only conclude that my son had murdered my grandson.

I went into my chapel, knelt before the altar, and prayed for both of them.

Rumors began to float about. Guibert, my seneschal, felt it his duty to keep me informed. He was a small-minded man, the kind who loves to share bad news. I kept him because his suspicious nature would unearth any cheating or wrongdoing in the palace.

The first tale he told me was that Arthur had been transferred from Falaise to Rouen and on the way tried to escape. In his haste he'd fallen over a cliff and died.

"Which may well be, my lady, since we know he was always an impulsive lad, who acted before he thought." Guibert's face, endowed with too much nose and not enough chin, shone with excitement and importance as he told me this.

Or, in another version, his guardians on the journey had taken aim at him as he ran from them trying to escape. An arrow had pierced him in the back. The wound had festered and killed him.

The worst story implicated John directly. It was said that after Arthur was imprisoned at Rouen John took him out in a boat on the Seine, ran him through with his sword, and pushed the body over the side.

"But nobody saw it, or at least nobody has come forward who's willing to bear witness. So far it's just talk. To my way of thinking, your son the King couldn't have done such a deed," said Guibert sanctimoniously. He may or may not have believed what he said. I sent him away. This was something I'd have to face up to alone.

Presently snippets of news of John's movements came, carried by traveling merchants, mendicant friars or roaming musicians. The latter often dropped in at the palace to see if any entertainment were needed. None of these sources was very reliable, but Guibert conscientiously repeated their reports to me.

It appeared that John was making sporadic forays in Brittany, in Normandy and along the Seine. But he was accomplishing nothing, while Philip roamed freely through Maine and Anjou taking castle after castle. Le Mans had fallen to him, also Saumur, the great fortress on the Loire.

At last when my spirits were lowest, William Marshal arrived with no forewarning. Though I doubted if he came with good news, he at least would be a friend I could talk to frankly. I received him at once in my private chamber. We sat facing each other in front of the fire. I craved its warmth.

William had aged. New lines spread downward from the corners of his mouth and across his forehead. It's not easy being a faithful vassal to King John these days, I thought.

Still he managed a cheerful smile over his shoulder as he leaned to warm his hands by the fire.

"I find you in good health, my lady Queen?"

"As well as can be expected," I replied, more tartly than I meant. I wasn't going to waste time by enumerating my aches and pains, troublesome as they were. "And you? You must be weary from your ride. I've sent for refreshments. In the meantime, tell me your news. First of all, William, tell me about Arthur's death. I've heard all manner of wild tales. I don't know what to believe. Is John guilty?"

"I don't know what I can tell you. John is close-mouthed. When he does permit the subject to come up he merely says the boy died of natural causes at Rouen. William de Braose may know more, but he won't say. I do know that John recently gave William some rich grants to English estates. It's not hard to put two and two together, though I grieve to say it."

I leaned my elbow on the arm of my chair and supported my forehead with my hand, my eyes closed. I had to accept the fact that John was guilty. It was a grievous realization for a mother, even one who had never truly loved her son.

I opened my eyes and looked at Sir William, who was watching in concern.

"You've seen us through many a hard time, my friend, but I can think of none worse than this. Let's move on. Tell me the rest of your news."

"It's not good, as you doubtless suspect. Your son seems to have lost his purpose. One day he is all for going out to fight Philip and the next he retires with his Queen and we don't see him for days."

"Where is he now?"

"In Rouen. I hope he stays there and holds to his intention to relieve Château Gaillard. Philip has been besieging it, and our men inside are trying desperately to hold out."

"But William, we can't lose Château Gaillard! What is John thinking of, how did he let things come to this pass?" I was outraged. The invincible castle on the Seine, built by my son Richard, had become the shining symbol of Plantagenet power in France.

"I agree, my lady. We mustn't lose it. If John acts quickly it may not be too late. But we must be realistic. When he gets discouraged, he talks of going back to England to raise troops and money for the war. From Rouen he'd have a short journey to Barfleur on the Channel, going through lands in Normandy still loyal to him. And from Barfleur it's a day's sail to Portsmouth. I greatly fear that flight is on his mind."

I'd been sitting up straight, listening intently. Now I sank back in my chair. What could I do, what could I do? I was weary.

After William left I sat on, pondering John's indecisiveness. I thought back to when he was a little boy. He'd shown the same behavior then: alternating between furious activity and silent sulking. Sometimes he'd run wildly through the palace corridors, shouting and laughing. The next time I'd see him, he'd be sitting withdrawn, apart from the rest of the family while we talked, quarreled, went about our business. Henry and I sometimes discussed his erratic behavior.

"Well, he's the youngest and smallest," Henry said. "With three older brothers, he probably feels nobody thinks he's important. He does anything to get some attention. When that doesn't work, he goes off in his corner to mope."

"That may be. I wish I could get Richard and the others to take him along when they go riding or hunting. But they say he's too much of a crybaby. I suppose I should find more time for him."

"Yes, that would be a good idea. He's completely devoted to you."

Then we'd tell each other he'd doubtless grow out of it, and we'd forget the whole subject. After all, with three sturdy big brothers in line ahead of him, it was hardly likely he'd ever be King.

And now he was King. God help us.

If God wouldn't, could I? Sometimes I thought I'd summon my knights and ride to Rouen or wherever John was and exhort him to some action. Then I'd give in to discouragement. Philip, the aggressor, had outmaneuvered us on all fronts. It was too late. Sitting in my tower room I looked out on my poplars, now leafless with bare branches sketched against a gray November sky.

I decided to go back to Fontevraud Abbey where I could quietly retreat from my cares. Where, in the tall severe church, the effigy of my husband Henry reposed, scepter in hand, and where I would presently join him.

Hugh le Brun
1206

Isabella sent me a message when I was imprisoned at Caen Castle. It came shortly after William des Roches had arranged for me to move up from my dreadful subterranean cell. I took the letter from the messenger, recognized Isabella's handwriting and read it hastily. She said she was sorry at my imprisonment and she hoped I wouldn't think she had anything to do with it. I was overcome. What a risk she'd taken, to write to me! What if John had found out? But Isabella had never lacked for bravery.

In all the time since I'd lost her, I'd done my best not to think about her. I'd concentrated instead on my hatred of John and my determination to have vengeance. But with her letter all the memories came flooding back: the happy days we'd known together, the pleasure we took in each other's company, the look on her face when we met after an absence. I had to admit to myself that I'd never stopped loving her. Did she too still hold those memories? Her letter gave no clue.

In the days to come, after my release, she'd often been on my mind. I longed to see her again.

I heard that she was to be at Angoulême in the autumn of 1206 to receive the homage of the vassals of her late father. I decided to go see her.

I hadn't been to Angoulême for six years, not since that strange meeting with Count Aymer when he and Countess Alix persuaded me to marry Mathilde. Good Mathilde! She was still bedridden, still uncomplaining, still willing to listen when I had something on my mind. Often she surprised me with her grasp of affairs and her advice.

Though I don't doubt she'd have wished me well if I'd told her where I was going, I didn't do so. Why risk giving pain to one who already bore so many burdens? I simply said I'd be away a few days.

Nor did I send word to Isabella that I was coming.

I rode through thick fog all morning. When I reached Angoulême about noon, it was like a mysterious shrouded city where I'd never been. In the palace courtyard everything looked ghostly. I could vaguely see, off to one side, blurred figures of men and horses near the stables. A man came from the garden bearing big pots of carnations that he carefully arranged on the steps by the massive door. I caught a whiff of their spicy aroma as soon as I dismounted. The low-lying fog didn't conceal the top of the tower where the pennant of the Taillefers waved languidly and damply. That meant that either Countess Alix or her daughter was in residence. Or maybe both.

I was announced and told to wait in the entry hall, a long narrow room with benches along both walls and rushes on the floor. Count Aymer had never been one to waste his money on unnecessary amenities. A stairway at the end led up to the family's living quarters, presumably more warm and welcoming. Lady Alix would have seen to that. Sitting in this joyless hall, I couldn't push the bitter memories the place aroused out of my mind. This was where I'd left Isabella, the last time I'd seen her, when John sent me off to Wales on that trumped-up mission. This was where, when I came back, Count Aymer and Lady Alix told me that during my absence Isabella had married John.

I sat on a hard bench, leaned my head against the hard wall and closed my eyes, remembering. A servant brought me a goblet of wine. I sat there for what seemed a long time.

"Hugh?"

She stood at the foot of the stairs, then walked toward me. She wore an exquisite gown of pale rose, with embroidery of silver flowers around the high neck. Her golden hair, coiled on top of her head, was covered by a lacy silver scarf. She seemed taller, more lissome. Her movements were as poised and graceful as a swan gliding over still water.

The carefree, disheveled girl I'd known had grown into a ravishing, self-possessed woman.

I rose. She held out her hand. I clasped it, staring at her, unable to say a word.

"Well, Hugh, aren't you going to greet me, and tell me why you surprise me like this?"

"I'm sorry, Isabella. It's you who surprise me. Somehow I thought you'd look the way you did half a dozen yeas ago."

"And you don't care for the new Isabella?" She posed in front of me with her arms raised and a toe pointed as though preparing to dance. She was enchanting. I believe she knew it and reveled in it..

"Of course I do. But I'm dumbfounded. You were always pretty. Now you're utterly beautiful."

"Thank you. I'm sorry I kept you waiting but I wanted to look my best for you. I'm glad if I succeeded. Now, shall we go out to the garden, and you'll tell me why you've come? Did you want to take something up with my mother? I'm sorry, she is hardly here anymore, and spends most of her time at her estate in Champagne. But she always instructs her seneschal to keep the palace ready, just in case."

As we walked she kept talking, as though she were afraid of silence.

"And of course, I've been getting ready for the arrival of the nobility tomorrow and the ceremonies. Aren't you glad you came today, Hugh? Otherwise you might have had to bend a knee to me."

We rounded the tower to sit on a bench in the rose garden where a few late blossoms still spread their pale pink petals. The fog was lifting rapidly. Behind us, puffs of steam floated off the gray stone walls of the palace as the sun reached them. Before us, a fountain tirelessly sent up spurts of water as though trying to reach the sunlight. I stared at it, watching as at last the sun broke through and each jet of water caught its light and glistened like sculptured crystal, only to fall back into the deep dark pool. I was acutely conscious of the extravagantly beautiful creature beside me. I felt as though I'd had a whole flagon of wine, not just a few sips.

"Why *have* you come, Hugh?"

"It's simple. Once we were very close to each other. Then we weren't. I'd gotten used to that until you sent me that message when I was in prison at Caen." I was looking at her, but she was looking at the fountain.

"Oh yes, so I did."

"Do you remember what you wrote?"

"I'm afraid not. That must be four years ago. I wrote it in a great hurry. I remember I was feeling very sorry for you and the other prisoners, locked up in those horrid dungeons. I didn't want you to blame me for what had happened."

"You wrote that you wished you could help me, and you asked me to think of you as my friend. I've never forgotten that. When I learned you'd be here I decided to come. I knew we couldn't change anything that's happened, but I just wanted to see you again. That's all." My words seemed lame and ineffectual, nothing like what was in my heart.

She glanced at me and smiled. It wasn't the guileless smile I remembered from when she was a fourteen-year-old whose moods changed so swiftly. It was the smile of a woman who knew she was charming, and who knew how to charm.

"And now that you see me, Hugh, what do you think?"

"I think you have become even more lovely, and that you've grown up. Are you happy, Isabella?"

"Of course I am, why shouldn't I be? How could the Queen of England not be happy? John dotes on me, you know."

"And you on him?"

"Of course."

We were both silent for several minutes, staring at the fountain. The sun had disappeared behind a cloud. The leaping spurts of water had lost their brilliance. I thought I might as well go. I was just rising when Isabella put a hand on my arm.

"Don't go yet, Hugh." Her eyes were fixed on me, eyes as blue as forget-me-nots. Now she was speaking with the openness of my young Isabella, speaking what was in her heart.

"I know what you're thinking. You're remembering how it was in Lusignan when we thought we would marry. And I'm sure you were dreadfully hurt when I married John so quickly, before I learned that you hadn't been killed after all. I blame my parents for that—and my own youth. It's grieved me that I never had a chance to try to explain it to you. Can you believe that?"

"I can, because it's what I've wanted to believe all these years."

"Then you must also believe this: After John and I were married I came to love him very much. It hasn't all been easy. He's not perfect, God knows. Neither am I. We've had our differences. But we always come back together, just like before. I simply can't imagine life without John. There, Hugh. I've been as honest as I can be. Maybe too honest. But I want you to understand me. Please don't go away still resentful, still maybe hating me for what I did. Your opinion means a great deal to me."

"I don't hate you and never did. I thank you for this time and your forthrightness. I'll always regret that things weren't different. I'll never stop caring for you. But I'm happy for you in your happiness. And I'll go away with a heart freed of resentment." I took her hand and held it tight. As I did so, it occurred to me that I'd never kissed her.

"May I kiss you goodbye?"

She didn't answer, simply turned her face toward me. Our lips met. Hers were sweet and yielding, so sweet that I had to force myself to pull away and get to my feet. As I did so I saw one of Isabella's servants standing at the corner of the tower looking agitated, wondering whether to interrupt or not.

Isabella rose too, composed and unruffled. "What is it, Alois?"

"My lady, I beg your pardon, but there's someone here who says he must see Sir Hugh at once."

I was nonplussed. Nobody knew where I was but my steward Pierre. I'd told him I'd be back within three days. He wasn't to tell anyone where I'd gone.

When I walked into the courtyard there was my son Hugh, just dismounting. Two of our knights were still on their horses. He grinned as he walked toward me.

"By all the saints, what is this about, Hugh? Why are you here?"

Another foolish escapade, no doubt. Ever since he'd come back from the ill-fated Fourth Crusade, Young Hugh had been aimlessly casting about for amusement and occupation. He spent more time with his cousin Simon de Lezay than he did at Lusignan. I'd often asked him to come with me when I went to see our important vassals. We had the same conversation many times:

"You go, father. You're much better at it than I am."

"But Hugh, one day you'll be the leader of our clan. You must establish ties with these men. You may count on them for your very life some day."

"All right, next time, depend on it, I'll go with you. But Simon and I are pledged to take part in a big tournament at Niort on Saturday. Next time though, for sure." And he'd be off before I could begin to argue.

Such were the unsettling thoughts that filled my mind this September afternoon at Angoulême. What was he up to now, this happy-go-lucky son of mine? At twenty-three, he should be showing some signs of maturity.

"I'm sorry father, I know you told Pierre nobody was to know where you were. But this is very important." Then he saw Isabella. She'd held back but was now walking toward us where we stood confronting each other in the middle of the courtyard. He transferred his attention and his smile from me to her.

"So you are Young Hugh. We've never met, though I believe I saw you once at Lusignan. But you didn't see me."

"I wish I had. I'd never have forgotten it."

Where did he learn to be so gallant? Looking at him I saw him in her eyes: tall as I was but more slender and with finer features. He had a head of smooth brown hair, unlike my bushy mop. His smile was infectious and even now, angry as I was, I felt a wave of warm love for this open-hearted, trusting son of mine.

"Well, we needn't stand about here. Do come into the palace."

"I'd better hear first what's so vital that he came here to find me. It may be we'll have to leave at once."

"Very well, I'll go order some refreshment for you. Come in soon."

We both watched as she went up the steps. I turned to young Hugh, waiting for his explanation.

"I think we'll indeed have to leave at once," he said. "A message came to you from King Philip. He's calling all his vassals in Poitou to meet him at Tours. John is bringing an army up from La Rochelle. Philip wants to gather enough men to move south and engage him."

So. The war was resuming.

"You were right to come. Now let's say our farewells to the Queen, and be on our way."

What a strange end to my sentimental visit to the past. The last time I'd said goodbye to Isabella, I was sent off to serve King John, soon to be her husband. This time, I was going of my own free will to do battle against King John, her husband.

Isabella

1207

On October 1, 1207, church bells all over Winchester pealed as though the bellringers were in some mad contest to see who could sound most discordant and demented. Loudest of all was the tolling from the minster near the palace. Every clang was like another hammer blow to my head.

In my close, warm room I felt smothered under heavy down comforters and overpowered by the smells of camphor, vinegar and something cloyingly sweet, like the white lilacs that grew in our garden at Angoulême. I lay exhausted while women pressed cool cloths on my forehead and made soothing sounds.

"There there, my lady. It's all over now. You must rest."

"Here, my poor dear. Try to swallow this, it will help you to sleep."

I drowsed a bit, then woke to ask in a panic, "The child? Where is the child?" I was fully awake now. The memory of the hours of pain and struggle was receding. I had to see the reason for it all. Was it well formed and healthy? Was it a boy? Was it even alive?

"They're just swaddling him now, my lady. And look, here comes the nurse!" The midwife's rosy face beamed and she pointed toward the door where a tall, brown-clad woman with a white wimple came in, stepping carefully and carrying something very small in her arms. Lady Anne and Adèle followed her.

The nurse walked to my bed and held the tightly swaddled baby toward me. She waited until I realized I should hold out my arms. That's what mothers did, of course. Only when I held him could I see that this was indeed a living if infinitesimal human being. I looked down at the red, wrinkled face. His eyes were tightly shut, showing only a fringe of long black lashes. I was surprised.

So babies were born with eyelashes? Hair too, I supposed, though his head was so snugly wrapped that there was no way to know. I'd never seen a newborn baby before, much less held one. He weighed so little in my arms that I could hardly believe he was real.

He opened his eyes. They were blue as my own. He stared at me as though taking in this strange new creature, wondering what to make of her. Then his little rosebud lips curved in a smile. I smiled back in utter delight, overcome by a surge of love for this helpless little being. My son! I held him to my breast and looked up to see the midwives, the nurse, Anne and Adèle smiling as broadly as I. It was a room full of exultant women, rejoicing in the miracle of birth.

The object of this rejoicing, however, took that moment to let out a squall that would have done a midnight-prowling cat proud. I looked up in alarm at the faces bent over me.

"What can be the matter, was I holding him too tightly? Is he all right?"

"He's just hungry, my lady," said the nurse. She lifted him out of my arms. "We'll take him to the wet-nurse and fill his little stomach."

I lay back on the piled-up pillows. Anne and Adèle were still there, one on each side of my bed. I put a hand to my forehead and smoothed back a few strands of hair. My head still ached, though not quite so agonizingly.

"So this is what it's like, being a mother," I said. "I'm glad it's a boy and John has his heir, because I don't ever want to go through that again."

"All first-time mothers say that, my lady," said Anne. "But you'll be surprised how quickly you forget the pain. And there'll come a time when you'll want to give your little lad a sister or brother."

I didn't believe her, but I didn't dispute her. I was too tired and sore.

Adèle gave me a sidewise look and a half-smile. "Well, no matter about all that, Isabella. You have two things to be grateful for right now. One, that adorable baby. And two, your stomach is flat again."

At sixteen, Adèle had blossomed. Hr face was a little fuller. So was her figure. She'd put up her long hair. I wasn't always sure what she was thinking, but I liked having her around because of her calm good humor.

I looked down to where I'd become accustomed to seeing a big mound. I'd hated how my body had swollen. I'd worried at how John had lost interest in me, the larger and more awkward I became.

"You're right, Adèle. And I *am* grateful. I just don't see why the good Lord couldn't have given us a less painful way to bring children into his world. Why must women be the ones to suffer while men take it easy? It's not fair!"

"But that's the way it is, and we must live with it," said Anne. "Now, my lady, speaking of men, your husband will soon be here. He'd gone hunting but a man was sent to call him back, as soon as you began having your pains."

I remembered vaguely that John had come into my chamber that morning to say he was going hunting. I'd wanted to get up and kiss him goodbye, but I'd hardly sat up and gotten one foot out of the bed before he was gone.

Anne was still speaking, in the same half-scolding, half-affectionate tone she'd used when I was a little girl refusing to do what I ought. "He'll have heard all the bells ringing, and he'll know what that means. The Queen has given birth! You'll want to look your best when he comes. Perhaps the blue capelet, and your pearl necklace?"

"Oh Anne, I'm so tired! Must I change?"

"Do you want your King to find his Queen all bedraggled and ungroomed? Come now, I'll help you sit up and get the cape on, and Adèle will brush your hair."

We were barely ready when John burst in. I'd had time to take a quick look in the mirror Anne held before me, and I wasn't displeased. I was pale, but my lips and cheeks were rosy, thanks to a few pinches. Adèle had brushed all the tangles out of my golden curls. The blue robe covered my disheveled nightdress, and Anne had smoothed the rumpled bedclothes and thrown a fresh white cover over them.

"My son, where is my son?" John roared, looking around as though an infant might be hidden in some corner. He still wore his muddy boots. His leather tunic was stretched tight over his torso—I'd not noticed till now that John was getting rather stout.

"We'll ask them to bring him at once, my lord," said Anne.

"Well, be quick about it." He pulled off his tunic and threw it on the floor. "Why do you keep it so infernally hot in here? Bring on my son!"

Anne took Adèle by the hand and left to call the nurse. At the door, Adèle paused and turned around to give a little bow to me and then to John. Now I was alone with this bellowing intruder, in whom I hardly recognized my husband.

Then his eyes fell on me. His face softened. He moved swiftly to the bed where I reclined. He took my hands gently as though they might break and bent to kiss them. I knew at once that I was still desirable in his eyes. He was mine again—if indeed he had been missing.

"My love, my dear Isabella, there you are. You look like an angel just come down from heaven. How are you, are you well?"

"Better now, my lord, since you have come."

I smiled up at him, deeply thankful that Anne had persuaded me to make myself beautiful for my husband. I know we were thinking the same thing: when, oh when, can these two lovers make love again?

There was a light knock on the door. The nurse came in and held the baby out to John. John took him eagerly and stared at the tiny face just as I had done, in wonder and disbelief. He sat down beside me on the edge of the bed. Together, we looked at our son. Our son looked up at us, then his blue eyes closed.

"He's sleepy, the little lamb, now that he's had his meal," said the nurse. She was about to take him but John insisted that she unwrap him so we could make sure he had the right number of arms, legs, fingers and toes. His round little head proved to be covered by downy dark hair, almost as black as John's.

"He has your eyes and nose, Isabella, but my hair. Maybe one of these days a black beard too." He tickled the baby's chin, but the infant slept on.

"We'll call him Henry, of course," John said.

"Of course," I said. It was right that he should be named for his grandfather. Maybe later, when we had other children, some could be called by names from my side of the family. Was it only an hour ago that I'd sworn never to have another child? Motherhood must grow on one.

The nurse succeeded in extricating her charge from his parents and left, wrapping him up again as she went.

John and I sat on, talking. He was mellow, full of the joys of fatherhood. We hadn't talked much for several months.

"My first son, Isabella! This is a great day for England."

"Truly, your first son, John? Are you sure?" I teased.

"Oh of course, there were a few bastards, years ago. That was long before I met you. Nobody pays attention to that anymore. And now they can't go on about how we've been married all this time, and still no issue."

I'd heard the nonsense. People said I'd bewitched John with potions and enchantments to keep him in my bed, while casting spells to protect myself from childbearing. It's true that for the first few years I had no wish for children, but presently I'd begun to worry that they'd never come. And then would John put me aside, as he had his first wife?

I reached up to run my fingers through his silky black beard and tweak him on the chin. "Yes, that's all past now. They'll have to find something new to gossip about."

He took my hand and kissed the palm, then held it. His face darkened.

"They won't have far to look. This argument with Pope Innocent about the new Archbishop of Canterbury is getting worse by the day."

"Why, what's the Pope done now?" I knew something of this dispute, thanks to Anne. She got information from William de Cantilupe and passed it on to me. He chose this means of keeping me informed rather than calling on me too often himself. He knew his suspicious master.

"He's consecrated that Frenchified Stephen of Langton as archbishop, when he knows I've already chosen John Gray, a stout Norfolk bishop, as learned as the best of them. What does Innocent know of England? Why can't I appoint my own archbishop in my own realm?"

"Dear me. We can't have two archbishops, I suppose."

He hardly heard me. He'd risen and was stamping about the room, each heavy footfall another blow to my aching head. He was getting quite red in the face.

"And now there's talk that he's threatening an interdict on England, just because I want to stand up for what's right."

"But surely the people are on your side, and the clergy too?"

"Yes, true enough. Most of the clergy anyway. But if the Pope actually puts an interdict on us I don't know how long they'll stay loyal. It's hard for a priest to stand up for his king when his parishioners are complaining about no church service, no sanctified weddings or burials."

I held out my hand and beckoned him.

"Come here John, and forget all that for now. No matter what the Pope does or who the archbishop is, we have so much to be happy about today. We have our beautiful son, our Prince Henry, sleeping safely in the next room."

He sighed and came back to my bedside. He looked down at me. His face relaxed. I realized that sometimes I forgot how much the running of this complicated, seldom peaceable kingdom weighed on John. I should try to be more of a helpmeet, if he would let me. I should encourage him to look beyond the day's problems.

"My dear John, we are blessed today with a healthy son. Let's resolve to bring him up so he'll be a strong and able English king and a credit to his father."

John bent to kiss me gently.

"You're tired, my love, I can tell by your voice. I'll bid you good night, and sleep well."

I was indeed tired. My women helped me undress, washed me and gave me a draught to relieve my pounding head. I sank back gratefully on the cool pillows.

I was nearly asleep when a picture flashed before my eyes, something I'd noticed fleetingly but pushed aside to think about later.

As Anne and Adèle had left after John's arrival, a look had flashed between Adèle and John. Reliving that moment, I realized it was like a secret message passed between two people who have a special understanding, unknown to any one else.

John
1208–1209

"Beware of kingship, my son."

Five-month-old Henry looked up at me as though considering my words while Isabella rocked his cradle. Perhaps he found my admonition amusing, because he gave us such an enchanting smile that Isabella and I had to smile at each other too.

"If only my mother had lived to see him. It would have eased her mind so much to know we'd finally produced an heir to the throne of England."

Queen Eleanor had died peacefully four years ago at her retreat at Fontevraud Abbey. I was always heartened to remember our last meeting at Mirebeau when she'd shown me the gratitude and respect I'd never had from her before.

"Yes. I'm sorry too. Maybe she'd have come to see her grandson. Maybe she and I could have gotten to know each other better. I'd have liked that."

She reached down to brush her fingers gently over the baby's cheek. He clasped a finger and tried to suck on it. She laughed. At twenty, she was lovelier than ever. The pretty adolescent girl I'd been captivated by seven years ago had become this poised young woman, secure in her beauty, her womanhood and her motherhood.

I'll admit, during the last few months of her pregnancy I'd been put off by the change in her looks. She'd become almost haggard with a disposition to match. I wondered if she suspected how often I'd gone elsewhere to find bed-companions.

Now all was as it had been if not better, at least domestically. We were taking our ease in the Queen's private chamber at Winchester, warm and surrounded by the new elegance Isabella had created. There were silver candelabra on beautifully carved tables with silver inlay. In a corner a gilded cage held a yellow bird that sulked and sometimes sang. My eye fell on a colorful wall hanging opposite me, with golden fronds and graceful snow-white swans on a crimson background. I pointed to it.

"I don't remember seeing that before. Surely it's not one of my mother's."

"No, it's new. I sent for some of our hangings and tapestries from Angoulême, and took down Queen Eleanor's. They seemed rather somber to me. I hope you don't mind."

"Of course not, my love." I was glad she'd made the Queen's apartments into such a pleasant haven. Here I could almost forget the state of the kingdom.

Almost. My rocky relations with the Pope were never far from my mind. I sighed.

"Another ultimatum from Innocent came this morning. He refuses to lift the cursed interdict until I accept his choice for Archbishop of Canterbury. Just when things are quiet on the Continent and Philip and I have signed a truce, the Pope decides to punish all England with this decree. He forbids sacraments in the churches. So good Englishmen can't get properly married, or buried in the churchyard. It's monstrous!"

"Well, at least we had Henry christened before it started." Isabella had heard all this before, but that didn't stop me.

"And a good thing. But I won't give in. I'll go to my grave before I'll see Stephen Langton as an archbishop."

I'd been expecting something like this, to be sure. The Pope and I had been disputing for years over one thing and another. Mostly, we disagreed about the will of my brother Richard. Richard must have been having one of his fits of fever when he made that will. Why did he leave so much to relatives who had no need of it, like our nephew Emperor Otto of Germany? And then there were the Pope's constant reminders of the rights of Richard's widow, Berengaria. I saw no reason why I, as Richard's heir and successor, shouldn't have the say over where his inheritance went. So I pocketed the whole thing and put off the various claimants.

Now things had come to a head with this matter of the archbishopric. I was holding out for my choice, the Bishop of Norwich, an ambitious and not over-scrupulous man. I was sure I could bend him to my will when necessary. But the Pope still insisted on Stephen of Langton.

"Calls himself an Englishman, does he, this Stephen?" My temper rose and I got up and paced about the room, rehearsing the arguments I'd use in my next message to Rome. Isabella was soothing Henry, who had begun to whimper.

"He hasn't been in England since he was a mere child. He's a Frenchman, that's what he is, after all those years at the University of Paris. And now he's snug in the Pope's pocket in Rome, a cardinal no less. And Innocent persuaded those spineless monks down at Canterbury to elect him in spite of me. May God curse me if I let any Pope tell me how to run my own kingdom!"

I'd come to a halt near the cradle. I was so worked up that I didn't realize how my voice had risen. I suppose my roaring frightened my son. At any rate he let out a wail that surprised me. How could such a small creature make so much noise?

"John!" cried Isabella over the baby's howling. "Do control yourself!"

I tried to. I sat down and clenched my teeth, glaring at the floor until I had calmed down. I looked up to see that Isabella had taken the child from the cradle and was comforting him. The nurse, alarmed by the uproar, came in and bore little Henry out of the room.

"I can't help it," I groaned. "Bad temper runs in the family. My mother used to tell me that mine was even worse than my father's, and God knows he was a terror when anyone crossed him."

"That may be, but let's try to avoid outbursts in front of the baby. Otherwise he might think that's what it takes to be a king, and grow up with a terrible temper himself."

She spoke with some testiness. Then she took pity on me, where I sat slumped over in dejection. She came to sit beside me and put her arms around my neck. She held her cheek against mine.

"Dear John, no wonder you have trouble with your temper. I know how this fuss about the Archbishop and the interdict troubles you. It's not fair for the Pope to interfere in your kingdom, but you'll find a way out of it. I know you will." She kissed me and smoothed my hair—I'd been tearing at it in my rage.

I held her close, and gradually I became calm. Sometimes I thought my love for Isabella was all that kept me going. She believed in me and encouraged me when no one else did. She was my refuge.

I didn't take the Pope's strictures lying down, though. As the months passed it became clear which of the clergy were with me and which supported Innocent's position. The latter had an unpleasant surprise. If they obeyed the interdict and closed their churches, my officers were on the scene at once to confiscate their property—churches, estates, homes, everything. Too bad for them, and all the better for my treasury, thanks to their unwilling contributions. I'd laugh at each new encounter and imagine the Pope's chagrin when he learned how much his stern measures were enriching me. I seriously considered sending him my thanks.

Instead, I gave Isabella a necklace of emeralds. I gave myself a cloth-of-gold girdle studded with pearls from the Orient. The fortunes of my London jeweler improved considerably.

To add to my good cheer, Isabella was pregnant with our second child. The more the better, from my point of view. A king needs a good supply of sons to stand in line to succeed him and daughters to marry off to the highest bidder.

We went to Windsor to keep Christmas, and a merry time we had. I wasn't going to let Pope Innocent ruin my holidays. On Christmas Day we heard Mass in the chapel, then went for our feast to the great hall in the Round Tower. I looked around in satisfaction as we entered. I'd spent many a Christmas here. The hall looked much as it did during one of those all-too-rare occasions when my family were on sufficiently civil terms with one another to gather for the festivities. A tall holly tree stood in a corner, its tip grazing the ceiling. Green garlands festooned the walls. Warmth spread from the hearth where a huge log blazed enthusiastically. Nearby, a group of minstrels, decked out in smart tunics and hose of red and green, struck up a cheery tune as we entered.

We were about three dozen at table, thanks to my council, Isabella's ladies, and the troop of courtiers who accompanied us on our many travels about the kingdom. Everybody waited expectantly to see what wonders the cooks had devised for us.

Cheers and applause broke out when three pairs of servitors marched in. Each pair bore, on a yard-long silver platter carpeted with grass, a whole rabbit baked in pastry, complete with tall pastry ears, puffy tail and raisins for eyes. Small roast birds had been set on the grass as though hopping about the rabbits. We admired the realistic effect, but that didn't stop us from demolishing everything in short order. After several more courses—eel pie, roasted quail, onion tart-- we were served platters of fig tartlets swimming in honey. By then everybody was ready to sit back and let digestion begin, with the aid of a glass of spiced wine.

We talked about what was on all our minds, the standoff with the Pope.

"The people are with you, my liege, no doubt about that," said Robert de Thorneham.

"I think they are, Sir Robert. But my people can be fickle. How can we make sure they don't lose heart, and perhaps let themselves be swayed by the arguments the Pope's agents are sowing all over the land?"

Isabella, who had been sitting quietly at my side, spoke up.

"John, isn't it true that many of your priests keep mistresses? I know the French clerics do, and I doubt if the English would want to be thought behind the times."

"I'm afraid you're right. Another black mark for the Pope. Why doesn't he enforce the rule of celibacy?"

"Then let me put this before you. What if you seized the concubines, held them for ransom, and forced the guilty priests to pay up in order to get their ladies back?"

Not a sound, except a smothered belch from some one down the table.

I laughed aloud—what an original, inspired idea! When the others saw how I'd reacted they began to titter, then let out roars of laughter.

I sent the orders at once. Within a week, sheriffs' officers began rounding up the unfortunate women, and a fine large number they captured. It didn't take long for the bereft clerics to pay up to retrieve their companions. Meantime, the good English folk were treated to a most entertaining spectacle. I doubt if the Pope, when he heard of it far off in Rome, found it so entertaining.

My glee over this caper was short-lived. At the New Year when we'd returned to Winchester Lady Anne rejoined our court. She'd been in France staying with her ailing mother for some months. Now the old lady had finally died. Isabella was glad to have Anne back. I wasn't.

Isabella was approaching her term. She was easily upset and short of temper. Late one afternoon, two days after Lady Anne's return, I went to my Queen's bedchamber, as was my daily custom. I asked her how she was feeling. She was sitting up in bed, with her long golden hair flowing over her shoulders. Her face was flushed and her blue eyes blazed. I anticipated trouble. At the same time, I thought I'd never seen her look more comely.

She brushed my polite questions aside and rushed to the attack

"So my lord, you've been amusing yourself with poor little Adèle, while her mother was gone? Seducing an innocent girl, charming her just as you once charmed me? Don't try to deny it. Adèle has confessed the whole sordid affair to her mother. Well, King John, what do you have to say for yourself?"

I was stunned. I'd taken precautions to keep my dalliance with Adèle quiet. With her mother gone and nobody keeping an eye on her, we had no trouble finding times and places to meet. At first she was prettily modest, then yielded when I told her that no one need ever know. It had been a long time since I'd enjoyed a young girl, especially one who proved so thrilled at this introduction to adult pleasures—and with a king!

In time, though, I lost interest in her. I didn't seek her out so often. As the affair petered out, she didn't pursue me, but I could see the hurt in her eyes when we chanced across each other. I suppose it was wounded pride that made her go to Lady Anne and confess.

There was no point in denial. But I had a secret weapon.

"Let the one who is without sin cast the first stone, Isabella. I've known for a long time of your assignations with Hugh le Brun, when you were in Angoulême. I didn't reproach you because I hoped you'd come to me and admit your infidelity, in which case I would have gladly forgiven you. Even now, if you'll acknowledge your misdeeds, I'll agree to forget they happened."

If I thought this would bring her around, I was sadly mistaken. Every word of her disdainful reply was like a spurt of venom.

"I will acknowledge no misdeeds. It's true that two years ago I saw Hugh in Angoulême—once. There were no 'assignations.' He came unannounced and uninvited. We spent about half an hour together. If he had any notion of resuming a relationship with me, I quickly put that out of his mind. I told him I was happy in my marriage, that I loved you and you loved me. Then we parted as friends."

" 'Friends,' eh? Then how do you explain that embrace and that kiss, just before Hugh was called away?"

"Your spies have been most observant. My congratulations. It's true Hugh and I exchanged a kiss, no more, in farewell. And farewell it was. We both knew we were unlikely ever to see each other again. You must remember, my lord, that I knew Hugh long before I knew you. We were attached to each other. We were to be married. I still respect him. I see no reason to wipe out that chapter of my history, and you can't force me to."

Her words only enraged me more. I had to strike back at her somehow.

"So, you hold yourself up as a model of virtue and goodness? That's not the picture the common folk of England paint of you. They don't have as high an opinion of their Queen as she has of herself."

"The common folk? When do I ever see the common folk, much less listen to them? You might as well tell me what they say. I can see you're dying to."

"And so I shall. They call you a witch, an enchantress. They say you've cast spells on their King that kept him from defending his kingdom. They say it's because of you that we have this damnable interdict on the whole land. That's what they say. And sometimes I think it's true!"

She gave me one last contemptuous look, then lay back on her pillow and turned her head aside. Silence. I couldn't tell what she was thinking.

It was our first serious quarrel. I felt depressed. Part of it was annoyance that she'd learned of my affair with Adèle. Part of it was my grudging admission to myself that she was probably telling the truth about Hugh. I sat there staring at my feet. The light was fading, and I thought dully that I should send for someone to light the candles. I heard a gasp and looked up. Isabella was clutching herself around the waist. She moaned, then she cried out. I ran to her.

"John, call my women, I think it's beginning!"

I'd had no idea she was so near to giving birth. I rushed out, told Lady Anne and the nurse, and made my way back to my own rooms.

Our second son, Richard, was born later that night. His arrival after a long, hard labor was such a relief and distraction to us both that we put aside the matter of our quarrel about Hugh. But I didn't forget.

Isabella

1209-1210

Excommunication! The word had such a horrid ring. It sounded just like what it was: the worst punishment God's vicar on earth could dole out.

Pope Innocent excommunicated John in the fall of 1209. John sank into one of his black moods where he stayed for two days. At last I persuaded him to walk out with me into the gardens behind the palace at Winchester. He was still glum, but willing to talk.

"Just what will it mean, being excommunicated?" I asked, partly out of curiosity and partly because I knew John rather enjoyed explaining to me the way the world works. "Besides forbidding you to go to mass and confess your sins and all that? I know King Philip was excommunicated because he refused to live with his queen and preferred Agnès de Méran. But as far as I could tell he kept right on doing as he pleased, in spite of the Pope. He certainly didn't send Agnès away. So what good was the excommunication?"

I wouldn't have been surprised if he'd snapped at me or refused to answer. On the contrary he took my question seriously.

"You're right, Isabella, as far as Philip's case goes. It didn't much affect his ability to govern. But Philip was lucky. Agnès died after she'd given him the heirs he wanted. So as soon as Philip was no longer living in sin, the Pope of course forgave all. What's more, the French didn't seem to hold it against him. I'm afraid the English aren't so frivolous and lighthearted." We walked on in silence, arm in arm. I could feel his arm stiffen as his tension grew.

"That Pope! He's as good as branding me a leper in the eyes of my own people! They're already angry about the interdict. Now when they learn I've been expelled from the church they'll respect me even less. I'll lose even more of the support of my vassals. They'll decide they have no more reason to obey me. By God's ears, I'll show them!"

His face reddened as his famous temper rose. He glared at a page who was passing and shook his fist as though confronting his enemy the Pope. The poor terror-stricken lad scurried out of sight.

John couldn't go to war with the Pope, but he struck out at his enemies at home. He'd become obsessively convinced that he was being assaulted from all sides. In Scotland, Ireland and Wales his barons were defying him. He spoke often of another expedition to regain the lands lost to King Philip. But first he'd have to put down his unruly subjects at home. He set about it with rare vigor.

First he took on King William of Scotland. John suspected him of conspiring with his enemies. He managed to muster a formidable army which he deployed on the Scottish frontier. William, old and tired, sued for peace.

Next John sailed to Ireland and chased a troop of rebellious barons the length of the country and into the sea. They fled to France.

What with all this warring, John wasn't present when our daughter Joanna arrived in the summer of 1210. She joined Henry, aged three, and Richard, not yet a year old.

She was smaller and more delicate than my sturdy sons had been at birth, with blue eyes and a fuzz of blond hair. Lady Anne was almost as enchanted with her as I was.

"She's identical to the way you looked as a baby, my lady. So I expect we'll have another beauty in the family."

Much as I loved my babies, I thought three in three years was enough. I was afraid of losing my looks. When John returned after Joanna's birth, sometimes I would try to put him off when he was eager to make love. I seldom succeeded, nor did I always want to. Even after ten years of marriage we could still fall into each other's arms as though we were honeymooners. I could see that, so far, my childbearing had not made me less desirable to him. Yet I worried.

Anne came in to my chamber at Winchester one day to find me examining my face in the mirror, searching for wrinkles. Satisfied that all was still well on that front, I asked her to help me into the blue gown I'd worn at my coronation, to see if I showed any bulges. I'd always seen to it that my ladies took good care of my favorite gowns because they had to last a long time. It was not easy to wheedle money from John for new clothes. Fortunately, this one still looked nearly new.

I stood in the light near the window so Anne could study me critically.

"Well, perhaps a bit tighter around the waist. But my lady, you've no need for concern. You're only twenty-four after all, and as slim and smooth as you ever were."

"But I want to stay that way. Anne, aren't there certain teas or possets a woman can take to keep from getting pregnant? Do you know how to find them?"

"I've heard vague old wives' tales, and I suppose I could ask around. But my dear, your husband would be very angry if he knew you were taking measures like that. He's a true Plantagenet, anxious to have as many children as possible."

"He needn't know. I think I'm entitled to a few secrets from John. Don't you keep some things from Sir William?"

"Of course I do, though not many. But that's different. We're not married."

"More's the pity."

She'd told me by now that she and William de Cantilupe were deeply attached to each other. Ever since she'd confessed to me about Adèle's affair with John, Anne and I had drawn closer. I think she was grateful that I hadn't blamed Adèle. As for me, I was increasingly glad to have one friend to whom I could talk freely.

"What's the word about his mysterious unmentionable wife who's hidden somewhere out in Wessex? Isn't there something we could do to hasten her demise?"

"That's a matter that William doesn't talk about. And I don't pry. All he says is that he can never live with her again. Is she demented, is she an impossible shrew? I have no idea. Yet there she is, his lawful wife. So what future is there for us?"

I'd seldom seen Anne despondent, much less so close to tears. I went to her and put my arms around her.

"There there, my dear friend. Let's not torment ourselves thinking of the future. At least you have the present. And as long as I can help I will."

She knew what I meant. She sniffled a bit, wiped her eyes, then regained her good humor.

"And how grateful we are to you, my lady."

While we were in Winchester, where I had my private apartments, I'd been glad to let Anne and William meet there, discreetly of course. They were always careful to avoid going in or leaving together. Anne's room was near mine so I could help them keep watch. I enjoyed the sense of intrigue. And what harm did it do?

Most of what I knew of John's doings when he was away I learned from William. Besides being chief household seneschal, he was John's deputy in several important shires so he traveled often throughout the kingdom. News also came during the council meetings, where Geoffrey Fitz-Peter reported on the King's campaigns. As justiciar and John's second in command, Geoffrey was the first to receive dispatches when John was campaigning. The council meetings were attended by the chancellor of the exchequer, the royal treasurer, the seneschals, the household stewards, and other officers and clerks who kept the realm's business moving. The primary reason for the gatherings was the perpetual need to find new revenue sources. Warfare was expensive.

In John's absence I presided at these meetings. I'd asked John if I could, and he'd said indulgently, "Of course." He doubtless thought I saw it as merely a ceremonial recognition of my status. That was largely true, though I fully intended to speak up if I saw the need. Maybe one day I'd take on Sir Geoffrey. His whole bearing, haughty and unsmiling, showed how he disapproved of the presence of a mere woman, queen though she be, in the council chamber.

At one such gathering in the fall of 1210 at Windsor Castle, some ten or twelve officials, courtiers and scribes met in the great hall to hear the latest about the King's Welsh campaign. I sat in my customary place at the left of John's empty throne. The others stood below me. I sat up straight on my throne, wearing my coronation crown and robe. The fires on the hearths, one on each side of the room, blazed away but the chamber was large and drafty. I was glad to be enfolded in the thick red wool with the warm ermine ruff around my neck.

"Welcome, gentlemen. Sir Geoffrey, what of the King?" I asked, when we were all assembled. He stood just below me on the dais and slightly to my left so he could face both the audience and me.

He bowed to me, then read from a parchment.

"The King sends greetings from Hereford to his Queen and his loyal counselors. We have confronted our rebellious vassal, William de Braose, who refuses to pay the King the just debts he owes. We have seized the castles in Wales of Sir William's wife, Matilda. Matilda and her children have escaped, but we shall pursue them and hold them hostage until the debts are paid. Meantime, we request that the Royal Treasurer send us forthwith the sum of four thousand marks, for the pursuance of our campaigns in Wales and Ireland. May God be with you all, as He is with us."

A good deal of noisy discussion broke out at this news, as well as anguished questions by the treasurer as to where he was to find four thousand marks.

While he and Sir Geoffrey conferred I stepped down and approached William de Cantilupe.

"There must be more to this story than those few words. William de Braose has always been one of John's strongest and most loyal supporters. What do you know, Sir William?"

He looked grave and drew me aside. His bearing was soldierly as always, his expression as reserved. Yet I knew by now that, though loyal to John, he was also my friend, an honest, principled man whom I could trust.

"A good deal more. I heard rumors of it while I was in Wales last month. Apparently King John has turned against the de Braose family because Lady Matilda has said in public that she can never give allegiance to a king who murdered his nephew. I can guess at the rest. William de Braose is probably the only person besides the King who knows what really happened to Arthur."

"Yes, I remember that he was Arthur's jailer in the castle at Rouen. I thought John trusted him completely."

"Well, now that his wife has spoken out so indiscreetly he's become John's enemy. I fear John may have brought up the matter of the unpaid debts to justify his attack on Sir William. He may be hoping to silence him by threatening his wife and children."

Nobody had ever spoken to me so frankly about Prince Arthur's tragic end. I'd refused to let my vague suspicions about John's involvement come to the surface. Now it appeared there was reason to believe in his guilt. Otherwise, why should he lash out so fiercely at William de Braose and his wife? Could I have married a man who could do such a barbarous deed?

It was as though an icy wind had swept over me and I shivered.

"Thank you, my friend." I tried to speak calmly. I was learning lessons in composure from William de Cantilupe. I thought I saw a glimmer of sympathy in his steady gaze as I turned, anguished, to leave the room.

I stayed in Windsor for another three weeks before John returned. For the most part I continued to bury my misgivings until I'd be able to talk to him and hear his side of the story.

Meantime I busied myself with our children. At three, Henry was old enough to appear in public as heir to the throne. It was amusing to dress him like a miniature king in rich velvet suits and teach him to walk by my side as sedately as he could manage. When we went into the state dining room or out into the city, he was much admired. It didn't take him long to find out what fun this was. I believe he inherited some of his father's fascination with fine clothes as well as his tendency to strut proudly before his subjects.

"You are becoming quite the little peacock, my pet," I told him.

He grinned at me in delight. "Let's go see the peapocks! I want to see who's prettiest, me or the peapocks!" he clamored. So we went out into the gardens where the peacocks were kept. Before long Henry was chasing them about and squawking at them like any three-year-old, prince or not.

When John finally came he looked so tired and worn that I hadn't the heart to confront him with my doubts. All I wanted to do was comfort him. All he wanted was to forget, for a little while, his grievous troubles. Our first night and for several thereafter, I comforted him to the best of my considerable ability. I persuaded myself that we could go on with the same trusting affection for each other we'd always had.

Then came Matilda de Braose.

I think John hadn't meant me to be there when she arrived. He'd urged me to leave for London and said he'd join me there as soon as he could. However, I'd given in to some kind of a fever and didn't feel well enough to travel. On a dour Monday morning when rain was coming down in sheets and I was glad not to be on the London road, I looked out to see a troop of soldiers gallop up to the palace. In their center was a pair of riders, chained together and wearing long black hooded cloaks that hid their faces. As soon as the company came to a halt John appeared, almost running, to confer briefly with the captain of the soldiers. Without a glance at the prisoners, he went back into the palace. I stayed at my window. The captain walked to the two black-clad figures and gestured to them to dismount. A pair of soldiers seized each of them and hurried them toward the rear of the palace. Just before they disappeared from sight one of them shook her hood loose. I caught a glimpse of a strong, square-jawed face with an expression of terrible anger and despair. Her long, gray, unkempt hair streamed below her shoulders.

That was the last time Matilda de Braose saw the light of day. Later I learned that she and her son had been locked away in the prison of Windsor Castle and left to starve to death. It took less than a month.

Hugh le Brun

1212

ear Hugh: I shall be at the castle in Angoulême during the month of October. Perhaps you could arrange to come see me. Isabella.

Was this an invitation, or an order? I wasn't sure. When I received it, October was already half gone. I'd have to make up my mind quickly.

At first I was a little annoyed and more than a little suspicious. After our last meeting when we'd said goodbye with such tenderness, I'd been sure I'd never see Isabella again. That was four years ago. What could she be up to now? Was this a plot she'd been put up to by John, to whom she'd said she was so devoted?

Finally I decided to go, just out of curiosity. I can't deny that the prospect of seeing my old love again had something to do with the decision. Isabella had by no means lost her fascination for me.

I sent a reply as impersonal as her invitation.

To Queen Isabella: I shall wait on you at Angoulême on October 20. Hugh IX de Lusignan.

She received me in a tower room, up a short staircase from the entry hall. The servant admitted me and left, closing the door behind him. The room, in contrast to the cold, sparsely furnished hall below, was warm, inviting and quiet. I had a vague impression of a great deal of gold and silver, dark red cushioning on divans and chairs, thick Turkish carpets and the scent of roses. Through a door to the next room I could see a high bed curtained in purple.

Isabella stood across from me, silhouetted by sunlight that streamed in through a tall arched window. The rays were reflected almost blindingly off a silver bowl and two crystal goblets on a table by her side. In the blaze of light

I could hardly make her out. She took a few steps toward me and I saw her clearly. She was smiling, but the smile seemed fixed, almost as though she'd been practicing for this moment. Beneath a silvery-gray, sleeveless cloak she wore a long-sleeved, high-belted, cherry-red gown that clung to her breasts, then fell in soft folds. I'd never seen her wear that color before. Her hair was a gilded cascade of curls that fell to her shoulders.

This wasn't the Isabella I'd met here four years ago, who'd seemed a more poised but still guileless version of the girl I'd loved at Lusignan. Now, she reminded me of the angels one sees in cathedral frescoes: carefully created works of art, existing only to be admired and adored from afar. I was dazed with the effort to reconcile this vision with the Isabella I remembered.

She broke the spell and held out her hand.

"Good morning, Hugh. Thank you for coming." I went to her and clasped her hand in both of mine. I glanced quickly at her face, then looked down at my feet like a shy schoolboy. I heard her rippling laugh.

"Oh, Hugh, this is so like the last time we met, when you stared at me as though I were some ghost."

I made a lame attempt at gallantry. "Not a ghost, Isabella. Rather a fairy queen."

"Prettily said, Hugh. Now your queen commands you to sit beside her, and we shall talk."

She led me by the hand to one of the cushioned divans. I sat erect, too nervous to yield to the seductive softness. She began speaking at once, with her eyes fixed on my face. I'd forgotten how they seemed to turn a darker blue when she was very serious.

"I've asked you to come because you're my oldest, truest friend. There's nobody else I can bring myself to talk to about what's been distressing me. I've just come from seeing my mother in Champagne, but she wasn't at all interested in hearing my tale of woe."

The speech, like the smile with which she'd greeted me, seemed rehearsed. I wondered where all this was leading.

"Poor lady, she's reached the age where she cares more about her aches and her pains, and her physicians and her poultices, than about what's troubling her daughter. You'd hardly know her, Hugh. I never thought I'd see my beautiful mother look old and gray and wrinkled."

The flawless façade of her face was softening, giving way to what might have been genuine emotion. She bent her head and covered her eyes with her hands. I knew how much Isabella had always loved and looked up to her mother. I tried to think of something comforting to say.

"That must have been hard for you. But what about John? Can't you talk to your husband about this tale of woe, whatever it is?"

She looked up at me doubtfully, as though wondering how much to tell me. Then her words came tumbling out.

"That's just it, Hugh. I can't talk to John because it's John who's made me miserable." Her voice was unsteady. "How could I have been so blind to what he's really like?" She hurried on, which was just as well. I couldn't believe what I was hearing, much less respond.

"Now I'll try to tell you plainly what's brought me to this state. You'll find it shocking. First of all, I've learned that John almost certainly murdered his nephew Arthur while he held him prisoner at Rouen."

I'd heard that tale. I'd brushed it aside. Why would John do it? He had no more sense of right and wrong than a wild pig, but he wasn't stupid. Surely he would have foreseen the political consequences of such a crime, the scandal that would attach to his name.

"That's a grave charge indeed, if it's true."

"It will probably never be proved. But I've put together everything I've learned, including John's absolute refusal to talk to me about it. I'm convinced he did it. But Hugh, that's only the beginning! Just this year John kept the wife and son of William de Braose shut up in the dungeon at Windsor without food or water until they died."

I was open-mouthed with disbelief. Even in an age when brutal punishments were commonplace this was abominable.

"Are you sure, Isabella? You know how rumors fly."

"Yes, I'm sure. John's steward, William de Cantilupe, who never lies to me, told me."

"But why would John do such a deed?"

"John said he'd imprisoned them because the de Braose family had refused to pay some tribute. But William says that what made John mad with anger was that Matilda de Braose had publicly accused him of killing Arthur. He had to silence her, permanently."

I didn't know what to say or do. Even though she'd been so frank with me, I didn't feel right in heaping invective on her husband. She shivered and put her handkerchief to her eyes. I saw what an effort it was for her to tell me all this. Without thinking, I put my arm around her shoulders. She turned her face to me, and I saw tears running down her cheeks.

"How can I go on living with him, Hugh? Especially when he…" she stopped and wiped her eyes. "Forgive me for making you hear these awful stories. But I've begun, so I might as well go on. In some ways this part is the worst."

She looked straight ahead and spoke in a weary monotone.

"I've known for some time that John hasn't been faithful to me. Nowadays he hardly bothers to hide it. He says he still loves me, and I believe he does, though not like before. It would be impossible for me not to know about his affairs. Everybody in the court talks about them, and sometimes I think they do it when they know I can hear. Maybe because they think I should have a comeuppance. That's what Lady Anne says. She says I mustn't mind, that some people are just jealous because I'm the Queen."

She paused and took a deep breath, as though to gather strength to go on. I waited. The room was quiet except for a subdued murmur, the sounds of the busy city that surrounded us muffled by thick stone walls. I caught the scent of roses again and looked down to see that the silver bowl on the table was filled with delicate pink petals.

"I'm so lonely, Hugh. I have very few friends at court. Just Lady Anne and one or two others. Anne's daughter Adèle—you remember her, Hugh? She used to be my friend. But she's become quite distant. She's talking of going back to France. So I'm surrounded by people who don't wish me well. They spread evil gossip about me. It's not true, but of course it reaches John's ears. Then he gets in one of his tempers and calls me a wanton and a strumpet."

She was getting quite worked up and her voice rose in her outrage. "He even accused me of having an affair with William de Cantilupe. Apparently somebody saw William leaving the Queen's chambers late at night. Well, almost everybody at court knows William and Anne are lovers. He often visits her in her room next to mine. But there's no way to make John listen when he's in a rage."

"Does he use force on you?" I couldn't bear the thought of that brute striking my Isabella.

"Not yet. And truly, there are good times still, when he woos me the way he used to and gives me rich gifts. I've learned to live with the bad times."

Even in distress, she was so beautiful and brave! I wanted to comfort her, to tell her I would make everything right again. But what could I do?

"I'm so dreadfully sorry, Isabella." My arm was still around her shoulders, and I tightened my hold. She put her hand on mine and stroked it.

"I knew this would be hard for you to hear, Hugh. I'm afraid there's more. I've just heard another dreadful story of John's wickedness. He was taken with a young girl, the daughter of Robert FitzWalter, one of his barons. She was a virgin, of course; John is quite partial to virgins. He thought he'd seduce her. She wouldn't have him, so he tricked her parents into letting her go off with him. He kept her shut up in some out-of-the-way castle. She still wouldn't have him. He was so enraged that he had her poisoned, and sent her body back to her parents. He told them she'd eaten some spoiled eggs."

She began to cry again. "Hugh, she was only fourteen. The age I was when John and I met. If things had been different, that could have been my fate."

The first thing I knew she was in my arms, her whole body racked by sobs. I held her close and smoothed her hair. Gradually she became calmer. She turned her head and our eyes met. I'd never seen her look more vulnerable or more lovely. I couldn't help myself. I drew her closer and kissed her. Our lips met hesitantly at first, then I pressed her to me with all my pent-up passion. It was unbearably sweet, that kiss. I wanted it to go on forever.

She drew gently away and rested her head on my chest. I could hardly hear her whispered words.

"I'm so tired, so tired." A deep sigh shuddered through her body. She felt like a little wounded bird in my arms.

"My poor dear love, try to rest."

"Yes, yes. I must rest." She stood and staggered a little. "I will go lie down. Will you help me, Hugh?"

I took her arm and supported her as she walked into the bedroom. I lifted her—she was so light, so fragile!—and laid her on the bed. She lay there looking up at me, then stretched up her arms and pulled me to her. I couldn't resist that invitation. I forgot all the reasons against what was about to happen. I forgot my doubts. I felt only exultation that at last, Isabella was to be mine.

Isabella

1212

fter five days with Hugh at Angoulême I was purring like a cat full of cream. Everything had been heavenly. I wondered why I'd waited so long to find diversion with someone other than John. Hugh had been tender, considerate and grateful. After ten years of John's impetuous, demanding lovemaking—to be sure, I'd been a willing partner—it was like discovering a new, gentler land where I could live for a while, a land I hadn't known existed.

But I had to cut the idyll short or John would return from Wales and be upset if I wasn't there.

On my last morning we came down from the warmth and comfort of my tower room to wait in the courtyard while Hugh's horse was brought around. It was a still, bitterly raw day. We stood under a sky like the inside of a pewter bowl, where low clouds hung gloomily over us deciding whether to pour down rain. I held the fur collar of my robe tightly closed and shivered. Hugh's arm was around me.

"When will I see you again, my love?" he asked. "Surely you'll have more business in Angoulême before long?"

We'd talked only vaguely about the future. Every time Hugh tried to bring it up I changed the subject.

"I don't know, Hugh. I'm not sure I'd be able to arrange it again. I couldn't have come this time if John had been paying more attention, but he was so busy preparing for his Welsh campaign that he hardly noticed when I told him I was coming to see my mother."

"But Isabella! Now that we've found each other after all these years, we mustn't lose each other again. Please tell me you'll try soon to find an excuse to come. Ah, if only I could go to England! But your King would have my head off the minute I stepped ashore."

"Well, of course I'll try. But no matter what happens, we'll have the memory of this time together. I'll never forget it."

He moved away and stared at me, stricken and unbelieving.

"You talk as though this were the end, not the beginning."

"Surely, Hugh, you didn't think we could keep on meeting when conditions are so difficult. Let's just say goodbye and be grateful for what we've had."

The groom brought his horse. I didn't want us to part in anger. I moved close and pressed my body against his. I put my arms about his waist, but his thick leather surcoat was unyielding. So was he. I looked up at him, willing him to bend and kiss me. When he didn't, I whispered, "My dear Hugh, this is so hard, so hard. I do love you."

He turned from me and mounted his horse. I reached up to press his hand, but he quickly withdrew it. His face was closed now. As he wheeled his horse, I called after him, "Truly I'll try to come back."

I don't know if he heard me. Suddenly the heavens let down their torrents. I couldn't see him anymore through sheets of rain. I ran inside. When I reached the shelter of the hall I flung off my dripping cloak and stamped my foot. Why had he ruined everything by leaving in such a huff?

Back at Winchester I found that John was still away, which as far as I was concerned was just as well. I was cross at men in general and glad to give my attention to the children.

Joanna, not yet one, had begun to be colicky and given to wailing through the night. The nurse thought it would soothe her if her mother spent time with her. So I would take the unhappy baby up in my arms, rock her back and forth and sing softly to her, as I barely remembered someone doing for me when I was very young. I doubt it was my mother.

Often Joanna would stop crying and stare up at me during the night hours we spent together. I'd stare back into those wide-open dark-blue eyes. I'd lightly caress her silky, gold-tinted hair, half-fearful that even that would be too much for the little head that felt as fragile as an eggshell. Though I was fond of my sons, Joanna was my pet. Partly, I was worried about her health. Besides that, I'd heard of the special bond between mother and daughter. When I was a child, the bonding had been all on one side: mine. I wanted Joanna to know from the start that her mother loved her.

John, though, had never paid much attention to her unless her crying disturbed him. He was far more interested in the little princes.

On a chilly evening in December when winds were tearing around the towers and steeples of Winchester and everyone was predicting a serious snowstorm, I was in my snug quarters in the Queen's House, sitting by the hearth with Lady Anne. Anne was occupied with her needlework. I held Joanna, who was almost asleep.

"Soon I'll call for the nurse to take her away," said Anne.

We weren't talking much, comfortable with each other, both looking forward to bedtime.

I'd asked that only one of the candelabra be lit, so the room was almost dark except for the pool of light the candles shed on Anne and her work. Her fingers moved smoothly over the brilliant, iridescent red silk on which she was embroidering, in silver thread, the letter "J." It was to be a coverlet for Joanna's cradle.

I looked at her, thinking for the hundredth time how lucky I was to have had her by my side all these years. Her hair, once a warm brown, was now nearly gray. She wore it pulled back and coiled in a neat knot at the nape of her neck. She'd always been strong and slender, but lately she'd grown a little plump and was beginning to have a double chin. There were lines on her forehead. It was still a serene, good-humored face.

A pitch pocket in a log caught with an explosive crackle. The sudden blaze pushed the shadows back. Joanna murmured and frowned, then returned to her slumber.

I gave myself up to remembering my time with Hugh, dreaming of lying with my head on his breast and his arms about me. Had I been wrong to bring our affair to such an abrupt end? To continue it would have taken so much conniving, so much risk of discovery and a scandal, that it would wipe out all my pleasure. And wasn't the pleasure men brought their main attraction?

Which took me inevitably back to the subject of John. God knows he'd given me more than my share of pleasure. But now I saw him differently. It was like picking up a stone to find black beetles running about underneath it. Not only was I disillusioned. Deeper down was the barely acknowledged fear that my day might come too, to suffer from his unbridled cruelty.

I knew our marriage would have to go on with at least a superficial appearance of normality. I was determined to continue to be Queen of England. I'd never feel the same about John, but I couldn't let him know. I'd have to learn to play the part of the compliant wife.

Joanna was getting heavy in my arms. I laid her carefully in her cradle and sat on, staring into the fire, trying to imagine the future, almost drowsing.

All at once the face of James Tourville appeared in my mind's eye. James was a golden-haired, brawny young courtier who'd been an acquaintance for several years. I'd begun to notice how he always managed to be around when I went walking, when I went to chapel, when an outing on the river was organized. I was flattered but not surprised; many of the courtiers sought my favor. James, though, had seemed more assiduous than most in his pursuit, which was persistent if inconspicuous. Thinking of James, I began to see intriguing possibilities.

"Now what does that little smile mean, my lady?" Anne asked. Before I could answer we heard the thud of the outer door slamming shut, then hurried steps along the corridor that led to my chambers.

John came in like a rooster into the henhouse, ready to crow. When he saw I wasn't alone, he frowned, flung off his snow-flecked cloak and stood, arms akimbo, glaring.

"What kind of welcome is this to your husband you haven't seen for six weeks?" He'd ceased to be the strutting rooster and was a snarling bear. "Didn't you get my message that I'd arrive tonight? Why are you sitting in the dark?"

I stood, cast a quick glance at the cradle, and put my finger to my lips.

"John, I beg you, keep your voice down. We've just gotten Joanna to sleep. No, I received no message. I supposed you were still in Wales. But of course, now that you're here, we'll send for whatever you wish and welcome you home."

Anne rose and took up the child, who was beginning to whimper.

"Don't you want to say goodnight to your daughter?" I asked John.

"Not if she's going to start her caterwauling." He barely glanced at her.

Anne was moving toward the door.

"Lady Anne, send Peter to me, and for God's sake have someone come in to see to the fire and light the candles. It's like a tomb in here."

Anne stiffened and almost stopped. I knew what she was thinking: *I'm your lady's companion, not your servant to be ordered about like that.* But she merely said, "Yes, my lord," and left the room.

Now I was all alone with the cross bear.

Alone and, for the first time in our marriage, not eager to be in the same room with him, much less go to bed with him. The time had come to try my hand at play-acting.

After Peter had helped him out of his damp, muddy travel garments and brought him a dry robe and soft slippers, John sent for food and drink. He plumped himself down by the fire and set to demolishing a slab of beef and an apple tart.

As usual, his temper improved with a full stomach and a pint of wine. I wanted to give it time to improve even more. I didn't want any scenes.

I rose and said as sweetly as I could, "You're feeling better now, aren't you, my lord? I'll just go to the next room and prepare for bed."

In my bedchamber, I went to the door and sent for Hortense. When she'd helped me into my favorite nightrobe—deep blue wool, soft as a kitten's fur—I nestled in its enveloping folds while she brushed my hair.

John called out, "Do be quick, Isabella, what are you doing all this time? Come have a glass of wine with me by the fire."

He still sounded irritable. I dismissed Hortense and rejoined him. I could see how strained his face was, with deep lines from nose to jaw and a tenseness in his effort to smile. He poured me a cup of wine. It was almost as though he sensed some new reluctance on my part to be in his company.

"Come sit on my knee as you used to do, and let's tell each other how things have gone for us since we parted, a month ago and more. I've missed you so, my Isabella." I knew he meant it. I was probably the only person who had supported him unquestioningly, through thick and thin.

"But John, I'm not the girl I used to be. You'd be quite uncomfortable if I sat on your knee now."

"Let me be the judge of that." He pulled me to him. Hardly had I arrived in his lap than he groaned. I jumped up.

"It's that cursed gouty leg of mine, there it goes again. It's been bothering me for a week. Bring me that stool and I'll prop it up. Oh, what a sorry thing it is to grow old."

"Nonsense, John. You're only…" I had to stop and think. "Forty?"

"Forty-four, I fear." He brooded in silence for a few minutes. I settled in a chair by his side. I was sleepy, tired, and not eager for conversation. The fire was reduced to glowing embers, hardly more lively than I was.

John reached to take my hand. "It's been such a miserable few months, Isabella. I'm glad to be back with you, but I'll have to be off again. Nothing's gone well since that wicked de Braose family turned against me."

He'd never referred to Matilda de Braose and her tragic fate. Maybe he thought I didn't know of it. Maybe he didn't care if I did. He went on. He wasn't expecting any response from me; he only wanted to tell someone about his troubles.

"Before I even started to Wales to put down the rebellion there, I learned that a clutch of William de Braose's cronies were conspiring to see that I failed. I heard they intended to get rid of me and put another king in my place."

That got my attention. If John weren't King, I wouldn't be Queen.

"John! How dreadful! They couldn't do that, surely?"

"Of course not. I still have plenty of men who'll stand by me. But it was shocking to find out who these traitors were. Robert Fitz-Walter was one of them. So was Eustace of Vesci. Those names might not mean much to you, Isabella, but they've been men I could count on up to now."

He wasn't looking at me so he didn't see how startled I was at the name of Robert Fitz-Walter. Not mean anything to me? I'd never been able to get the story of John's murder of Fitz-Walter's daughter out of my mind. He must have heard my smothered gasp.

"I know, it's alarming to find out men you thought you could trust are turning against you. I suppose part of it is because of the interdict and the excommunication. I don't know, maybe I'll have to give in to the Pope and accept Stephen as Archbishop of Canterbury one of these days." Usually when the subject of the Pope came up John raged like a baited bear. Now he only sighed. He shifted his leg on the stool and slumped in his chair.

He was pathetic. I steeled myself not to feel sorry for him. Two of the men whom he'd cruelly wronged had turned against him. What else did he expect?

"And then there's Philip. My spies say he's getting ready to invade England. The effrontery! To invade England! But he'd find plenty of traitorous lords here, eager to collaborate. To say nothing of the commoners and the rabble. They'd probably come out with their pikes and their pitchforks, ready to march along and depose their king."

He drank from his goblet and sat glowering at the hearth. I could almost feel the sullenness and self-pity radiating from his body.

"It's all because of that foolish fellow up in Yorkshire who's making those ridiculous prophecies," he growled.

"What fellow in Yorkshire? What prophecies?"

"Oh, he's called Peter of Wakefield, a crazy hermit. Somehow he's persuaded the common folk that he's a messenger from on high. He insists that God appeared to him in a vision and told him that my reign will end after fourteen years. He doesn't say how."

"Well, I hope you don't take that seriously."

"I don't, but the ignorant country people he preaches to take it as gospel. The word's spreading: 'God will punish King John and take away his crown. He will remove him from his throne on Ascension Day in 1213.'"

He sat there brooding. I really did feel sorry for him now, so weighed down with so many troubles. They weren't all of his own making. Drowsy as I was, my brain must not have been shut down because an idea came to me.

"John, you need to get your people's minds off your problems with the church and your wicked barons. Why not steal a march on King Philip? Launch an attack on him before he knows what's happening! Regain the lands he took from you! A victory in France would silence all these enemies at home."

He sat up and looked at me in such surprise that I almost laughed. I didn't often venture an opinion as to matters of state.

"Not a bad suggestion, Isabella." He actually seemed to be considering it. Then he let out another of those sighs that were almost groans. "But it wouldn't work. I'd have the devil's own time getting an army together, what with all the disaffection. And the Royal Treasury is in poor shape so it would be impossible to hire enough mercenaries." He sank down in his chair again. His head was bowed so his chin nearly rested on his chest. I could hardly hear his next words.

"Maybe King Philip isn't really planning an invasion. Maybe someone will silence Peter of Wakefield ..." his voice trailed off. Neither of us said anything for a good five minutes. I could hardly keep my eyes open.

John gingerly removed his leg from the stool and stood up. He took my hand and pulled me to my feet.

"Come, Isabella, let's go to bed. At least we still have our love to console us, no matter what."

We were both very tired, very sleepy. Yet we consoled each other quite creditably. I had no need to pretend. As soon as we lay together and I felt John's touch, body took over from mind. I forgot everything else and gave myself to our lovemaking. I'd hoped that at the moment of climax I'd be able to imagine myself in Hugh's arms. But no. The face that appeared before me was that of James Tourville.

John
1212-1213

When Isabella told me that she'd like to go visit her mother in France I'd been surprised. Except for the very earliest days of our marriage, she'd hardly mentioned her mother. I supposed, though we never talked about it, that she'd turned against her parents when she learned of their part in the scheme to get her to marry me instead of Hugh. I still fumed when I thought of that busybody Queen Berengaria, and her part in the disclosure.

"Why this sudden concern for Countess Alix?" I'd asked.

"Well, she is getting on in years. And it seems, now that I have a daughter, I wish I'd been closer to my own mother. Maybe it isn't too late."

"Oh, very well. But don't be gone too long. This trip to Wales shouldn't take more than a month. I'll want to find you here when I return."

And I'd gone back to my preparations. But I harbored a faint suspicion about Isabella's sudden interest in her mother. She'd seemed withdrawn lately. I wondered if she could be pregnant again—but surely she would have told me. Just before I left I sent for my agent, Walter Mauclerk, and instructed him to cross to France and watch Isabella's movements.

I'd heard nothing from Walter by the time I returned to Winchester. I was so tired and so glad to be with Isabella again that I put my doubts aside. All I wanted was to rest in her arms and try to forget my worrisome kingdom.

All too soon I had to be off again, this time to Ireland. I was on a crucial mission. King Philip was now seriously threatening to invade England. I had to confer with my barons about how we'd repel him.

Thanks to William Marshal, good faithful William Marshal, my journey was fruitful. William had laid the groundwork for a rapprochement with several

Irish vassals who'd been at odds with me. We met at Offaly Castle in Leinster and came to an agreement quickly. After they left I stayed on in the hall—a rather mean, drafty chamber but the best the half-ruined old castle had to offer. At least the castellan had swept the floor and put down fresh rushes. And the fireplace drew properly. I dismissed my household knights and ordered supper to be brought to me there. I wished Isabella were with me so I could tell her about this happy resolution of at least one of my problems. She was still the only person I could bare my heart to.

Missing her and seeking consolation in wine, I was interrupted by a discreet knock on the door. Walter Mauclerk sidled in. Walter was my most skillful spy. He was so adept at looking nondescript that sometimes I hardly recognized him. He was neither tall nor short, fat nor thin, with an ordinary sort of face and brown hair that he wore medium long. I counted on him for my most secret, confidential missions.

"I apologize for interrupting you, my lord. But I thought you would want to hear what I've found out." In a voice without much expression and certainly without judgment he told me what he'd learned. The servants at the palace in Angoulême had been only too glad to report, for the right price, that Hugh de Lusignan had called on their mistress and had stayed for five days.

Walter left as unobtrusively as he'd come, before my anger could erupt.

I was mad with jealousy. So! My suspicions had been justified. Now I knew exactly what she'd been up to. It was a good thing for her that she wasn't nearby. I might have strangled her. All I could think of was confronting her with her infidelity.

Sitting there alone in front of the fire, gnawing on a greasy, overdone rib of lamb and washing it down with sour wine, I gloated as I imagined the encounter.

First, I attack:

"I accused you once before of having an assignation with Count Hugh of Lusignan in your palace at Angoulême, but you persuaded me that I was mistaken. Now I have proof that on your recent trip to France, instead of visiting your mother you met Hugh and the two of you spent five days together at Angoulême, despite your marriage vows. You are an adulteress, Isabella! Can you deny it?"

She tosses her golden curls and smiles sweetly. But what's this? She gives the conversation a turn I hadn't expected.

"Before I answer that impertinent question, my lord, let me ask one of my own. Can you deny that you have seduced the Baroness of Vesci, the Countess of Granville, Lady Margaret of Haworth, two of my ladies-in-waiting, and the milkmaid at Gloucester Castle?"

She has a point there, no question. Even before Isabella had become less fond of my company I'd often sought pleasure elsewhere. I'd made no effort to hide my affairs. Most of my partners were willing. If some demurred I'd generally find a means of persuasion, such as threats of retribution to their husbands or fathers. What's the point of being a king if you don't take advantage of your power?

Nevertheless I continue the discussion.

"Might I remind you, my Queen, that if you had not seemed so unwilling of late to share your bed with me, I might have been more faithful to you?"

No smiles this time. Each word is bitten off as though she were attacking a dry crust of bread with her sharp little teeth.

"Conversely, my King, if you had been more faithful to me I might have been more willing to share my bed with you."

I sighed and adjusted my throbbing leg on its stool. She'd won, for now. I decided it might be best to keep quiet and try to forget. A time would come when the knowledge of her affair with Hugh could prove a useful tool.

Yet in spite of everything, I thought that if I could only go back to the days when Isabella and I were so in love, so trusting of each other, I'd give half my kingdom. And even now, I looked forward almost feverishly to seeing her again, to finding solace in her embrace.

During the long, tedious return journey from Ireland I had plenty of time to worry and plenty to worry about besides an unfaithful wife. Reluctantly, I had to admit to myself that even with the support of a good number of my barons we wouldn't be able to withstand Philip's invasion army. I'd have to find some other way to put off the evil day. Maybe it was time at last to yield something to the Pope.

When I reached London I was glad that Isabella was still in Winchester. I wasn't sure I'd be able to stick to my resolve to avoid a violent confrontation. Besides, I had to do a great deal in a short time.

First I sent an urgent message to Pope Innocent that I was ready to negotiate. He wasted no time in dispatching his papal legate, Pandulfo. I was waiting with a party of my knights to greet him when he disembarked at Dover.

I saw a man of slight build, about my height but somewhat stooped—perhaps from years of nodding and bowing to the Pope his master. He was black-haired like me, but beardless. His face had a chronically sour expression as though he had bitten into a lemon. When he smiled, which wasn't often, it was more sardonic than amused. I took to him at once. Here was a man I could deal with, unlike the oily, pompous high lords of the church the Pope had sent as emissaries before. Pandulfo was only a subdeacon. When I knew him better I realized he was more interested in quietly furthering the Pope's projects by any means necessary than in making a show of power.

I had horses ready. Together we rode up from the pier to Dover Castle. That very night, in the cold great hall of the massive stone keep that my father had built, we came up with our plan. I'd already decided I'd have to give in. All I needed were the best terms possible.

I agreed to accept Stephen of Langton as Archbishop of Canterbury. I agreed to reinstate the clergy I'd exiled. Most painful, I agreed to repay the church the moneys I'd confiscated.

The next and final provision was my suggestion.

"My lord Pandulfo," I said, "what if I were to cede my kingdom to God and to Pope Innocent III? And what if Innocent were then to make me responsible for governing the kingdom as his vassal? This should please His Holiness. And when they've had time to take it in, it should please my people. They'd be saved from the French invasion. No Christian ruler would dare invade a land under apostolic protection."

Pandulfo's thin lips twisted in his version of a smile.

"Excellent! This was the outcome the Holy Father hoped for. I was empowered to suggest it to you if you didn't propose it yourself. I believe we are now in complete accord."

All that remained was to inform a few of my most powerful nobles and obtain their guarantee of my pledge. The Pope had particularly asked for that assurance, though I told Pandulfo I thought it unnecessary.

"Why wouldn't I keep my word, with so much at stake?"

"His Holiness requires it of all his vassals on whom he confers lands in fief. Especially those who have in the past not kept their promises to him and whom he has had to chastise." Pandulfo's eyes bored into mine. I took his meaning and said nothing more on the subject.

My four guarantors agreed at once: anything to end the misery we'd been living in for the past half-dozen years under the interdict and my excommunication. Beyond those four, not a soul knew of my plans until I called an assembly in the Church of the Temple in London.

I deliberately chose this modest church rather than Westminster Abbey because I didn't want this to be seen as a grand ceremonial occasion. It was more of a business transaction. No incense, no chanting, no ritual. I selected one of the kingdom's lesser archbishops to preside: Henry of Dublin. Besides my four guarantors, I'd invited a small company of peers and clergy to witness the proceedings.

On May 15, 1213 Archbishop Henry stood in the church's bleak, circular nave. I knelt before him on the bare, cold stone floor. I wore my customary black and my crown but no jewels, rings, or cross. The archbishop, in contrast, was splendidly garbed in a scarlet cassock with a white stole. His white mitre soared above his head like the sail of a ship.

Kneeling there, my knees already sore from the rough stone, I looked around at the thick rough-hewn walls of this church the Templars had built, so like a fortress that it could have withstood a Saracen siege. I saw how the walls bristled with carved heads of demons, snarling beasts and fantastic creatures. Not an angel to be seen. Perhaps that's just as well, I thought. Our business here has more to do with skullduggery than with holiness.

The archbishop read from a document I'd given him. His voice rather resembled the bray of a donkey, but it was a donkey with good lungs. His words carried to every listener.

"These are the words of King John:

We have deeply offended our Holy Mother the Church and it will be hard to draw on the mercy of Heaven. Therefore, we would humble ourselves, and without constraint, of our own free will, by the consent of our barons and high justiciars, we give and confer on God, on the Holy Apostles St. Peter and St. Paul, on our Mother the Church and on Pope Innocent III and his Catholic successors, the whole kingdom of England and Ireland, with all their rights and dependencies for the remission of our sins; henceforth we hold them as a fief, and in token thereof we swear allegiance in presence of Pandulfo, Legate of the Holy See."

Behind me I could almost hear the stunned silence of the assembly. I imagined their open-jawed amazement at what they'd just heard. Pandulfo was sitting near me on the throne I'd ordinarily occupy. I looked up to catch his eye while the archbishop spoke. I winked. Since he was facing the audience he couldn't reply in kind, but I knew from his narrowed eyes and the merest twitch of his lip that we were of like mind: "Haven't we given them a fine surprise!"

Playing my role as penitent son of the church to the hilt, I took off my crown and handed it to Pandulfo. He held it up for all to see: the gleaming gold coronet with its rubies and emeralds and its five upstanding fleur-de-lis inlaid with pearls. He placed it on a cushion on the table at his side. He stood to address the spectators, who had begun to murmur in their confusion. He raised his hand for silence. His black cassock and stole couldn't rival the archbishop's brilliance. His words, however, were even more startling.

"In the name of His Holiness, Innocent III, God's vicar on earth, we accept the kingdom of King John. Taking account of his penitence and his sincere desire for forgiveness, we name him vassal of The Holy See, with responsibility to govern the kingdom in the Pope's name. We abjure him to govern wisely, in accordance with the tenets of the church and in such manner that all his acts will redound to the glory of God. In token of the Pope's faith that King John will obediently carry out these admonitions, we restore to him his crown, which he may wear so long as he remains a faithful and obedient son of the church."

More murmurs and gasps, while Pandulfo replaced the crown on my head.

The archbishop concluded with a "God bless us all" or some such parting message. The ceremony was over. The lords and bishops hurried out to spread the strange story. The good people of London would have a lot to conjecture about.

The next day Isabella rejoined me at Westminster. I was still so puffed up with what I'd accomplished, and she was so amazed at the news, that any coolness in our relationship was thawed by our shared rejoicing that we were still King and Queen of England. Late in the afternoon we left the palace to walk by the river along with several of our courtiers. Isabella's hand was tucked in my arm and her face turned to me while I described the events in the Church of the Temple in every detail. She hung on my words, an adoring wife. It was easy to forget that I'd been recently so enraged at her.

"How I wish I'd been there, John! To see you humbling yourself, then getting your crown back! Couldn't you have sent for me to come?"

"No, my love, that would have made it seem a state occasion, with my Queen at my side. But I have a mind to invite the world—or at least the world that resides on this isle—to rejoice with us at our improved fortunes. You'll certainly be at my side for that."

On Ascension Day I held a grand celebration on the Kentish Downs. The crown that the mad hermit had predicted I'd lose this day sat comfortably on my head. I lounged on my throne in front of my royal pavilion. It was a bright breezy day, the kind that England can produce to reward us for surviving the dreary winter. Daisies had popped into bloom on the greensward. I could hear the snapping and fluttering of the Plantagenet pennant that flew from the tent's peak, as though the three golden lions were trying to claw their way off of their red field and join the festivities. I surveyed the scene before me. Tables were laden with every kind of meat and fowl and pudding, vats of wine and barrels of ale. Wandering minstrels were tootling and plucking and sawing away. Lords and ladies, bishops and even an archbishop or two sat at the tables partaking with gusto.

Looking beyond the merrymakers, I saw an endless expanse of green, where the downs rolled on to Dover. I could almost imagine I saw the Channel. But it was only a low-lying cloud shining in the sun. No matter. I knew the Channel was there. And I knew that on the French side, King Philip's armies and navies, primed to invade England, had been halted by a formidable if invisible barrier. If they invaded now they'd be attacking a papal fief. To do so would incur the Pope's wrath, perhaps his excommunication. For Philip it wouldn't be worth the risk. Pandulfo had promised when he left that he'd make a point of seeking King Philip out and assuring him that his cause was lost.

I looked around for Isabella, who'd been sitting beside me but had risen a few minutes ago to speak to friends in the crowd. I caught sight of her at once, chatting with a cluster of lords and ladies. She was wearing a gown new to me, the same color as the cherries that were ripening in the Kent orchards. Her hair hung in ringlets like coils of spun gold. She was laughing. She looked up and caught my eye and blew me a kiss. I thought in my euphoria that I could forgive her much if she continued to be the lovely, loving wife she was at this moment.

But who was this—this tall man who took her arm and led her away? He looked familiar but I couldn't place him. They stopped. He spoke earnestly while she stood listening, smiling. She looked up at him with the same coquettish come-hither invitation I'd seen so often when we were first married. He leaned down and she raised her face to his, but at the last minute turned her head so his kiss landed in the air instead of on her lips. It was so quick that I almost missed it. She laughed and gave him a little push. He went one way, she returned to the throng.

"Peter!" I roared. My man was busy in the pavilion behind me, preparing a table with my repast. He jumped at my shout and came running.

"Peter! Who is that tall yellow-haired man, just sitting down at the farthest table to the left?"

Peter squinted into the sun, found the man I referred to, and said, "Why that's one of your Norman knights, my lord. Surely you've seen him around your court this past year. That's James Tourville."

Isabella

1213

When we came back to Westminster Palace after John's extravagant celebration in Kent, I felt uneasy and adrift. It was as though, having fallen out of love with John, I no longer had a center to my life.

I asked Lady Anne: "Have you heard whether the English have a term for what we call *joie de vivre*? I find myself strangely lacking in it these days."

"I doubt if they have a word for it, since they so seldom display it. Too bad we aren't back at Lusignan with Countess Alice. Remember how she'd brew up a spring tonic when we felt out of sorts? It tasted so horrid that we forgot all our other troubles."

I smiled at the memory of good Aunt Alice, so solicitous. Then I fell to brooding again. Should I pursue my flirtation with James Tourville? It enlivened my spirits somewhat, though it hadn't gone very far. He was heartbreakingly handsome, but so callow and predictable that there wasn't much sport in the relationship.

John was busy arranging his settlement with the church and planning a new expedition to France. We were civil with each other and got along well enough, though we seldom shared a bed. When we did I managed to make a good pretense at enjoying the experience. I didn't always have to pretend. Much as I fought against it, his touch could still excite me.

Sometimes at dinner in the great hall or during a service in the chapel, I'd catch him staring at me as a hangman stares at his hapless victim. I'd shiver when I saw those black eyes fixed on me. I supposed he'd learned something of my meeting with Hugh. I didn't care. If he brought that up, I had a long list of misdeeds I could accuse him of.

At the end of September the new papal legate, Cardinal Nicholas of Tusculum, came to London to prepare to withdraw the interdict. England was to be restored to the Communion of the Church. This required endless meetings at Westminster Palace. First out of boredom, then out of curiosity, I attended many of them.

I'd met the first legate only briefly and was expecting another like him. Cardinal Nicholas turned out to be the exact opposite of Subdeacon Pandulfo. He was plump, outgoing, and so affable that John, even at his sourest, soon became cheerful in his company.

Their first task was to see that new clerics were elected to fill all the vacant sees and abbeys. This could have been a delicate project because John wanted only men he approved of. I'm sure he expected arguments from Nicholas. But it seemed the Pope had instructed his legate to be conciliatory (and why not, since he had so easily won suzerainty over the kingdoms of England and Ireland!). All of John's choices were accepted.

Negotiating the financial terms of John's capitulation to the Pope was a little thornier. How John hated to part with money! After a good deal of hammering away at each other, the two came to a sort of agreement. It was at the end of a long, heavy meal in the grand dining hall of Westminster Palace. Most of the diners had wiped the last crumbs of plum tart off their chins and departed for naps. The nurse had taken off the two youngest children, Richard and Joanna, long ago. Of John's council, only Geoffrey Fitz-Peter the justiciar, William de Cantilupe and Brian de Lisle remained. Sir Brian had taken over from Robert de Thorneham the year before as chief household steward.

I was still there, as was little Henry. John had decided it would be educational for him to be present at some of these meetings.

"It's none too soon for him to see what it's like to be a king. He spends too much time with you women. Time to put some backbone in him."

So here was six-year-old Prince Henry, dressed in a fine red velvet tunic, his curly black hair well brushed, doing his best to pay attention and stay awake. He sat between Cardinal Nicholas and me. Over the clatter of the servants taking away empty dishes and mopping up pools of spilled soup and wine, I heard the cardinal's genial voice.

"An excellent meal, my lord king. I've never had such succulent goose in Rome. I thought I detected a whiff of tarragon. I must talk to your cooks and ask them what herbs and basting seasoning they use."

"Yes, I suppose it was passable," said John. He was far more interested in quantity than quality of his provender, and was doubtless surprised at Nicholas's enthusiasm for anything as ordinary as roast goose.

The cardinal put a hand over his mouth to smother a barely audible belch and spoke. I loved his voice. It was like warm treacle flowing over smooth pebbles.

"Well, we have more weighty matters than that to discuss, don't we? I believe we're close enough to an agreement to see the interdict lifted within the next few months. Have you made your final decision on the amount you are willing to pay the bishops?"

Henry looked up at me and whispered, "Why does my father have to pay the bishops? Don't they work for the Pope and doesn't the Pope pay them?"

Cardinal Nicholas overheard. He patted Henry on the head. "A good question, Prince Henry. Let me explain. The bishops are indeed responsible to the archbishops, who are responsible to the Pope. But the Pope doesn't actually pay them. Like any other barons in England, the bishops depend on their woodlands and their farms for money to live on and to do their good works. Many of them lost a great deal of land during the last few years, as well as the castles they lived in. So King John has promised to make it up to them."

Henry, very serious, had kept his eyes on the cardinal's face during this explanation.

"Thank you, sir. I think I understand."

I sent a grateful look to Nicholas. He'd said not a word about how John had confiscated the bishops' castles and farms and cut down their woodlands. Henry was a little young to learn the unpleasant side of John's way of ruling. I was glad to let him believe that his father was making recompense out of the goodness of his heart.

"Yes, well, as to the amount," said John. "I've decided that we'll offer them one hundred thousand marks. And I think you agree, Sir Geoffrey?"

Geoffrey Fitz-Peter nodded his grizzled old head but said nothing. He looked tired, hoping the meeting would soon end. I'd never liked him, not since the days when he'd done his best to ignore me when I presided at the council meetings. Now though, looking at his stooped back and his gray, drawn face I had to admit he had served John—and before John, Richard—with complete loyalty, for decades. John had precious few loyal men about him now.

Nicholas considered. He turned to his small companion and asked him, with all the gravity of a potentate consulting his most trusted adviser, "What do you think, Prince Henry? Is that a good offer?"

Henry screwed up his face, thinking. Then, in his piping little voice, "It does seem like a great deal of money. But if the bishops can prove that they really need it, I think they should have it."

Nicholas smiled and thanked him.

"I agree with Prince Henry, my lord. The amount seems ample to me. But the bishops and the Pope will have the final say. I'll inform them of our agreement and tell you their response."

So the matter was settled. I strongly doubted if John meant to pay the entire hundred thousand. As it turned out, he didn't. When the interdict was at last lifted the next year, he'd shilly-shallied and procrastinated so successfully that he was out only thirty thousand marks. He never got around to paying the rest.

With his papal relations taking such a satisfactory turn, John could now devote himself to resuming the war with Philip. The very thought of more battling wearied me. After fourteen years as Queen of England, it seemed to me that the one constant was preparing for war, going to war or planning the next war.

John had already told me I must accompany him to France. He was still unwilling to have me far from him. When things went well, he needed someone to hear his bragging. When they didn't, he needed an audience for his angry complaints.

It was the former he was full of on a late fall day in 1213.

We were at Winchester, John's favorite of all his royal residences. I liked it too, chiefly because of my elegant private lodgings in the Queen's House. I often wished Queen Eleanor were still alive so I could show her that I too had elevated taste.

John had just returned from Oxford where he'd held a council of war to make final plans for the Continental expedition. He found me walking in the gardens with the children and a group of my ladies. It was the first halfway fine day after a dreary week of steady, depressing rain. I'd felt the need for fresh air and knew it would do the children good. The paths were still damp underfoot, the trees were dripping, and a few bedraggled chrysanthemums drooped in discouragement. Only the herb garden with its vigorous stand of rosemary showed any spirit. Even when the sun escaped from scudding clouds it didn't send down much warmth. I held three-year-old Joanna's hand while she skipped along at my side. Lady Anne was trying to keep the little princes in check without much success. Richard had decided he was a horse and trotted about, whinnying. Henry entered into the game, but only so he could push Richard down and leap onto his back.

"If you're a horse why can't I ride you?"

"Because I'm a warhorse and you're not a warrior," Richard squealed. "Besides I can run very fast so you can't catch me!" He galloped off to hide behind the dovecote. Henry screamed after him, "Yes I can! Just you wait!"

John walked out from the palace into this bedlam. He frowned.

"Henry, don't shout so! Isabella, what are you thinking of, bringing them out in such foul weather? Come in. I want to talk to you."

"Yes, and there's something I want to tell you too. I'll come soon, after they've had a little more time to play. The more they're allowed to run about, the better they'll behave once they're inside."

He harrumphed and stomped back into the palace.

When I joined him in his chamber in the tower, his clerk was just leaving, carrying a box of parchments, pens and inkwells. John liked the view from this room. I found him standing by the window looking out at the huge golden weathercock atop the cathedral belfry, glowing in a rare beam of late-afternoon sun. He glanced at me, then continued to watch while a robed brother climbed into the belfry and began pulling at the heavy bell-ropes. Four mighty peals rang out, signaling to the whole city that at least at this moment, all was well in God's heaven and in our world here below. John smiled, then settled himself in his big chair before a table that was littered with long strips of parchment dense with writing.

"Now Isabella, you must sit here and look at what we've put together in the way of support. These are the names of men who have pledged themselves to join us against Philip, and the amounts of money they're prepared to provide."

I sat beside him. It was an impressive array. How had John inveigled so many to join his cause? On closer examination I saw few familiar names—only a half-dozen of the English barons who should have rallied around. Instead there was entry after entry like "From Wessex, twenty freemen" and "From Kent, fifteen freemen and forty-two hired soldiers." It looked as though John's army would be mostly mercenaries and lowborn soldiers. Then my eyes fell on another list. It was led by the name of Otto the Emperor of Germany, John's nephew, followed by others almost as distinguished: counts from Flanders and Holland, dukes from Lorraine and Brabant, nobles from Poitou and Boulogne.

"Mercy on us, John, are all these really pledged to you? How have you managed this?" I was truly amazed.

He smirked. "Bribes and flattery, mostly. Keep reading, Isabella."

I did. At the bottom of the list, scrawled in John's hand, was the name of Hugh le Brun de Lusignan.

Frozen-faced, I stared at it. I felt as though my heart had stopped beating for a moment. John watched my reaction.

"Surprised, eh? How did I lure your dear friend Hugh to join my ranks? Shall I tell you?"

I couldn't speak for shock and confusion.

"Actually, he hasn't yet done so, but I am confident he will. I sent Walter Mauclerk over to track him down. Walter is familiar with Hugh's habits and whereabouts by now. This is exactly what I told Walter to say to Hugh: 'If you will support King John in his wars with King Philip, and encourage the rest of the Lusignans to do the same, King John will offer to your son and heir, Hugh, the hand of his daughter, Joanna. As advance on her dowry he will present you with Saint-Onge and the Island of Oléron. With the Lusignans' present holdings, this will give you a domain far larger than Philip's Ile de France, as well as ports on the Atlantic Ocean.' I told Walter to tell Hugh to discuss this with the rest of the clan and that I'd expect their answer before our forces arrive in France."

He folded his arms and waited, self-satisfied and patient as a cat that's maneuvered a mouse into a corner.

I didn't know where to begin. Anyway, what was the point of objecting? Hugh would probably agree. He'd think I'd plotted this with John, glad for a chance to humiliate him further after I'd broken off our affair.

But I couldn't let John think I approved.

"My lord, why wasn't I consulted? I am the Queen and the child's mother. I believe that I have a say in her future."

"You weren't consulted because I knew you'd object. You'd have nattered on that she's only three, that it's far too soon to think of her marriage. You might even have said it was unseemly to betroth your daughter to the son of your former fiancé. I myself think it's a brilliant solution to several of my problems." His lips curled in a grim smile while he waited to see if I'd go on arguing. I believe he was disappointed when without a word I rose and left the room.

Back in my own chambers it was blessedly quiet. I'd made myself a comfortable, semi-private little retreat, a screened corner before a tall arched window. I settled here and looked out across the gardens where we'd just been walking. On the far side, against the high castle walls, a row of poplars flaunted their golden leaves—all too soon they'd fall.

My fury at John had given way to melancholy. I'd intended to give him my own news. But he'd driven it out of my mind with his insane proposal to marry Joanna to young Hugh. Now, to spite him, I decided to keep it to myself for a time.

I'd just discovered that I was pregnant.

John would have been pleased. Another child to marry off. I was far from pleased. I didn't look forward to months of discomfort, discontent and unloveliness.

My brooding was interrupted when Anne knocked and came in.

"I didn't know you'd returned, my lady. I'll have them come stir up the fire."

"Thank you, Anne. And a brazier for my feet? I think I'll sit here a little longer."

"Of course. You do look a bit tired. Would you like a bowl of broth?"

"No, thank you. You're very good."

"I'll be off then. Oh, I almost forgot. I was asked to give you this." She handed me a small pouch of purple silk tied with a rose-colored velvet ribbon. I could tell from her tone that she disapproved of whatever it was.

When she'd left I opened it. Inside were a heart-shaped silver brooch and a note.

"My lady Queen, you have been avoiding me! Therefore I send you my heart, in hopes that you will take pity and I may be restored to your friendship. May I meet you somewhere, anywhere, soon? Yours, James Tourville."

What a foolish lad! was my first thought. It was followed at once by *Well, why not? I need something to take my mind off John and his maddening ways. I've earned a little diversion. And James has earned a reward for his devotion.*

Before I had time to think I walked to my writing table, found a pen and an inkwell, and scrawled at the bottom of the note:

"Yes. Here. Now." I put it back in its silken pouch.

When the man came to see to the fire, I handed him the pouch and asked him to find James Tourville and deliver it to him.

Within fifteen minutes James knocked on my door. He looked disappointed to find me fully dressed. Perhaps he'd envisioned me lying languidly on my bed, waiting for my lover, needing no coaxing to yield to him. I suppose being so extraordinarily handsome, he'd never had to learn that a lady likes to be wooed. His previous conquests had doubtless been women who couldn't wait for him to bed them.

So our lovemaking found him more of a pupil than a conqueror. But I will say he was a willing and eager pupil. I decided it would be instructive for him, and amusing for me, to continue his education.

I felt, though, that I should caution him. As he was leaving, after kissing my hand most properly, I asked him, "Have you thought, James, of the danger you're risking if John should find out about you? He's insanely jealous and can be incredibly cruel."

"No matter. One hour with you, my lady fair, is more precious than life itself."

I recognized this as a line from one of the troubadours' ballads. If he insisted on being so foolishly romantic, I couldn't help it. I'd warned him.

John
1214

Know you that we and the loyal followers who came with us to Poitou are safe and well, and that, by God's grace, we have already taken steps to confuse our enemies and bring joy and satisfaction to our friends. On the Sunday before Mid-Lent we besieged the castle of Milécu, which had been armed against us, and on the following Tuesday we captured it.

John

I sent that message home to my justiciar and other officers in England on March 8, 1214, less than a month after landing on the shores of France. To my surprise, King Philip hadn't ventured out to do battle with me though we had a few skirmishes with his son, Prince Louis.

Walter Mauclerk had had no trouble in convincing Hugh le Brun that a betrothal of his son and Joanna was an excellent idea, in view of what I was offering in exchange. It's amazing what the promise of a near-doubling of your vassals' holdings can accomplish. At the end of May I could still send cheerful dispatches:

On Trinity Sunday we were at Parthenay when the Counts of La Marche and Eu, together with Geoffrey of Lusignan, did homage and fealty to us. Having already discussed the marriage of our daughter Joanna and the son of the Count of La Marche, we now granted this to him…Now, thank God, we are ready to attack our chief enemy, the King of France, beyond Poitou. We inform you that you may rejoice at our success.

John

I'd arranged to meet the Lusignans at Parthenay, not far from their ancestral domain. For some years I'd been sending subsidies to the local lord, who'd remained a faithful vassal in spite of the blandishments of King Philip. He'd used them well in building and strengthening the fortifications and in providing lodgings for the pilgrims who stopped here on their way to Santiago de Compostela in Spain. Entering the town I looked around with satisfaction at his work. It was gratifying to see how my patronage had put the fear of King John into the hearts of my enemies, and gratitude to King John into those of the faithful.

Our large party rode in great ceremony through the massive city gate and along the Pilgrims' Road that went straight through the city to the Citadel. Three heralds rode before me, one bearing the Plantagenet pennant and two blowing lustily on their horns to clear the townsfolk and the countryfolk out of our way. My palfrey was caparisoned in red and gold. I wore my crown and my jeweled signet ring. My long black cape, richly embroidered with golden lions, fell in regal folds almost to the ground. Isabella rode beside me, nearly as splendid. Her sky-blue cape glittered with silver fleur-de-lis, always a sure reminder to any doubters that the kings of England were also monarchs of a good part of France.

As we neared the entrance to the Citadel, I laughed when a bumpkin had to leap aside to avoid my horse's hooves. He was agile as a court dancer. How comical he looked, watching while his basket of turnips and onions spilled over the muddy cobblestones and were pounded into mush by the riders who came after. I looked at Isabella to share my amusement, but she was staring straight ahead, her face set in the same stiff, uncommunicative expression I'd seen so often since we'd left England.

She hadn't wanted to come. She'd told me she should stay quietly at home to await the birth of our child, who was due in the fall. I'd reminded her that she'd traveled about during her previous pregnancies with no ill effects. She'd countered that those travels had been in England, a relatively peaceful land, not embroiled in strife and open warfare as France now was. Running out of arguments, I'd simply ordered her to come with me.

"You'll be safe enough with our hundreds of armed knights protecting us at all times, and with your own ladies to see to your needs. It will do you good to get away from the court and all the distractions." I think she knew what I meant. I hadn't any proof yet that she was having an affair with James Tourville, but I was watching carefully.

We reached the Citadel walls and stopped at the Church of Saint-Pierre, just outside. I'd decided it was appropriate to hold both of the ceremonies I'd planned here, rather than in the castle. Coupling the oaths of fealty of the Lusignans with the betrothal, and in a holy place, would suggest that both were blessed by God. The small courtyard in front of the church filled quickly with horsemen; lords and ladies dismounting, conversing and exclaiming; knights noisily unbuckling their armor and tossing it to their squires; and the odors of sweaty beasts and horse dung. I helped Isabella to dismount, then took Joanna down from the arms of her nurse and set her on the ground. She looked up at me wondering what she should do. She was wearing a long-skirted ruby-red gown that covered her from neck to wrist to toe. She looked very small and very young, more like a doll than a little girl. I hadn't bothered to explain to her what lay ahead of her. I assumed Isabella had.

Isabella's gown was the same color as Joanna's. She wore a gold circlet that sparkled with pearls. She bent down to place a similar circlet on Joanna's head. The child put her hand up to touch the circlet carefully, and looked up at her mother with a shy, proud smile. For a moment I was transfixed by the beauty of the picture: mother and daughter, both in glowing red, both golden-haired and blue-eyed, smiling at each other. My heart gave a little lurch. It was a long time since Isabella had looked at me with such love.

She took Joanna's hand and we went into the church. The bishop greeted us. He looked quite young to be a bishop and extremely nervous, twisting his hands together and searching the crowded nave for any signs of impropriety or candelabra that hadn't been lit. He'd probably never had a visit from royalty. While I conferred with him, explaining the order I wished for the ceremonies, I looked around. The church was filling rapidly. The Lusignans had arrived before us, some twelve or fifteen men, standing at the front on the right. There was Hugh le Brun, Count of la Marche, looking a little older and stouter than when I'd last seen him when I took him prisoner at Mirebeau. On the whole he was the same bushy-haired, earnest-faced man I remembered though his brown hair was graying. The tall young man next to him must be his son, the future Hugh X. I had no trouble recognizing Geoffrey and Ralph. I'd had the satisfaction of receiving their fealty long ago, just after I inherited the throne. Then they had treacherously gone over to King Philip. And now they were returning to the Angevin fold.

Isabella and Joanna were seated at the front on the left, with her ladies standing nearby. Neither then nor throughout the afternoon did I see a single glance exchanged between my queen and Hugh le Brun.

While our party of knights, nobles and ladies found places, the bishop led me to the dais above the nave where I sat in one of the two thrones that had been set up there. I gave the signal to the trumpeters who were waiting at the outer entrance. They let out a fanfare that, though more like a contest than a duet, did get attention. Chatter and scuffling of feet stopped.

The bishop uttered a blessedly brief prayer, than gave a little bow in my direction. I spoke from my throne.

"My lord bishop, lords and ladies, loyal subjects both English and French, greetings. We are here, first, to welcome back as vassals of the English King the noble leaders of the Lusignan clan. We are gratified that they have seen the wisdom of taking this step. We assure them that so long as they remain faithful and true, combating their king's enemies as though they were their own, so will we support them in the defense of their lands against all assaults. Sir Geoffrey, Seigneur of Moncontour and Vouvant; Ralph, Count of Eu; and Hugh, Count of La Marche, come forward."

The three men stepped up to stand before me. Normally a vassal kneels, but I didn't ask this. My purpose wasn't to make them grovel, which would only have added to their resentment. I was simply interested in their public pledge of loyalty.

I turned to Geoffrey first. I was glad I wasn't standing up because he would have towered over me like an oak over a sapling. I held out my hands. Geoffrey placed his two hands within mine, as is the custom when a vassal swears fealty to his lord.

"Do you swear to serve King John as your liege lord, providing him with aid and counsel, so long as he stands by you, protects you and deals fairly with you?"

"I do so swear." His voice was gruff. He looked into my face almost defiantly. I knew how much it cost him to give up the enmity that had fueled his resistance all these years. Still, he swore.

So did Ralph, with less bravado.

So did Hugh. If I'd thought Geoffrey a simmering cauldron of rage, Hugh was nearly boiling over. His swarthy face was mottled red. He hesitated a moment before placing his hands in mine, as though he had to force them. How the man hated me! Yet like his uncle and his brother he was a realist.

I nodded to the bishop, who came forward. The three Lusignans knelt and bowed their heads while the bishop blessed each in turn, in the name of the Holy Trinity. They stepped down and resumed their places.

I signaled the trumpeters to send out their triumphant tune. The pause must have done them good because this time they nearly succeeded in playing the same notes at the same time.

Now it was time for the betrothal. This was the bishop's business. He asked Isabella to bring Joanna up to the dais and told young Hugh to stand beside her, both facing him. Isabella sat on the throne by my side. The bishop droned on about fidelity and marriage vows and chastity. The onlookers smiled and whispered, enchanted with the exquisite little girl and her tall fiancé.

Isabella kept her eyes fixed on her daughter as though willing her to be brave and not cry. Joanna, standing stiffly, stared back at her wide-eyed, doing her best to be the good girl that Isabella had doubtless told her she must be. Every now and then Isabella would glance up at Hugh, as though assessing him to see if he would make a good husband for her child. He looked satisfactory enough to me: more handsome than his father, tall and well-built, with the same brown hair but less unruly. He too looked as though he were trying to be the good boy his father had told him he must be. His expression was good-natured, though it hadn't been his idea for a thirty-year-old man to become engaged to a four-year-old girl.

And still, though he was almost in front of her and not ten feet away, Isabella sent not even a fleeting look at Hugh le Brun.

The bishop was nearly finished.

"Now, Hugh de Lusignan and Joanna of England, do you promise to be true to each other until the day of your marriage?"

Hugh's "I do" rang out loud and clear, but Joanna's was almost a whisper. By now she looked close to tears, confused and frightened. Isabella rose and took her hand, preparing for our procession out of the church.

A pair of vergers in red robes with white stoles swung censers, sending the sweet spicy odor of incense wafting through the church. A small choir had materialized from somewhere. The bishop prayed to God to bless this union. While the choir sang a closing anthem we all marched out. The trumpeters, thank heaven, were no longer in evidence. Perhaps on hearing the choir they realized they'd met their betters.

Out in the courtyard while I waited for the rest of the company I looked up at the elaborately carved figures on the church façade. I was intrigued by a stone horseman holding his spear high. He might have been going into battle full of brave hopes, or returning victorious. A fitting symbol, I thought. I'd just won my battle with the powerful Lusignans—luring them away from King Philip and to my side. And now I was about to engage Philip in a battle to regain my lost French kingdoms. I had no doubt I'd emerge victorious.

Then just two months later came the Battle of Bouvines.

I wasn't there. I was in La Rochelle, a seaport far to the south, trying to rally my forces after a humiliating desertion by my Poitivin barons. They'd turned tail when they heard that Prince Louis was advancing with a great army. I'd sent for reinforcements from England so I could take up the fight again but none had arrived.

Meantime, my allies were preparing to meet King Philip in pitched battle, north of Paris. They were a formidable coalition: Emperor Otto of Germany, Fernand of Flanders, Renaud of Boulogne and other lords from Holland, Lorraine and Brabant. With their thousands of knights and foot soldiers, the force seemed invincible. Yet,

"When the borders of Flanders had been surrounded and the troops organized, a battle took place on the bridge of Bouvines between Mortain and Tournai on 27 July, a Sunday, and having killed many in the conflict the French king held the palm of victory."
Anonymous Barnwell chronicler

I didn't have to wait for the chronicler to describe the defeat. Terric Teutonicus, a Germanic knight who'd long served me faithfully, escaped capture and rode night and day to bring me the news. He told me that Otto of Germany had lost interest and left the field, and the coalition army had fallen apart. Philip had dealt my allies an overwhelming defeat. He was free to march into and claim for his own my lands in Normandy, Maine, Anjou, the Touraine and Poitou.

Bereft of my lands, without an army, I could do nothing in France now. I prepared to retire to England.

I was accompanied on the voyage only by Terric, my steward Brian de Lisle and a half-dozen of my household knights. Isabella and Joanna had returned shortly after the ceremonies at Parthenay. The journey seemed interminable, up the coast of Aquitaine, around Brittany and across the channel. I brooded and raged. Terric, Brian and my retainers kept out of my way as well as they could on such a confined vessel. If Isabella had been with me I could have made her listen to my tirades. Well for her that she wasn't, though. I might have struck out at her, half-believing the old tales of how she'd used fiendish powers to bewitch me and bring me ill fortune.

William Marshal met me when I stepped onto the pier at Dartmouth. I could tell from his gray, frowning face that he wasn't bearing good news. We rode up to the castle through the cold October twilight. The wind whipped at our cloaks and made our horses shake their heads and snort. There were few people about. Those whom we met, muffled up against the chill and with their heads low as they fought the gusts of wind, paid no attention to us. How different, I thought, sunk in my bitterness, from another royal visit to this port. As a much younger man, I'd watched when my brother Richard had embarked from Dartmouth on his Crusade in 1190. It was a time full of hope, with thousands of brave knights setting off on the greatest adventure of the age. Now Richard's successor was arriving here after defeat and betrayal, deserted by his allies, not even recognized by his indifferent subjects.

At the castle I ordered supper and mulled wine to be brought to the upper room that looked out at the estuary. Over our roast beef and apple tarts William told me that a good number of the barons, perhaps two-score, were almost in open rebellion. Archbishop Stephen Langton was encouraging them to demand that I restore the rights I'd taken away from them.

"What are they talking about? They have the same rights they had under my brother and my father."

"Apparently they've found an old document that they call a charter of liberties. They claim, and Archbishop Stephen backs them, that it goes back to King Henry I and promises the king's noble subjects freedom from all manner of obligations. I haven't seen it. I doubt if it's as broad a charter as they think. But it gives them something to rally around."

I got up and stamped about the room. I could feel the anger rising until I felt I might explode.

"By God's body, I'll give them something to rally around! I'll impose a tax on every one of them who refused to go to France with me. Rights, they say. Ha! A king has his rights too!"

William said nothing. He was used to my temper. Finally I calmed down enough to resume my seat. I downed my goblet of wine in two gulps.

"My lord king, I suggest that you call a meeting of your council as soon as you arrive in London and also call in the barons who are still loyal to you. You'll need their advice and counsel."

I agreed.

Then William gave me a final bit of news. He probably thought it would cheer me after all his dismal tidings.

The week before, my Queen had been delivered of a daughter, whom she'd named Isabella. Mother and daughter were well.

My first reaction was disappointment that it wasn't a son. My second was a fleeting bit of resentment that she hadn't been named for my mother, as I'd intended for the next girl-child.

But now that I'd lost nearly all my French possessions and had to face this infuriating rebellion at home, what was another daughter to me?

Isabella

1215

"You will welcome me to your bed or I will see that the body of your lover James is hung lifeless before your eyes!"

I was rigid with terror.

John gripped my arm so tightly that I felt it might break. I struggled though I knew it was useless. The more I tried to escape the stronger his grasp. He pulled me to him and kissed me so savagely that my face was bruised. He dragged me to the bed, threw me down and fell upon me. I beat at him and tried to hold him off, but he only became more violent. At last he shuddered so it racked his whole body, then rose and stared down at me.

Between gasps he snarled, "Not like what you've been enjoying with your namby-pamby Monsieur Tourville, was it? Let this be a lesson to you, Isabella. Nobody denies the King, not even the Queen. Especially a Queen who has cuckolded her husband!"

I turned my head aside and closed my eyes, almost fainting with outrage and pain. I heard the door slam behind him. I don't know how long I lay there in agony before I heard a light knock. Anne came in. She must have heard my sobbing.

Bless her. She didn't speak, but gently and efficiently helped me out of my torn gown, washed my tear-ravaged face, wrapped me in a warm robe and led me to my nook by the window. We were at Winchester, in my private apartments. Always up to now John had been here only at my invitation or with my agreement. Now I felt that my Queen's House had been violated, just as I had been.

Anne sat beside me with her needlework. I'd never had to confide in her about my relations with my husband. She knew how things were without words from me. It was always an enormous comfort to sense her unspoken support. I'm sure she disapproved of my affair with James Tourville, but she'd never said anything.

Now, though, it was more than I could bear alone. All the fears and forebodings I'd been suppressing came out.

"He's become a monster, Anne. What happened to the man I married, who loved me as I loved him? Everything is changed, and I don't know what to do. I'd go away but where? Wherever I went he'd find me and compel me to come back. And there are the children. I couldn't leave them. They're mine as much as his."

"As to the man you married, my lady, there's no doubt he's changed a great deal. But…" She paused. I could tell she was wondering whether to go on. She took a deep breath. "You may have brought this on yourself to some extent. You may have provoked him more than you realized, without thinking through the consequences."

This was beginning to sound like criticism. I didn't like criticism.

"Now my dear, just listen a moment. Do you remember when you were a girl and we left Angoulême to stay at the Lusignans' castle? When your mother entrusted me with your care she was very frank.

" 'There's no doubt Isabella is going to become a beautiful woman,' Lady Alix told me. 'Men will be attracted to her. My dearest hope is that when she and Sir Hugh are married they'll grow to love each other and be true to each other, as her father and I have been for twenty years. But Isabella is headstrong. If things don't go well in her marriage it will be up to you to use what influence you can to keep her from doing something foolish.' "

Now I was angry.

"Why couldn't she have said some of that to me? I thought she was pushing me out of the nest, glad to get rid of me. She never said a word about what might lie ahead for me as a wife. Not then, or later when I married John."

"Would you have listened, Isabella? You *were* headstrong. And you were very young. "

I sighed. "I suppose you're right. But Anne, why are you telling me this now? Is it because you want to warn me against doing something foolish? I fear it's a little late for that."

"I almost spoke, several times. I thought of warning you about how John would take it when he found out about you and James Tourville. But I don't think you would have listened to me either. Now of course that's over. John will undoubtedly banish him from court, or worse. Let's hope that when all this trouble with the rebellious barons dies down your husband will be easier to live with."

We sat quietly for some minutes. She was probably right. I was partly to blame for my misfortune. But why couldn't I have some little amusement, when John was free to be as unfaithful as he chose? Why was I held to a higher standard than he was? I didn't know the answer. Anne's last words came back to me.

"But will the trouble with the barons die down, Anne? It seems to me it just keeps getting worse. Whenever there's more bad news John's more out of control. I suppose it was their taking London that set him off this time."

"William says there might be better news soon. He says he and the others on the council are urging John to be more conciliatory and to listen to the rebels' demands. Apparently John has agreed to meet them near Windsor in June. If he does listen, and can bring himself to make some concessions, we may see better days. At least that's what William says."

"And we all know Sir William isn't one to be hopeful unless he has good solid reasons. Well, I'll try to be hopeful too. But if I know John, he may pretend to give in without any intention of keeping his promises."

Anne said nothing. What was there to say?

"I think I must try to sleep now, Anne." I stood up and suddenly felt so weary that I wondered if I could even make my way to bed. "Will you send Hortense to help me? And will you please stop at the nursery and tell the children I won't be able to come say goodnight because I'm unwell?" I took her hand. "Thank you, dear friend, for sitting with me and being here when I need you."

For some months after John's rapacious attack on me we managed with moderate success to avoid each other. Nothing can heal such a wound, but time can dull the outrage somewhat. In time I was able to look at him without utter loathing and to be civil in what speech we had to exchange. I told myself that he was to be pitied rather than condemned. I tried to pray for his redemption, but I have never been very good at praying for others than myself.

As for poor James Tourville, he simply disappeared. I never saw him again or knew what his fate was.

Sure enough, as William had predicted, John arranged to meet the barons and discuss their written demands. It was to be a ceremonial gathering on June 15, 1215, near Windsor. He asked me if I would come. I suppose he wanted his Queen by his side to augment the royal presence and impress the rebels with a display of majesty united.

I declined. He didn't press me and left without me.

I'd just discovered that I was to be a mother, again. How could a child have been conceived out of that loveless, vengeful act? When the child was born could I look at it with anything but resentment? I was desperate to get rid of it. I knew better than to ask Anne for help. But I'd heard my lady of the bedchamber, Hortense, speak of an ancient aunt who was a wizard at potions to cure every ailment. I asked her, promising a generous reward, if she could procure a draught to cause a miscarriage. She was glad to oblige.

When she brought me the vial of a clear, harmless-looking liquid, she said her aunt had cautioned her to tell me that sometimes it was a day or two before it took effect, and that it might cause me a great deal of pain. It looked like nothing but water to me. I wondered if I was being cheated. Nevertheless I drank it down. It tasted horrid, like vinegar mixed with nettle broth.

Nothing happened.

The next morning we received our first word of John's meeting with the rebel barons. We heard from a wayfarer who had just come from Windsor that the two opposing parties met at the field of Runnymede on the banks of the River Thames. We heard that the weather was fine. We heard that there was a good deal of argument and that after four days the two sides eventually hammered out a seventy-article document. They called it Magna Carta—the Great Charter.

Later that day we had word from John himself.

As a grand finale to the week's events he'd decreed that a tournament be held and that his court, the barons and their ladies and any of his subjects who chose to come would be welcome. He sent orders to me to bring Henry and Joanna at once. I had no choice but to obey. I still felt perfectly well, and had reluctantly decided the potion was worthless.

Henry was excited at the thought of going to a tournament. Though only eight, he'd been preparing himself for jousting and battle for a year or more. His tutor had been William Marshal no less, the most skilled and admired knight in the land. Sometimes I'd go out to watch William schooling Henry. At William's signal the boy would trot his pony toward the quintain, the straw man that hung from a post on which knights practiced their swordsmanship. He'd slash at it with his small sword. If his aim was good the quintain would spin around as though suffering a mortal blow. William would call out "Well aimed, Prince Henry!"

Henry knew he couldn't take part in a tournament yet. But he could watch the knights and cheer his favorites. And his idol William Marshal would be there.

Joanna was less enthusiastic but, as always, obedient.

As for me, in spite of my worry I looked forward to the spectacle. I'd have a chance to see, face to face, the fearsome barons whom John so despised. Even more, I looked forward to finding out just what Magna Carta included. Had John given up many of his jealously guarded prerogatives? What had the barons won that moved them to sign? It was more than curiosity on my part. If this document limited the power of the King, it diminished his Queen as well.

On the day of the tournament, a warm day with light winds, we rode out in procession from Windsor Castle to Runnymede. John and I rode side by side. Nobody watching would have doubted that this was the happiest royal couple in Christendom. John's face, usually phlegmatic unless he was angry, was positively beaming. He smiled occasionally at spectators who'd lined up along the road. Once he even sent a smile my way. I didn't return it. John had always been good at forgetting his past misdeeds. Sometimes I envied him that.

Behind us rode Prince Henry and Princess Joanna, then a long line of dignitaries. Archbishop Stephen Langton led the way, his spare frame robed in voluminous folds of scarlet so he looked twice his actual size. His tall white mitre bobbed along like a beacon to guide those who came behind. These included William Marshal; the new justiciar, Hubert de Burgh—I had not yet come to know him; Pandulfo, who'd been reinstated as papal legate replacing Nicholas; the Grand Master of the Knights Templar; and various other bishops, barons and lords who'd remained faithful to John. Though it seemed a substantial party, I saw when we arrived at the fields of Runnymede how our number was dwarfed by the assembly of barons.

Well above the marshy stretch by the smoothly flowing river, brightly colored tents and pavilions dotted the meadow. The jousting grounds were laid out in their midst. The pennants that lined the course snapped in the breeze, cavorting like frisky pups on a leash. Rows of raised seats had been set up on either side of the lists, many already filled. Those barons who wouldn't be taking part in the tournament had shed their armor and milled about with much shouting and loud laughter. Townspeople had left their shops and country folk their fields to settle on the slopes above. Enterprising vendors were crying their wares—ale, pasties, pickled pigs' feet, fresh cherries, treacle tarts. When I got a whiff of roasting pork I felt an uneasiness in my stomach.

A page escorted us to our seats at the center of the stands just as trumpeters announced the start of the tournament with three piercing blasts. Henry, sitting between his father and William Marshal, jumped up and down in his seat and cried, "Here they come!" Two knights emerged from their tents, one at either end of the lists. Each was sheathed from neck to hips in silvery mail and wore a visored helmet of burnished steel. Each held a shield in his left hand, a long lance in his right. Their squires helped them leap on their waiting horses.

I'd seen many tournaments, but never failed to get caught up in the excitement. The children were full of questions.

"Is that a real lance with a steel tip?" Henry wanted to know. "No," said William. "It has a blunt iron point. They'll try to hurt each other but not to draw blood."

"Why will they try to hurt each other?" Joanna asked me. This was her first tournament.

"It's a game, a contest," I replied. "They have to hurt each other at least a little bit, or knock their opponent out of the saddle, or we won't know who wins."

"I think the knight with the red and gold shield will win," said Henry. "He looks a little bigger. And his horse is a lot bigger."

"You may be right," said William Marshal. "That's Richard de Percy. He's seldom been unhorsed."

"Well, I think the one with the silver and black shield will knock him right down," said Joanna.

The herald who stood midway between the two opponents raised his flag. With a flourish he let it fall. A roar came from the crowd. Both chargers galloped toward each other, their riders holding lances level, arms drawn back, ready to strike. Sure enough, red-and-gold hit silver-and-black with such force, in the very center of his shield, that he tumbled out of his saddle. He landed on the dusty ground with such a crash that I flinched. He lay there for half a minute while I, and many others I'm sure, thought he was dead. But no, he picked himself up and led his horse off while the victor doffed his helmet and accepted the cheers of the crowd. Henry did his best to add his voice to the acclaim. Joanna looked glum.

I didn't know if it was the shock of seeing the fallen warrior, but I suddenly felt a pain shoot through my whole body, so sharp that I doubled over in my seat and clutched my midsection. I think I moaned. John, William Marshal and the children all looked at me in alarm. The first to move was Lady Anne, who was sitting behind me. She hurried to my side, just as John reached me. I managed to straighten myself. The sharp pain had lessened but I hurt from head to toe.

"Isabella, what is it?" John asked, taking my hands in his.

"I don't know, but it's better now." I fought to get my breath. "I'll be all right. Just let me get back to Windsor where I can lie down. You must stay,

John, please, it's important for you to be here on your day of triumph. And the children must see the rest of the tournament. "

"I'll see to getting her away, my lord. We'll send word to you if you need to come," said Anne, helping me to my feet. William de Cantilupe and Anne guided me from the stands.

Back in Windsor Castle, Anne and my ladies put me to bed and watched over me. I went through hours of wrenching pains, of retching until there was nothing more to bring up, of praying for death—anything to end my agony. By morning I was free of pain but so weak that I could hardly move an eyelid.

I had not lost the child.

It took John, aided by the wily Pandulfo, only four months to persuade the Pope to annul Magna Carta. The civil war began again. It was John with his ruthless mercenaries from the Continent against the barons with their new ally Prince Louis of France, to whom they'd offered the crown of England as an inducement to join them. This made John even fiercer. He fought them up and down England from the Firth of Forth to Dover, from London to the Welsh Marches.

I didn't see much of him. When I did, I still served as audience for his diatribes. Where only a year ago I would have listened idly, not much caring who was doing what to whom, now in spite of myself I admired his ability to seize the advantage from his enemies. From everything I heard from him and from others, John was absolutely tireless in his pursuit of the rebels, chasing them from one place to another, besieging any castles they'd taken, reinforcing the garrisons of the ones he held.

"If they called him John Softsword in France, he's become John Sharpsword here at home," said William de Cantilupe. He'd come from Rochester Castle, which John had just taken, with messages from the King. We were in my apartments in Winchester. In the seventh month of my pregnancy and feeling far from well, I'd asked William to give his report there and to assemble the household knights, the lords and ladies of the court and others who should hear how their king fared.

Henry and Richard listened open-mouthed while William described the taking of Rochester. It had to do with John ordering tunnels to be dug under the formidable stone keep; having the tunnelers shore them up with wooden supports as they went; greasing the supports thickly with the fat from forty pigs; bringing in straw and brush; and throwing in a burning fagot.

"The whole place exploded like a bonfire in hell. The keep collapsed and you should have heard the crash!" The normally reserved William was remarkably animated as he told the story. I wondered if perhaps he had had something to do with devising the scheme.

"Taking Rochester was a great feather in King John's cap," said William. "But this is just the beginning. The barons are on the march. So, my lady Queen, the King has directed that you and the young princes and princesses are to go to Corfe Castle, where you will be safe. He will come to see you there as soon as he can."

I didn't want to go. I was perfectly content at Winchester. But William explained to me that Corfe Castle in Dorset was the most impregnable fortress in the entire realm. John wanted his Queen and his children to be as far as possible from the war. So we went.

In November 1215 my third daughter, the child I'd never wanted, was born at Corfe. When I held her in my arms my resentments melted away. She was tiny, innocent, defenceless. It wasn't her fault she'd been born. I wanted to love her and I did.

I named her for John's mother, Eleanor. I had an idea she might need strength, self-confidence and an indomitable spirit. Beauty would help, too.

Henry 111

1216-1217

"Look mother, how beautiful!"

Corfe castle looked like no other castles I'd known in my whole life. I liked it from the first day I saw it. It could have been a fairy-tale castle with its white battlements against a blue sky. It wasn't in the middle of a town or city, but right at the top of a hill, floating above the village below. All around it was nothing except more green hills.

We arrived there about noon on a late-October day. We were a very large party--my mother, my sisters and brother and I, as well as all our lords and ladies of the court. We'd brought our cooks and grooms and other retainers too.

We were all tired. I hadn't wanted to come. Neither had my mother. She grumbled all the way about having her baby in a strange godforsaken place instead of in Winchester where she felt so at home

The constable of the castle, Peter de Maulay, was waiting at the outer gatehouse. I liked him right away. He wasn't as noble-looking as William Marshal, or as neat and proper as William de Cantilupe, but he was very friendly. He was tall and burly and usually looked somewhat rumpled. His head was quite bald. He smiled often.

He led us on to the inner bailey. Now I had a good look at the keep. It was just as my father had described it to me before we left Winchester. He said the castle keep was a huge, tall white tower in the middle of the other buildings.

Sir Peter saw me staring up at it. He must have read my mind. He grinned at me.

"Can't wait to get up there, eh Prince Henry? Well, let's get the Queen and her ladies settled, then I'll take you and Prince Richard up to the top."

With his wife, Lady Isabelle, he gave us a tour of the castle. After that all of us, even my mother, felt better about our new home. She was especially pleased with the royal apartments.

"That long vaulted hall is nearly as big as the one at Westminster. I think this will do very well indeed!" I heard her tell Lady Isabelle when she was looking over her own rooms. "Just look at those blue damask hangings on the wall and these thick Persian carpets. And what a handsome bed, all curtained in blue and yellow! If John had told me more about Corfe Castle I would have begged to come long ago."

Within the hour, as good as his word, Sir Peter conducted my brother and me, as well as his own son Roderick—about my age—up the keep's long coiling stairway. Narrow windows along the way gave me slivers of view, mostly of sky.

While we climbed I thought about what my father had told me about the keep. He'd sounded so proud of it.

"Did you build it, father?" I'd asked him.

"No, old King William's son, King Henry the First, built that keep. He made it strong enough to hold off a thousand Vikings, if any had still been around. But I added the high outer curtain wall. You'll see it the minute you get the castle in sight. Now when you are at Corfe, my son, you must make yourself familiar with every inch of the castle. You must be ready, in case you ever have to defend it when you are king."

I'd nodded. I was proud that my father was advising me about my future role as a king.

"And don't forget the dungeons. Make sure they're secure. We may have to send a new batch of prisoners there before this war with the malcontent barons is over. No prisoner has ever escaped from Corfe. And none ever will, Henry, as long as we're vigilant."

I'd shivered at the thought of the dungeons. Now that I was here I decided I'd let that part of my father's instructions wait. What I wanted most of all was to get to the top of the keep.

Finally when I thought we'd climbed halfway to heaven we came out onto a square platform with a low wall.

Richard and I peered over the edge at the bailey below us. The other buildings, with tiny figures moving about between them, looked like toys. We knelt at the low points in the wall and pretended we were shooting arrows at invading armies. Looking around, I could see for miles across rolling fields where flocks of distant sheep were like clusters of white flowers on the green. I'd never been so high above the ground. Roderick pointed out the sights.

"All the ridge to east and west is the Purbeck Hills. You can see where they've dug into the cliff for the stone to build the castle walls. We call it limestone but it's really marble. And way down there"—he pointed toward the south—"is the Channel. You can't see it, but I've been there. Maybe my father will take us riding that way while you're here. "

"I will indeed," said Sir Peter. "It's important for the princes to see that precious body of water that protects England from enemies abroad. But if by some chance some marauders should make a landing, Corfe Castle would stop them in their tracks."

I could well believe it.

Just as I'd liked Sir Peter and his son Roderick at once, my mother soon became fast friends with Lady Isabelle. For one thing, she was the daughter of our old household steward Robert de Thorneham. For another, she was only a year younger than my mother, lively and pretty. They found they had a lot in common besides their names, like the fact that they were both pregnant. Lady Isabelle's child wasn't expected for some months, but my mother's was due any day. This would be her fifth child.

When her fourth, my baby sister Isabella, was born I was only six and hardly knew what was going on. I felt much older now, at nine. I told my brother Richard and my sister Joanna that we were going to have a council meeting to discuss the upcoming event. We'd hold it at the top of the keep. I led the way.

Joanna had a hard time keeping up, what with her short little legs and the steepness of the stairs. When she puffed her way out to the open air she was red as a poppy. She mopped her face with the hem of her long skirt and flopped down on the stone paving, getting her breath back. She lay there looking up.

"I don't see what's so special about this place. I can see the sky just as well from down below." So of course we had to pull her to her feet and make her look around. She agreed it was wonderful.

I thought it was time to get down to business. I had it all planned.

"Since I'm the oldest, I'll open the meeting of the King's Children's Council. We've excused Isabella from coming because she's so little. You all know that our mother the Queen is going to have a baby. We have to talk about three things: when it will come, whether it will be a boy or a girl, and what it should be named."

"We can't decide when it will come, that's up to God," objected Joanna. "God says, 'Now I think I will send a baby down to Queen Isabella,' and that's when it's born."

"We can't decide whether it will be a boy or a girl, either," said Richard. "I think our mother and father decide that, or maybe God."

"It's God," said Joanna. "I asked my mother, and that's what she said."

"Well, I think it's too bad the baby's own parents can't say whether they want a girl or a boy."

The discussion was getting out of hand.

"Never mind all that," I said. "We aren't here to *decide* those things, but to make bets on what will happen, and to pick a name for a girl or a boy. Now everybody keep quiet and think, then I'll give the signal and we'll make our wagers."

Joanna frowned and thought hard. Richard knew his answers right away and jumped up to march around the battlements. After a couple of minutes I called the meeting to order.

"You first, Richard."

"It will come Tuesday week and it'll be a boy. His name will be Edward."

"Why Edward?" Joanna asked.

"I just like it. Besides, I think there were a lot of Edwards in our family, way back."

"Well, I think it will be a girl, and it will come day after tomorrow, and we'll call her Eleanor. That was our grandmother's name and it's a pretty name."

My turn now. "It will be a boy, and he'll come on All Hallows' Eve, and he'll be called Geoffrey. My father told me once that he'd named his sons for his brothers. So if he has another son I know he'll name him Geoffrey, that's the only one left."

Joanna came closest. In three days our mother gave birth to a baby girl, and named her Eleanor.

Life went on quietly enough for the next few months. We three older children had occasional lessons in reading and writing Latin from the priest who came up from the village. I thought he was rather bumbling and absent-minded. I doubted if he'd ever had to teach anybody anything before. My mother joined us when she could. Her Latin was better than the priest's so when she sat with us she saw that we learned a lot more, though we couldn't fool around so much.

Roderick and I, and sometimes Richard when we'd let him, practiced our jousting in the outer bailey, where Sir Peter had set up a course with a quintain for us to try to demolish.

We did get our ride to the sea. It was calm and sunny when we rode out from Corfe. But by the time we reached Swanage on the Channel the wind was blowing hard and heavy gray clouds were spreading over the sky. I stood on the clifftop and looked out at the sea. It was gray-green, and the waves had white manes like horses. The waters went on and on until you couldn't tell where the sea stopped and the sky began. Just below us the breakers were dashing against the rocky shore. It was exciting to see the showers of spume they shot up and hear the roars.

"How far to France?" I asked Sir Peter.

"A good two days' sail. More, for any sailor foolish enough to set out in weather like this. Are you thinking maybe of a voyage across the Channel, Prince Henry?"

"No, I was just wondering if this might be where the French would land if they invaded England, and how long it would take them, and whether we'd try to have an army here to meet them, or if we'd wait for them at Corfe Castle."

"Good questions, my prince. Most likely they'd choose a shorter crossing, like from Calais to Dover. If they did land here on the Dorset coast we'd probably wait at Corfe, though that would depend on how much advance notice we had."

"I think we should push them right over the cliff and back into the sea!" cried Richard. "What a great splash they'd make!"

Sir Peter laughed.

"So they would, Prince Richard! That's one battle tactic that hadn't occurred to me. I'm glad you're both thinking about how to defend this land of ours. When your father comes, which I hope will be before long, I'll tell him his princelings will soon be ready to join him on the field of battle."

That was the first hint I had that my father might be coming. I knew he was far away in the north, fighting the barons who had been so disloyal and risen against him. If he could find time to come see us that would mean the war was going our way.

I was right. He arrived in June of 1216 with William Marshal and twenty knights.

I hadn't often seen my father in such a good mood. Much of the time he was either so gloomy he wouldn't talk to anyone, or so cross that he snapped at the nearest person. Sometimes I was that person. I knew better than to answer back. All I wanted to do was escape. My mother told me I shouldn't mind this, that he wasn't cross at me, just very upset about matters of state. I tried to believe that, but I couldn't help feeling I'd failed him somehow.

As soon as he arrived at Corfe Castle he asked Sir Peter to assemble everybody in the Long Hall. He seated himself on his throne at the far end. William Marshal stood at his right, Sir Peter at his left. My mother and we four children sat at the side. So did the nurse holding Baby Eleanor, and Lady Isabelle with Roderick. Standing below us were Sir Peter's deputies, my father's knights, my mother's ladies in waiting and the husbands of those who had husbands, the castle knights and their squires. We must have been about three dozen. I'd never seen this hall so crowded. As soon as everybody was assembled a group of musicians struck up a tune. It was very lively. A lutist and an oboist played the melody and the drummer beat out the rhythm. I saw some of the ladies begin to tap their toes.

"Will there be dancing later? Oh, I hope there will!" Joanna said to my mother. Joanna loved dancing. I'd been helping her to learn the steps.

"Shhh. Maybe. I hope so." My mother loved dancing too. "Now be quiet. The King is going to speak to us."

My father looked different. In the nine months since I'd seen him he seemed to have become fatter and older. He was growing bald and what hair he had was nearly gray. So was his beard that used to be so black. Another thing that was different was his good temper. He was actually smiling while he looked around the room. As usual, he was dressed like a king. His heavy gold chain with the cross was around his neck. Whenever he moved the jewels on his finger-rings and in his crown flashed.

He spoke while seated on his throne. I'd noticed before that my father preferred not to stand in the presence of others who were taller. William Marshal and Peter de Maulay were both much taller.

He raised his voice so everybody in the hall could hear.

"My loyal friends, I bring you good news. Thanks be to God, we have routed the insurgents from the Scottish border, from Yorkshire and the Midlands and Essex. They are penned up in London with their cowardly French allies. Prince Louis beats on our castle walls to no avail. Try as they might, they shall not defeat our brave defenders.

"We are grieved that some of our supporters have seen fit to desert our cause and join the rebels. Yet if they repent and return to our service there will be no penalty. This word is being published throughout the land. We will welcome any good trusty warrior who cares to join us. I ask all of you to spread this message too. With God's blessing, we shall prevail."

Some people in the crowd cheered. I heard cries of "We shall prevail!" and "God bless King John and God bless England!"

My father smiled and raised his hand for silence.

"Now, my friends, we shall feast together and if you will, celebrate our good fortune with music and dancing."

More cheers. I felt like cheering too. It hadn't been often that our family was all together and all in such good humor.

My mother rose and took baby Eleanor from the nurse. She walked over to my father and held the baby out to him. Since I knew he hadn't been here when Eleanor was born, I'd have thought he'd want to hold her now, when he saw her for the first time. But he only glanced at her and didn't move to take her. He looked up at my mother. I could barely hear his words, but it sounded like "How do I know it's mine?" I couldn't see her face. She walked quickly out of the room, still holding the baby.

Soon after that my father left. I saw him only once more. In July he sent word for my mother and me to join him at Chester in the West Midlands. She was to bring some of the royal treasure that he kept in safekeeping at Corfe Castle. I suppose he had to sell it to pay for this war, which seemed to go on and on. I saw him for only a few minutes when he came out to meet us. He didn't look well. He was limping with his gouty leg, stooping over the way I do when I have a terrible stomach-ache. We'd hardly arrived in Chester than he was off again. We heard he was fighting all over the Midlands, Essex and Lincolnshire.

Toward the end of October when we were staying at Windsor Castle, William Marshal brought us the awful news: King John had died of a fever at the castle of the bishop of Lincoln in Newark.

"I wasn't with him at the end, my lady Queen. But he did everything that needed to be done. One of his last acts was to designate Prince Henry as his heir. He ordered his companions and me to swear allegiance to Prince Henry. He sent letters to order his sheriffs and constables to accept Henry as their king. I think you would want to know what message he left for me:

" 'My loyal friend: I place my son Henry in your keeping as his protector. He is only nine and will need your guidance. I implore you, for the sake of God, to act in Henry's interest.' "

"Did he leave a will?" my mother asked.

"He did. He named twelve of his longtime loyal friends and supporters as executors."

"No mention of me?"

Sir William didn't answer right away. I could see that he didn't want to hurt my mother.

"None," he said.

Isabella

1216-1217

Nine days after John's death, my eldest son was hastily crowned King Henry III of England. I sat by his side in Gloucester Cathedral for the ceremony.

I'd dressed soberly with only a few jewels. I intended to be seen as the loving caretaker of this child, the Queen Regent who would watch over him and advise him until he was old enough to rule on his own.

During the brief ceremony I managed to look suitably solemn, but I was hardly the grieving widow. I was sorry for John's sake that he'd died before succeeding in driving out the French invaders, yet I can't say I missed him or mourned him. Nor did most of his subjects. Everybody was ready to forget the past and to find in their new king, though he was only nine, their hope for a more peaceful and prosperous England.

I hoped nobody watching would laugh when the bishop of Winchester placed a strange-looking crown on Henry's head. How typical of John! One of his last rash acts was to insist on hurrying to ford a river that would soon be swollen by the incoming tide. He and his men barely got through the flooding waters. His baggage train and all his treasure, including the coronation crown, were lost. We'd improvised a crown of sorts from one of my gold belts and some jeweled brooches.

Perched on two thick pillows, Henry looked very small on the big throne. He knew what was expected of him, though, and did his best to live up to it. He was a handsome boy. The black hair he'd been born with had lightened to a chestnut-brown, with ringlets falling to his shoulders. Already he had dignity and a natural gravity, tempered by his sunny disposition. I hoped and believed he'd turn out to be less choleric and more merciful than his father.

As soon as we were back in Winchester, I received William Marshal, who asked to discuss Henry's future. John had named William as protector of the kingdom and of Henry. I was glad—he'd be an excellent mentor.

But though the war was winding down, it was far from over. William would be away a great deal, organizing the resistance to Prince Louis and the rebels.

"Because of his youth, I wouldn't wish to take the King about the country with me. I wish to entrust him to a guardian to supervise his learning and to prepare him, little lad that he is, for kingship. We have named Peter des Roches, the bishop of Winchester, to this post." Courteous as always, he bent his silvered head deferentially as he waited for my reply. I guessed that the decision had already been made. However, Sir Peter suited me very well since that meant we could make Winchester our main residence. It was the favorite home of my children as well as mine.

"A wise choice, I believe. I don't know the bishop well, but I remember that he fought on John's behalf for many years before being named bishop. Thank you, Sir William. And Godspeed as you go out to protect the kingdom."

Henry took to the bishop at once and he to Henry. He saw that the boy was schooled in Latin, both reading and writing, as well as in soldiering. Sometimes William Marshal sent word that Henry should join the army for some march or maneuver. Then Sir Peter would conduct him to where the action was and stay by his side, as both guardian and instructor. Everybody on the council was eager for Henry to become a warrior and leader of warriors as soon as possible. I was learning that I had very little say in the matter.

In fact, I had very little say in anything these days. Nobody consulted me or informed me about affairs of state. After some time I decided that since Bishop Peter seemed a reasonable man I'd tell him how I felt. I thought it more diplomatic to go to him rather than command him to come to me. So I arranged to meet him in his chambers in the bishop's palace near the cathedral. After I kissed his ring he asked me to be seated. He looked more like an ordinary priest than a bishop, with no red robes or white stole, just an unadorned purple surplice with a modest silver cross on his breast. A genial-looking man with iron-gray hair and impressive eyebrows, he was courtly but not subservient.

"I'm honored at your visit, my lady Queen. May I assist you in some matter?"

"I hope so, my lord bishop. But first I wish to thank you for your good care of my son Henry. He has a high regard for you and often says so."

"He's a fine lad who should prove a worthy king. It's my pleasure to help point him on the way."

"Thank you for that. Now, you can help me too if you will. As you have seen, I'm not invited nowadays to be present when the council meets, so I'm woefully ill-informed on the progress of the war. I've heard there was a great victory over the rebel barons at Lincoln. Does that mean we'll have peace?"

"Ay, we'll have peace, and before long, with God's aid. Both sides are ready for it. Prince Louis has asked for a truce. He holds little besides London now. We'll probably meet with him soon to begin talking terms. Would you wish to be present at such a meeting, my lady?" He cocked his head and looked at me shrewdly from under his bushy brows, knowing perfectly well what I wished.

"I would. I've come to believe that the council doesn't want to hear my opinions and is unwilling to grant me the title of Queen Regent. Nevertheless I knew King John's wishes for his kingdom as well as anyone. I believe I should be present when such important matters are considered."

"I think William Marshal would agree with you. So do I. So would the papal legate Gualo, in all likelihood, and most of the others. We have only the justiciar Hubert de Burgh to persuade. I'll do what I can to convince him that inviting Queen Isabella to join us at our meetings with Prince Louis will not do irreparable harm to the Kingdom of England."

I thanked him for his promised aid. He thanked me for being so gracious as to favor him with my presence. Both of us knew we were playing a game. But I felt that the bishop was on my side in the game now.

I still felt so when I was asked to be present in September 1217 at the signing of the peace treaty with Prince Louis. It was to take place on the neutral ground of an islet in the Thames near Kingston. Along with my son the King, William Marshal and the new papal legate Gualo, I was rowed out to the island in a long, broad boat with a red silk canopy and the Plantagenet pennant flying. Other boats brought other members of the council and supporters of the English King. We watched while Prince Louis approached over the water from the other side of the river. With him were a good number of the dukes and counts of France, all gorgeously attired, besides many of the English barons who'd risen against John.

We too had dressed with care. The barons, earls and knights were all in velvets and fine woolens with well-polished gilded swords at their belts. The legate Gualo was in scarlet even to his biretta.

I'd given some thought to Henry's costume and my own. I didn't want him to be in the black his father had favored. We settled on a deep blue tunic and leggings, the former embroidered with golden lions around neck and hem. By now a proper crown had been made, similar to the lost coronation crown though with fewer jewels. I too wore my crown as well as my coronation robe. I wasn't going to let anyone forget that I was still Queen of England. I was pleased with my appearance. Anne had concurred.

"My lady, you have never looked lovelier. Nobody would guess you were a day over twenty." I was thirty-one.

The meeting itself was anticlimactic as far as substance went. Both sides had agreed on the provisions ahead of time. First the legate Gualo reminded everybody that England was still a possession of the Pope. So Louis, who had been excommunicated for going into battle against the Pope's kingdom, knelt before Gualo and swore on the Gospel to be faithful to the Pope and the church from that day forward. Next, he swore to release from their fealty to him all the barons and men of England who had joined his cause. He even promised to try to persuade his father, King Philip, to restore to King Henry the English rights to their former possessions in France.

"Could that really happen?" I asked Bishop Peter.

"That he tries to persuade his father? Probably. That King Philip agrees? Hardly likely. But it makes Louis sound nicely conciliatory. They're going to pay him a sizable sum to get himself and his army out of England. He should at least make a gesture toward giving something in return."

That was my last public appearance in England.

Just before Christmas of 1217 the justiciar, Hubert de Burgh, came to me and told me I was to leave the country.

I was so shocked I didn't say anything, just stared at him. He must have taken this for acquiescence, and began at once to talk of getting me to Dover for the voyage.

I'd never taken to Sir Hubert. I knew he'd remained faithful to John when many others deserted his cause. To reward him John had named him justiciar, that is, his second in command and chief dispenser of justice in the kingdom. He was, besides, sheriff of Kent and several other counties. He was constable of Dover Castle, which he'd defended with great bravery against the forces of Prince Louis. He was also one of the men John had named to Henry's council. He was, in short, one of the giants of the baronial community. John had trusted him. That didn't mean I had to.

"Sir Hubert, wait a moment, I beg you. Why do you tell me I must leave my kingdom? Am I not still Queen? Doesn't my son need me at his side while he's of such a tender age? By whose authority do you give this order? Until I hear it from my son and from his protector William Marshal I must decline to obey."

This huge man, bulging with muscles and authority, wasn't used to dealing with women, much less argumentative women. His face turned so red I feared he was going to have a fit. He glared at me like a maddened bull. We were alone in the outer chamber of my rooms in Winchester Palace. I began to wonder if I might need to call for help. But I was as angry as he was.

"Sir Hubert, when Queen Eleanor was widowed, did the council evict her from England? No! She remained to guide her sons and to act as their surrogate in the governance of the kingdom when they were absent. Why is it so different for me?"

He managed to regain enough control to reply. Calumnies erupted from his snarling mouth like anathemas from an angry god.

"Madam, this order is by authority of the King's council, the men King John named to govern England before he died. If William Marshal had given you the word he might have been gentler but he has agreed that your departure is necessary in view of the mood of the English people. The people hate you. They lay to your door all the woes that have beset this country since you tricked our King into marrying you. They call you a sorceress, a temptress, a Jezebel. In short, the council does not see you as a fit person to influence your son or to be associated with the government of England."

I didn't believe him. I'd never achieved the popularity with my English subjects I'd hoped for, but I'd never felt they hated me. I ignored that part of his tirade.

"If I'm not fit to be part of the government, why did the council ask me to join them in guaranteeing the truce of last summer? Why was I present at the ceremony when the peace was signed, along with my son the King, the papal legate and all the council that you say wish to push me out?"

"That was solely at the urging of William Marshal and the bishop of Winchester. Most of us advised against it. Now madam, I have no more time. I shall arrange for a ship to be ready at Dover on any date you choose within the next three weeks. You will take your daughter Joanna with you, since she is betrothed to Hugh of Lusignan. Of course you will send her to stay at the Lusignan castle until her marriage. Richard and the two younger princesses will remain in England."

He left before I could gather my thoughts to continue the argument. It was fruitless anyway. Without William Marshal and the bishop to support me, I had no allies.

I sat on, shocked, trying to come to terms with this cruel exile. I'd no longer reign as Queen of the country I'd come to think of as my own. Equally grievous, I'd have to leave Henry and the younger children. They'd be left to the mercy of Hubert de Burgh and his kind. How I regretted now that I hadn't taken more time with them! The two little girls, only three and five, would hardly realize what was happening. Doubtless in time they'd be married off to suitable princes. I only hoped their marriages would be happier than mine. But Richard, at nine, though intent on growing up as fast as he could to be a warrior, was still young enough to depend on me for affection and support. And Henry—my Henry, my firstborn—would grow into his role as King of England while I was far away.

When I said goodbye to him he was more composed than I was. At twelve he'd been King for two years. I thought I was seeing signs of some independence of thought in the face of his council. I hoped so.

We sat facing each other in my chamber. I was determined not to cry. I tried to think of something wise to say, something he'd remember in the time to come.

"Henry, as you know I'm not leaving of my own free will. If I could I would stay in England and watch as you learn to be a strong, good king. Even so, I'll be able to follow your progress from my home in Angoulême. I'll never forget you and I'll always love you."

I couldn't help the tears that ran down my cheeks. Henry tried to comfort me, when I'd thought it would be the other way around.

"Never mind, mother. You won't be so very far away. Maybe you'll come back sometimes and maybe I'll be able to come to see you. Maybe Richard and I will bring an army and make the King of France give us back our lands."

"Yes, maybe you will. If you do, you'll have help from me and from Joanna and her husband. That's something to look forward to, isn't it?" I wiped my eyes.

"And we can always write to each other."

"Yes. I'll write to you often. And Henry, you must watch over your brother and sisters. Don't any of you forget that your mother loves you."

Lady Anne came in to say the horses were saddled and waiting. I rose, took Henry in my arms for a last hug, kissed him, and left.

Isabella

1218-1219

49

What a change from my unkind ejection from England was my welcome in Angoulême!

I settled easily into the palace of the Taillefers, my family's ancestral home, glad to find little had changed. Anne had come with me, of course. I was also permitted to bring three of my ladies, including Hortense my lady of the bedchamber, to see to my needs and those of Princess Joanna. The only other retainers who'd come with me were Terric Teutonicus and his brother Walerand. The council had delegated these two knights to be my protectors. I wondered if the assignment included spying on me.

Two days after my arrival, the mayor of Angoulême put on a great show of presenting me with the keys of the city. He, the bishop and their retinues marched through the narrow streets from the cathedral to my palace. I met them in the courtyard and led them into the great hall. The mayor ceremoniously took the keys from a red velvet cushion and with a little speech handed them to me. Next he read a document expressing the gratification of the civil and ecclesiastical authorities that once more a Taillefer countess was in residence in the noble city of Angoulême. I was asked to acknowledge their gratification by signing my name at the bottom of the parchment. I gladly did so: Isabella, Queen of England and Ireland, duchess of Normandy, duchess of Aquitaine, countess of Anjou and Angoulême.

It took me some time to get used to a quieter life. No flights from enemy armies, no moving the court from one palace to another. No more stormy encounters with John—or passionate reconciliations. For the first time in my adult life, no man around to love, hate or fear.

I missed my children. I sent them messages but received no replies. I wondered if the council might be teaching them to turn against me.

Joanna was a comfort. Now eight, she still depended on me and followed me around, yet she was beginning to be her own person. I knew the day would come when I'd have to send her away to stay at the Lusignans' castle. I remembered my own misery when I'd had to do the same thing. Joanna, of course, had known ever since her betrothal to Hugh at Parthenay that this would happen. I, on the other hand, had had very little warning from my parents; I'd been whisked away within days of learning of my betrothal.

Before I was ready the decision was made for me. In June 1219 a message came from Hugh X. It was full of information and surprises. It was also rather long-winded. Was my future son-in-law a blatherer?

To Queen Isabella, greetings. I was pleased to learn of your arrival in France. I hope that you and your daughter the Princess Joanna are well. I would have written sooner to ask when the Princess might be able to come to Lusignan, but I wanted to make certain improvements in the castle. I wish her to be perfectly comfortable. Now I believe you and she will find it to your taste. My father tells me that when you were here your chamber had no window and was very small. I have enlarged it and now there are two windows giving a good view of the inner bailey. I also wish to tell you that Princess Joanna will be in the care of Lady Alice, Countess of Eu. You will remember that she and her husband, my Uncle Ralph, were your guardians when you were here. My uncle, I am grieved to say, died earlier this year. Lady Alice has come as companion to my father's wife, the Lady Mathilde, who is bedridden. My aunt has asked me to tell you she looks forward to seeing you again and to meeting your daughter.

My father, Hugh le Brun, also sends a message. He regrets he will not be here to greet you because he leaves tomorrow on Crusade. Please send a reply by the messenger and let me know when you will arrive. Your loving son, Hugh X de Lusignan.

My first reaction was a little jolt at the mention of Hugh le Brun. I'd been trying not to imagine what it would be like to see him again. Now I wouldn't have to. Then, rereading the message, I felt amusement that this man, three years my senior, signed himself as my son—my loving son! Yet he seemed well intentioned and agreeable.

At dinner that afternoon I told Joanna that it was time to start packing.

She didn't seem to dread the idea. She saw it as an adventure. She was full of questions. "What will it be like? Is their castle like our palace here in Angoulême?"

"When I was there, nearly twenty years ago, I thought it rather dreary. I was spoiled, of course. I'd never lived anywhere but right here in this palace. But I believe they've made it more pleasant since then. We'll see."

"Will Elizabeth be able to come with me?" Elizabeth was Hortense's seven-year-old daughter. She and Joanna had naturally been thrown together since our arrival and had become fast friends. The girls sat next to each other at table. Joanna clasped Elizabeth's hand. The gaze from my daughter's blue eyes fixed on mine and her tensed posture told me how much this meant to her.

"I don't know why not. You'll need some companionship. Her mother would have to go too. But I suppose I could get along without Hortense." I smoothed her hair, the color of ripe wheat, and kissed her.

The journey to Lusignan was so filled with memories for me that I was often close to tears. I relived the despair I'd felt at fourteen, leaving my beloved home and my idolized mother. But this time, instead of on a cold, damp February day we arrived in bright June sunshine. The bailey was tidy and the outbuildings seemed in good repair. There were even a few flowerbeds with pink and yellow primroses along the walks. Nobody was crying. All my gloom was dispelled

As soon as a groom helped Joanna dismount she ran to Lady Alice, who'd come out to meet us, and put out her hand.

"You must be my Aunt Alice. I am happy to meet you. This is my friend Elizabeth."

Alice's face, plumper and not so rosy and with a whole new assortment of wrinkles since I'd last seen her, hadn't lost its good humor. "Bless you, my little princess. I'm happy to meet you too, and your friend Elizabeth. Now here's my lady, my Isabella." We hugged each other. When I felt her strong old arms about me I realized how much her uncritical affection had meant to me in my youth. Probably I'd never told her so. I hugged harder.

Hugh came from the stables to add his welcome. He seemed much the same as when I'd seen him five years before at the betrothal, except that then he'd been dressed in finery whereas today he was in a workmanlike roughspun tunic and muddy boots. Obviously he wasn't the kind of lord who left all the work of the castle to others. He had a cheerful smile for everyone and a kiss on the cheek for Joanna.

When he'd taken my hand and greeted me, he asked, "Will you be able to stay with us a few days, Queen Isabella?" (I noted he didn't call me "Mother"!) "It would give us pleasure. We could make you very comfortable. I'm only sorry my father had to leave before you came."

Something about his words and manner hinted at a tendency toward flattery and perhaps a little guile. His father had been free of both.

"I wish I could. But urgent matters in Angoulême will call me back. I'm expecting the seneschal of the county of Angoulême to visit me and I must be ready. After I see Joanna settled I'll need to be on my way."

"That will be our loss. Perhaps I could help. I'm acquainted with Bartholomew de Puy, the seneschal. Before he left my father named me head of the clan of Lusignan. He must have finally decided I'd grown up enough to do the job. So I'm not without influence in these parts. Do let me know if there's any service I can provide you."

"Thank you. After I find out what he wants to see me about, I may call on you. It would be good to know I have an adviser in the family, as it were. The local lords are getting fractious. I must act quickly to assure their loyalty."

I looked around and saw that we were alone. While we'd been talking the others had gone in.

"I must go see how Joanna is and make my departure."

He walked along with me and opened the tall oaken door that I remembered so well. In the hall he stopped and asked, "So you don't plan to be a figurehead countess, content to reign snugly in your city of Angoulême? You're determined to assert your suzerainty throughout the county, if I'm not mistaken?"

"Of course! Wasn't my father, Count Aymer, feudal lord over all the land from Perigord to your own La Marche?"

"Your task won't be easy. Especially with your son's council taking such an interest in Aquitaine and Poitou. Well, we can at least look forward to the day when Joanna and I are married. Then all of La Marche will be joined to your Angoulême."

"True. But that's far in the future. A lot can happen in the meantime."

"Yes. A lot can happen. You might find some powerful lord to marry and ally yourself to, for example, and change the whole picture. You're young, beautiful and mistress of a good part of France. I predict you'll be much sought after."

I'm afraid I blushed. Nobody had called me beautiful for some time. He smiled slightly and went on.

"Or Joanna could change her mind, just as her mother did. That could alter the picture even more drastically." A pause while I took this in. "Or so could I." Another pause. "I assure you, however, I don't intend to."

I couldn't at once think of a response. I was glad when Joanna ran out and took my hand, pulling me off to see her room.

What a surprise this Hugh was turning out to be! I'd thought him good-looking, agreeable, without much depth. But the man had a nimble and possibly calculating mind. He was adept at steering a conversation any way he wanted. One had to be on the alert to keep up with him, but I liked the challenge. Yet I realized that I mustn't be influenced by his apparent goodwill.

It was possible that beneath his generous offer of help, he was looking for ways to turn my affairs to his own advantage.

I had a lot to think about on my return journey. For one thing, I decided I'd come to see my daughter much oftener than my mother had come to me at Lusignan.

Hugh X
1218-1220

"You should marry, Hugh."

That was my cousin, Simon de Lezay. Ever since my father's death he'd been assuming a parental role.

My father had died on Crusade at Damiette, a city on the border between Palestine and Egypt. Though the Crusaders took the city, hundreds of them died not in battle but from the agonies of the plague. My father was one of these. I was deeply grieved at the loss, but I had to step quickly into my new role as leader of the Lusignans.

Simon, though only six years my senior, was free with advice. As carefree youths we'd gone careering about the countryside, hunting and jousting and sowing our wild oats. Now he was forty-two and I was thirty-six. Life had become more serious.

"Marry? I will marry, as you know perfectly well. In good time. As soon as we get to Lusignan you'll meet my little bride-to-be, Joanna. She's a pretty thing."

"How pretty?"

"Have you ever seen her mother, Queen Isabella?"

"No, but I hear she's a famous beauty."

"Quite so. Ravishing. And I do believe her daughter Joanna will be the same."

While Simon digested this morsel of information we rode on. I'd just completed a circuit of the strongholds of my kinfolk to gather a few of my closest friends and advisers to come with me to Lusignan. Ever since Queen Isabella had arrived in Angoulême there'd been signs of unrest in her lands and mine. I needed counsel.

We rounded the last curve and crossed the little bridge across the Vonne. I looked up at the castle. Rover though I was, I always felt a deep sense of security and homecoming at the sight of that long stout wall anchored at either end by a round tower. The rocky, rutted road gave way to cobblestones as we rode up through the village. Shopkeepers and laborers went about their business, giving me a respectful nod as I passed. The September sun warmed us gently, filtered through the leaves of the linden trees beside the road. I smelled the sweetness of newmown hay from nearby fields. From the baker's open door I caught the aroma of fresh-baked bread. It reminded me how as a child I used to run down to the castle kitchen and beg for a thick slice off a loaf just out of the oven.

I became eager for dinner.

So were the others. When we were slowed behind a cart laden with vats of wine lumbering up the hill, I heard grumbling behind me. Simon turned in his saddle and called out, "Stop your complaining! That's very likely the wine you'll have with your dinner. The longer it takes to get there the more it will improve with age." This was met with grudging laughter.

We rode into the inner bailey where Pierre, my father's old steward, limped out to greet us. I saw Joanna and her friend Elizabeth hovering in a doorway, watching the bedlam of seven big men dismounting from seven big horses while their squires saw to the saddlebags and led the horses to the stables. The girls decided this had nothing to do with them and disappeared.

"Bishop Etienne is already here, my lord Hugh. He's waiting in the dining hall," Pierre reported.

"Good," I said. "Please tell them to serve dinner at once."

Etienne Delorme, who'd been priest at our village church for years, had only recently been named bishop of Poitiers. He'd been a great friend of my father's. "The wise man of Poitou," my father had called him. I was glad he'd been able to come.

We'd hardly sat down and attacked our platters of roast chicken and mutton stew when I asked Simon, "Now what did you mean, I should marry? You know that I'm already betrothed to Princess Joanna."

"Just this: it may be ten years before Joanna will be old enough to bear you any children. A lot can happen in ten years. A lot can happen in *one* year, the Lord knows. The sooner you have an heir the more secure your Lusignan clan will feel and the more willing to follow you. Besides that, it gives you a bargaining piece in this never-ending game we play with King Philip and King Henry."

"And now we're playing games with the Countess of Angoulême too," said

Henri de Chizé. His castle was in the south of the Lusignan territories, not far from the borders of the County of Angoulême. "I know two of your vassals in Saintonge that she's approached. Told them that her son King Henry has given them suzerainty over them and they must swear fealty. They said nonsense, that Henry gave you Saintonge as part of Joanna's dowry. Not only that, she's dismissed Bartholomew de Puy as her seneschal. Apparently she means to govern the county personally. She's making enemies fast."

"All right, Simon, assuming I go back on my agreement to marry Joanna, won't I join the list of Isabella's enemies? And whom do you suggest for my bride?"

"As for your first question, you needn't make a formal declaration that you're rejecting Joanna. Just let it be bruited about that you might, a bit of gossip for the good folk to spread. When Isabella hears about it she'll be eager to do whatever it takes to keep you on her side. As for who might be your betrothed, I haven't gotten that far. But preferably she'd be from a family loyal to King Philip."

"And highborn," said another.

"Right, a princess if possible," said Simon. "Remember, you're jilting a princess."

We considered the subject of princesses for a time.

"Doesn't King Philip have several sisters?"

"Yes, but they're either too old or thoroughly married."

"What about the one who was engaged to John's brother Richard until he threw her over for Berengaria? Alice, was it? I heard no one would have her after that. She must be available."

I spoke up. "I don't want some old princess who's the worse for wear. Maybe we should lower our expectations. What about a countess?"

A few names were bandied about: a countess of Toulouse, a cousin of King Philip's first wife.

Etienne had been uncharacteristically quiet. Usually he rattled on like a jaybird, but making a lot more sense. My first memories of him were of the wiry, energetic, middle-aged priest who used to sit for hours laughing and gossiping with my father. Now he was white-haired and less spry, but his brain was as agile as ever.

"Well, my good bishop, what's your thinking?" I asked him.

He broke off a chunk of bread to sop up the last of his mutton stew, then drank meditatively from his goblet while we watched and waited.

"I know just the lady. First, though, do you remember Arthur of Brittany?"

"Poor lad," said Simon. "Murdered by his uncle. A terrible business. But what's that to do with finding a bride for Hugh?"

"Arthur had almost as good a claim to the English throne as John. Some still say he was the true heir. So though he's gone, wouldn't his sister be next in line?"

I objected, "But Etienne, Arthur's sister Eleanor's been a prisoner in England for years. John didn't dare murder her, but he made sure she'd have no chance to get back and stir up the Bretons to do him some mischief."

"Ah," said the bishop, "but I'm not talking about Eleanor, I'm talking about his half-sister Alice. Now listen carefully. This gets complicated. Alice's husband is Peter Mauclerc, a great grandson of King Louis VI of France. Their daughter must be about fourteen. Not exactly a princess, but still in the direct line of succession to the throne of Brittany if there were one, and indirectly to the French throne. You could send a message to her parents, just to feel them out. If the messenger is suitably indiscreet, the news of his mission will spread to various interested parties. Then we'll see what we shall see."

"Clever!" cried Simon. He spoke for all of us. "My good bishop, how can you come up with such fiendishly inventive schemes?"

Etienne laughed and with an effort stood up. I could almost hear his joints creak. "It's my hobby. Some call me a meddler. I prefer to think I'm furthering God's work on earth by removing obstacles in good people's way. Now my friends, it's time for an old man to seek his bed. If you like the fiendish scheme, I'll leave it to you to decide who'll take the invitation to Peter and Alice." He waved to us and left.

Henri de Chizé volunteered as emissary.

"If it's indiscretion you want, I'm your man. And I have nothing much else to do this next month."

The scheme worked. The news spread that Hugh X of Lusignan was seeking a bride. In a few weeks Isabella sent word that she planned a visit to her daughter. She hoped I'd be able to receive her to discuss matters of mutual concern. She signed it Queen Isabella. I'd noticed she never referred to herself as a mere countess.

I replied that I'd be delighted.

In the meantime my fortunes had improved. I'd done a great favor for England's seneschal of Poitou and Gascony, Geoffrey de Neville. He'd been trying unsuccessfully to put down some rebellious barons and was badly in need of money to finance his efforts. I advanced the money. Geoffrey, suddenly my dearest friend, felt I deserved some recognition. He wrote to King Henry to tell him that without my invaluable help, he wouldn't have been able to restore order.

King Henry, or rather his council, took the hint. They must have decided I was someone to be reckoned with. They made me seneschal of all Aquitaine—which included Isabella's Angoulême.

I was sure this information would reach Isabella before she left for Lusignan. I relished the thought of her stunned surprise.

I planned a state dinner that would impress a queen. Poor old Pierre was almost worn out, seeing that my orders were followed. I had the great hall cleaned of cobwebs and dust. I ordered fresh rushes for the floor. It was nearly Christmas so I had green boughs and holly brought in to make garlands to hang all around the walls. I ordered the cook to produce a procession of courses of meats, fish, puddings, tarts, pickled this and honeyed that. I engaged a couple of musicians. One could blow a tune on a pipe and simultaneously beat on a tabor. The other could both strum the lyre and play a small harp (though not at once). I practiced one of my own favorite songs. I imagined that Isabella wasn't aware of my reputation as a troubadour. That would give her another surprise.

As to the guest list, besides my own Lusignan kin and allies I invited several lords who were sitting on the fence regarding fealty to Isabella. The bishop of Poitou would be there, of course. To add interest, I invited Bartholomew de Puy, whom Isabella had ousted as seneschal of Angoulême. Like Geoffrey de Neville, he was now my fast friend.

Finally, I told Pierre to instruct the knights and minor lords who would be seated at the lower tables to refrain from loud and unseemly behavior.

Isabella arrived in the morning, spent a few hours with her daughter and rested. I sent word in late afternoon that I would be pleased to escort her to the great hall. When we met I saw that she too had risen to the occasion. She was dressed like a queen. Her flowing blue gown was festooned with strings of pearls around the hem. She'd chosen the perfect color to offset her creamy complexion and her golden hair, which she'd pulled back into a loose knot. Her silver tiara was lavished with pearls. From the gold chain about her neck hung a huge sapphire, the same color as her eyes. I supposed the English hadn't allowed her to bring her crown jewels, but she'd managed very well.

Even a plain woman would have gotten attention in such dress, but Isabella, so slim and poised, her face alive with anticipation of what the evening would bring, looked positively magnificent. I told her so.

"Why thank you, Sir Hugh. It's an honor to be here. I thought I should try to live up to it."

The evening went very well, I thought. Isabella was charming, by turns, to Bishop Etienne on her left and to me on her right. Joanna and Elizabeth, farther along and under the watchful eyes of Lady Anne and Lady Hortense, behaved impeccably. Bartholomew de Puy received a brilliant smile from his countess and a few polite words along the lines of "I am delighted to see you again, my lord." The knights were by and large well behaved. When any loud laughter or shouting did erupt, the well-trained musicians simply increased the tempo and volume.

Isabella and I conversed but skirted the subjects we both had on our minds. She complimented me on improvements she'd observed. "I noticed new tiles on the Tour Melusine, and the inner courtyard looks ever so much nicer than when I lived here."

"That's mostly my father's doing. He wanted to get the castle in good shape before he left on Crusade. I expect you've had the sad news of his death." I knew, of course, that she and my father had nearly become man and wife. But I had no idea if, or how much, she'd been attached to him.

"I have heard the news and with great sorrow." She sounded genuinely moved. "You must miss him very much. He was a good man."

"He was indeed. He set me a fine example. I wish he were here to see that I'm taking my duties as lord of the Lusignans seriously. He thought I'd never grow out of my irresponsible ways."

"From what I hear, you're taking your position very seriously indeed."

She turned to the bishop. I heard him invite her to visit him in Poitiers where he'd show her the new cathedral.

When most of the guests had eaten their fill or more and sweet wines were being poured, my cousin Simon prevailed on me, without much urging, to give the guests a song. I joined the musicians. A page handed me my vielle, fashioned of cherry wood and polished until it glowed. I drew the bow across the three strings and stood there a minute, as though trying to decide what to sing. I knew that in my somewhat more modest way I cut as fine a figure of a man as Isabella did of a woman. My tunic and leggings were the color of purple plums. My belt was woven of silver threads. For my performance I'd put on a cap of plum-colored velvet with a silver tassel, in the troubadour fashion.

I sang a song my father had told me was composed by King Richard.

> Brightly beam my true love's eyes
> Like twin stars sparkling in the skies.

278

When upon me her glance doth dart,
I swear it pierceth to my heart.
Yet, pleasuring in cruelty,
She turns her lovely face from me.
Oh lady fair, turn not away
But hear my plea. Oh lady, stay!

There were calls for more, but I declined.

"Thank you, good friends. But the hour is late, we've all earned our repose, and I'll bid you goodnight." I went back to the head table to take my leave of Isabella.

"Thank you for gracing our gathering tonight. We've seldom had such a charming and ornamental guest. I hope you're not too tired."

She didn't look tired.

"Not at all. But I fear Joanna is. I must get her to bed."

Joanna, in fact, was resting her head on her arms, sound asleep. I gave her a gentle pat on the shoulder. She looked up, suddenly wide awake and with a big smile for me.

"Did I miss anything? Have you sung a song yet?"

"I'm afraid you did miss it, but I'll sing you another tomorrow."

Then to Isabella, "And I hope that tomorrow you'll be able to give me some time. There are several matters I think we should discuss."

"There are indeed."

"Shall we say at eleven, in the lower hall of the Tour Melusine?"

A good half hour past eleven the next morning Isabella came into the small audience chamber, looking flushed and happy, her hair a little disheveled. She took off her cloak and flung it on a chair.

"I beg your pardon for being late, Hugh. I wanted to take Joanna riding down by the river, where I used to go so often with your father. It was a little chilly, but we had a glorious ride!"

"I'm sorry I haven't taken her there. In fact, I haven't spent nearly as much time with your daughter as I should have."

"Don't worry about it, she seems perfectly contented. And you, of course, are bound to be busy, what with all your serious responsibilities."

We sat across from each other at the oval-shaped table that occupied the center of the room. While Isabella looked around I looked at her. She was so contained, so self-possessed. I wondered if there could be any softness under that porcelain façade.

"This room has been greatly improved, I see. It used to have only the table and these chairs, no other furniture at all. The fireplace looked as though it hadn't been used in years. Now you have that fine chest, and an armchair, and even a few tapestries. And someone's lit a fire for us. Very well done, Sir Hugh!"

"Thank you. Now, my lady Queen, will you tell me how your affairs are in Angoulême, and whether there's a way I could help you? Let's be frank with one another."

She leaned toward me and spoke carefully, considering her words. "I think there may be a way you could help me. First, let me tell you how I stand. You undoubtedly know some of this. I don't receive loyalty or revenue from most of the barons of Angoulême, in spite of inheriting from my father the suzerainty of the county. I've told them they owe me fealty but they laugh and go on as before. I've written to my son to tell him that without England's support I won't be able to defend his domains here. I do believe Henry wants to help his mother. He's always loved me, as I love him." She sat a moment looking down at her folded hands. I kept silent, waiting to see where this was leading and what kind of help she might be asking for.

"But Henry's so young, so malleable. I don't think he's to blame that I've had no answer to my pleas. It's clear the council has the upper hand. They succeeded in sending me away from England and from my children. They deprived me of the regency. Now they've named as seneschal of Aquitaine the man who will marry my daughter one day."

Now she wasn't the mournful mother but the embattled queen.

"They've named *you*, Hugh! I've been shunted aside as though I were of no consequence whatever. I cannot accept this!"

I was caught in the blaze of her blue eyes like a butterfly on a pin. How beautiful she was!

"I understand completely. Of course you feel mistreated. But Henry's council controls Henry, and they've made their decision. For your sake, I'm deeply sorry to be the recipient of England's largesse and the cause of your distress. But what can be done?"

The anger disappeared. She reached across the table to place her hand on mine. I tried not to show my surprise. I didn't want that gentle pressure to go away.

"Hugh, I've given this so much thought. I've prayed for guidance. Here is what I propose to you. I shall forget about the English and their effrontery. I shall ignore King Philip and his half-hearted efforts to enlist my aid in holding the English off. I shall rely instead on the ancient feudal ties that bind the barons of Aquitaine and Poitou to their historic suzerains—you and me. I ask you, Hugh, to become my husband, to join your lands with mine. This would have happened in any case when you and Joanna were married. But we can't risk waiting five or six years until Joanna can give you children. Forgive me for being blunt, Hugh, but as you said, we must be frank. I'm thirty-four and you're what, thirty-seven? You and I could begin at once to insure the succession to La Marche and Angoulême."

She brought my hand to her lips. I was mesmerized by the blue eyes looking into mine, no longer flashing with anger but gently pleading.

"Hugh, I need your help now."

The touch of her lips on my hand transformed me in an instant from adversary to ally. She was offering herself, her exquisite self, and begging for my protection. I wanted to protect her and I wanted to possess her.

When I could think more clearly I was struck by how her argument echoed the reasons my friends had given me for breaking my engagement. Yet not one of us had thought of this logical resolution.

She released my hand and looked at me, waiting. I had to say something.

"There's much in what you say. I suppose we can assume that Joanna, young as she is, wouldn't feel hurt at being rejected. I suppose King Philip would care very little one way or another. But what of the English? Won't they see this as such a threat that they'll have to restrain us by force?"

"We'll explain to them that we're acting purely in their interest, to preserve their French claims. We'll promise that we and all our vassals will support them in any new war with King Philip."

"Indeed, you've thought this through." I walked around the tale and looked down at her. "There are plenty of political reasons for us to marry. Can you think of any personal ones?"

I drew her to her feet. I put my arms around her waist. I'd expected her to pull back or to be passive. Instead, she laughed up at me and moved closer into my embrace. She held her face up to be kissed. The kiss, tentative at first, lengthened and sweetened. We drew apart and stood there holding each other.

"I've been wanting to do that for some time," I said.

"And so have I."

Henry 111
1220

Hubert de Burgh, the justiciar, blustered into the audience chamber in Westminster Palace where my tutor, Father Jerome, was giving me dictation in Latin. Father Jerome didn't like Sir Hubert any more than I did and excused himself.

Since William Marshal had died in 1219 Sir Hubert had taken over as my protector. I'd always liked Sir William. He'd been my friend and adviser since long before my father died.

Sir Hubert, on the other hand, was overpowering. I wasn't exactly afraid of him, but he made me feel helpless. Whenever I questioned him he'd turn me aside with a sharp word, as though I didn't have the sense to see how right he was. Now that I was nearly thirteen, though, and had been King for four years, I wasn't feeling quite so small and young in his presence.

"I've brought you a letter from your mother," he said.

I was excited. I thought surely she'd say she was coming for my recrowning, which was to take place in two days. I still missed her a great deal.

"Thank you, Sir Hubert! It's so long since she's written me. I think only twice since she went to France. Why do you suppose she doesn't write more often?"

"Perhaps she's too busy, or perhaps she's forgetting about her children that she deserted."

"I don't think she'd forget about me. When she said goodbye she told me that she loved me and would always keep in touch even though she was forced to leave me."

"That may be what she told you, but it's time you faced it the facts, my lord King. When she found out she wasn't going to be able to queen it over the good men your father had appointed as your council she decided she'd rather go back to Angoulême where she could do as she pleased. She didn't mind giving up her children. She's been making trouble ever since."

I didn't believe him but I'd learned there was no point in arguing with Sir Hubert.

"Well, at least she's written this time. I hope she says she's coming for my crowning."

"She doesn't. You aren't going to like what you read there."

"Do you mean you've already read it?"

"Of course. The council always reads any letters that come to you. We must be on the lookout for anything that affects your safety and England's."

"Do you read the letters I send too?"

"We do."

I'd been suspecting something like this. The council had been neither sending my letters to my mother nor giving me hers. Hence the silence.

There wasn't a single thing I could do about it, though, until I figured out a way to stand up to Sir Hubert. One of these days I would. Meantime, I spoke as coldly as I could.

"Please give me the letter. You may leave me now."

"Very well. The council has given some thought to a reply. We'll wait on you in an hour to get your approval." Out he stamped.

I sat down and spread out the parchment.

My beloved son: After the death of Aymer of Taillefer and that of Hugh IX of Lusignan, Count of la Marche, the present lord of Lusignan and of Poitou, Hugh X, found himself without children. His counselors advised him not to marry your sister, she being too young, and to choose a bride in France who could provide him with an heir. If he should do so all your land in Poitou and Gascony, and ours too, would be lost. We therefore, seeing the great danger that might arise if such a marriage should take place, and getting no support from your counselors, have taken the said Hugh, Count of La Marche, to be our lord and husband. God knows that we have taken this action more for your advantage than for our own. Your loving mother, Isabella, Queen of England

The letter was so formal and cold. I was sure it had been written more for the council's eyes than for mine. I stared at it, trying to take in the fact that my mother had married some Frenchman. Then I noticed that the bottom of the page seemed to have been torn off. I guessed at once that my mother had added a personal note, and someone on the council hadn't wanted me to see it. I wondered if I should complain about that. I read the letter again, then tried to concentrate on my Latin lesson without much success.

When I heard shouting and singing, I jumped up and ran to the window that looked out over the river with its constant stream of waterborne traffic. A procession of three gaily decorated boats was floating slowly downstream— slowly, I saw, because the oarsmen were busier passing the jug about than they were in using their oars. Each boat was crammed with merrymakers, decked out in their finest, singing loudly and discordantly and tossing flowers onto the water. Then I remembered that it was Mayday, the Feast of Saints Philip and James. This was when the English celebrated the beginning of summer. I wished that I could go boating too. But I couldn't imagine Sir Hubert agreeing to such a frivolous wish. I sighed and went back to my Latin.

The council arrived at the appointed time. Besides Sir Hubert there were my uncle, William of Salisbury; my guardian, Bishop Peter of Winchester; the papal legate Pandulfo; and several others. I knew all these important men well by now, especially Bishop Peter, who oversaw my lessons. Except for Sir Hubert I liked and trusted them.

The legate Pandulfo had taken over the regency of England from William Marshal. He was the senior member of the council. I'd liked Gualo, the legate before him, better. He was jollier. But Pandulfo and I got along all right. He was sour and not very chatty, but at least he was respectful and didn't treat me like a child. Furthermore, he wasn't huge and intimidating like Sir Hubert. In fact he was quite short.

Pandulfo showed me the letter they wanted me to sign.

It wasn't very long. It was addressed to Hugh de Lusignan, Count of La Marche, and to Isabella, Countess of Angoulême. In the council's words, I told them that I approved of the marriage. I hoped it would prove mutually beneficial to England and to them, as custodians of lands under English sovereignty. Finally, I requested that they send my sister Joanna back to England. Since she had been destined to marry Hugh de Lusignan, some other alliance would now have to be arranged.

I sat at the table looking at the parchment, wishing there were some way I could add a few words. I wanted to tell my mother I hoped she was well and that she was happy in her new marriage. I wanted to tell her I was sorry she wouldn't be at my coronation. I wanted to tell her I missed her.

In the silence, someone coughed. It was Sir Hubert, standing right behind me. "Is there some difficulty with signing the letter, King Henry? Do you see some errors in the Latin?"

Without answering I picked up the quill pen, dipped it in the inkwell and signed my name: Henry Rex Anglorum.

He snatched the parchment up with a curt "Thank you, my lord King." Ignoring him, I addressed Pandulfo.

"My lord Pandulfo, will you please tell me whom the council is considering to be the husband of my sister Joanna?"

"Certainly. We believe it will be most advantageous to marry her to Alexander II, King of the Scots. That will mean peace along our northern borders. We hope shortly to arrange a meeting between you and King Alexander."

At the name Alexander I remembered something that happened when I was about three. I heard my father complaining to somebody about "that little red fox, King Alexander, who's nipping at our heels along the border." For several years I'd thought there was a king up in Scotland who was a fox. I'd wondered if he had a bushy tail. Now I was almost sorry I was going to meet him and find it wasn't true.

First, though, there'd be the coronation.

The Archbishop of Canterbury, Stephen Langton, had explained to me why I was to have a second coronation.

"When you were crowned at Gloucester just after your father died, my lord King, we had to do it so quickly that the ceremony didn't have all the proper ritual. The Pope has decreed that you should be recrowned. He wants it to be done 'with due solemnity, according to the custom of the realm and in the place which usage of the kingdom requires.' That means at Westminster."

I looked forward to it. At my first crowning I'd been only nine and hardly aware of what was happening. Now that I was four years older I was getting quite used to the ceremonies that went with being a king.

Archbishop Stephen also summarized for me the order of the ritual. I'd march into the church behind him, the bishops and abbots and followed by the council and the nobles. I'd stand before the altar and swear an oath to protect the church of God, to preserve the peace of both clergy and people and the good laws of the realm.

"Then I will anoint your head with holy oil. I'll hand you the seal and insignia of royal office, and place on your head the crown of the most holy King Edward." That was King Edward the Confessor, one of my earliest ancestors and the king who had built the first abbey church at Westminster.

Then there'd be a prayer, the organ would play the Te Deum and we'd all march out.

It went just as he'd said. When the archbishop placed King Edward's crown, heavy with gold and jewels, on my head I felt that now I was truly King of

England.

Much later I read what the chronicler had written about my coronation:

And this crowning of the King was done with such great peacefulness and splendour,
that the oldest men among the nobles of England who were present asserted that they never
remembered any of his predecessors being crowned amid such concord and tranquillity.

Walter of Coventry

Unfortunately, though concord and tranquillity were widespread in England now, they didn't prevail in all of my domains. There was trouble in Aquitaine.

First, my mother said she wouldn't send Joanna back until the council gave her and her new husband the dowry lands promised to her when she married my father. She also asked for the inheritance due her as the widow of King John. My counselors replied that they wouldn't send the money or give up the lands until Joanna was returned, and Hugh and Isabella gave up their claim to Saintonge and Oléron. These lands had been granted to Hugh as surety for Joanna's dowry when they were betrothed.

It was all very complicated. I did my best to understand what went on at the council meetings. It helped when I could ask questions of Bishop Peter afterwards. I signed a great many letters, including one to the Pope and his cardinals. In it I asked that Hugh be compelled to right the wrongs he had done to me, because "regardless of his plighted vow, he has taken our mother to wife instead of our sister and now refuses to give our sister back to us, wishing by his detention of her to compel us to buy her back."

I didn't mind signing that. I was sure that Hugh, not my mother, was responsible for all this trouble.

But it took a while for the muddle to get sorted out. The Pope threatened to excommunicate Hugh. Both sides met to try to sort out their claims. Finally they had to call in the Preceptor of the Temple in London to arbitrate. At last it was resolved. Joanna came back to England. Hugh and my mother gave up their claims to Saintonge and Oléron. My mother received her dower lands and her inheritance.

Thanks to all this I began to see that being a king involved much more than wearing a crown and receiving cheers from one's subjects. Very soon, I thought, I'd speak up more in council meetings.

I was glad to see Joanna again. Hortense, the mother of Joanna's playmate Elizabeth, was now officially Joanna's lady in waiting. Hortense brought my sister up to my rooms in Winchester Palace. We stared at each other, getting used to the differences that two years can make. Joanna was ten now. Like me, she was finding out at an early age what princes and princesses are obliged to do.

"You've gotten taller," I said.

She took this as a compliment. "Thank you."

She was prettier too, and I told her so. She blushed a little. She was doing her best to act grown-up. I expect it helps one to mature to be engaged to a thirty-one-year-old French count at the age of four, to have that engagement broken off at ten, and to be instantly promised to a twenty-three-year-old Scottish king.

"Did my mother send any message to me?" I asked.

"Yes, she said to tell you she loved you, and she is very pleased that you and your council have resolved your differences with her and Sir Hugh."

"Do you think she'll ever come back to see us? Will she come to your wedding?"

"I doubt it. But she said I was to tell you to take me under your care until I'm married."

"I'll do that. You'll stay with me here at Winchester, or wherever I am, and I'll travel with you when you go to meet King Alexander."

Still, I wasn't sure whether marrying a little red fox up there in the wilds of Scotland was the best future for her.

Isabella

1220-1225

It was hard to say goodbye to Joanna. I only hoped that at ten, she felt secure in my love. That would give her strength when she returned to the land of her birth, where Henry's council would doubtless dispose of her in the manner they thought most advantageous. In November of 1220, I could put it off no longer. She had to go.

"You must be sure to tell Henry and Richard and your two little sisters that I send them my love," I told her. "And tell Henry that I depend on him to keep you safe and well."

"I will, mother."

We were in the bailey at Lusignan, where Hugh and I had come after our marriage in April. Joanna was already in the saddle. So was Hugh, who was to take her to La Rochelle and deliver her to her English escorts. So were the rest of the party—Lady Hortense, her daughter Elizabeth and six of Hugh's knights. Everybody was thoroughly cloaked and hooded against the cold. An early snowfall had blanketed everything with a soft white coat, hiding all the mud and making little white mountains out of haystacks and woodpiles. I looked up at Joanna's small figure through a gauzy curtain of gently falling snowflakes. I felt she was already receding from me into her unknown future. It was perfectly quiet except for the muted jangle of the riders' harness. I heard the bells of the village church toll eleven. As though that were a signal, Hugh waved, wheeled his horse and led the riders out through the gate.

Watching them disappear in the swirling snow, I felt very tired, as though I'd come to the end of one long journey and needed to catch my breath before setting out on the next. All the children of my marriage to John were now out of my life, except for whatever ties I could manage to maintain from this great distance. I would need to maintain ties to Henry, certainly. Not only was he my firstborn and best-loved son, but also as King of England he was our overlord for all our lands in Aquitaine.

As I went back into the castle, though, England seemed very far away. I was beginning my new life, the next stage of the journey. I was expecting my first child by my new husband.

Marriage to Hugh had already proved vastly different from marriage to John. I'd never felt that John saw me as his equal, even during our first years when we were infatuated with each other and he would do anything for me. Increasingly he'd treated me not as a partner but as a subject—and finally as a victim. I still shuddered when I thought how filled with anger and discord our last years had been.

I'd resolved never to let that happen to me again.

Hugh and I married out of prudence, not passion. We saw no other way for both of us to keep a firm hold on our possessions. We knew we'd have to work together against those who would deprive us of our domains. We were both well past the age of youthful illusions about love matches. So it was a surprise to find how compatible we could be not only in the council chamber but in the bedchamber as well. Our marriage proved extremely satisfying. It was also remarkably fruitful.

Our first child was born in January 1221. His father expected a son and was given one.

"Well done, my dear!" he said when he came into my chamber after Lady Anne gave him the good news. We were at Angoulême. I'd wanted to have the child there. I thought it would be a sign to my people that I hadn't deserted them for the Lusignans.

"And you look none the worse. In fact, you are positively blooming. And so is this young man." The nurse had handed him the well-swaddled infant. "We'll call him Hugh, won't we? Hugh the Eleventh, Count of La Marche and Angoulême. How does that sound, my son?" The baby kicked and squawked. Hugh gave him hastily back to the nurse. Hugh was new to fatherhood, while motherhood was an old story for me.

When little Hugh was not yet two and I was well into another pregnancy, his father decided it was time to talk about his son's future.

We'd gone out to take the air, and were strolling along the winding brick walk through the rose gardens at the palace in Angoulême. I tired quickly these days. I sank down on the bench near the fountain. Even now, so many years later, this spot reminded me of Hugh le Brun. Here was where we'd exchanged a chaste farewell kiss that led to John's first attack on me for supposed infidelity. And here, six years later, we'd sat during the long summer evenings of that stolen week when we were so briefly lovers. Bittersweet memories, fading fast.

My husband's voice roused me. He was standing, arms akimbo, gazing at the fountain and musing about the prospects of the latest Hugh.

"He should be able to command a princess as his bride. What do you think, Queen Isabella?" He knew I liked it when he gave me my title, even though I suspected a bit of irony.

"I agree completely, but from what I hear eligible princesses are in rather short supply these days."

He grinned. He'd told me how he and his advisers had tried in vain to come up with a suitable princess for him to marry if he gave up his betrothal to Joanna.

"We do have a few years to make this decision, Hugh."

"True. Nevertheless, my love, I think I'll ask Bishop Etienne to start some subtle inquiries. While he's at it he could ask about young princes. I feel our next child will be a daughter."

"What a schemer you are! But I suppose it can do no harm. Meantime, we have a more immediate problem. Do sit down and listen."

He sat obediently.

"Don't you think, Hugh, since our family is growing so fast, that we should contrive to make more room for us all? My father always meant to add another tower to the palace. But he never got around to it. I've asked old Jean d'Aunat if he remembered talking to my father about it. Jean was castellan here for years and years. He does indeed remember. The tower was to be there, where the north and east walls come together." I pointed to a spot off to our right where nothing towered except a spindly pine tree.

Hugh peered at the corner I'd pointed to. "Well, I suppose that would make sense. For one thing, it gives us more strength and a good lookout post on the north wall. And I think we can afford it. The revenues are coming in regularly, for the most part. We're at peace for the moment with both King Philip and King Henry." The more he spoke, the more enthusiastic he became. "Yes, now would be a good time. We'll begin at once. Let's call it the Tour d'Isabelle."

"Not the Tour des Lusignans?" I teased him.

"Oh, plenty of time for that later. As our family grows we can add tower after tower!"

I laughed up at him and held out my hands for him to help me to my feet. There were so many things about Hugh that I loved: his good cheer, his optimism, his energy without the vacillations I'd observed in John. I liked the way our aspirations for our joint future meshed so smoothly. Most of all I liked how he listened to what I said, took my suggestions seriously and usually agreed.

We needed all our optimism and energy during the next few years.

In July of 1223 King Philip died. He'd been King of France since before I was born, a force to be feared, respected, reckoned with. In his place we now had Louis VIII, less canny and less inclined to sit back and watch events take their course than his father. He'd been chafing under Philip's restraint for years. Now at thirty-six he could wear the crown and brandish the sword. His first objective was the County of Poitou.

Both Hugh's La Marche and my Angoulême were in Poitou. In exchange for England's recognition of our rights to them we'd given our allegiance to King Henry. Since we'd sent Joanna back and my dower lands had been restored to me we'd had no serious quarrels with the English. In fact, we'd heard very little from Henry and his council even when we'd asked for help in keeping the Poitevin barons in check. Still, our affairs were going well. We saw no reason to make any changes. We hoped that Louis's threats were merely bluster.

But within a few months Louis sang a new tune. He stopped blustering and made us a direct offer—a very tempting offer. In exchange for our fealty he'd give us some of the richest lands in Poitou to add to those we already held. Once all Poitou was in French hands, he'd make Hugh his general for an attack on Gascony to the south. He'd assign to him two hundred mounted knights and six hundred foot soldiers.

If Hugh succeeded in capturing the prosperous seaport of Bordeaux during this campaign Louis would grant him its revenues.

We talked it over at length.

"We'd be taking a big chance," said Hugh. "What do you suppose your son would do if Louis marched into his Poitou? Wouldn't he send an army over?"

"He might, I suppose. But he'd hardly have time if Louis acts quickly enough."

"We'd be very rich."

"And very powerful. Especially if we became masters of Bordeaux. This puts things in a new light, Hugh. For two years the English haven't answered our requests for help. I think we'd now be justified in renouncing our allegiance to them, though of course it troubles me. But facts are facts. They've ignored us."

"Right! We've had no thanks and no compensation for keeping the peace in Poitou. And they named a new seneschal of Aquitaine without bothering to tell me."

So we agreed to switch masters. To ease my conscience I wrote to Henry, explaining how necessary it was in view of the lack of English support during the past few years.

On Midsummer Day in 1224 Hugh went to war, leaving me with three small children—Guy had been born in 1222 and Isabella arrived in June 1224, just before Hugh's departure. The name was Hugh's idea.

"I'm so happy with the Isabella I have," he said, "that I'd like to add another."

I didn't see him again for four months. I received a few messages, not very detailed. Other reports and rumors came our way from a hodgepodge of travelers--merchants, pilgrims, wounded soldiers returning to recuperate. All in all, Louis and his army seemed to be doing quite well in Poitou, but I was thirsty for real news.

In October we were reunited.

I hadn't realized how much I'd missed him until Pierre knocked on the door of my chamber at Lusignan and poked his head in, his creased brown face split by a grin.

"He's home again!"

Hugh was right behind him.

"My own Queen Isabella!" he cried. "There you are, bewitching as ever." He gave me a hug and a kiss, then stood back to look at me.

"Actually, I believe you are even more bewitching. How can you bear to acknowledge this old man as your husband? Here I am, baked black by the sun, wrinkled by worry, bowlegged after weeks on horseback, and starved to a skeleton by soldiers' rations."

"A good wash and some fresh clothes are what you need, old man. Then we'll have some supper and you'll tell me everything. Oh Hugh, I'm so glad you're back!"

"What's the hurry about supper? Let me get cleaned up and I'll meet you in your chamber. Then you can show me just how glad you are."

Eventually over our supper table he told me his story of the past four months. It was mostly a string of successes.

"There wasn't much blood shed by either side. We took Niort in July. St-Jean-d'Angély gave up without a battle. We were far busier galloping from town to town and searching for a place to sleep than fighting. Apparently the towns had asked King Henry for support but no help came. So they had no choice but to submit to us."

"Yes, I heard that from Sir Terric. He still has his mysterious ways of knowing what's going on in England. He learned the Irish had been rising and rebelling and the English had to send a large army to put them down. So they couldn't do much about the requests of their vassals over here. I'm just as glad. I can't say I'd have liked going into battle against my son's forces."

"Nor I, of course. I'd rather think of Henry as my stepson, not my enemy."

"I dearly hope the day will come when you can meet him as a son. Now do have another bowl of this lentil soup. It will do wonders for your starved skeleton."

"Thank you, I believe I will. But let me tell you about La Rochelle. That was the biggest surprise of all. We'd expected a hot defense because as you know the city has been loyal to the Angevins for some seventy-five years. King Louis ordered up the siege engines and we got ready for a long siege. First though, as a formality he sent envoys to negotiate with the city fathers. We'd hardly lobbed a boulder or two over the wall when the garrison marched out and surrendered, and the citizens swore fealty to Louis. I think some of our men were disappointed. They do like a chance to give a well-defended fortress a good battering, and then take the place by storm."

"So Louis secured Poitou. Which of course he couldn't have done without you, my love." I patted his knee. "What happened next?"

"A great deal. The King decided things had gone so well that he could return to Paris. He wants to start planning his Crusade against those heretics in the south, the ones who've broken away from the church. It seems the Albigensian heresy has spread from the common people to his own noble vassals. So he left and ordered me to lead the forces down into Gascony. That wasn't so easy."

While he finished off his soup, I refilled our wine goblets. I was anxious to hear about Bordeaux, the city whose revenues we'd been promised. But Hugh seemed determined to tell his story in the order of events as they happened.

"Well, at first it wasn't hard. We took four of the big towns to the east of Bordeaux. We thought we'd have a hard time at La Réole on the Garonne. It's built on a steep hill with the castle at the very top. But the garrison was pretty careless. I suppose they counted on hearing the clatter of hoofbeats long before any attackers got to the castle. We fooled them--left the horses down at the bottom and crept up on foot. There was only one guard at the gate so we got in with no trouble. They didn't even have time to post any archers. And where do you suppose I spent that night, Queen Isabella?"

"I hope not with some camp follower or loose-living lady of the town."

"Certainly not. I was lodged in solitary splendor in the grand Hotel de Ville.

That's the palace King Richard built some thirty years ago as a gift to the city after they supported him in one of his raids down toward Toulouse. The mayor was all settled in for the night, but he quickly gave up his own rooms to me when he saw which way the land lay. I found them quite comfortable. I must say, I felt grateful to your brother-in-law."

I was beginning to suspect Hugh was rattling on like this to put off telling me the outcome of the campaign hadn't been a happy one.

He took a handful of raisins and chewed them thoroughly. He saw that I was getting impatient. He looked at me mischievously.

"They sweeten the stomach, you know. Good for the digestion. After that fine meal, my stomach deserves a sweet finish."

Serious again, he sighed.

"Well, now comes the bad news. In spite of meeting so little resistance around Bordeaux, we couldn't take the city itself. God knows it wasn't for lack of trying. We tried to force our way in. When that failed, we tried to persuade their officers that they'd be better off under Louis than Henry. They just laughed. They don't care a farthing which king claims to rule them. All they care about is the cozy relationship they have with the English. It's a city of merchants and shippers, that's what it comes down to. As long as the English are so thirsty for French wine, the Bordelais will keep selling it and sending it across the Channel. They doubt King Louis would let them. I doubt it too."

"That's bad news indeed. King Louis must have known what a hopeless mission it would be, why did he send you?"

"I've decided he dangled the prize of Bordeaux before us so we'd support him in his other campaigns. We'll have to learn to be more suspicious of our monarch's motives, my dear."

"Yes, and maybe come up with some schemes of our own. Well, in any case, you've helped him regain Poitou and a good part of Gascony. We won't let him forget that."

A servant came to remove the remnants of our supper and light the candles. We sat there a while in silence. Poor tired Hugh was slumped in his chair and almost nodding off. A shaft of golden light from the declining sun lit the room and warmed my face. I caught the sweet scent of lavender from a bowl of dried blossoms on a table behind me. Perhaps they're right when they say lavender stimulates the brain. Ideas about what we should do next were buzzing about in my head like agitated bees.

"Hugh my love, what do you think of this?"

He came to with a jerk.

"What do I think of what?"

"This: King Louis will be very busy in Paris for some time, getting ready for his Crusade. We shouldn't be idle. Let's go out into Poitou and call on the barons who've just come back into the French camp. We'll remind them that fealty to Louis means fealty to us too, because the King has charged us to maintain order and peace in his name. And let's suggest, ever so subtly, that they can count on us more than on the King of France to keep their interests paramount, just in case—God forbid—the English once again become their overlords in Poitou."

He was wide-awake now.

"Yes, I see what you're getting at. We should build some bridges before the next flood comes, as it's very likely to do. I assume, my Queen, that in these subtle hints of our support in case of a change of masters we'll imply that you, as mother of the King of England, may have some special influence you could bring to bear."

I smiled at him and poured the last of the wine. As we raised our silver goblets they glittered in the sunset rays.

"To Angoulême and La Marche, against all others!"

We did make our forays out to call on our vassals and those we hoped to enlist as vassals, with considerable success. Over the next few months we divided our time between that and seeing to the improvements to our castles. Besides the new tower at Angoulême we'd begun building an addition at Lusignan to serve as the Logis de la Reine—the Queen's Chambers. I'd persuaded Hugh that we needed more space for my ladies and me as well as the children. As a matter of principle he demurred at first—he was more frugal than I was. But I pointed out that as King John's wife I'd had my own Queen's House at Winchester. He came around.

For a time we felt we reigned in our own golden kingdom where all went well. Then in March 1225 came news that tarnished the gold considerably. My son Richard with a sizable army was on his way to Bordeaux, aiming to retake Gascony for King Henry.

Henry 111
1225-1227

A few months after I officially came of age at eighteen my brother Richard turned sixteen. I knighted him and granted him the earldom of Cornwall and the countship of Poitou. Now he was equipped to lead our forces into battle. He could go overseas and launch a bold new campaign to retake the lands recently lost to King Louis and to our stepfather.

I'd worried about his going off so young to such a difficult task. I'd offered to go myself. Hubert de Burgh dissuaded me.

"No, King Henry, your best service to your kingdom is to stay here and give your people a sense of stability and purpose. You'd do well to travel to the North, to Ireland and Wales, let everyone see that their young King cares about their welfare and safety. Richard will be in good hands, with his uncle Earl William and Philip d'Aubigné to accompany him. They're the most seasoned warriors we have."

The assignment suited Richard perfectly. Though I knew war was necessary and had always acquitted myself well, I thought it a chore. Richard saw it as glorious recreation and always had.

Once at Windsor, when I'd been practicing at jousting under William Marshal's supervision, ten-year-old Richard had begged to take a run at the quintain, though he'd never done it before. I dismounted and gave him my lance. He mounted and set of with the speed of a falcon dropping on its prey. He launched the lance with such force that it went clean through the straw body and buried itself in the post.

William Marshal watched in amazement.

"By the saints, young man, you're a born warrior. I've never seen any but a grown man do that. You must take after your uncle, Richard the Lionheart. He was always one to dash into the thick of the battle as though the enemy were so many straw men, like that poor wounded fellow there. And he'd come out the victor, ten times out of ten."

Richard went scarlet with pride. After that he had his own horse and lance. And now he had his sword. Everybody was full of hope and confidence.

"He'll be a brave leader," said William de Cantilupe, who had continued as my steward after my father's death.

"I predict that in two months we'll hear that Gascony is ours again," said Sir Hubert.

I still didn't like Sir Hubert, but I'd come to respect him. He was stern, unbending, even pig-headed sometimes. I'd never forgiven him for the way he sent my mother away. But he was loyal to me and had England's best interests at heart, as he understood them. As far as I knew, he wasn't more likely than the next man to try to enrich himself through his office of justiciar.

I asked Richard to come to my audience chamber at Westminster Palace just before he was to leave. He was so excited he couldn't settle down. His short blond curls were tousled. He didn't wear his hair long as I did—"With short hair your head won't get so hot and sweaty in your helmet," he'd said when he was nine and insisted on having his hair cut. That was years before he'd worn a helmet. Now my tall young brother wore a coat of supple chain mail and carried his helmet under his arm.

"So, brother, you're about to go to war at last. I wish I were going too, but they tell me I mustn't. So be it. Now, there are a few things I want to say before you leave."

He settled himself in a chair before me. He stretched out his long legs and looked attentive. Maybe he expected a lecture on bravery, fighting for the honor of England and setting an example to the troops.

"Your enemies will include our mother's husband, Hugh de Lusignan. We don't know much about him except that he seems ready to serve any master who makes it worth his while. You may never even come across him. But if you can, try to find out what kind of man he really is, what people think of him, whether there's any way we could persuade him to become an ally and to stay faithful to England. I wish you might have a chance to go to Angoulême or at least to send a message to our mother, but I suppose that will be impossible."

"It's not so far from Bordeaux, where we'll land," Richard said. "I've been studying the maps. But I doubt if it would look well if the leader of the English forces left the battle to call on the wife of our chief enemy. Henry…" He paused, then took a deep breath. "Henry, you really should face the facts. Our mother left England and married Hugh, she's raising another family with him and she's never bothered to keep in touch. It's plain to me and should be to you that she doesn't care about us anymore."

I didn't say anything. I had nothing to go on besides my memories of my mother. But I knew he was wrong.

A man knocked and came in to tell us that Sir Hubert, Pandulfo and the rest of the council were waiting in the courtyard. The knights were mounted and Richard's horse was saddled and ready.

"Let's go out, then," I said. "It's time for us stay-at-homes to wish you and your men Godspeed and send you bravely on your way."

Hubert de Burgh's prediction about how soon Richard would succeed was almost on the mark. Our forces were warmly welcomed at Bordeaux. Within a few months he sent word that most of Gascony was again solidly pledged to King Henry. Only a few towns held out.

In October Richard sent another report. The council met at Westminster to hear it and to discuss our strategy.

The others were already seated at the council table on the dais of the great hall when I came in. I looked around at the enormous room where I'd attended so many banquets and gatherings. It hadn't changed much over the years. Red and gold Plantagenet pennants still hung along the walls between the tall arched windows. They looked as though they'd benefit from a good shaking out. Fires blazed in the two fireplaces, but whatever heat they released floated at once to the cavernous upper reaches of the hall, shadowy with the network of stout wooden buttresses holding up the distant ceiling. It was chilly and drafty and smelled musty. I pulled my fur-lined cloak closer about me and seated myself at the center of the table, surrounded by familiar faces.

Sir Hubert sat on my right. My uncle, Earl William of Salisbury, was on my left. He'd been fighting alongside Richard and had brought this latest message. Strictly speaking he wasn't a full uncle, being the natural son of King Henry, my grandfather. He'd always served his half-brother, my father, with bravery and devotion. Looking at the tall, commanding figure, I remembered when I'd first heard him referred to as "William Longsword," and realized it was a deliberate and unkind comparison with the name they gave my father behind his back, "John Softsword." But Earl William was far too honorable to bring that up.

Also at the table were the legate Pandulfo, Archbishop Stephen of Canterbury, William de Cantilupe and Brian de Lisle. My old tutor and friend Peter des

Roches, bishop of Winchester, was no longer asked to attend council meetings. He'd had a serious falling-out with Sir Hubert two years before.

"Welcome," I said, looking along the table and nodding at each man. "Earl William, let us hear the message my brother sends."

My uncle unrolled the parchment.

"To our brother the King and all his loyal subjects, greeting: We rejoice that all Gascony is now safely restored to England. We have taken the last two towns to resist us, Bergerac and La Réole, to the east of Bordeaux. At La Réole we came very near to capturing the enemy leader, Hugh de Lusignan, while he was making a stealthy retreat during the night. He escaped us this time, but we will be vigilant. We await your instructions. With Gascony ours, we may now with good hopes make incursions into Poitou and drive King Louis from his strongholds there. Richard, Count of Poitou."

Until recently Sir Hubert would have taken charge at this point. Now he deferred to me. I'd thought the day would never come. I addressed the council.

"We must build on my brother Richard's successes. Sir Hubert, speak first. What is your advice?"

The big man seemed to swell even larger in his chair, almost overflowing it with the bulk of his body and his opinions, bursting to be expressed.

"Thank you, my liege," he said in his rumbling growl. "Our course seems clear to me. We must keep the initiative and move as quickly as possible into Poitou."

"And the sooner the better," said Earl William. "Before I left, we heard what King Louis has been up to in Poitou since he regained it. He's been settling differences with the cities, donating to churches and religious orders, acting the part of the generous overlord. The Count of La Marche and the Countess of Angoulême are right behind him. If we don't act now we'll find it devilishly difficult to regain any of our old vassals."

"On the other hand," said canny old William de Cantilupe, "we mustn't neglect Périgord and the Limousin. They haven't gone over to King Louis yet, but without our attention they might. We know King Louis will soon go on his Crusade. I'd suggest we do what we can in the South now, then when Louis is out of the way, go up into Poitou."

I asked Pandulfo, "What's your opinion?" As papal legate, his first loyalty was to the Pope. But since the Pope was still technically the ruler of England, Pandulfo had to be equally devoted to the well-being of his master's kingdom. He looked around the table. With his sharp nose, long chin and hooded eyes he'd always reminded me of a lizard. Sometimes I expected an angry tongue to flick out from those tightly closed lips.

"We mustn't leap into an assault on Poitou while King Louis is absent on his Crusade. My information is that he will be leaving very shortly. As you know, this Crusade is dear to the heart of Pope Honorius, who wishes once and for all to stamp out the heresy of the Albigensians."

"And King Louis wishes to stamp out the rebellion of the Count of Toulouse, who's taken up the cause of the heretics more out of politics than religious zeal," said Sir Hubert. "How convenient that the Pope's and the King's aims coincide." Sir Hubert was always suspicious of everybody's motives. Yet I think we all agreed with him.

"That may well be," Pandulfo went on. "But you may not be aware that the Pope has threatened to excommunicate anyone who attacks the domains of King Louis while he is on his holy mission."

This gave everybody pause.

Archbishop Stephen spoke up. "I must concur in my good friend's cautions. England has already suffered the pains of excommunication. I'd be most distressed if, out of an eagerness for quick conquests, we subjected our people to that disgrace again."

Nobody wanted to the first to advocate bringing disgrace on the nation. After a moment Archbishop Stephen went on.

"Furthermore, as good Christians it's our duty to support King Louis, or at least not hinder him. The Albigensian heresy threatens the very foundations of the church. The misguided believers claim they are the only true Christians; unfortunately they have refused to listen when good Catholics have tried to explain to them the error of their ways. Much as we deplore it, this may be a time when war is the only answer."

"Still, it's not our war," Sir Hubert muttered. "Our war is in Poitou. Why do we have to suit our actions to the whims of King Louis?"

For some time the opposing views were noisily aired around the table. To add to the confusion, Brian de Lisle remembered that a respected astrologer had predicted that King Louis would die during the Crusade. If that were true, we might do better to wait until he was dead before we took action. Yet if it weren't true, we'd lose valuable time by holding off.

Finally I spoke up above the clamor.

"Good friends, listen to your King. I believe, in view of the Pope's threat, we should postpone action. Let us instruct Count Richard to assemble his forces and march north to the Poitou border. That will keep our enemies unsettled and alarmed. In their indecision some may decide to come over to our side. When we see how King Louis fares we can decide on the next steps."

At this, Hubert de Burgh grew quite red and sat scowling at his clenched hands. Pandulfo gave me a quick glance of what looked like approval. William de Cantilupe looked noncommittal. Archbishop Stephen smiled blandly. Brian de Lisle, a crony of Hubert de Burgh, looked glum. Only Earl William spoke.

"A wise judgment, my lord King. I believe Count Richard will agree. He is eager to pursue his advantages, but he is also aware that his army needs time to recover from the campaign. This gives him that time." My uncle was a diplomat as well as a soldier.

So hostilities ceased at the end of 1226 while King Louis was battling in the south. In November of that year we had the news that the astrologer's prediction had come true. Louis VIII of France died while returning to Paris from his Crusade.

The council had to scramble to adjust to these new circumstances. The late King's son, Louis IX, was only twelve. For some time his mother the Queen Regent, Blanche of Castile, would rule France. From everything we'd heard about her, she'd be hard to ignore. We thought we should capitalize on the uncertainty and probable unrest in France and seize the moment for attack. We sent envoys to feel out the lords of Poitou, Anjou and Normandy.

Then we had some unexpected good news: the commander of the important port of La Rochelle had opened the gates of the city to Richard. This put us in a considerably stronger position. Yet I was still reluctant to begin any major action that could mean all-out war against my mother and her husband.

Queen Blanche made my decision for me. She offered a truce to last until Midsummer of 1227. In spite of the reservations of some of my more battle-hungry advisers, I sent instructions to Richard to sign the truce. It was signed on the other side by Queen Blanche, Louis IX, Hugh de Lusignan and some of his adherents.

In the first year of my majority I'd made war, made peace and, I believed, begun to act as a king—a prudent king.

Isabella

1227-1240

When Blanche of Castile became Queen Regent of France I intended to be friendly, even magnanimous. I felt Hugh and I were in a strong position to receive special favors from the French monarchy.

My English sons were clawing ferociously at the lands their father had lost to the French. Richard had already retaken Gascony, the longtime seat of English power in southwestern France with its prize, the port of Bordeaux. Blanche must have known that my son Henry was maneuvering to take back Poitou, where Hugh and I held sway. It would certainly be in her interest to cultivate the goodwill of the invaders' mother.

Besides, we had so much in common: We were widows of kings and had sons who were kings. We were almost the same age. We even had a family tie. Her mother, Eleanor of Castile, had been the sister of King John, so through my marriage to him I'd become her aunt.

I was gratified but not surprised, therefore, when we received an invitation to visit her at Vendôme in June of 1227.

"This could be a very interesting meeting," I said to Hugh. "We must make a good impression. I think we should take at least six of our courtiers."

By now we'd attracted a small group of lords and ladies who were with us at Angoulême and Lusignan and accompanied us on our travels about our lands. To my sorrow Lady Anne was no longer one of them. William de Cantilupe's mysterious hidden wife had finally died and he'd sent for Anne to come marry him at last. I was happy for her but bereft at the loss of this last tie with my past. I felt that with her going I was finally saying goodbye to my youth.

"Who will tell me I'm still beautiful in spite of having passed forty? Who will keep me from being foolish and headstrong?" I asked her. We were at Lusignan, where she'd brought me as an uncertain fourteen-year-old, so many years ago. Though she was nearly sixty, the years had been kind to her. I looked at the wise, affectionate face of this woman who knew me so well. I clung to her hand, unwilling to let her go.

"My dear lady, I've done all I can for you in that respect. At least I leave you with a kind husband and fewer temptations to stray."

We hugged, and after one last kiss on my cheek she was gone.

Now, two weeks later, Hugh and I and our party made our way up "La Montagne," the eminence above the River Loir where the castle of Vendôme perched in lonely majesty. Before we went through the gates we stopped to look across the deep gorge of the river to the town that clung to the hill on the other side. At the crest was a sprawling abbey with the tallest bell tower I'd ever seen.

"Strategically speaking," said Hugh, "this castle is as fortunate as Lusignan, high on a cliff with unobstructed views of any enemies approaching."

"I agree as to the location. But we don't have such a fine prospect. When we look out from our castle we don't see anything but the insignificant little farms down below and the woods on the other side of a river half the size of the Loir."

"Well, never mind. If Queen Blanche thought she was going to make us discontented with our humble lot by asking us to her grand castle, she'll have to think again. I wouldn't trade our Lusignan for this or any other castle in France."

I tried to agree, but when we were inside the walls and I saw the exquisite garden that occupied almost all the big courtyard, I felt stabs of jealousy. Pebbled paths bordered by neatly trimmed hedges ran in precise lines, crisscrossing the space and framing flowerbeds. White lilies filled one bed, next to it were roses in bud with a few blushing pink rosettes just unfolding, then a square of regal purple iris, and so on through all the colors of the rainbow. Two gardeners were hard at work plucking out any rash weeds that dared to peep above ground. I saw a white-clothed table set up in the center. A blue canopy decorated with golden fleurs-de-lis shielded it from the sun.

The whole scene made our gardens at both Angoulême and Lusignan look haphazard and untended. I resolved that when I returned I would order some changes.

Queen Blanche was waiting at the foot of the broad flight of stone steps at the castle entrance.

I'd feared I'd find a ravishing beauty, tall and imperial. This unsmiling woman, hardly taller than I was, was far from beautiful. I saw a dark-complexioned face, dominated by black eyes, heavy black eyebrows that almost met, and a nose a trifle too large for harmony. Her Spanish heritage was evident not only in her face but also in her costume, of unadorned black from head to toe except for a gold cross at her throat. I was surprised that when she spoke her French was flawless.

"Welcome, Sir Hugh and Lady Isabella." (My first clue as to how she saw me: She didn't call me Queen Isabella.) "I am so happy that you could come. If you please, come in to refresh yourselves before we dine."

When we came out, we found King Louis, an untalkative lad of thirteen, seated at the head of the table. An indigo-blue silk tunic hung loosely on his thin frame. From time to time he poked at his crown to make it sit more comfortably on his narrow head. His mother asked Hugh and me to sit on either side of him. She took the place next to me. Our courtiers and hers arranged themselves at the remaining places.

I was completely charmed by the ambience. It was pleasantly warm. Our pavilion was an island of civilized elegance in the midst of a disciplined, colorful floral sea. The scent of roses and lilacs hovered in the air. Servants brought course after course of a long meal that began with tiny succulent roasted ortolans and ended with sweet pastries in the shape of fleurs-de-lis. Nothing of moment was discussed during the meal. Blanche and I settled on childhood memories as a safe topic. She'd been brought up under the strict supervision of her father, King Alfonso, and her mother, Queen Eleanor. They taught her to be devout and obedient to her elders, including the nuns and priests who schooled her in Catholicism and the duties of a princess. She professed wonder when she heard of my relatively unsupervised childhood.

When the last pastry had been consumed and the crumbs swept away, Queen Blanche suggested to her majordomo that he give the others of our party a tour of the gardens and the castle. She, King Louis, Hugh and I remained at the table. It was time to get down to business.

Our negotiations were indeed most businesslike. By the time we had been there an hour, we had come to an understanding. His mother spoke for the young King. From time to time she'd look at him inviting comment, and he would murmur a word or simply nod his head. He may have been uninterested, or he may have learned that his mother ran his life and there was no point in having an opinion.

Our agreement amounted to Blanche's buying our support for King Louis vis-à-vis King Henry. She offered 10,600 French livres to compensate me for the portion of my dowry that John's council had never paid me, and to compensate Hugh and me for the loss of revenues from Bordeaux that the late King had promised us. Then we discussed matrimonial alliances between our families. We agreed that our eldest son, Hugh XI, was to be engaged to Isabelle de France, King Louis's sister. Our daughter Isabella was promised to Alphonse, King Louis's brother. Not one of the four was older than seven.

In return we promised to come to the aid of the Queen Regent and her son against all enemies. We wouldn't give asylum or supplies to any enemies of France or lend them troops. That meant, of course, that neither King Henry nor Prince Richard would receive any help from us if they should invade or attack.

"I am satisfied," said Blanche when the bargaining was over. "To celebrate our accord, shall we have a toast with my favorite wine, which is brought to me from Portugal?" She beckoned to one of the servants who were lined up behind us. He brought a crystal decanter and poured each of us a glass of the wine—sweet and potent, glowing ruby-red in the sunlight. We raised our glasses. Hugh made the toast.

"To Queen Blanche and her son King Louis, may this mark the beginning of a mutually beneficial relationship. Queen Isabella and I will cherish the memory of this day when we enjoyed the hospitality of the gracious Queen." Hugh could be quite the courtier when he put his mind to it.

We spent that night at Vendôme, lodged in a sumptuous upper room in one of the towers that were spaced along the battlements.

We were both tired, maybe a little dazed by the day's events. After we'd changed into our night robes and the servants had left we sat down to talk.

"I think we came out rather well, don't you?" I said.

"Especially if she's prompt and honest in sending the money."

"Yes, that remains to be seen. Do you think we should have asked for more than she offered? She might have been willing to go higher."

"It was considerably more than I'd expected. No, I'm content with 10,600 livres. That's almost as much as we get in a year from all our fiefs in Poitou."

"I suppose you're right. And as for the marriage arrangements, they're advantageous to both our sides. I'll confess I was halfway hoping that she'd suggest betrothing King Louis to our Isabella. I suppose she's holding out for some royal princess for him."

"Probably." Hugh yawned and stretched. He looked toward the enormous bed, canopied in blue and gold silk. "It's time to get our rest."

I wasn't quite finished.

"Hugh, did you notice that Blanche never called me Queen Isabella and all the time we were discussing terms she addressed you, not me?"

"Indeed I did. I was gratified that you didn't point out to her how bad-mannered she was. Your restraint was admirable."

"Thank you, my lord. I thought so too."

I went to stand by the window, looking over the castle walls at the town on the other side of the river. It was nearly dark. I could still make out the abbey's tall tower. One small light shone from a window halfway up. Maybe a monk was reading his scriptures, waiting until time to ring the bells. I wondered if some day we could add a tower like that to the Church of St. André in Angoulême.

The breeze freshened and I shivered. I turned around. Hugh was already in bed, sitting up and not looking so sleepy now.

"I've been thinking, Queen Isabella. Since we may lose two of our children to the royal house of France, we'd do well to begin producing a fresh supply. Come, I can't do it all alone. Will you help me?"

I believe that was the night our fourth son, William, was conceived.

I suppose Henry learned of our agreement with the Queen Regent. At any rate, he began to send counter offers, which we rejected or ignored. Like his father, he was determined to get back England's lost lands. Gascony wasn't enough; he wanted Poitou. That would restore Aquitaine to what it was when Queen Eleanor brought it as her dowry upon her marriage to King Henry. For forty years, the French had been nibbling away at Aquitaine and the English had contested every lost morsel. Even before I was exiled from England I'd seen how Hubert de Burgh and the other members of the King's council had carefully nurtured my son's obsession with reclaiming it.

In early 1230 we were in Angoulême, discussing with the builders, masons and carpenters our plans for a new palace. We'd decided that instead of merely adding a tower to the four-hundred-year-old palace of the Taillefers we'd start afresh. I envisioned a capacious three-towered residence, appropriate to our status. Two of the towers would be round and one octagonal—a nice contrast, I thought. There'd be an interior courtyard where I could create a garden as impressive as the one I'd seen at Vendôme. Hugh objected at first to the cost, despite our new prosperity. Then he saw how we could surround the palace and its bailey with thick defensive walls, linked to the existing city walls. That would give us a palace that was also a fortress. Hugh had been worrying for years about the meager defenses of Angoulême in case of an attack.

While we were discussing these matters with the architect, a messenger came from King Henry. The man had been riding hard through a spring downpour and water was dripping off his cloak when he was ushered into the audience chamber. He insisted on delivering his message at once. It was urgent, he said, and was too important to be trusted to writing. He had to deliver it orally. He'd memorized it well.

"To our beloved mother Queen Isabella and our stepfather Count Hugh, from Henry, King of England, greetings. We trust that you and your sons and daughters are well and prospering. We also trust you have received favorably our several invitations to support us, for which support we have promised you suzerainty, as our vassals, over any lands in Poitou that we reclaim. Now we hereby inform you, in utmost confidence, that King Henry and Count Richard are on the eve of launching an invasion of Poitou from the north. We beg you, in view of the love and respect that we hold for you and that we believe you hold for us, to join us in this endeavor. We plan to arrive at the port of Nantes during the first week in May. We shall hope and expect to find you there. Please send your reply by the messenger who brings you this. Your loving son, Henry."

We sent the messenger down to the kitchen to dry off by the fire and have some hot soup while we considered our answer.

"I see no reason to change loyalties," said Hugh. "We have a perfectly satisfactory arrangement with Queen Blanche and King Louis. They leave us to ourselves without making demands. If we went over to Henry it would mean raising armies, doing battle, alienating many of our vassals, and for what? What chance does he have? The minute he begins his advance he'll find not just the barons of Poitou to subdue, there'll likely be resistance from Brittany, not to mention an army mobilized for Louis."

I understood his reasoning. Yet it wasn't easy to turn down this plea from my son. I could sense the hope and desperation behind the formal words. Over the years since I'd last seen Henry I'd held the memory of him as a beautiful little boy, still learning to rise to what was expected of him, still willing to listen to his mother. I knew that was foolish. He was now twenty-three, he'd been King of England for fourteen years and all that time he'd been dreaming of victories in France. If only that wicked Hubert de Burgh hadn't sent me away I'd have been Queen Regent, just like Queen Blanche. I could have helped my son rule during his minority. Part of me wanted to help him even now.

Hugh was looking at me, wondering why I didn't speak up in agreement.

"But Hugh, think of what it might mean for us if the war went his way—our way? If he brings a large enough army he might succeed this time. We'd be masters of twice as many lands as we now hold. We could forget about Queen Blanche and King Louis. We could leave magnificent legacies to our children. Shouldn't we at least talk about the alternative?"

"Isabella, my dear Queen Isabella, even if by some miracle Henry succeeded, we'd be trading one master—who asks so little of us—for another who would require every service a vassal can provide. The English would be looking over our shoulders every minute, demanding our support for one scheme or another."

We were still sitting side by side at the table, strewn with the papers and parchments we'd been going over with the workmen. Hugh put his arm around me and spoke earnestly. "I know you'd like to help your son. But you have other sons now, and daughters. We mustn't forget our own best interests as well as theirs. We need to fortify our castles and build support in the lands we hold now. Remember our pledge? To Angoulême and La Marche, against all others!"

I sighed, then nodded. He was right, of course.

We instructed the messenger to tell Henry that we were deeply sorry, but we would be unable to meet him at Nantes. But we would be wishing him well and asked him to keep us informed of his progress. I insisted that we leave that small loophole in case he had spectacular success and we decided it would be in our interest to come over to him.

His invasion failed. Though he made some inroads in Poitou, the forces of King Louis were too much for him. By the end of September he went back to England, dejected and, I heard, humiliated that his own mother had refused to come to his aid. The next year he signed a peace treaty with King Louis.

We had a rare opportunity now to look to our own interests. The new castle in Angoulême was our first concern. I sent secret agents to inspect Queen Blanche's gardens at Vendôme and to report to me in detail, so mine could outshine them. We also went ahead with another of my favorite projects, the "Logis de la Reine" at Lusignan. The Queen's Lodgings would be within the ramparts and across the bailey from the old castle keep, joined to it by a long gallery. I could imagine the stately processions of the Queen and her court along the gallery to the castle's great hall.

Throughout Poitou we examined our vassals' defenses and helped them make improvements. We also built a completely new castle at Crozant on the Creuse River at a strategic point that had been woefully undefended. In this and other constructions we were greatly aided by the Lusignan clan. Among the most enthusiastic were Hugh's cousins, descendants of his father's old companions at arms, Geoffrey de Lusignan and Ralph of Eu.

I'd never known Geoffrey, but I had many fond memories of Ralph, my guardian when I was a girl at Lusignan.

"What do you suppose Uncle Ralph would say, Hugh, to the way we're spending all this money to secure Poitou for the interests of the Lusignans and the Taillefers? Would he approve?"

Hugh also remembered his gruff old uncle. "He'd probably say, 'You go ahead if you think it's so important. Just leave me out of it. I have a pain in my belly and I'm going home.'"

Hugh X
1241

55

ow the money poured in!

Isabella and I kept finding new ways to assert our rights of governance over most of Poitou and tap into undreamed-of sources of revenue. Isabella was particularly ingenious.

One Sunday afternoon in Angoulême we went to mass at St. André and were strolling back to the palace. Our eldest sons, tall strapping Hugh and almost-as-tall Guy, had become impatient with our slow pace and had gone on ahead. I was enjoying the fine day, thinking how prosperous and tidy the city looked, when Isabella stopped suddenly and pulled on my arm. "Hugh, I've just had the most marvelous idea. Stand still and let me tell you. "

When Isabella had a marvelous idea, her whole face tensed and her blue eyes positively blazed with her sense of urgency. There was no way to avoid hearing her out.

The narrow street was crowded with other Sunday strollers, who moved around us, looking curiously at their count and countess so deep in conversation. No doubt they wondered what we were up to now. I fear we'd earned a reputation for shaking things up.

"Remember that large tract of vineyards along the Charente River that we own? I think I know how we can get a better price for our wine. Hugh, don't we have the right to set the date of the market when the vintners offer their new wines?"

"We do, as lords of the county. Though we've never bothered to make any changes to the usual date, second week in October."

"Suppose that we postpone the date for the wine market this year."

"Why would we do that?"

"Why, because we can then offer our own wine well before the market and charge whatever we like. There'll be plenty of thirsty folk who can't wait to fill their empty cellars. They'll be glad to pay a little extra."

I laughed in delighted admiration. "How clever! How simple!"

A few days later she came up with another clever idea.

"Hugh, did you know that we permit the Jews to live in their own districts in our cities, and we don't even charge them for the privilege? They should be paying us for protecting them."

I did know that there were Jewish enclaves in the larger cities like Poitiers and Angoulême. It hadn't occurred to me that we were protecting them.

"Of course we are. If we wished we could drive them out, and you may be sure King Louis would support us. He'll do anything to convert Jews to Christianity, but he doesn't care a fig for the ones who prefer not to give up their faith. Yet we let them live peacefully in their neighborhoods. They're rich enough, they could afford to pay something."

So we charged the Jews rent, which they paid without argument.

Sometimes the seigneurs who owed us fealty were surprisingly willing to increase their monetary contributions when we requested it. I explained to Isabella why we were so fortunate. It had to do with the peasants.

"You must have noticed, Isabella, how they toiled at the plowing, with those slow plodding oxen? Now they can plow up a field twice as fast."

"How, by harnessing more oxen? Or whipping them harder? I must confess I've never paid much attention to peasants or oxen."

"No, now their seigneurs are encouraging them to use horses. They move a lot faster. And they're managing to get two crops a year instead of one. So now their lords can demand higher rents which means they can afford higher payments to us."

We also found we could levy tolls on travelers who wished to cross our bridges or pass through our city gates.

There were, of course, grumblings. Sometimes I worried that we'd be seen as greedy.

"Never mind. We'll do more for the church and the holy orders," said Isabella. "That will show people that we're devout and generous."

So we founded two orders of mendicants in Angoulême and provided the wherewithal for the Abbey of La Couronne to enlarge the dormitory and build a chapel where the monks could pray for our eternal souls. Abbot Vital had respectfully asked if he might not spend our donation on a scriptorium instead of the dormitory remodeling. But neither of us was particularly interested in the boring work that scribes did. We thought it far more important for the monks to have a few more inches of space between one cot and the snoring brother in the next one.

"So they'll be rested and in a serene state of mind," I said, "when it's time to go the chapel and pray for their benefactors."

Once we'd settled that matter, Isabella came to depend on the abbot as her spiritual adviser. She'd often visit him to tell him her concerns. He would listen to her when she had doubts about whether our subjects, not to mention God, would think she had acted wisely in this or that affair, or when she wondered if she'd be seen as selfish or vain. I'd overheard complaints about her highhandedness, though I never mentioned them to her. But she probably had an idea she wasn't universally beloved.

At any rate, the abbot must have been reassuring. Isabella would come away from the abbey so full of self-confidence that she couldn't resist telling me all about it.

Our royal overlords in Paris left us alone for the most part. Though King Louis had long since reached his majority, Blanche still acted as co-ruler. Their lack of attention suited us. We liked the freedom to do as we pleased. Then Isabella began to worry. Were King Louis and his mother ignoring us because they thought we weren't important?

She was gleeful, therefore, when in June 1241 a messenger in the blue-and-silver livery of the Capetian kings appeared at our palace in Lusignan with an invitation to a royal assembly at Saumur. This castle on the Loire River had been a favorite of the King's grandfather, Philip Augustus, who had restored it and maintained it as one of his royal residences. With such a distinguished history and with its present fame as a place frequented by the highest nobility of France, the castle of Saumur was like a magnet for Isabella.

"I must have two new gowns," was her first pronouncement.

"Certainly, my dear. As many as you like," I said.

"And we'll need to decide how large a party to take with us. Surely we should include young Hugh, since he's betrothed to the King's sister. And Isabella too, who is promised to the King's brother Alphonse."

"I don't think so. The invitation was directed to Count Hugh of La Marche and Countess Isabella of Angoulême. Nothing about anyone else. If they'd wanted our children they'd have said so. Queen Blanche is probably responsible for planning this event, and she's most punctilious about proper etiquette."

Whereupon my Isabella pouted and we almost quarreled. She insisted on taking our daughter Isabella at least, as well as four of our courtiers.

We found Saumur to be an enormous and confusing conglomeration of towers, inner and outer courtyards and walled enclaves, with a dreary, tall keep in the midst of it all. But it was considerably brightened by the throng of elegantly dressed lords and ladies who milled about, then gathered in the large interior courtyard for King Louis's grand reception. Tables were draped and canopied in blue silk embroidered with silver fleurs-de-lis. The attendants wore tunics of the same blue, bearing the coat of arms of our County of Poitou.

"Why do you suppose they're bearing that insignia?" I said to Isabella. "Saumur isn't in Poitou. It's in the Touraine."

Isabella stopped a passing servant who was carrying a tray of little cakes. They gave off a marvelous aroma of cinnamon and nutmeg.

"Why are you all wearing the coat of arms of Poitou? Why not the King's own insignia?"

The man looked at her haughtily.

"All I can tell you, my lady, is that the tunics were made up especially for this occasion on orders of King Louis." Holding his tray high, he marched off.

"Maybe it means the King is going to give us some special honor, as lords of Poitou." She smoothed down her rose satin skirts and straightened our daughter Isabella's sash.

The King wasn't flaunting any Poitevin insignia, but a tunic and surcoat of blindingly white satin and a scarlet mantle trimmed in ermine. Most of the guests were only slightly less splendid. I was put off by the ostentation but Isabella reveled in it. Her spirits fell somewhat when she found that I'd been asked to sit at the King's table while she hadn't. My tablemates, besides the King and his mother, were his brother Prince Alphonse; the Count of Brittany; and Jean de Dreux, the King's uncle and one of his close advisers. A beautifully gowned young woman, unknown to me and wearing a tiara and a fixed smile, sat next to Queen Blanche. Isabella and our daughter were at the next table down but still surrounded by counts and countesses.

Nobody imagined this was a purely social occasion. Sure enough, at the end of the meal the King rose to address the gathering. He'd been seated when I arrived. Now I saw that he'd grown from the frail-looking, diffident boy I'd last seen into a tall, well-built man, as dignified as a deacon and as humorless.

He told us, after welcoming us and thanking us for gracing his assembly, that he was pleased to make two announcements that he knew would give us joy. First, his younger brother Alphonse, recently knighted, would henceforth be Count of Poitou.

"This was my father's last wish," said King Louis. "He regarded the rich

County of Poitou as one of the jewels of his domains. He instructed me to safeguard it, to keep it from falling again into the hands of the English, and to grant its overlordship to his son Alphonse, as soon as he attained his majority. That day has come."

The significance of the Poitou coat-of-arms was now shockingly clear. Isabella and I had come to see ourselves as de facto lords of Poitou, ruling independently of any monarch, French or English. I looked down to where she sat. Her face was strained. She was fighting not to show her anger. All around her, others were murmuring their approval and smiling as broadly as though they themselves had been granted countships.

The King continued.

"Furthermore, we rejoice to welcome Jeanne, daughter of Count Raymond of Toulouse, into the royal family of France. She was only yesterday joined to our brother Alphonse in matrimony." He gestured to the young woman in the tiara. She stood, smiled even more radiantly at everybody, and sat down again.

I believe I felt this affront fully as much as Isabella did. Without a word to us the King had annulled the engagement of his brother to our daughter Isabella. I looked at him in angry disbelief, then saw Queen Blanche send a malicious glance in my wife's direction. Isabella caught it and sent it back. So much for conciliation. The battle lines were drawn.

"Now," said the King, "I ask all my loyal vassals from Poitou to come forward and pledge your homage to our brother Count Alphonse of Poitou and to his Countess, Jeanne de Toulouse."

One by one we advanced to where Alphonse and his still-smiling wife sat enthroned. Count Alphonse, a good-looking youth of twenty-one, was almost as richly dressed as his brother. When I'd bowed to them both, knelt and placed my hands in his and made my oath, I stood and returned to my seat. I looked toward Isabella to see how she was taking this new insult. Her face had reddened. She suddenly rose, took her daughter's arm, pulled her to her feet and led her away. The girl looked bewildered. Her mother had decked her out for this occasion in a new gown and a cape embroidered with the coats of arms of La Marche and Angoulême. How meaningless those symbols of our power were now!

I stayed until I thought I could leave without being noticed. The guests had risen from the tables and were strolling about, chatting, seeing and being seen. Before I could disappear, though, I heard the King call my name. Perhaps he was going to explain and apologize.

"Sir Hugh," he said while I stood before him respectfully, "I was desolated to see that your lovely wife was so suddenly unwell. I hope it is nothing serious, and I can understand your desire to see to her. Before you go, however, please accept our invitation to join us at the royal palace in Poitiers, in two days' time. We are asking all the new vassals of Prince Alphonse to come to reaffirm their homage to him and agree on various matters to do with his assuming the countship. I hope we may see you there." I had no choice but to say, "Of course, my liege." I added, "And I assume you will want me to bring the Countess of Angoulême." Isabella would be even more unwell if she weren't invited.

"Perhaps the countess, in view of her indisposition, will find it wiser to remain quietly at home for a time."

All the way back to our lodgings I worried about how I'd tell Isabella that King Louis and Count Alphonse didn't want her at Poitiers.

When I got there I found that Isabella had left, taking young Isabella with her. One of her ladies had remained behind to tell me that if I wished to see my wife, I would find her at Angoulême.

Well, that would have to wait. Perhaps it was just as well; I had an idea she would need some time to cool off. Meantime, I'd go to Poitiers.

I'd returned from Poitiers to Lusignan and been there for several days when Isabella arrived from Angoulême. At first I thought everything was going to be all right. She seemed calm. During dinner, where Young Hugh, Guy and Isabella joined us, she spoke to the children and her ladies, with not a word for me. Studying her, I saw the signs. This was the ominous, oppressive quiet that precedes a violent storm. We'd had disagreements, of course, but they seldom lasted long. Often I gave in, just to avoid unpleasantness. Often we settled our differences in bed. Tonight that might not work. Nevertheless, after dinner I accompanied her along the gallery to the Logis de la Reine.

The minute we were in her chamber and before I'd had a chance to sit down, she began.

"So, Hugh, what new shame did you bring on the houses of La Marche and Angoulême at Poitiers?" She was still calm but barely so. Her eyes were cold and blue as icy ponds. She stood straight and rigid, as though she were afraid she might break if she moved. She was clenching and unclenching her hands. The rage that had been building up for a week was boiling to the surface.

"I agreed only to what was necessary to safeguard our interests and those of our children."

"Such as?"

I thought I might as well get it all out at once.

" First I renewed my homage to Alphonse."

"For your La Marche alone, or for the County of Angoulême as well?"

"For both."

"And then?"

"I agreed to hand over to Alphonse the cities of l'Aunis and Saint-Jean-d'Angély."

"*What*? Those were awarded to us as part of the dower that Louis's sister Isabelle will bring when she marries our son Hugh."

"Apparently that's not going to happen. They've affianced her to someone else."

She flung herself into a chair and looked up at me, pale with shock and disbelief. Then she loosed a torrent of invective.

"This is too much, too much. Hugh, how could you let them insult us so? How could you give up our independence, our prospects of advancement? And for what? What did you get in return? Nothing! Oh I wish to God I hadn't listened to you and that we'd kept our allegiance to Henry. My son would never have treated us so basely. If only I'd been there! I would have made it plain that as Queen of England, I will never, never bend the knee to that nobody from Toulouse, countess though she calls herself."

When Isabella was in such a passion, she could be powerfully persuasive. Also strikingly beautiful. Over the years her face had sharpened somewhat and lost its youthful softness, yet gained character. The tilt of her chin, the flash of her eyes, told the world that this was a woman to be reckoned with. Over twenty years of marriage I'd seen her in many moods. The embattled queen stirred me fully as much as the bewitching temptress.

"Isabella…" I began.

"Leave me!" she cried. "I cannot bear the sight of you. I never want to see you again!"

Obviously there'd be no reconciliation in the bedchamber tonight. I left.

The next morning she gathered up all her linens and clothing and the hangings from her rooms, packed up her chests, tables and whatever other furnishings she could remove, and took herself off to Angoulême. She refused to see me before she rode away.

I was anguished. I followed her, but she wouldn't let me into the palace. I had to stay at the lodge of the Templars, across the square. Finally after three days she sent word that I could be admitted.

I found her tearful, wearing a clinging lilac gown that I was sure had been chosen to present her at her most seductive. The presentation was successful.

She allowed me to put my arms around her and kiss her. She looked up at me, with tears still welling in her eyes.

"Oh my dear Hugh, do you see now why I had to come away? I couldn't bear the humiliation and the injustice of our treatment by King Louis and his brother. I couldn't bear to think that you had been a party to it. Hugh, we cannot permit them to push us around like pawns on a chessboard!"

I was deeply moved. She was my wife, the mother of my children, but beyond that she was so fiercely devoted to our cause. I burned to match that devotion. Above all I wanted to restore myself to her good graces. I was ready to promise anything.

"My own Isabella, you are right and I was misled. Will you forgive me? I swear from now on I'll listen to you. Surely the two of us together can find a way to right these wrongs."

She looked at me, unsmiling and deadly serious.

"If you'd said otherwise, my lord, I would never again admit you to my bed."

We were united once more. She permitted me to play the master again as I took her hand and led her to her bedchamber. I believe that was the night our daughter Alice was conceived.

The very next day we began planning a complete reversal of our allegiances. We'd launch a new campaign. It would involve her sons Henry and Richard, our supporters in La Marche and Angoulême and all the barons of western France, to be deployed against King Louis, Queen Blanche and Alphonse.

Henry 111
1241-1242

I n the autumn of 1241 I received a surprising letter from my mother.

To our beloved son, from Queen Isabella, Countess of Angoulême and Hugh de Lusignan, Count of La Marche, greetings. The barons of the West are ready to rise against their Capetian king and his brother Alphonse, whom he has named Count of Poitou. That title is rightfully your brother Richard's. Will you join us in their good fight? We can promise you all the support you lacked when you came across to France ten years ago. The barons' feudal authority is being undermined. They think with longing of the days when they were pledged to the Plantagenets, who were open and generous and who understood their traditions. Will you come to lead them? Your loving mother, Isabella.

How well she knew me! I desperately wanted to believe that the vassals who had failed to answer my call during my last, disastrous invasion would flock to my banner today. Should I have another try at fulfilling my dream? Might it at last be possible to reclaim Aquitaine, Normandy, Brittany?

The days were long past when I had to let my council decide England's course. The men who'd run the country during my early years as king were no longer around. William Marshal, long dead. The papal legate Pandulfo, returned to Rome. Peter des Roches, dead three years ago. Hubert de Burgh, now grown old and weary, retired to his estates in Surrey.

At thirty-four, I felt that I'd learned a great deal about kingship. Now was the time to prove to myself, to my mother and to my people that I could succeed in what had become almost a crusade for me.

But I'd been misled before. I decided I should learn more about the situation before committing myself.

I invited my mother and her husband to come to discuss the matter. They arrived in early December. I'd chosen the small city of Reading for our meeting because I didn't want this to appear as a state visit, pompous and ceremonial. I knew there'd be resistance in England to another Continental venture.

My young wife, Eleanor of Provence, came with me. I'd married her for political advantage, to cement relations between England and the south of France. To my great joy we proved to be fond partners, perfectly suited to each other. We were equally devoted to England and the monarchy. Also in my party were Peter d'Aigueblanche, the bishop of Hereford; Peter of Savoy, Eleanor's uncle, whom I'd come to admire greatly for his circumspection and discretion, and my trusted old household steward William de Cantilupe.

We met at Reading Abbey, one of England's noblest monastic centers, and were lodged in a commodious house adjoining the cloister. These quarters were always reserved for royal guests, because my ancestors had founded the abbey and given it many donations. I'd often come to stay at the peaceful abbey when I needed an escape from the cares of state.

We'd hardly paid our respects to Abbot Richard when our visitors from overseas arrived. They were quite a large party—some dozen lords and ladies besides my mother and my stepfather. My mother entered the hall first.

I thought at first she hadn't changed a bit. She was slim and graceful and walked with the quick, assured step I remembered. She'd tucked her hair under a little jeweled cap, but the tendrils that escaped to frame her face were as golden as ever. Her long purple cloak swept the floor. Her lips were parted in an eager, expectant smile. She was dazzling.

"Henry, my dear son," she said. She reached out her arms and we held each other. I felt like the twelve-year-old boy who'd said goodbye to his adored young mother twenty-one years before. All the anguish of that day came back to me, the day she'd told me that though she was leaving England she'd follow my progress and pray that I'd become the great king she'd always known I could be.

"I am so glad to see you, mother. And how well you look!"

"I am well, thanks be to God. But older, as you see."

Now I did notice a few fine wrinkles fanning out at the corners of her eyes and a little fleshiness under her chin.

"No, I don't see. You're just as lovely as I remember you. And here's another beautiful queen, come to meet her mother-in-law."

Eleanor had been standing at my side waiting to be introduced. They appraised each other. Eleanor was only eighteen, in the first blush of young womanhood and disposed to make a friend of her mother-in-law. My mother was in her fifties, serenely self-confident and with every reason to enlist Eleanor on her side. They smiled at each other, and Eleanor took my mother's arm.

"I'll show you and your ladies to your rooms so you may rest a little before the meal. There's someone there who's waiting most impatiently to see you."

"I do so hope you mean Lady Anne. When I saw Sir William in the hall I thought surely he'd have brought her. Thank you, my dear. You couldn't have brought me a better present."

After they left I greeted my stepfather, whom I was meeting for the first time. He was grayer on top and thicker about the middle than I'd expected. By and large, though, he was good-looking and good-natured with a disarming smile for all. I could see how my mother would be attracted to him.

"A charming city, Reading," he said, "at least what I've seen of it as we rode along the Thames into town. And the abbey is marvelously imposing. But tell me, why did you choose this out-of-the-way spot instead of meeting at Westminster or Winchester? Isabella had so hoped and expected to go to Winchester. She remembers it with great fondness, and I've always wanted to see it."

He looked around the uninspiring room, doubtless comparing it with the imagined splendors of Winchester Palace. It was large and well proportioned. It was perfectly clean and scrubbed; the monks saw to that. The furnishings were adequate—a table now set for dinner but also suitable for parleys, a well-drawing fireplace, performing admirably on this cold December day, and ample illumination from candles on the table and in sconces around the walls. As I saw it through his eyes, though, I realized it was woefully lacking in any attempt at beautification.

"Yes, I can understand that she might have wanted to meet in Winchester. I'm sorry to disappoint you. But we anticipate a great deal of opposition to any new Continental engagement from the lords and barons of England. I didn't want our meeting to draw too much interest. Better to keep quiet for now."

I didn't tell him the other reason. My mother was still enormously unpopular in England. I'm not sure she or Hugh knew that. I wanted to spare her from the rude, even dangerous, public censure she might have met in London or Winchester.

We made our way through the meal quickly so we could get down to our discussions. There was a great deal to go over. During that afternoon and the next day we hammered out a formal alliance between the Lusignans and myself.

Hugh and Isabella promised faithfully to help me recover my possessions, in exchange for certain considerations.

I agreed in return to grant in perpetuity to them and their children the rights to a dozen or more cities and fortresses in Poitou as well as the archbishopric of Bourges and bishoprics of Limoges, Périguex, Saintes and Poitiers. It was an impressive list, including most of the onetime holdings of the Plantagenets in Aquitaine.

Of course, at the moment it was only promises on parchment.

We talked at length about raising an army in France. They assured me I'd find enthusiastic support the moment I came ashore. I reminded them, most politely, that I'd been told the same thing eleven years before.

"This time it's a totally different climate, isn't it, Hugh?" He nodded and my mother went on. Her face was tense and I noticed how thin it had become. But her blue eyes blazed with conviction. She was beautifully persuasive. "Truly, Henry, you'll find most of the powerful lords eager to fight under your banner. What's more, we'll publicly announce that from now on we'll give you our fealty instead of King Louis and his brother. The fact that we're openly defying the King will encourage even more of our vassals to join our cause and bring with them their own knights and foot soldiers. They've grown quite resentful of the way King Louis meddles in their affairs."

They described how they'd already traveled all over Poitou exacting pledges of aid. They named names, very impressive names. All that was needed was for me to gather as many troops and as much money as I could and sail across the Channel.

On this optimistic note we parted.

I plunged into preparations. My counselors weren't as enthusiastic as I was, but they didn't try to dissuade me. The most supportive was Eleanor's uncle, Peter of Savoy, who had more ties to France than the others. The most cautious was William de Cantilupe.

Early in January 1242 he came to me with an astonishing tale. William had ways of learning useful information. If he took it seriously enough to pass it on, it had to be reliable.

It seemed that Prince Alphonse had invited Hugh and Isabella to Poitiers for the Christmas festivities.

"They'd never have been asked, of course, if Alphonse had known of their plans to desert the Capetian cause," said Sir William. He went on to tell the story as it had been told to him, in such detail that it could hardly have been invented.

Alphonse and his court were feasting in the great hall while musicians filled the air with carols. Into the noisy and joyful scene strode Hugh with Isabella close behind him. Hugh went straight to Alphonse. He cried out, so loudly that he could be heard above the trilling of the flutes and beating of the tabors, "Now let it be known to you, Prince Alphonse, that I am no longer your man. I withdraw my homage from you, in protest against your stealing the countship of Poitou from the rightful count, Richard of England, while he is on Crusade to the Holy Land. I am no longer your subject or subject to any son of Queen Blanche. Henceforth I owe homage only to Henry of England!"

William seemed uncomfortable telling this story. He paused to see how I was taking it.

"By our Lord, Sir William! This is remarkable, if true. Last December my mother and my stepfather promised they'd publicly withdraw their homage to Alphonse. But I'd never imagined they'd do it *quite* so publicly. I can't say I approve of such brazen defiance."

"Unfortunately, it's true. And there's worse to come. They left in as much of a rush as they'd arrived, before anybody could put out a hand to stop them. They rejoined their troops who'd been waiting outside and rode to their lodgings. They set fire to the house, then galloped off to Lusignan."

"What possible reason could they have for making such a scene?"

"I've been turning that question over in my mind, and talking to my wife, who knows your mother so very well. I believe that the grievances Queen Isabella holds against Queen Blanche and her sons have festered to the point where she will do anything to let the world know how she despises them. You know, my liege, that your mother is a woman of strong passions. So strong that she can easily persuade others to go along with her. Both she and Hugh are fearful that King Louis will take away from them the power they've amassed in Poitou. And it may be that when word of this outburst gets around it will build even more support for their—for our—rising against Louis. A headstrong baron minded to declare his independence can't help but applaud it."

"I suppose not. So, strange as it is, I don't see how it can do our cause any harm."

"In itself, no. Let's only hope it isn't a sign there may be other impulsive acts that could have more serious consequences."

Our preparations for the invasion proceeded. Sir Peter urged me to hurry. He was impatient to go into battle. But I wanted to take every precaution and leave as little as possible to chance. I went over lists, inspected the knights and their equipment, and sent emissaries out to exhort bishops and barons, lords and laymen, to turn over every last penny to the cause.

Finally when I was satisfied that all was ready we set out for Portsmouth. My wife Eleanor accompanied me. Though we'd just learned she was pregnant, she was eager to come and be part of the triumph we all looked forward to. My brother Richard had come back from his Crusade in time to join us. He was keen to finish the task of conquest he'd begun ten years before. With us, also, were a half-dozen of my powerful barons, several hundred knights and many coffers of treasure.

We embarked to the cheers of crowds on the shore and with nothing between us and victory but a two days' sail. Then we would land on the coast of France, find Hugh and an eager army waiting, and march on to vanquish King Louis. The Plantagenets would reclaim their lost dominion.

Henry III
1242

The King of France gathered a formidable and overwhelming army, a multitude of men on horseback and on foot, who marched like a river flowing to the sea.
Matthew Paris, chronicler of the reign of Henry III

We landed at Royan, near Bordeaux, on May 13.

But no cheering armies met us. Instead, Terric Teutonicus and six other knights were waiting on the pier. I was surprised to see Sir Terric still in Isabella's and Hugh's service. He must have been seventy. He wasn't quite as tall and terrifying as he used to be, but still bulging with muscle and combativeness.

He told us King Louis was on the march. In only a month he'd taken city after city in western Poitou. I pressed him to tell me more. Reluctantly, he admitted that as Louis advanced, barons who had pledged themselves to my stepfather and my mother had deserted their cause and gone to Louis. He said that Hugh de Lusignan was waiting for me at Saintes, a day's journey to the east, and wanted me to join him as soon as possible.

I sent Eleanor, in the care of Richard and fifty knights, to wait in safety at Bordeaux, which was still ours. I promised Richard I'd send for him as soon as I had a better grasp of the situation. Then I led my troops to Saintes, worrying all the way at the turn things had taken, hoping Hugh would have better news.

Terric took me to the pilgrims' hostel within the city walls where Hugh had made his headquarters. It was a tall narrow building, at the moment uninhabited by any pilgrims. I found Hugh pacing the floor in the big second-floor room where meals had been served. Dirty, rusty pots littered the floor and tables. Messages had been scrawled on the walls—some prayers to God to keep the pilgrims safe, others leaving word for those who would come later as to where the town's best brothels were.

Hugh's face looked drawn and as grim as the run-down hostel. "So you've come at last. Thank God. We've just had word that Louis's army is within sight. Some of the vanguard may already be in the city. I haven't had time to inspect the defenses, and the citizens are surly and may turn against us."

"How many men do you have?"

"About fifty knights on horseback, and another hundred foot soldiers."

"That's all?" In my shock I couldn't keep the outrage out of my voice. "What about those thousands of loyal barons you said would rush to our sides?"

He didn't answer. There was no point in berating him, facts were facts. "So. Even with my forces we hardly have enough men to make a successful attack. We'll have to prepare to withstand a siege. How are your supplies—food, water, fodder?"

"Very low. And the shopkeepers refuse to sell to us even at the exorbitant prices we offer. I doubt if we could hold out more than a week."

Sir Terric came in to report that Louis's army was already surrounding the city. Even from our thick-walled hostel we could hear shouts, blaring trumpets and the rumble that might be siege engines being drawn up to the walls. We climbed the stairs to the rooftop in hopes we'd be high enough to get an idea of what was going on.

We were. It was a horrid sight. Far below and beyond the city walls a horde of tiny figures ran about. At first they looked as aimless as ants on an anthill. But we soon saw what they were up to. Amid the crowd the tall, ungainly trebuchets loomed, as men toiled to trundle them into place a stone's throw from the walls. I counted six of the infernal contraptions, looking like huge wooden insects. Other men were urging on the mules that dragged carts laden with the stone balls that would soon be launched from the trebuchets toward the city. Toward us. We wouldn't have a chance.

"With luck, it will be at least another hour before they're ready to attack," said Hugh. We looked at each other, both realizing what our course must be. "So do you agree that we'll have to get out of the city before they have their men and machines in place?"

I nodded. Without another word we went down to assemble our forces.

Before we gave the order to our troops I asked Hugh to draw apart with me. I didn't want to waste time arguing but I couldn't repress my fury any longer.

"You promised me thousands of troops. You said King Louis would fall back before us and his forces would melt away. Yet here we are at the enemy's mercy. I will continue to fight at your side, Hugh de Lusignan, for my mother's sake. But from this day forward I will not trust your word."

He looked surprised and in fact I'd surprised myself. I had no reputation for forthright speech. I knew men had called me Henry the Softspoken.

"I can only say I'm sorry things haven't turned out as we'd hoped. I'm afraid Isabella may have misled you about how many from Poitou would join us. She sometimes lets her wishes outrun the facts."

I didn't dignify this with an answer and turned to mount my horse while he was still talking, his resentment growing. He had to shout to be heard over the noise of the men and the horses.

"But the blame's not all on my side, by God. Nobody could have foreseen how few troops you would bring and how long it would take you to get here. Why did you delay so? That gave King Louis time to take the initiative. And how could we have guessed how cowardly our allies would prove?" He paused then went on, still angry but resigned. "But now we have only one choice--to fight on together. You are my liege lord, and my sons and I are here to serve you."

I was furious that he blamed me for our situation and that he criticized my mother for deceiving me. But this wasn't the time for recriminations. And he was right: Our only hope was to fight our way out of the city and take Louis by surprise.

We mounted and gave the order to advance. With heralds holding our banners high and with Hugh's two sons close by, we led the charge. The trumpets blared the battle call. I heard cries of "To victory with King Henry!" and "Lusignan! Lusignan!" from the men behind us. We trotted in an orderly fashion through the town, heading for the bridge across the Charente that connected the two parts of Saintes.

We rode across the bridge unopposed, but the moment our vanguard reached the other side hundreds of mounted men pounded down the narrow streets to pursue our troops. We were almost deafened by the clangor of hoofbeats and shouts echoing off the stone walls. Somehow we managed to get out through the city gates. Just as we did, we heard, rather than saw, the frightful whir of the first missile from the trebuchets and the boom of its smash against the city wall. Then the crews manning the machines saw us and left their work to try to stop us. But we reached the fields and vineyards beyond the city. There we made a stand against an army that must have outnumbered us three to one. Many of our men were struck down by showers of arrows and by well-aimed lances. Many were captured. Many were wounded, to lie moaning between the rows of vines.

Yet we too struck out vigorously. I saw young Guy de Lusignan charge at a huge French knight and strike such a blow that the man tumbled from the saddle, clutching his bleeding right arm with his left. Guy's brother saw the action, wheeled his horse, grabbed the reins of the fallen knight's steed and led it back to where one of his comrades had been unhorsed. I heard Sir Terric roaring horrible Germanic oaths and saw his sword arm flashing and slashing, like a scythe mowing a field of grain.

Despite such acts of bravery we couldn't withstand the enemy's superior numbers. I saw the horseman who bore Hugh's standard fall from his saddle with blood gushing from his neck. The banner was trampled in the dust. The sun was sinking.

As it grew darker both sides fell back, exhausted. The French retired to the other side of the river. All through the battle I had looked in vain for King Louis. He must have been watching from a distance. Perhaps he'd seen this as such a minor, easily won encounter that he felt no need to be on the scene.

When night fell we brought in our wounded and made camp. We English kept to ourselves, a short distance from our Poitevin allies. The latter shouted taunts at our men for coming too late, for fighting too cravenly. From my tent I saw, across a field, Hugh and his sons huddled around a fire. When the flames shot up I could see how haggard and utterly discouraged they looked. I was glad that my two half-brothers were still alive, but I was too tired and depressed to want to speak to them, much less their father. What was the point? The campfires of the French army were blinking from the hillsides around the town like all the stars in the sky. It would plainly be hopeless to resume the fight against such superior forces.

During the night I gathered the remnant of my troops and rode toward Bordeaux. I didn't know whether Hugh managed to escape. Nor did I care.

Isabella

1242

While Hugh was waging war in the south I was trying to encourage our vassals in La Marche to rise up and march to the aid of my son and my husband. Even those who had vowed on their honor to join our battle were holding back now. They were alarmed at how King Louis had seized the high ground. As always, they saw which way the winds of war were blowing and adjusted their loyalties accordingly.

Nevertheless I felt optimistic. If things went well with Hugh and Henry, the wavering barons might discover the wind was blowing in their favor after all. I returned to Angoulême, hoping to find a message from Hugh.

The next day Terric Teutonicus arrived from the south. He'd come to resume his duties as my personal bodyguard. He looked even more sober than usual. After a brief greeting he handed me a letter from Hugh and excused himself while I was still unrolling the parchment.

To my dear wife, Queen Isabella: We have lost the battle to hold Saintes. King Louis has gained the city. King Henry and his paltry army have fled to Bordeaux from where they will undoubtedly take ship as soon as possible for England. Without the help we had hoped for from the barons of Poitou we can fight no longer. King Louis promises to be merciful, but he demands that you, our sons and I make a formal submission to him. He will receive us at Pons, on the River Seugne, on July 26. I beg you to come. Hugh de Lusignan.

I let out a scream so loud that my maid came running. When she saw me tearing the parchment to shreds she escaped as fast as she'd come. If Hugh had been there I would have rushed at him and clawed at his face. How could he have surrendered when there was still hope for reinforcements from the north? I was just as angry at Henry for deserting with his troops. Where was the courage I'd tried to instill in him? Was he a true son of his father after all, ready to turn tail when he felt threatened?

For a day and a night I kept to my rooms, weeping and pacing the floor. I alternated between wretchedness and desperate hope—perhaps I could think of a way to salvage something from the debacle. I sent for Abbot Vital of La Couronne and poured out the story. In the past when I'd sought his advice, he'd always counseled me to keep fighting for what I thought was right. He knew what I wanted to hear. This time, though his voice was as soothing as ever, his words were discouraging.

"My daughter, God has indeed dealt you a grievous blow. I can understand your wish to find a way to deflect it, to strike a blow in return for yourself and your family. But the time may have come to accept the fact that, at least for now, you must humble yourself and place yourself under the wing of God's mercy. If that means submitting to your enemy, so be it. Trust in God and he will help you to survive your tribulations."

I stared at his pink, plump face and at the fringe of white hair that encircled his pink, bald pate. How could he look so calm and sound so bland when my world had fallen apart?

"*That's easy for you to say,*" I thought, clenching and unclenching my fists. "*You aren't about to lose everything you've been fighting for these past twenty years.*"

But he'd made a crack in my assurance that I could prevail. Was this really a punishment sent by God that I'd have to accept? I'd never imagined God as anything but a distant deity who was generally on my side as long as I said my prayers and went to mass.

For the first time in my life I felt uncertain about what path to follow.

Maybe Abbot Vital was right. In any case, I'd have to go to Pons.

"Father, will you come with us? If King Louis sees that I'm befriended by such a respected churchman he may be more lenient."

"Gladly." He became even pinker. "I welcome the opportunity to meet the King, such a saintly man. I understand he intends to go on a Crusade very soon. It may be, my daughter, that you'll find him kinder and more forgiving than you expect."

I'd never been to Pons. I'd always tried to keep informed of the condition of our defenses in Poitou, but Pons was far to the south in Gascony, on the frontier that had so often been the battleground between the English and the French. I asked Sir Terric if he knew anything about it.

"As it happens, I do know a good deal about Pons." Terric loved to be asked difficult questions and often had answers that tended to be more informative than one needed. "I was in Pons long ago, before I ever came to England. Your late husband's brother, King Richard, had knocked down the keep during his battling in Aquitaine. When I was there, the lord of the city had just rebuilt it, and a big brute of a fort it was. Then I was with your son King Henry when he had the castle walls strengthened while he was battling in those parts back in 1230 or so. I haven't seen it since then, but I expect it could withstand quite a siege."

He sounded wistful, as though he'd like to be mounting a siege of Pons. He probably resented having to leave Hugh's army and come back to dull Angoulême.

"Well, we're not going to besiege it. On the contrary, we're going to yield like cravens to the King of France as we've been ordered to do."

When we reached the Seugne River and looked across at the castle I saw how accurate Terric's description had been. A sheer rock cliff rose from the very edge of the river and the castle soared above it like a seamless continuation of the cliff. Assault from below would be impossible. High walls encircled the castle on the other three sides. The tall square keep in the center of it all looked impregnable. Yet with the afternoon sun full on the tawny stone it had an odd harsh beauty. My spirits rose a degree or so.

At the castle gates the King's steward greeted us courteously. He led us to the rooms where we'd be lodged and said we'd be expected in the great hall as soon as possible. I'd hardly had time to take off my cloak when he reappeared to conduct us to the meeting place.

The great hall was not very great, about half the size of ours at Angoulême. It was dingy and not well lit, with only two narrow windows to let in some light. This castle, I had to remind myself, was designed for defense, not royal spectacles. The King's people had obviously done their best to make it look regal. They'd spread blue-and-gold carpets on the grimy cold floor. The French fleur-de-lis blazed from banners hung on all four walls.

My eyes flew to King Louis, seated on an ornate gold-inlaid throne at the far end of the room. I wondered if he took his throne with him when he went to war. He was conferring with a man I took to be his secretary. He was surrounded by courtiers decked out in bright reds and purples and deep blues, cloaks with gold embroidery, ermine capes; the ladies hung with gold chains and flaunting their rainbows of jewels. I almost regretted my decision to wear a modest gray silk with discreet silver embroidery and no jewelry except a cross at my throat and my crown. But if it would help my case to forsake the finery I loved, I'd dress as a humble supplicant.

When the steward led Abbot Vital and me to the front of the crowd and I could see the King more plainly I felt better about my restraint. When I'd seen him a year ago at Saumur, he'd been so enveloped in satins and furs, gold and silver, that I could hardly make out the man within the wrappings. Today he wore an unadorned black tunic and leggings and a short red cape. His crown wasn't the huge gleaming gem-laden one he'd worn then, but a simple gold circlet with only a few modest diamonds. His face, framed by gently waving yellow hair that was cut short just below his ears, was calm, judicious, almost kindly. Under other circumstances I might have liked this man.

"They say he wears a hair shirt all the time now, while he prepares for his Crusade," Abbot Vital whispered to me.

A row of chairs had been placed directly in front of the King. Hugh and our sons Hugh and Guy were already seated.

The steward seated the abbot and me, bowed and left. Hugh was on my right. We glanced at each other. He tried a thin smile. When I didn't respond he sighed, then took my hand. I snatched it away and looked straight ahead. He leaned toward me and spoke in a low voice. Though the room was still noisy with conversation and movement, we were undoubtedly the center of attention.

"Isabella, I beg of you, even if you can't be civil to me, don't argue with the King. No matter how much we may disagree with his judgment, our only hope is to be submissive. I've already instructed young Hugh and Guy. Will you promise that you'll join us in a contrite plea for mercy? A few tears wouldn't be amiss. You can look so piteous and beautifully helpless when you weep."

I looked at him suspiciously. Was he joking? No, he was as serious as I'd ever seen him.

"I will be contrite. I will weep. I will refrain from ranting and raving at the King. I know as well as you what's at stake." I bit back the angry words I longed to spit out at him. There'd be time for that later.

"And please, Isabella, if the King asks if we have anything to say, let me be our spokesman. It will be hard for you to play the part of the dutiful wife but this is one time when you'll have to pretend."

I nodded.

The King took several parchments from his secretary, then looked out over the room. He raised a hand. Silence fell immediately. I heard the rustle of damask skirts being adjusted and, through the windows, the soft cooing of pigeons.

"My counselors, my lords and ladies, my noble guests, welcome. We are here to bring a peaceful conclusion to the wars we have been waging against the rebels in our realm. We thank God for granting us the victory." He bowed his head for a moment. Abbot Vital instantly bowed his head too. He almost quivered with his approval of such saintliness.

"We have already received the submission of Renaud de Pons, lord of Saintonge. Today we will receive that of Hugh le Brun, Count of La Marche and of his wife and sons."

No matter how many times it happened, I flinched when I was referred to merely as Hugh's wife. My back stiffened but otherwise I tried to look indifferent.

The King beckoned to us. His expression was that of a stern but loving father who regrets that he must reprimand a wayward child. The four of us knelt before him.

"Hugh de Lusignan, you have renounced your loyalty to your rightful lord and taken arms against us. You have incited others who owed us fealty to do the same. You have joined forces with our enemy, Henry of England. What say you to these charges?"

Hugh spoke up in a strong but respectful voice. I wondered if he'd rehearsed his reply. He was unable to produce any tears but he put on a remarkably sorrowful face.

"Sire, most honored King, I freely admit to the truth of what I am charged with. I have betrayed you most wickedly and presumptuously. I can only hope for your forgiveness. You are known and revered for your justice and mercy. I will comply with whatever punishment you deem fitting for such transgressions."

King Louis listened attentively to this groveling. I bowed my head so nobody could see how my cheeks had turned an angry red.

Hugh went on. "I plead with you to bear no malice toward me, my wife and my sons, as we bear none toward you. I beg you to accept my promise to serve you loyally from this day forward."

I looked up to see the king fixing his gaze on me. "Isabella, Countess of Angoulême, have you anything to add to your husband's submission?"

"Nothing, my King." I had no trouble summoning the requisite tears; they were already flowing. But they were tears of helpless fury, not penitence.

He asked each of our sons the same question and received the same answer.

"Then rise. Sir Hugh, you and yours are pardoned."

Some of the spectators must have thought this was an unnecessarily soft judgment. There was a good deal of murmured conversation and argument. The King ignored it. He asked Hugh to meet with him and his council in his own chamber to discuss the terms of the surrender.

With my sons, I went back to our lodgings. They seemed stunned. They'd gone so sturdily into battle with assurance of victory. Guy wasn't yet twenty. What a sorry finale to his first foray onto the battlefield!

But with the optimism of youth, they rallied.

"If he's pardoned us, that must mean we won't have to give up any of our possessions," said Hugh. At twenty-one, he was already thinking of when he'd be Lord of Lusignan. "What do you think, mother?"

"After this shameful day I don't know what to think. We'll have to wait and see. When your father comes back he'll tell us how much of your and your sisters' patrimony he's given away."

Toward evening Hugh came in where we were waiting, bored but apprehensive, in the cramped chambers we'd been allotted. When I learned that the King's brother Alphonse had been present at the discussions I was glad I hadn't been invited. I doubted if I could have kept from lashing out at the man who had jilted my daughter and assumed my son Richard's rightful title to Gascony.

I'd never seen Hugh look so tired and dejected. He'd lost every trace of his customary good humor. He threw himself into a chair and made his dismal report without looking any of us in the face.

First, Louis had demanded that the lords of Poitou and Saintonge who had previously been our vassals must renounce their fealty to us and swear to serve him. This would mean lost revenues for us. And the payments we'd received from the king to defend Poitou would end.

Next, we were ordered to renounce our suzerainty over all the cities and fortresses that Louis's armies had taken from us in the recent war. Hugh had to give up our three major strongholds in Lusignan, including the splendid castle of Crozant we'd so recently rebuilt. All in all we lost about a third of our territories. Some of them were to be garrisoned by French armies at our expense.

"He did promise, though, that if after three years he was assured of our loyalty they'd revert to us."

"Three years!" said young Hugh. At his age, that seemed an impossibly long time.

"So. We've lost lands and revenue. Our expenses will nevertheless increase. Is that the last of it, or have you brought even more disgrace on your family?" I couldn't dredge up a morsel of pity for him.

"His last demand was that I serve for three years in his army, at my expense, when he begins his assault on the Count of Toulouse and his other enemies in the south."

The words snapped out before I could think. "Then the sooner he begins, the better. We'll be rid of you and your new master before the two of you can do us any more mischief!"

I slumped in my chair and stared at the floor. I was drained of anger. I didn't look up when I heard Hugh and the boys leave.

How could I have imagined I saw signs of mercy and clemency in the King's face? True, he had pardoned us. Then he had ruined us.

The next morning we prepared for the homeward journey.

"Will you come to Lusignan?" Hugh asked me.

"No, I will go to Angoulême."

So he, with his sons, went to his ancestral home and I to mine, where we would, each in our own way, try to come to terms with this humiliation.

Back in Angoulême I still felt the depression that had overcome me in Pons. I spent hours in my familiar, beloved chamber in the palace, looking out at the gardens and the barely-begun new tower. Heretofore, when I suffered a setback I began at once to think of ways to fight back. This time I felt helpless. Whether it was God's will, as Abbot Vital suggested; or Hugh's and Henry's failure at the battle of Saintes; or the miserable cowardice of our supposed allies in Poitou; or King Louis's vindictiveness—for whatever reason, the fortunes of the Lusignans and the Taillefers had sunk like a stone to the bottom of a well.

Hugh and I had dared to think we could steer our own course, independent of the monarchs of France and England. We'd failed. In my weariness I was beginning to wonder if our marriage, our partnership, could survive this debacle.

But I clung to one tenuous hope. Our children need not fail.

For now, though, I wanted only to rest. Maybe my will to fight would come back.

Abbot Vital sent word that he'd come see me a week after my return. He'd left Pons before King Louis had meted out his punishment to us, but he must have heard all the horrid details. Still, he didn't bring it up nor did I. I liked the abbot because he never told me to fall on my knees and implore God's forgiveness for my unspecified sins. Rather, he let me ramble on with my complaints and murmured his sympathy, interjecting the occasional wise platitude about submission, patience and forgiveness.

I asked him to sit beside me before the fire where a servant had placed his usual comfortable chair and a cushioned footstool. I'd ordered a plate of his favorite honey-soaked figs and a goblet of sweet spiced wine. He beamed to see them and his round face looked even more like a jovial man-in-the-moon. The good abbot had a well-developed taste for the finer things of life.

"Welcome, my lord abbot," I said. "You've come at a good time. I need your counsel."

"If I can help in any way, you know I will try." He ate a fig, then daintily wiped his fingers on a snowy napkin he produced from some cavity in his voluminous red habit.

"I'm sure you can imagine how deeply I feel the misfortunes that have fallen upon my husband and me."

His response was a noncommittal "Mmmm" and a sip of wine.

"But I'm not plotting revenge. I'm still trying to accept my fate. I feel now that I must find a quiet retreat where I can rest and think about what to do next."

"I can understand that. It would do you good to retire for a time to some tranquil spot, far from reminders of your worldly concerns. Might I suggest, my daughter, our own Abbey of La Couronne? It's beyond the city walls, in as quiet a spot as you could find hereabouts. We'd be honored by your presence. We could lodge you comfortably. And my lady Queen, you'd be sure of a snug, dry sleeping chamber, thanks to the generosity of yourself and Sir Hugh."

I'd almost forgotten that Hugh and I had paid for the abbey's new roof the year before.

"An interesting suggestion. I'll think about it. Thank you, father."

After he left I did think about it. Then suddenly in my mind's eye I saw another abbey: Fontevraud.

I believe I'd held the thought of Fontevraud as the ultimate refuge ever since John and I had stopped there to see Queen Eleanor. How long ago that was—forty years and more. Now perhaps the time had come.

Hugh X
1242-1243

59

For two months after Pons we didn't see each other or communicate. The bonds that had held our marriage together—bonds of mutual regard and shared ambition—had weakened under the weight of King Louis's punishing judgments.

I kept myself busy repairing and raising the castle walls and finishing another tower.

"Tell me, Hugh, why are you so set on strengthening your fortress?" asked Etienne Delorme. "Lusignan Castle hasn't been attacked for a hundred years. I doubt if it's likely to be attacked any time soon in view of the peace that King Louis has enforced."

We were comfortably settled before the fire in my tower room. A jug of wine was mulling and chestnuts were roasting on the hearth. My friend Etienne was planning to retire from the bishopric of Poitiers and had come to supervise the readying of the house near his old church where he'd live.

"It seems, my good bishop, that as one approaches sixty one gives a great deal of thought to the little time one may have left, and what one will leave behind for one's children. After I finish my service for King Louis, I'm thinking I might join him if he goes on Crusade to the Holy Land. That was my father's ambition at the end of his life, but he never got to Jerusalem. Perhaps I'll be able to make that pilgrimage for him. Maybe like my father, I won't come back again. So, to answer your question: before I leave, I want to make sure my son Hugh will inherit a strong, well-fortified castle. Just in case he has to defend it some day."

"Ah yes. You see war as the one constant in life. You are probably right. My seven decades of observing man and his foibles haven't taught me any differently.

But speaking of inheritances, children, and all that, I hear that Geoffrey de Rancon is casting about for a wife. I don't know much about him except that his first wife has just died without producing a son. Isn't your eldest daughter Isabella still available, or have you carelessly betrothed her to someone without seeking my advice?"

"She is indeed available and at eighteen she should have been married off long ago. After the betrothal to Prince Alphonse was annulled we thought some of affiancing her next to Count Raymond of Toulouse. But that doesn't seem like such a good idea now, since King Louis has ordered me to go to war against Raymond. Yes, Etienne, I salute you." I sipped my wine. "This Geoffrey might serve very well. He's one of Louis's loyal vassals down in Saintonge. There'd be no harm in such an alliance and maybe some good. The girl is with her mother in Angoulême. I'll look into it."

I was glad to have a plausible excuse to get in touch with my wife. The next day I sent a message explaining the proposal and asking her what she thought. I didn't actually invite her to come to Lusignan but tried to make it plain that she would be welcome. To be sure, I'd enjoyed the peace of this respite without her. I was weary of our arguments and differences. Yet I sometimes missed the stir that she produced wherever she went. I missed the drama of wondering what she'd be up to next. I had to admit that Isabella was a stimulating presence.

She replied that she thought it would be useful for her to come so we could discuss this and other matters. She'd leave at once.

I didn't know what to expect. Tantrums? Cold disdain? Efforts to enlist me in new plots and intrigues? I wasn't prepared for the Isabella I found when I walked over to the Logis de la Reine.

She was calm and withdrawn, though when she permitted me to kiss her she warmed just a bit and let me hold her close for a moment. She seemed to have forsaken any ostentation in her dress. Her gown was fine enough—she didn't own any that weren't—but she wore no jewels whatsoever. She'd pinned up her hair and covered her head with a white wimple. Without that crown of golden hair her face looked thinner, her features sharper. Her blue eyes were even bluer in such a pale face. Could it be that at fifty-seven Isabella had lost her vanity?

"Hugh, before we even begin to talk, let me say this. I would prefer that we not go over the misfortunes that have fallen on us. We'd only end up quarreling about who was to blame. We need to devote ourselves now to the future—the future of our children."

"I agree completely."

I'd had a table prepared near the window where Isabella used to like to sit, looking out at the gardens. I sent for Pierre and asked him to bring us our meal. It was mid-afternoon, past my usual dinnertime.

I raised my goblet and said, "Do try this fine red wine, Queen Isabella. See if you can guess where it came from."

She took a sip, then another, and laughed.

"Indeed, it's from our vines on the Charente. Is that vineyard still ours, Hugh?"

"As far as I know, it is. Our lord King must have missed it when he was going after our possessions."

This was getting dangerously close to forbidden topics, so I urged her to try the pickled fish. I went at my own with gusto, then helped myself to roast mutton. Isabella ate sparingly. She wanted to get down to business.

"Now Hugh, as to the betrothal of Isabella, I think we'd be very wise to propose it to Geoffrey de Rancon. He's considerably older but certainly well endowed with lands and vassals. The poor girl is beginning to feel like an old maid, with both her younger sisters already betrothed."

"Good. I thought you'd agree. I'll start the negotiations."

I munched on a thick slice of bread and looked at her, wondering whether it was safe to bring up the next subject. I decided to plunge ahead.

"My dear, before we go on, let me tell you of a wicked tale that is being spread about. I'd like you to hear it from me before it comes to you from some mean gossip."

She put down her knife and sighed.

"A wicked tale about me? Well, I'm used to that. What is it this time?"

"It has to do with an attempt to kill King Louis. Etienne Delorme told me that he'd heard it from several disreputable sources. He scoffed at it, but he said—rightfully, I believe—that we should be aware of the lies that are being told. It seems you are accused of hiring two men and sending them to poison the King while he was at Saintes. This would have been after you heard from me that our cause was lost, and just before you left for Pons. The cooks at the castle in Saintes where the King was staying caught the men in the act of pouring poison into the King's meat and his wine. When they were apprehended they said you'd sent them."

"What!" The Isabella I knew so well was on fire again. "How dare they!" she screamed. She sprang to her feet and stood glaring at me and then at the servant who had come running at the shriek. He was new in my service and not familiar with her ways. When he saw that nobody had been stabbed or fallen in a fit he left in haste.

"How dare they spread such a story? I would never, never do such a thing. I am not a murderess! Hugh, you know that! You know I am not a murderess." She sank in tears to her seat. I tried to comfort her. I knelt beside her and put my arms around her. I told her I believed her, all right-minded people would laugh at the story, she was not to give it another thought.

"If King Louis had suspected you he would certainly have said so when we met him at Pons. It's his opinion that matters. The tales will die away, when people find something else to blather about."

She wiped her eyes. "I suppose so. But who would spread such a vile rumor? It must have been that prissy Jeanne de Toulouse, who snatched away the husband who'd been promised to our Isabella. I knew from the moment I saw her she was a trouble maker." The anger threatened to take over again, but she sank back and looked at me helplessly. "Hugh, why are people so ready to believe the worst about me? I'm so tired of it all, so tired."

She did look tired. Tired and dejected. She leaned back in her chair and closed her eyes. Her hands were clutching her damp handkerchief.

"I think you should rest now. I'll leave you. We can talk more later."

"No, Hugh, don't go." She sat up straight and gathered herself together. I could see the energy flow back. "We have matters to discuss that are far more important than malicious gossip. I don't want to put this off."

So I stayed, and she told me what she thought was so important: nothing less than her belief that from now on we should live apart, and that we should agree on a division of our lands and properties among our children.

Somehow I'd been expecting this. I think she was relieved that I didn't resist.

"As you wish, Isabella. Perhaps at least for now we should maintain our separate residences. God knows, we have plenty to occupy us. In spite of what Louis did we both have sizeable lands to govern and vassals to keep in line. As to a legacy for our children, I'd like to have young Hugh with us when we work out the terms. He's at Poitiers now but he'll be here tomorrow. And I'd want my cousin, Simon de Lezay, to join us. Whatever we decide affects the whole Lusignan clan. If you agree, I'll send for him."

She agreed.

It took the better part of two days for the four of us, with the help of my secretary, to agree on the will. As was only right, Hugh XI as future head of the clan was to have suzerainty over the county of La Marche, my heritage. That meant he would eventually be master of the castle at Lusignan. He would also inherit Isabella's County of Angoulême. Even without the fiefs that King Louis had taken from us, Hugh's legacy would be considerably larger than what I'd been left by my father.

To our second son, Guy, we left several fiefs in Angoulême and Cognac. To this Isabella added a proviso.

" I'd like to add that, with the consent of his brother Hugh, he is to have the rights to the city of Angoulême, as long as he lives. He has always taken such an interest in building the new palace. It's still many years from being finished, and I think we can count on him to see it through."

Nobody objected to that. To our other three sons we left various fiefs in Saintonge and Poitou. They included those that we'd surrendered to King Louis on the understanding that they'd eventually be restored to us, dependent on our obedient service to the King. We trusted that by the time our sons were of an age to receive their inheritances this would have happened.

"That's assuming the King remembers what he promised you," said Simon. Simon took a jaundiced view of the trustworthiness of kings.

"True," I said. "But what choice do we have? And if need be they can fight for their rights, as I did and my father before me."

When the documents had been properly drawn up we signed them with great solemnity. Isabella, as always, signed herself "Countess of Angoulême and Queen of England."

That night when Simon had left, young Hugh had gone back to Poitiers and we were alone, Isabella asked me to come with her to her rooms. We walked along the gallery with a servant ahead of us lighting the way.

"I'm so glad we settled all that. Have you thought, Hugh, that we've achieved what we said we'd do when the Count of La Marche married the Countess of Angoulême? We've combined the two parts into a whole that's almost powerful enough to stand up to the King of France. Just because we didn't quite succeed doesn't mean that our son Hugh can't win back what we lost when he's in sole charge. Especially when his brothers are so well endowed, in such strategic locations. Not to mention his sisters, who'll be married to men of consequence and power."

I didn't reply. I wanted no more of her grand schemes, even if these were for our children and not for us.

We reached her chambers where I thought I'd say goodnight. The servant lit a few candles and threw a log on the fire, then left. Isabella unpinned her wimple and tossed it on a chair. Her golden hair, now turned silvery, was loosed to cascade to her shoulders. In the dimness with the flickering firelight playing on her face she looked as young and desirable as the Isabella I'd married. She took my hand.

"Hugh, will you come to bed with me?"

We hadn't slept together for months. I'd resigned myself to a life of celibacy.

"I would be honored, Queen Isabella."

That night we made love without passion but gently, considerately, soberly. It was like an envoi to our life together.

In the morning I opened my eyes to see her already awake and watching me. She smiled.

"Thank you, Hugh, for a lovely last time."

"Last time? What do you mean? We'll still visit each other. Now that I know you haven't crossed me off your list of bedmates, I hope we'll visit often."

"No, I'm afraid not. You're about to go fulfill your pledge to serve King Louis in Provence. Long before you're back I'll have been admitted to the Abbey of Fontevraud."

Isabella

1243-1246

hen I came to Fontevraud Abbey, I looked forward to the calm, orderly atmosphere I'd been impressed with during my first visit with John. Here, if anywhere, I could find peace, or at least rest. I was weary of the efforts to reconcile my various loyalties: to my son Henry; to Hugh's and my self-interest as lords of Poitou; to the future well being of our children.

I was even weary of Hugh. Though I was still fond of him I couldn't think of any reason that we should continue to live together.

Perhaps, too, there was some vanity in my wish to retire to the abbey. After a lifetime as a beauty, I was dismayed at the signs of aging. I had to face it: now in my fifty-seventh year, no ointments, potions, poultices or herbal infusions were going to bring back my youth. In this relative isolation, away from those who knew me, maybe it wouldn't matter so much.

With my small party I rode down the broad avenue, through the gate and into the great sprawling community, centered on the huge abbey church. Though I'd been here only once, all those years ago, I felt I was coming home. I pointed out the sights to my companion, Louise de Beaufort.

"There are the convents for the nuns and monks with their houses and cloisters. There's the shelter for lepers. There's even a home for fallen women but it's tucked away. And down that lane are the lodgings for rich and titled ladies who wish to retire from the world. That's where Queen Eleanor had her apartments. I expect we'll be lodged there."

I remembered so well the opulence of Eleanor's rooms and the respect accorded her by everybody from abbess to humble lay sister. As a former Queen of England I looked forward to commanding the same respect.

At the house the abbess greeted me civilly but coolly. She told me at once that I couldn't be lodged in Queen Eleanor's old house.

"We keep that ready for King Henry's queen, if she should decide to visit us." That was my son Henry's wife Eleanor. As far as I knew she'd never visited Fontevraud and wasn't likely to any day soon. Nevertheless the abbess, like all her predecessors, knew how important it was to show obsequiousness to the reigning Plantagenets. The abbey owed a great deal to the dynasty. John's father Henry II, as well as Queen Eleanor, had endowed it richly. John and I had also been generous. But since I'd committed the indiscretion of marrying again after my royal husband died, it seemed the new Queen of England had superseded me.

I fumed but there was no point in arguing. I had to be satisfied with a smaller suite of rooms. We were barely able to fit in all the furniture I'd brought from Angoulême. However, it was self-sufficient with its own dining hall as well as lodgings for Louise and the two servants. I was glad I'd thought to bring my cook.

The abbess told me there were only three other ladies in residence currently, all widows of noblemen.

"They generally take their dinners in the refectory of La Madeleine. Since it's nearly the dinner hour, would you like me to show you the way?"

"Not today, thank you. I'm tired from the journey and more in need of rest than food. Perhaps tomorrow."

"As you wish." She flounced out.

So began my new life.

My acquaintance with the three other ladies languished after I heard one of them tell the others that I was "that woman who tried to poison our blessed King Louis." If they were silly enough to believe that, I wanted nothing to do with them.

After that I depended mostly on my own company and on that of Louise de Beaufort. I'd chosen her to come with me because she seemed to have good sense and discretion. Though nobody could replace my old friend Lady Anne, who'd seen me through so many tempestuous years, Lady Louise proved a good companion. She was about five years older than I was, a widow of a minor noble of Poitou. Her face was square-chinned, her nose was prominent and her white hair generally flew about as though she'd just been through a windstorm. She tended to chatter. But I soon found she didn't care whether I took part in the conversation, so I let her ramble on; it was rather restful. She was certainly good-hearted. If I chanced to say something that amused her, she'd look at me with a wide smile, her cheeks would turn pink and I knew that Lady Louise was on my side, no matter what. In my hall with its view of the abbey church we'd sit for hours with our needlework, looking out at the comings and goings of our fellow inhabitants of this little self-contained world.

On the whole I was content at Fontevraud. I took pleasure in walking in the gardens with Lady Louise. She knew a great deal more than I did about herbs and flowers. When we first arrived there were no flowers to be seen, though in the kitchen garden the sturdy plants that didn't mind the cold flourished: sage, rosemary, thyme. Throughout the winter we'd see the silent nuns with their little spades and their baskets, digging up carrots and beets. Later Louise would point out to me the bright green leaves of mint popping up through the brown earth, a sign of spring. Soon after that we'd see violets and daisies dotting the meadow grass. Still later there was such a profusion of flowers that I simply enjoyed them without needing to know what they were.

Sometimes I wondered about Hugh. I hoped that no harm would come to him in King Louis's service. On the whole, though, I felt pleasantly removed from my past life, as though a door had closed behind me to shut off all the turmoil, all the entanglements with family, friends and enemies. Now I was in a new and quieter room.

Just when I was congratulating myself that I didn't need the outside world it intruded. In September of 1243 a messenger came from my son Henry. I'd supposed he'd gone back to England after the terrible defeat at Saintes. But no, he and his wife were still in Gascony.

His message was brief: He had learned of my retirement to Fontevraud. Could he come to see me, as a dutiful son calling on his mother, and for no reason other than his love for me? (By which he meant, I supposed, that this wasn't a political mission and I wasn't to persuade him to embark on any hopeless new schemes.)

I sent the messenger back to tell Henry I'd be overjoyed to see him, and urged him to come soon. He replied that he'd get to Fontevraud before noon on September 27.

When he arrived I was waiting at my door, looking out at the bright autumn day. Gusty winds were blowing the leaves off the trees that lined the road, swirling them about so we seemed in the midst of a golden rainstorm. The high prioress, Lady Blanche, conducted Henry. I could tell by her preening, self-satisfied look that the arrival of the King of England was a great honor for the abbey, much more so than that of his mother with her questionable reputation.

I'd last seen Henry only two years ago, when we met at Reading to plan our uprising against King Louis. So much had happened since then! After a hug and a kiss I stood looking at him, noticing how he'd changed in just that short time. Losing that war had certainly aged him. Yet this wasn't the face of defeat. It was the face of a man who'd learned to accept setbacks and recoveries, a man comfortable with his kingship, a man who'd become used to commanding respect.

I invited him into my hall, which he surveyed carefully.

"You haven't lost your good taste, mother. Such a handsome chamber! I suppose those tapestries are French, but surely I remember these two fine chests from your Queen's House at Winchester?"

"Yes, when I left England I was permitted to bring some of my favorite things. They've been with me at Angoulême all these years, and I couldn't bear to leave them. But tell me, my dear, how you are, why you are still in France, how your wife Eleanor is—I have so many questions! But you must remember to speak plainly and directly to me. Your poor old mother doesn't hear as well as she used to."

He laughed and hugged me again. "Very well, poor old mother. And the first thing I'll say plainly and directly is that you look neither poor nor old to me, but as beautiful as ever and hardly poor—I believe I see a gold ring on your finger with an emerald the size of my thumb."

I led him to a windowseat. He bounced a few times on the thick cushion, well filled with goosedown.

"And I see you still insist on your comfort." He grinned at me.

"Well, why not? At my age one's bones get very close to the surface, and the softer the seat the better. But do answer my questions. Oh Henry, I am so very glad to see you!"

"And I you." He looked at me with such kindness, such open love, that I saw once more the little boy who had thought his mother was the most wonderful person in the world.

"All right, to your questions. I'm still in France because Eleanor was so near to giving birth when the war ended that we stayed in Bordeaux rather than risk the voyage back to England. And I'm happy to tell you that she's been delivered of our second daughter, Beatrice, and both are doing well. Then I had to make peace with King Louis and sign a truce. And since Gascony is still largely ours, Richard and I had a great deal of business there. He'll stay on, but Eleanor and I must return in October. While I was so close I couldn't deny myself the pleasure of coming to see my mother before we left."

"Thank you, my dear."

"But what of you, mother? Where is your husband, why are you here?"

"Hugh has gone on King Louis's service to the south, trying to bring Toulouse into the King's domain. It was a condition of the peace we signed. And I'm here because Hugh and I finally had to admit we'd both be happier apart. No need to go beyond that. I'm far more interested in you. I have so little news from England. How are your sisters? I know about poor Joanna, of course. I still mourn her." My eldest daughter, who'd married the King of Scotland and gone to live in that harsh cold country, had died four years ago.

"I grieve to tell you that Isabella died only last year, but Eleanor is very well, and is now the wife of Simon de Montfort. I was happy to give her my permission."

Then we fell to reminiscing about his childhood. We spoke of happy times he and his brother and sisters had had at Winchester and at Corfe Castle. "I fell in love with that castle when I was only ten," he said, "and I still go back whenever I can."

Two subjects we avoided: his father King John and his unhappy last years; and the recent debacle when Hugh and I had persuaded Henry to join us and try to reclaim England's lands in France.

Before he left I asked him if he would go with me to the abbey church to pay our respects to the tombs of his grandparents, Henry II and Eleanor of Aquitaine, and his uncle, Richard the Lionheart. We walked along the short path to the church courtyard, meeting a few nuns on the way who looked deferentially at my son and bobbed their heads. Maybe I'll get a little more respect, I thought, now that they've seen me with the King.

The sun was hiding behind a cloud. The wind had died down after depositing a thick carpet of yellow leaves that rustled as we walked through them. The autumn day that had earlier seemed the last bright fling of summer was now a sober harbinger of winter.

In the vast church we walked along the nave, flanked on both sides by marble columns. Henry, who'd seen many churches in his time, looked up to where the columns arched gracefully to support lofty domes. "Very fine," he said. "As fine as anything we have in England."

At the transept we found the tombs with their stone effigies recumbent. All looked calm and regal, Henry and Richard with scepters and Eleanor holding an open book. I'd always wondered about that; she wasn't known as a scholar. But it was probably meant to show her piously saying her prayers.

"I wonder why my father isn't here too. Did he especially request that he be buried at Worcester?"

"He did. Your father was always a complete Englishman. No doubt he thought he'd rest more easily in an English cathedral. Whereas the three we see here were as attuned to France as they were to England. What do you think, Henry, would you like to lie in this church some day?"

"I've not given that much thought. Wherever it is, I'll want my wife at my side."

"Well, I've given my final resting place a great deal of thought. I want it to be right here. But I suppose when the time comes someone else will make that decision."

"If I have anything to say about it, and I trust I will, you'll get your wish."

After we said goodbye and I watched him ride away, I felt such a sharp sense of loss that tears came to my eyes. I was sure I'd never see him again.

It was about this time that I realized that along with advancing years came ailments. I'd always been fairly healthy with enough stamina to keep me going through a variety of ordeals. Now my body was failing me. I walked more slowly. Sometimes I woke in the night with severe pains in my back and my legs. I took little pleasure in eating; Lady Louise had to urge me or I'd have sent everything back to the kitchen.

"You're getting altogether too thin, my lady," she'd say. "It's all very well to be as slim as you were at sixteen, but you don't want to waste away so you're practically invisible. Now, try some of this nice borage tea. It's very good for inspiring the appetite."

Sometimes she persuaded me to go for a meal in the refectory with the other ladies. "Even if you don't like them it will do you good to get out and show them you haven't given up and taken to your bed." I believe she thought I'd eat more in company, and she may have been right.

But I didn't enjoy it. As my hearing got worse I found it aggravating to have to ask people to speak up, to repeat. I hated this, especially when they were people I cared so little about—the prioress, the nuns, the abbess, the other noble ladies. Before long when they found it too difficult to have a conversation they stopped trying. So I was spared the company of those I despised. Not only that, but as I grew more silent they assumed I'd lost my hearing entirely. This could be amusing sometimes, when I overheard remarks never meant for my ears. At other times it was painful when I was the subject of their gossip. Fortunately for my peace of mind, I had the steadfast companionship of Lady Louise all this time. She went along with the little game I was playing.

One day I overheard something more alarming than idle chatter. The prioress told a friend that if I should try to leave the abbey I would be prevented. "We've been given these instructions from the very highest authority," she said.

I was outraged. Wasn't I a countess, a queen? Wasn't I free to go where and when I pleased? Poor Louise had to listen to my invective.

"I came here of my own free will, I can certainly leave if I wish. Who could give an order to prevent me?"

"Forgive me, my lady, but I think I know. I've befriended one of the abbess's confidantes. She told me she understood that King Louis had given the order that you were to be detained here to keep you from making more mischief. I didn't want to tell you this because I knew it would only anger you and add to your sorrows."

Though this was shocking, I didn't burst out in an explosion of anger. Nowadays, along with the rest of me, my temper wasn't as robust as it had been. I merely said "Ha!" Then I thought about what to do.

"You were right to tell me. And perhaps you were right to keep this to yourself up to now. You know me very well, my dear friend."

Being told I couldn't leave made me suddenly want to escape. I had to test the King's decree and find out if I were indeed a prisoner. But where would I go?

The answer was obvious. I wrote to Hugh. I was sure he must be back from his service for King Louis.

My dear husband Hugh: I hope and trust you have returned unharmed from Toulouse. I find that I am not wholly contented with my retirement here at Fontevraud. It is far too quiet. I miss the active life we used to lead. I miss our children. Most of all, I miss you. I regret that I left you so abruptly. May I come to you at Lusignan? Your loving wife, Isabella.

Just writing those words made me look forward to resuming our life together. Maybe after all this time apart we'd find it easier to get along. I waited anxiously for a reply. I packed my belongings so I'd be ready to depart the moment I heard. In ten days his answer came.

My dear Isabella: Yes, I have returned, safe and sound, from my service for King Louis. I thank you for your concern. Your suggestion that you return to me at Lusignan comes too late. I have decided to undertake a Crusade to the Holy Land, something I have wished to do ever since my father did the same and lost his life there. All is ready. I will leave in three days. Our son Hugh and his wife Yolande are already here. Hugh will take over as head of the clan when I leave. Of course they would welcome you if you came. Otherwise, I hope you will become reconciled to your quiet life at Fontevraud. May God shed his mercy on you. Hugh.

I read and reread the letter. If Hugh had really wanted me to come back he would have changed his plans. Only now did I realize how much I'd been counting on his welcome, his affection. Not for a moment did I consider going to Lusignan if he weren't there. Fond as I was of my son Hugh, I knew that he and Yolande would have taken over my Logis de la Reine. I'd be sent to stay in a tower room, as poor ailing Mathilde, Hugh le Brun's wife, did for so many years. I'd never submit to that.

Well, perhaps I could go to Angoulême. When I'd packed up and left for the abbey, I'd told Guy that he might as well move in whenever he liked, since we'd left Angoulême to him. I hadn't heard whether he'd done so or not. In any case, there was plenty of room there for both of us. I wrote to tell him that I intended to leave Fontevraud and come back to my home. He replied at once.

My dear mother: I grieve to hear that your life at the abbey is not what you had hoped. I have been at Angoulême for two months, and you would be pleased to see the progress we have made on the new tower, though it is years away from completion. My sister Agatha is here too. As you know, she was to marry William de Cauvigney, but the arrangements are going very slowly. My brother Hugh is handling that. In the meantime, of course I told Agatha she was welcome here. She is living in the apartments that you once occupied. I believe that we could make you quite comfortable in the old tower where you lived as a girl. Please send word as to when you plan to arrive. Your loving son, Guy de Lusignan

The message was clear. He didn't really want me. I couldn't imagine going back to the little room where I'd spent so many lonely hours during my childhood. Nor could I imagine accepting a secondary position in the home of my son and my daughter.

With this, my zeal to escape died. If I couldn't be lady of the castle I'd have to content myself with staying at Fontevraud for whatever years were left to me. Here at least I had my independence.

And time. I had plenty of time. Time to reflect on all the turns my life had taken. These days I found myself dwelling more on the past than on the future. How vivid the memories! How often I'd risked so much, to assert my right to live my life as I thought best. And as often as not I'd won. When I didn't, it hadn't been my fault.

It wouldn't be too bad, I thought, looking around at my comfortable room with all its familiar furnishings. I'd have Lady Louise's company and her restorative teas. Maybe I'd study holy works. It couldn't do any harm and might do some good. I'd go to mass more often, and pray to the Virgin Mary to prepare a place for me in heaven.

Then at last, I trusted I'd be laid to rest in the abbey church. That was surely my due as a Queen of England.

Epilogue

I sabella died at Fontevraud Abbey in 1246, aged sixty. Her son Henry saw to it that she was buried in the abbey church. Her recumbent effigy lies near those of King Henry II, Queen Eleanor and King Richard I, the Lionheart. Isabella wears a crown over a wimple that hides her hair. She is dressed in a simple blue gown, belted at the waist, and a cloak trimmed in gold braid. Her hands are folded on her breast. In eternal repose, her face is calm but not meek.

After Isabella's death her husband, Hugh X of Lusignan, seemed to shed his enmity toward Louis IX. He was one of some four thousand knights who joined the Seventh Crusade, led by King Louis. The Crusaders' first conquest was Damiette. They intended to take Egypt before marching on Jerusalem. Hugh died at Damiette in 1249—fighting at the side of his onetime enemy, the king's brother Alphonse. Hugh's father, Hugh le Brun, had died at the same place thirty years before.

Encouraged by the easy capture of Damiette, King Louis led his army toward Cairo. He was disastrously defeated. The Egyptians took him prisoner, then released him and forced him to pay indemnity. His army was greatly depleted. He spent the next six years in the Holy Land, negotiating unsuccessfully with the Muslims in an effort to acquire Jerusalem without fighting for it. He returned to France, and launched his last Crusade in 1270. This too was doomed to tragic failure. Louis died of the plague at Carthage before reaching the Holy Land. Canonized in 1297, he was the only French king to become a saint.

Isabella's son Henry III ruled England until his death in 1272, when his son Edward I succeeded him. After his defeat in 1242 Henry made no further attempts to regain the English lands in France, having ample occupation at home dealing with the fractious Welsh and Scots. As his father King John had been at Runnymede in 1215, Henry was challenged by the magnates of the realm who demanded more say in the government. Also like his father, toward the end of his reign Henry presided over an England riven by civil war. Unlike John, he survived to rule another seven years.

One of the most curious sequels to Queen Isabella's life story is the tale of how Henry befriended his half-brothers and -sisters, children of Isabella and Hugh, after his mother's death. As far as we know the only ones Henry could have met were the elder sons, who were with Hugh when he and Henry were defeated by King Louis's forces at Saintes. Under those conditions of battle and hasty retreat there couldn't have been much time to get acquainted with one's brothers.

Yet in 1247, the year after his mother's death, Henry--who was genuinely attached to all his brothers and sisters, English as well as French--invited his Lusignan relatives to come to England. Guy, William, Aymer and Alice accepted with alacrity. Geoffrey came a few months later. As the younger children in this large family, with relatively small inheritances and not having found advantageous marriages, they may have seen more opportunity for advancement on the other side of the Channel. Henry was generous to them, ostentatiously so. He loved pageantry, and they gave him a good excuse. One of his first acts on their arrival was to arrange a magnificent spectacle to mark the knighting of William, complete with a full ceremony in Westminster Abbey and a lavish banquet to follow. Later he arranged a brilliant marriage for William to a wealthy heiress. He also showered the others with honors and riches. Aymer became Bishop of Winchester. Alice married the Earl of Surrey. Geoffrey and Guy were given impressive amounts of money, much of which they took back to France. When it was safely stowed away, they came back for more. The chronicler Matthew Paris reported that when Guy left England for a trip home in 1247, "his saddle bags were so heavily loaded with new money that he had to increase the number of his horses."

No wonder this didn't sit well with the English barons, nor did their monarchs' similar largesse granted to Queen Eleanor's relatives from Savoy. They saw these foreigners usurping the honors and rewards that good Englishmen were entitled to. By 1258 the barons had had enough, and rose up to demand that Henry evict his "beggarly relatives" from the kingdom. Henry had to comply. So back the Lusignan brothers went, considerably better off than when they had come.

It would be hard not to conclude that Queen Isabella bequeathed to her children her ambition for power, wealth and recognition, and that her husband Hugh's more equable, temporizing nature died with him.[1]

Later generations of Lusignans did not fare so well. They fell heavily in debt. The temptation to occasionally ally themselves with the English against their own king resurfaced from time to time. The last count, Guy, imprudently joined Henry's son Edward I in Edward's last assault on France, which failed. On Guy's death in 1308 King Philip le Bel of France, citing the Lusignans' enormous debts, took over their lands. After three centuries the powerful Lusignan house sank into oblivion.

Edward I and his successors continued the battles with the French that had embroiled the English since the reign of Henry II. Not until 1453, the end of the Hundred Years' War, did the struggle end. The English had to give up all their possessions in France except the port of Calais, which they finally lost during the reign of Mary I, "Bloody" Mary, daughter of Henry VIII. Yet the rulers of England continued to call themselves kings and queens of France until 1802. Isabella would have approved: once a queen, always a queen.

And what of Isabella's legacy, as recorded by history? There is no doubt that her contemporaries saw her as unpopular. The chronicler Matthew Paris, a monk who wrote in the thirteenth century about King John and King Henry III, was harshly judgmental of both of them and by extension of Queen Isabella. He claimed that the French called her a Jezebel, after the fiercely energetic Biblical queen who disregarded the rights of the common man and defied the prophets Elijah and Elisha. She was described to Queen Blanche, mother of King Louis IX (probably before Blanche met her) as a shrew, a termagent and an inciter to rebellion. Others accused her of attempted murder, adultery, and betrayal of her own son. Though later historians have made only glancing references to her character, they were seldom kind. One called her the Helen of the Middle Ages, chiding her for exploiting her extraordinary beauty to influence men and events.

The French historian Sophie Fougère (see bibliography) imagines Isabella's thoughts during her final seclusion at Fontevraud. She sees her musing on her life, admitting her follies and finding humility and repose. We have no way of knowing what her state of mind was. I prefer to believe that this strong-minded woman was convinced to the end that fate had been unfair to her, but accepted the fact that there was nothing she could do about it. She did find a measure of repose. But humility? No.

---

1 For a full account of this post-Isabella chapter in the Lusignans' history, see the article "The Lusignans in England" by Harold Snellgrove, cited in the bibliography.

A Selective Bibliography

Castaigne, Jean François, *Notice Historique sur Isabelle d'Angoulême, Comtesse-reine.* Angoulême, 1836

Centre d'Études Supérieures de Civilisation Médiévale, *Isabelle d'Angoulême, Comtesse-reine et son temps (1186-1246).* University of Poitiers, 1999

Costain, Thomas B., *The Conquering Family.* Tandem Books, 1973

Duby, Georges, *William Marshal, The Flower of Chivalry.* Pantheon Books, 1985

Fawtier, Robert, *The Capetian Kings of France: Monarchy and Nation, 987-1328.* Macmillan, 1960

Fougère, Sophie, *Isabelle d'Angoulême, Reine d'Angleterre.* Edit-France, 1998

Joinville, Jean de, *The Life of St. Louis.* Penguin, 1963

Kelly, Amy, *Eleanor of Aquitaine and the Four Kings.* Harvard University Press, 1950

Lloyd, Alan, *The Maligned Monarch: A Life of John of England.* Doubleday, 1962

Marvaud, François, *Isabelle d'Angoulême, ou la Comtesse-reine.* Lafraise, 1856

Norgate, Kate, *The Minority of Henry III.* Macmillan, 1912

Painter, Sidney, *The Reign of King John.* Johns Hopkins Press, 1966

Roger of Wendover, *Roger of Wendover's Flowers of History,* Vol. II, 1170-1235. John Allen Giles, tr. Bohn, London, 1849

Snellgrove, Harold, *The Lusignans in England, 1247-1258.* University of New Mexico, 1950

Strickland, Agnes, *Isabella of Angoulême, Consort of King John.* In *Lives of the Queens of England,* Vol. I. London, 1857

Vincent, Nicholas, *Isabella of Angoulême, John's Jezebel.* In *King John: New Interpretations,* S.D. Church, ed. Woodbridge, 1999

ISBN 1412092128-4